S0-AFI-959

MOONLIGHT EMBRACE

"I don't think you understand," Catherine said, her voice trembling.

"Oh, I understand perfectly, Cate." Nick stepped toward her as he spoke.

Catherine found it difficult to speak, to even breathe. His presence in her room was overpowering. She swallowed nervously, trying to think of something to say. He looked rakish and dangerous as he stalked closer.

"I never meant for this to be part of our agreement," she whispered.

"Didn't you?"

He stood so close that Catherine had to tilt her head to look into his face. Moonlight gilded his tousled hair, his piercing eyes, and his wide, beautiful mouth. Catherine locked her knees to keep from falling toward him. "No, I . . ."

He silenced her protest as his warm lips touched hers. Catherine reached out to push him away—to draw him nearer—as his kiss drove everything but him from her mind . . .

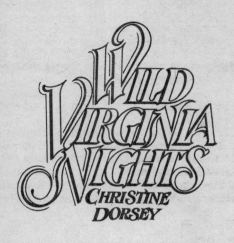

WILD VIRGINIA NIGHTS

CHRISTINE DORSEY

ZEBRA BOOKS
KENSINGTON PUBLISHING CORP.

ZEBRA BOOKS

are published by

Kensington Publishing Corp.
475 Park Avenue South
New York, NY 10016

First printing: September, 1990

Printed in the United States of America

To Ben, Chris, and Elizabeth, who make their parents proud. And, as always, to Chip.

A special thanks to Maude Kerby, bookseller and student of Midlothian history, for her inspiration.

He putteth forth his hand upon the flinty rock;
He overturneth the mountain by the roots.
He cutteth out channels among the rocks;
And his eye seeth every precious thing.

Job 28:9-10

Prologue

New Castle, England
March, 1831

Damn!

The thought struck Nicholas Colton just before the beefy fist exploded against his jaw. Flashing lights interspersed with midnight black momentarily interrupted his view of the havoc the miners' brawl wrecked on the tavern's common room.

A much-used sixth sense of survival cleared Nick's head in time to duck the follow-up right aimed at his nose. With a growl, barely heard above the sound of flesh pounding flesh and shattering glass, the burly miner lunged forward. Dodging to the side, Nick used a well-placed kick in the groin to send the man sprawling across an oak table. Twin tankards of ale, miraculously unspilled to this point, sailed off the well-worn surface, before the table splintered, collapsing around the stunned man.

Wiping sweat from his eyes with the back of his

sleeve, Nick scanned the smoke-hazed room. He'd stopped by the Devil's Pit tonight hoping—needing—to see a face from his past. Someone who didn't curl their pinky finger when sipping tea, or sip tea at all for that matter. He hadn't been disappointed. Some of his buddies from shaft number nine had hailed him when he'd entered the tavern. They'd all been peaceably sharing a bottle of whiskey and watching the local dart champion defend his title when this donnybrook erupted. There'd been little choice but to join the free for all.

Nick caught a glimpse of his friend, Jack, his wild red hair flying, leaping atop an already prone adversary. Grinning, Nick shook his head. Obviously, Jack didn't need assistance at the moment.

Turning to search for the others, Nick saw the enraged face of the miner he'd sent crashing into the table. What he didn't see was the board the man swung until just before the splintered wood collided with the side of his head.

The room tilted and wide sawdust covered planks rushed up to meet Nick. Acrid odors of rum and ale pierced the last shreds of his consciousness as he slammed face first to the floor.

"Have you taken to brawling?"

Nick moaned. It wasn't bad enough that every bone in his body ached, now he was hearing voices. And not just any voice. The voice of the last person he wanted to see right now.

"Nicholas."

Oh God, there it was again. Even through the fog

8

enveloping his brain Nick knew this to be no hallucination. Tentatively he slit open an eye, abruptly closing it when the light accelerated the drums pounding in his head. But that split second glance had confirmed his foreboding. Travis Fielding stood glaring down at him.

Nick moaned again. "How in the hell did you get here?"

"With much greater ease than you, I'd warrant," the owner of the Fielding Mining Company explained. "Where as you were dragged, I simply walked."

Dragged? For the first time Nick realized a soft mattress and clean sheets cushioned his battered body. Throwing an arm across his eyes, he squinted, noting with some consternation that he lay in his own bed. "How *did* I get here?" Nick interrupted his employer before he could respond. "Dragged, I know, but by whom? And who opened those damn drapes?" The sun streamed through his window, another painful revelation he'd gained from prying his eyes open.

"The drapes were my doing. I thought perhaps the light would help bring you around. As for your inauspicious arrival home, two of my men accomplished that feat."

Levering himself up—relieved to discover he could still move—Nick stared directly into his employer's light gray eyes. "You had me followed?"

"Hardly. Though perhaps I should. Will you *ever* give up this penchant for such establishments?"

"I was born in one of those *establishments,* if you recall." Nick swung powerful legs over the side of the

9

bed, resting his forearms on his knees a moment before attempting to stand.

"I remember. You are the one I thought wanted to forget."

Nick shot Travis Fielding a sharp look over his shoulder as he made his way slowly to the heavy mahogany wash stand. Though walking did nothing but emphasize his aches, he seemed to be in one piece. "Is there a problem with the way I do my job?" Grimacing into the mirror, Nick examined the swollen bruise on his jaw through bloodshot gray eyes.

"Don't be ridiculous. You know as well as I do you're one of the best mining engineers in this part of England."

Nick shrugged. If that were true, he had the man sitting by his bed to thank. It had been nearly thirteen years ago that Nick had been called up from the depths of shaft number nine. Told the owner of Fielding Mines wanted to see him, the sixteen-year-old Nick had been scared out of his wits. But he'd covered his reaction with the same cocky arrogance that had served him well since his mother had died, and he'd been thrust alone into the world.

After her death he'd been alone and barely more than eight. He'd spent the first few years trying to decide which would kill him first; the cold, or the hunger. Luck, and the prospect of stealing a few chunks of coal to burn against the winter chill, had brought him to the mines on the same day a pit boy had gotten kicked in the head by a cantankerous mule. The unfortunate boy had rendered his life to God and his job to Nick.

He'd also taught Nick a valuable lesson. Nick never took the mines or anything in them for granted. He'd worked hard, memories of his caved-in stomach and numb blue feet added strength to his arms when he finally began digging the coal. The work was grueling but steady, and the jingle of change in his pocket was all he'd thought he'd wanted till that day he sat waiting in Travis Fielding's fancy entrance way.

"I've never had a problem with the way you do your job. You know that." Travis Fielding's words interrupted Nick's recollections.

"Just my social life," Nick quipped, glancing over his shoulder. "I went to that damn reception last night." Hell, he still wore the black evening trousers and silk shirt to prove it. Of course, they were both a little the worse for wear. Nick stripped off the torn shirt and splashed water from the porcelain pitcher into the bowl.

"You left early."

"It was damn boring. Besides, you weren't even there." Cupping his hands, Nick threw water on his face, wincing when the cool liquid came in contact with split skin. Rivulets ran down his muscled forearms, playing in the golden brown hair, and splashing onto his broad chest.

"Granted, Margaret Ellsworth doesn't host the most exciting soirees." Travis appeared to ignore Nick's cocked brow. "However she does have a daughter who—"

"Travis!"

"All right." The older man held his hands up in a placating manner. "That's not what I wanted to

11

discuss with you."

Nick grabbed a linen towel, drying himself carefully, and said nothing. He knew Travis wanted to see him marry and settle down, and there was very little he wouldn't do for the man. Nick owed Travis more than he could ever repay. Instead of doing any of the dreadful things, Nick's sixteen-year-old mind had imagined all those years ago, Travis, for reasons known only to himself, had taken Nick from the mines and given him an education. And then a job. Now the only one more powerful at Fielding Mining than Nick Colton was the owner himself. But still the thoughts of having Margaret Ellsworth as a mother-in-law, of watching her daughter grow more like her every year, set Nick's teeth on edge.

The damp towel draped around his wide shoulders, Nick turned. His steely gray eyes watched as Travis rose, covering the space between them in purposeful strides.

"I have a favor to ask of you, Nick."

Even assured this had nothing to do with Margaret Ellsworth's nondescript daughter, Nick had the feeling he wasn't going to like the request. And hearing it did nothing to prove him wrong.

"I want you to go to America."

Chapter One

Virginia
April, 1831

Catherine Brousseau laid her pen on the desk's polished surface and pinched the bridge of her nose between her thumb and forefinger. She'd added the last column of figures three times, and each time had gotten a different sum. The three answers had one thing in common. Not one of them was enough. Not enough coal was coming from the mine, not enough money was coming back to Greenfield. In less than a week she owed her neighbor, John Parker, his biannual deposit for the use of his slaves to work the mine, and she didn't have it. Catherine had hoped help would have arrived by now, but . . .

A fuzzy fat fly wandered in the open window, lighted on the sill, then as if changing its mind, flew back into the late afternoon haze. Catherine followed its flight with her gaze, wishing a breeze would enter the stuffy room. Even a faint one would be welcome—a lot more welcome than the noise that did drift past the lace curtains.

The voices were part of the reason she'd been unable to add the numbers. The twittering giggle of her sister, accompanying the deep baritone laugh of the man with Marie, had annoyed Catherine as much as if that fly had come in and buzzed around her head.

"Catherine?"

"Yes, Grandmere." Looking behind her toward the room where her grandmother lay abed, she answered the thin reedy voice. Catherine tried to keep the exasperation she felt from washing into her tone. Her grandmother couldn't help that the predinner nap Catherine had taken a quarter hour to prepare her for had lasted only twenty minutes.

"Is that Henry returning, Catherine dear?"

Catherine let her head fall forward till it rested on her ink-stained hands, heedless of the dark auburn tendrils escaping her heavy chignon to brush the side of her face.

"No, Grandmere, it isn't Grandpere." What Catherine left unsaid was that it couldn't possibly be her grandfather. Henry Brousseau had been dead for nearly ten years. But nothing would be accomplished by saying it. Grandmere refused to believe her. It was the same with Grandmere's son and daughter-in-law, Catherine's parents. To the elderly lady, they were all alive in a world created from fond memories and more than a dash of senility. Unfortunately, the real world offered no such easy escapes from its problems for Catherine.

"Who's that talking on the porch, dear? It sounds like my Henry." Her grandmother's words brought

14

Catherine from her musings and made her realize that the couple on the porch had disturbed more than just her.

"It's just one of Marie's friends, Grandmere." Catherine rose and walked to the connecting door between the library and her grandmother's room. She'd moved grandmother's bed and dresser down to the back parlor when it became difficult for the older woman to climb the stairs to the room she'd slept in since Greenfield was built.

"Do you want to get up or do you think you can sleep some more?" Catherine moved across the room, bending to give the parchment-thin skin on her grandmother's cheek an affectionate pat. Catherine's eyes misted as the old woman reached up and covered Catherine's hand with her own.

"You're so good, dear, for taking care of me like this."

"Nonsense. I simply do what must be done." Catherine spoke briskly, fighting the urge to break down and spill out her frustrations at her grandmother's knee as she'd often done as a child.

The sound of deep masculine laughter winged through the air, sending tiny vibrations dancing up Catherine's spine. She turned toward the doorway almost expecting to see . . . She didn't know what she expected.

"What is it, dear?"

The obvious anxiety in her grandmother's voice freed Catherine from the spell that that sensual sound had caused. "It's nothing, Grandmere. Do you think you could sleep some more if Marie and her gentleman caller weren't quite so loud?"

"Maybe. But I don't want to cause any trouble," Grandmere was quick to add.

"Don't worry." Catherine brushed her lips across the wispy white hair on her grandmother's head. "You just rest. I happen to know that Betsy is fixing rabbit stew for supper, and you know how she goes on if we don't all do her cooking justice."

Catherine backed out of the room and paused only a moment to frown at the figures in the open ledger on her desk before heading for the front door. She would tell Marie and her friend in no uncertain terms to keep their flirtatious laughter quiet. Or take it elsewhere. Catherine cared not a whit as long as they didn't disturb Grandmere's nap again.

The thought of combing back her escaped curls or shaking the wrinkles from her plain cotton dress was quickly suppressed. Whoever Marie's visitor was— and Catherine was a little surprised that she didn't recognize his voice at all—it was unlikely that he'd give Catherine more than a passing glance.

Nick Colton leaned his hip against the porch railing, feigning interest in what Miss Brousseau said—something about the gigot sleeves on her new gown. He heard the door to the house open and looked up but could see no one in the heavy shadows inside the house. His hostess appeared not to notice the noise or the loss of her audience as she babbled on.

Nick had been at Greenfield for only a short time, but already he was surprised at how things differed from his expectations. When Travis Fielding had requested he come to America and help a friend's daughter with her coal mine, Nick had assumed the

16

lady in question would be rich. After all, Mr. Fielding was extremely wealthy. But, from what he could see, this house didn't belong to anyone in the same financial league as Fielding.

The house itself was fairly large, with two large chimneys at either end of the expanse of white-washed wood. The door that had opened was one of a pair that graced the front of the building. From a distance, Nick had thought it very impressive. On closer inspection, he noticed the paint peeling from the weatherboarding and the weeds that clogged what must have once been a lovely garden.

And Miss Brousseau. Nick's gaze strayed back to the blue-eyed, dimpled blonde who sat across from him on a porch chair, stirring a small breeze with her ivory fan. She was nothing like he'd imagined. Mr. Fielding had read him part of her letter—an impassioned plea would be closer to the truth—asking him to send someone who could help her run her mine. Somehow Nick couldn't imagine this lady becoming impassioned about anything.

Of course, her obvious lack of interest in her property would make his job easier. Nick had been afraid Miss Brousseau's well-meant suggestions might cause him some trouble in getting the mine working at peak performance. He'd also thought she might resist Fielding's offer to buy the mine if Nick decided it would be a good investment. Not much chance of that. Miss Brousseau appeared not to care about much more than having enough money to pay her dressmaker to clothe her lovely body.

Nick glanced back at the young woman, nodding at something she said and then laughed because she did. He wasn't even certain what she'd been talking about. He definitely had to pay more attention.

Miss Brousseau was a pretty thing, all soft yellow curls and ruffles. At first Nick had been resentful about being sent to America, but as he leaned back against the porch railing he decided it might not be so bad after all.

"Grandmere is trying to sleep." Unable to help herself, Catherine had watched Marie and her guest for a moment before speaking.

The low, steady voice that came from the house startled Nick, and he found himself straightening, looking back at the open doorway. A young woman moved from the comparative darkness inside to the shaded sunshine of the porch. The dress that covered her slight build from high starched neck to toes was painfully plain, and Nick's first thought was that she must be a servant. But the moment she lifted her determined green eyes to his, he knew differently.

"Oh fiddle, Catherine. She sleeps all the time. Besides, what do you want me to do about it?" Marie fanned herself in agitation.

The newcomer let her gaze shift toward Miss Brousseau, and Nick thought he caught a glimmer of disgust shine in those expressive eyes before she spoke again.

"Grandmere is old and requires much rest. As for what you can do about it, all I ask is that you and your guest respect her right to peace and quiet."

The green-eyed woman's gaze raked over Nick once more, and he had the wild urge to apologize profusely for whatever he may have done. But she gave him no chance. With an economy of motion she

18

turned on her heel and started to reenter the house.

"He's not my guest, you know," Marie said sulkingly. "Actually, he's yours."

Catherine stopped, glancing over her shoulder at her sister. "Mine?"

Maria snapped her fan shut and rose, fluffing nonexistent wrinkles from her ruffled skirt. "Well I certainly didn't invite anyone here to discuss mining. That is what you wanted to talk about, isn't it Mr. Colton?"

Nick's slate gray eyes narrowed and he felt a trickle of annoyance as he looked from one woman to the other. When he'd ridden up to the house a few minutes ago, the blonde had introduced herself as Miss Brousseau, and he hadn't thought any further. But now . . . "I've come to see a Miss Brousseau about running her mine."

Catherine stepped forward, not at all impressed with what she saw. Oh, he was easy enough to look at, she'd noticed that while watching him from the doorway. His thick wavy hair was a warm brown, shot through with strands teased by the sun till they shone like clover honey. The face that now watched her with the same sexual assessment she'd noticed earlier when he looked at Marie, was lean and tanned. Dark brows and lashes emphasized his gray eyes and the slightly pugnacious bent of his nose and chin.

Ruggedly handsome he might be, but she'd expected—hoped—that Travis Fielding would send her someone older, more experienced. He looked experienced all right—with women. But what she needed was an expert on coal mining.

Catherine cocked her head to one side. "Travis Fielding sent you?"

"Are you Miss Brousseau?" Nick asked, though looking into her eyes he had no doubt she wrote the letter he'd read.

"I'm Miss Catherine Brousseau, owner of Greenfield Mine."

"Then Mr. Fielding sent me," Nick answered, a grin splitting the handsome planes of his face in reaction to her haughty tone. She sure was full of vinegar. He reached into his frock coat pocket and removed the envelope containing his letter of introduction. "Mr. Nicholas Colton, at your service." He bowed over the hand that reached for the packet of papers, a gesture Miss Catherine Brousseau seemed not to notice.

Catherine sat on the edge of the porch chair that Marie had occupied and opened the cream-colored envelope. For the second time today she fought the unaccustomed urge to break down and cry. Catherine had counted on Travis Fielding to help her. Contacting him had been the last resort of a desperate woman, and to discover that he'd sent her this . . . this flirtatious miner dressed as a dandy was almost more than she could bear.

"I hope you find everything in order." Nick watched as the young woman read the letter for the second time. He knew what was in it—nothing to warrant such a lengthy study. It contained Nick's qualifications and a brief outline of why he'd been sent.

Travis had explained to Nick that many years earlier he'd met James Brousseau at a gaming table in

20

London. Brousseau, on the tails of a tremendous run of luck, had quickly wiped out Travis's cash. Obviously, Brousseau had loved gaming over winning, for he'd proposed another bet. When Travis had mentioned his lack of funds, Brousseau had asked for a favor as payment. "Not now," he'd said, grinning at his pile of winnings, "but to be called in at some future date."

"Apparently that date is now," Travis had said that morning he'd asked Nick to go to America.

"Excuse me?" Catherine looked up from the letter, realizing Mr. Colton had spoken to her. "Oh, yes. You come highly recommended." Catherine just wished she could believe everything written about him. Of course the other information in the letter she knew. Her father had once told her about Travis Fielding's wager and had even shown her the signed promise. A favor from a wealthy mine owner, her father had found it amusing, almost like a trophy, and he'd never cashed it in.

But Catherine had. And looking again at the miner Travis Fielding had sent, she almost wished she hadn't.

Marie bristled, obviously not enjoying being ignored while her sister and Mr. Colton surveyed each other. "Why don't I show Mr. Colton to his room?" she said, sweeping past Catherine, but keeping her eyes on the manly form of their visitor. "I'm so glad you'll be staying with us for a while."

"Mr. Colton won't be staying in the house, Marie." Catherine ignored the look of surprise in the wide, baby-blue eyes. "As most of his time will be spent at the mine, I'm certain he would prefer the cabin down

21

by the creek." Catherine stared at Nick, daring him to question the arrangements.

He didn't have to. Marie was quick to intercede on his behalf. "That old ramshackle thing? Catherine, you can't be serious. A gentleman like Mr. Colton would be far more comfortable in the house."

Catherine shot her sister a warning look that Marie missed because she'd yet to take her eyes off Nicholas Colton. Marie seldom bothered to make any decisions, and certainly nothing that concerned the mine ever troubled her. Why now did she question Catherine's authority?

Why? Catherine cast a surreptitious glance at the large, broad-shouldered man. Why, indeed. There was no question that Nicholas Colton was too handsome for his own good—or hers—with his tall, muscular body and cool gray eyes. He was going to be trouble. Trouble she didn't need.

"Miss Catherine's right."

Catherine heard the words, but she couldn't believe he was saying them. She'd been expecting an argument in favor of staying in the house.

"It would be more convenient if I were closer to the mine. Besides, then I wouldn't worry about disturbing you two ladies when I leave each morning." Nick almost laughed aloud at the expression on Catherine's face when he agreed with her. Her soft, rosy mouth dropped open, and he had to stifle the urge to lift her rounded chin with his finger. There was no doubt she'd expected him to fight staying in the cabin. Hell, he had no idea what the place was like, but Nick was confident he'd lived in worse.

"Mr. Colton will be taking his meals with us,

22

won't he, Catherine?" Marie cajoled, the beginnings of a pout forming on her face.

"Of course." Catherine rose and started toward the porch steps. Certainly she'd let the man eat with them. After all she wasn't cruel. Just because she didn't want Marie around him—or to be around him herself—any more than necessary didn't mean she'd see him starve to death. "If you'll follow me, Mr. Colton, I'll show you the cabin."

Catherine waited in the gravel drive while Marie said her good-byes. "Dinner is at seven o'clock," she heard her sister purr.

"Is that all you brought with you?" Catherine motioned toward the saddlebag that Nick had thrown over his shoulder. He'd taken the pouch off his horse after he and Catherine led the animal into the stable.

"The rest of my things are at the tavern where the Richmond-Lynchburg Stage let me off. I paid a boy to deliver the trunk later this evening."

Catherine nodded. Leaving the stable, she led the way down the path through the woods that led to the mine and, beyond that, to the creek.

It was cooler under the pines, with only a lacy filtering of sun to heat the air. Catherine's skirt swished along the carpet of pine needles, fanning their pungent fragrance around her and the tall man at her side. Hardly a day went by that Catherine didn't follow this path. She knew it so well that she could find her way in the dark, and often had. Why then had she never noticed before how narrow and intimate the trail was?

You're beginning to think like Marie. Catherine

swallowed the lump in her throat that had suddenly appeared when her shoulder grazed against Nicholas Colton's muscular arm and looked up at him. "I suppose you'll want to see the mine after you've put your things in the cabin?"

Nick grinned. The words themselves were a question, but her tone brooked nothing but a positive response. No resting after the long journey for him. "Yes ma'am, Miss Brousseau," he answered, his voice thick with sarcasm. But if the little lady noticed the acerbity, she gave no indication.

The path widened, then disappeared completely as they entered a clearing. At the far end, surrounded by wild dogwoods, stood a small cabin. Covered with weatherboard similar to the main house, the structure exceeded Nick's expectations.

"My grandmother and grandfather lived here until they built the big house," Catherine said in a way of explanation. She opened one of the two front doors. "I'll have Betsy come down and clean later. I swept it out last week but I wasn't certain when you'd arrive." *Or if you'd arrive*, she added silently.

The room they entered had a large fieldstone fireplace against one wall and a handmade table and chairs in the center. A few shelves lined the white-washed walls, but save that, it was bare.

"The other room," Catherine motioned toward the interior door trying to ignore the blush she knew had stained her cheeks, "contains a bed. I changed the ticking, too." Catherine retreated outside, thankful that there was no need to discuss the bedroom anymore. She'd done her duty, now they could get down to serious discussions.

24

Minutes later Nick joined her. He'd draped his saddle bag over the bed, and had seen to his relief that the bedding was indeed clean. When he came out the door, he found Catherine nervously picking the petals off a violet, but at the sound of his boots on the porch, she dropped the flower and faced him, a determined gleam in her eyes.

"Before we go to the mine and meet the other men, I think we should talk about money." She'd worried about this since she'd sent the letter to Travis Fielding. "I intend to pay you a salary." Catherine hesitated, then lifted her chin a notch. "I simply can't do it right away."

Nick stifled a grin. He had to hand it to her. Catherine Brousseau had a lot of brass, bringing up the topic of a wage, then telling him she couldn't pay him. "Mr. Fielding pays me a salary."

"Yes, but while you're here, I think I should pay you, also." How much could Mr. Fielding be paying him? "The favor I asked of Travis Fielding was to send someone to help me, not to finance you."

"All right," Nick agreed, deciding she would have it no other way. He turned toward the path.

"Mr. Colton. There are a few more things we need to discuss." Nicholas Colton seemed agreeable enough about a salary, but what would he think of her next demand? While waiting for him to come out of the cabin, Catherine had decided she didn't much care for the man Travis Fielding had sent her. Well, what had she expected? Fielding probably wasn't happy, having to pay off an old betting loss. Maybe he even sent someone inexperienced on purpose, to cause her trouble. Maybe he—

"Well?" Nick leaned against the rough trunk of an oak and folded his arms across his chest. She'd said she had things to say, and then she just stood there.

The man's impertinent manner didn't improve Catherine's opinion of him. She stretched to her full height, though she still felt dwarfed by him. "You are to manage the mine, but I am ultimately in charge." Catherine saw the telltale signs of a grin begin on his face and continued. "All major decisions are to be cleared with me first."

Nick's countenance sobered. "And what do you consider major decisions?"

Catherine sucked in her breath at his insolence. Her hands formed tight fists at her side and she silently cursed the circumstances that had led her to this point. "Perhaps you should just let me know about all the decisions you need to make and I'll let you know which ones I consider major."

Nick took a menacing step forward, ready to tell this bossy little wench exactly what she could do with her decisions. Only a memory of Travis Fielding putting his confidence in him stopped Nick. He owed the old man, and this was what Fielding had asked him to do. Besides, if the mine could be made profitable, Fielding wanted to buy it and other mines in the area. Like it or not—and he definitely didn't like it—Nick had to do this job.

Catherine had fought the urge to back up when Nicholas moved closer to her. There was something almost savage about him, and at that moment she'd decided her first impression of him as a dandy was wrong. Now she watched as his manner became less aggressive.

"All right, Miss Brousseau. You make the decisions."

After his initial reaction, Nick's soft-spoken capitulation took Catherine by surprise. It also gave her courage to set down her last rule.

"There's one more thing, Mr. Colton." Catherine took a deep breath and plunged on. "You are to stay away from my sister."

Chapter Two

"There really is no reason to be so upset."

Catherine spoke the words that had been dancing through her mind since last evening. The sound of her own voice in the early morn quiet of her bedroom caused Catherine to cease the bothersome task of pinning up her thick chestnut hair.

Now she was talking to herself. Catherine sank into the rocking chair in front of the fireplace and let out a sigh of frustration.

Why had she asked Travis Fielding to send her help? Certainly she could have found someone as experienced as Nicholas Colton in Maryland or Pennsylvania. Why did it have to be this man that she must look to for guidance?

He hadn't blinked an eye when she'd told him to stay away from Marie. He'd just looked at her with that hint of a grin playing along the wide curves of his sensuous mouth, just looked at her until she could abide it no longer and turned to start down the path to the mine.

"Miss Brousseau?" his deep, gravelly voice had stopped her retreat, for that was exactly what it had been.

"Yes?"

He hadn't answered until she'd looked back at him. He'd advanced on her then, and Catherine found the hypnotic pull of his gray eyes had held her prisoner. When he was nearly close enough to touch her, close enough for her to detect the aroma of outdoors and heady male scent that clung to him, he'd halted. "Am I to stay away from you, also, Miss Brousseau?"

It had been a simple question. But there had been nothing uncomplicated about the way it made her feel. Her breath had caught in her throat and her skin had tingled—the way it did now just thinking about his words.

"This is silly." Catherine all but jumped from the chair and marched to her dresser. With quick, efficient motions she finished securing her long curls, not noticing the way the morning sun shining through the window played in the mahogany highlights. A passing glance in the mirror convinced Catherine that her hair was relatively neat, her dress clean and tidy.

She would think of her encounter with Nicholas Colton no more, Catherine decided as she left her room and walked down the narrow stairs to the library. After all, this was her house, and he was an employee. She was paying him—or at least she would when she got some money—to do her bidding. And do it he would. She certainly expected more from him than insolence. Never again would she sit at the dinner table too flustered to speak as she had last night. She'd show Mr. Colton his little games didn't bother her, Catherine thought as she sat down at the desk and opened the ledger.

"Miss Brousseau."

Catherine jumped as though she'd been shot, but it wasn't the shock that caused her heart to race and her stomach to tighten. There was no mistaking that voice, nor the affect it had on her. With an iron will Catherine forced herself to calm down before she looked up at Nicholas Colton.

"I didn't mean to startle you, Miss Brousseau. Please accept my apology."

He leaned against the door jamb, a low, black, wool hat held carelessly in one hand. Yesterday he'd worn all the trappings of a gentleman—fawn trousers, rich brown frock coat, and cravat—but not today.

Catherine pulled her gaze from his long lean legs encased in heavy trousers, past the sailcloth shirt that did nothing to disguise the thick corded muscles of his chest and arms, to his face. His mouth was sober. Catherine could almost believe he meant this apology. Then her gaze met his. He watched her with such amusement that the slate-gray color of his eyes now shone silver-bright.

Realization that he found entertainment at her expense straightened Catherine's backbone, and she glared at him, ignoring his words. "Did you want something, Mr. Colton?"

"I did." Nick walked into the room uninvited, rested his hip against Catherine's desk and made a point of examining the inkwell, wondering just how long it would take until she demanded to know why he was here.

Nick hadn't come to the house with the idea of playing games with her. He wasn't even sure why he was doing it. Ever since he could remember, Nick had little trouble attracting women. When he was younger, it had been tavern wenches who'd vied for his attentions. Now it was the so-called ladies of society. In either case, there were damn few females impervious to his charm. Damn few, except Miss Catherine Brousseau.

Maybe that was the reason she intrigued him, Nick told himself, though he felt there was more to it than that. He found her large green eyes and haughty airs more attractive than he liked to admit. As for her body—Nick stole a glance her way—it was difficult to be certain what those drab, serviceable dresses concealed. But he could imagine, and one of these days, he was going to find out. For now, he just wanted her to stop ignoring him.

Catherine watched Nick's finger circle the opening of the inkwell. His hands were nicely shaped, their long, slender fingers were lightly sprinkled with golden brown hair. Sensitive, aristocratic hands, she thought. The mesmerizing movement stopped and he forged a path down the small container's smooth metal side. It was then that she noticed the nicks and scars that roughened his knuckles and palms. They were hardly the type of imperfections you'd expect to see on a gentleman.

It took her a moment to realize she was puzzled by his hands and their ability to fascinate her. *Good heavens.* What was she doing? How could she allow one of her employees to bother her senses like this?

With a quick motion, Catherine reached out and grabbed the inkwell, spilling some of the black liquid in the process. Annoyed with her reaction to him, and the result of her temper, Catherine looked about for something to wipe the ink from her hand. Before she could find anything, Nick pulled a handkerchief from his pant's pocket and, leaning over the desk, wrapped her fingers in the soft linen.

"It's clean," Nick informed her when she looked up at him questioningly. "At least it was until now." Nick smiled as he traced the cloth down the satiny skin of her finger to her nail's small half moon. "There will be a stain, I'm afraid."

"I could wash it for you."

Nick laughed and put the handkerchief back in his pocket, letting go of Catherine's hand with a reluctance he hadn't expected. "I was speaking of your fingers, Miss Brousseau, not my handkerchief. I couldn't get all the ink off of them."

"'Tis no matter." Catherine folded her hands, then hid them in the folds of her skirt. Her skin still tingled where he had touched her, and no amount of twisting or rubbing her hands together seemed to stop the sensation. Catherine wondered if he knew of her reaction to him, and the thought helped to clear her head.

"You wished to see me about something?" She was proud of her steady voice.

"I've been down in the mine this morning," Nick began without preamble.

"And . . ." Catherine had a feeling she wasn't going to like what he had to say. Their trip to the mine last evening had not been very informative. Catherine had been unable to forget the look in his eyes when he'd asked if he must stay away from her, so the tour had been cut short. She'd planned to go back with him this morning, never dreaming he would have gone already.

"And, there are some areas we need to discuss."

He didn't say, "If I'm to stay here," but Catherine thought by his tone that he implied it.

"Such as?" Catherine tucked an errant auburn curl behind her ear.

Sitting in the straight-backed chair in front of the desk, Nick answered her question with one of his own. "Are you familiar with the pillar system of mining?"

"Of course." Catherine took a deep breath, then described the method of supporting the shaft that Greenfield Mine used. "Pillars of coal are left unmined to bear the weight of the tunnel's roof. It's not unusual. Most of the mines in the area use it. As a matter of fact, I believe the idea was first brought from England."

"And how much coal must remain standing to ensure safety?"

Catherine sighed in exasperation. "The pillar must be twice as large as the area mined. Mr. Colton, I—"

"Bear with me, Miss Brousseau." Nick's voice was deceptively calm as he interrupted her. "Have you ever heard of the phrase 'robbing the pillars'?" Her expression told him she had.

"What are you saying?" Catherine leaned forward on her elbows and stared into Nick's clear gray eyes, demanding an explanation.

"I'm saying, Miss Brousseau, that the pillars in Greenfield Mine have been robbed. By the look of things, it's been going on for some time. That's one of the reasons for the accidents and costly delays you've had recently."

"B-but that's impossible," she stammered. "I've explained it all very carefully to my bottom boss."

"That would be Sam Stevens?" At Catherine's nod, Nick continued. "I fired him this morning."

"You what?" The chair no longer restrained Catherine. She jumped up and started around the desk toward Nick. "By whose authority did you do that?"

"My own." Nick had known her reaction would be intense, though he hadn't expected her to stand over him, hands on hips, and eyes flashing green sparks. He resisted the urge to rise and dwarf her with his size.

"What right do you have to come into my house and tell me you've fired one of my men? I thought I made it perfectly clear yesterday that I was to be consulted before you made any decisions!" Catherine was so angry she thought she could easily slap his insolent face.

Nick gave in to temptation and stood. The effect was all that he could have hoped for, and it was immediate. Catherine backed up, and the hands that had been knotted into fists, now fluttered to her side. But Nick was too furious to gloat over her reaction. How dare she worry about a breach in her authority when men's lives were in danger.

"You have a lot of nerve, Catherine." Nick heard her gasp when he used her Christian name but ignored it. "There are men working in your mine—slaves who have no choice in the matter, I might add—and it isn't safe. And your main concern is playing boss lady."

"Don't you speak to me that way!" Catherine's mind was racing, trying to absorb all he'd said. Had Sam been robbing the pillars? If so, was her constant press for him to produce more coal the cause? But she would never, never have condoned this. Well, she would take care of it, but not before she'd put this meddling troublemaker in his place. Catherine crossed her arms and glared at Nick, daring him to try and intimidate her.

"You are dismissed Mr. Colton. I will write Travis Fielding and inform him that circumstances have changed, and your services are no longer needed. Greenfield Mine and her miners are now none of your concern."

Catherine whirled around, hoping to terminate the interview before he noticed the tears that blurred her vision and threatened to spill over her long, dark lashes. What was she to do now? Without the mine she had nothing. And whatever Nicholas Colton might believe, Catherine would never allow anyone to work where she knew it to be unsafe. But what would happen to Grandmere and Marie? What would happen to her?

"The hell they aren't." Catherine didn't know if it was the quiet determination in his voice or the feel of his large hands gripping her shoulders as he turned her back toward him that shocked her more. Whatever the cause, she just stood there, staring into the stormy gray of his eyes, listening to the contained

36

anger of his words. "That mine is unsafe, Catherine, and those men are in danger. And I'm not going to walk away from it."

"Why do you care about those miners?" It was a stupid thing to say and Catherine knew it even before the question left her lips, but she resented his implication that without him to see to the right of it, she'd continue to endanger the men.

His hands tightened and, though there was no pain, Catherine was more aware than ever of his restrained strength. And something else. There was no denying the sensual excitement his touch evoked.

"I care about the miners, Catherine, because I am a miner. I handled the mules as a pit boy until I was big enough to swing a pick. Six years I worked underground, and the reason I'm here to tell about it is that someone kept it safe, whether it was because it made more sense financially or because it was a matter of caring about the men in the tunnels."

Nick finished his impassioned speech feeling foolish. Why would she care what his life had been? He never told people about his past. Ever since Travis Fielding had taken him from the mines, Nick had worked hard to capture the persona of a gentleman. At Mr. Fielding's suggestion, he had studied, learning to do more than the rudimentary reading and writing he'd picked up from his mother before she died. Fielding paid him well, and Nick used the money to buy the clothes, books, and lodging that went along with being well born.

Now he had let this woman be privy to his background—all because of a handful of slaves. She was right. They were none of his concern. But, dammit, he cared about what happened to them. Nick looked into Catherine's upturned face, and a new and disturbing thought filled his mind. He cared about what happened to her, too.

He said he was a miner; yet, at times, he dressed like a gentleman. Catherine didn't have time to think what this meant. She didn't have time to think at all. Without knowing why or even how, Catherine felt a change come over Nicholas. It stole the air from her. Her lips parted to help her breathe, and her breasts rose and fell under his hot stare.

Catherine knew he was going to kiss her even before he began lowering his head. Stop him, her mind screamed. You are Catherine Lorraine Brousseau, proud descendant of the French Huguenots who have owned this land for seven generations, and he is but a miner who disguises himself as a gentleman, a flirt who teases your sister, and now you.

But even as her mind preached reason, her body rebelled. His lips were too tempting not to want them pressed against hers, his arms too strong not to want them wrapped around her. She moved into his embrace softly, willingly, all too aware of the long, hard length of his thighs and chest against hers.

"Catherine, is that Henry you're talking to?"

The voice, the words, she heard every day of her life startled Catherine so that all she could do was jerk away from what her senses still craved. Catherine's hand flew to her throat and she frantically tried to calm the pulse that fluttered madly against her fingers. It took several moments and a second call from her grandmother before Catherine felt composed enough to answer. And all this time, she studiously ignored the man who had ignited her passions without so much as a kiss.

"No, Grandmere. It's Mr. Colton." Catherine started back toward her grandmother's room. It was past time to help the older lady rise, a task that Catherine never failed to do. There was no need to question what had kept her from her duty today.

"Is he that kind gentleman I met at supper last night?" Grandmere's voice was weak but easily heard.

Catherine stole a glance at Nick. He stood, his back to her, staring out the window. "Yes, Grandmere. That was Mr. Colton."

"Such a nice young man, Catherine. Don't you think?"

Nick heard Catherine's grandmother and smiled to himself. Nice was probably the last word Catherine wanted to use to describe him. But he listened while she did just that. Though agreeing with her grandmother was hardly a testimonial, Nick was surprised at how good it made him feel.

"Mr. Colton."

Nick looked around and into the leaf-green eyes of the woman he'd almost kissed. Though he knew the encounter had flustered her, she seemed to have regained control of her emotions and now spoke to him in a very businesslike manner. Nick decided to answer in kind.

"Yes, Miss Brousseau?"

Catherine ignored the sarcasm she was certain

laced his words. "I will be busy for a while. Please meet me later at the mine."

She had dismissed him. Right now Nick wasn't certain if it was a temporary measure or something more permanent. If he were a betting man, he'd go with the temporary. Miss Catherine Brousseau needed him, and he was pretty sure she knew it. The thought made him whistle as he retraced his steps to the mine.

Nick decided to use the time waiting for Catherine to do a more thorough inspection of the tunnel. Before he came out of it earlier this morning, Nick had called up the underground crew. He'd set them all to work at the tipple, sorting the coal and loading it onto the cars of the inclined railroad. The train, powered by gravity, was one advantage Catherine had going for her. Before the local mine owners had gotten together to build tracks that ran down hill, thirteen miles to the James River, the cost of shipping coal had been eight to ten cents a bushel. Now it was less than three.

The miners were still busy when Nick arrived at the mine, although he knew it wouldn't take them all day to complete the task he'd given them. Hopefully, by the time they'd finished, he'd have talked Catherine into letting him take a crew into the forest. He wanted to look for trees that might provide some sturdy timbers to shore up the mine ceiling.

After talking briefly with a few of the men he'd met that morning, Nick went into the lamproom for a Davy lamp. Nick could have called on the gas man to accompany him into the pit, but there was really no need. He'd done this job before. When he was about fifteen, Nick had been the one to go down in the mine first to check for pockets of methane. If the highly explosive and suffocating gas was encountered it extinguished the flame on the Davy lamp, a sure sign to clear the mine immediately.

Nick stepped into the large woven basket and on his nod was slowly lowered into the shaft. Some thirty minutes later when he signaled to ascend, he rose toward the ever growing circle of light. At the top he found Catherine waiting for him.

"Well?" she asked, standing with her hands folded at her tiny waist.

"Nothing's changed since this morning." Nick walked toward the dressing room, Catherine close by his side. "There's not enough support for the amount of area dug out. The grain in coal runs on an angle. If the coal shifts . . ." Nick left the rest unsaid. They both knew what would happen.

"What can we do about it?"

"We?" Nick's rakish brow arched with that single word before he disappeared inside the rough board structure the miners used as a washroom. He was covered head to toe with coal dust and would feel much better talking to Miss Brousseau after he'd cleaned up, especially since it seemed the little lady had come around some since their earlier discussion.

Catherine leaned against the shed and kicked a forlorn-looking clump of grass with the toe of her leather shoe. The small group of miners who'd stopped their work to watch her talking with the new manager had been all that kept her from following

41

Nicholas into the building. He had a lot of nerve, treating her this way, especially since she'd come down to the mine to let him know he wasn't fired. If this was the way he was going to act, maybe she'd just forget about giving him another chance.

A sigh escaped her. Who was she trying to fool? Catherine needed Nicholas Colton and he knew it. She just hoped he could offer a solution to her dilemma.

"Well, do you want to know what *we* are going to do about the mine?" Nick came out of the washroom, watching for the expression on Catherine's face as he deliberately baited her. He figured that after all her dos and do nots, he owed her one. She didn't disappoint him. Her full bottom lip thinned and tightened, and her eyes darkened till the green was the rich deep shade of a pine forest. Her face came alive, and even if he was the cause of her anger, Nick decided he preferred this to the look of dejection he'd noticed when he'd stepped out of the shed.

Impossible! She simply could not work with such an arrogant man. Catherine had it on the tip of her tongue to tell him so when something happened. Her gaze lowered. Catherine was sure she'd seen men's chests before. After all, she spent a lot of her time at the mine. Certainly other men had cleaned up and left their shirts unbuttoned. But if they had, Catherine could remember it no more than she could take her eyes off the broad expanse of hair-covered flesh revealed by Nick's open shirt. Catherine's mouth went dry and she had the wildest urge to test the texture of the golden brown curls that covered his bronzed skin.

"Well, do you want me to tell you or not?"

Nick's voice helped focus Catherine's attention back on the subject at hand. She swallowed, hoping he hadn't noticed her foolish reaction to seeing his chest. "Yes." The word was little more than a squeak. Catherine cleared her throat and tried again. This time she sounded less giddy. "I am interested in any suggestions you may have."

Nick grinned and shook his head. The little lady was set on being the boss. "Well then, Miss Brousseau, I suggest we shore up the tunnel with timbers."

"Timbers." Catherine worried her bottom lip. "That could be expensive."

"Not if we take them from the woods around here." Nick motioned to the trees beyond the mine. "I checked this morning and I think there are several trees that are large enough."

Catherine just shook her head. "I don't own these woods. Oh, they used to be part of Greenfield, but no more. The house, the mine, and the trail between are all that's left." Catherine started walking past the shed, farther away from any miners who might be listening. Nick fell in step beside her, buttoning his shirt as he went along. "I'm afraid I haven't any money to buy timbers, or anything else for that matter. I've saved almost enough to pay my neighbor for the lease of his slaves to work the mine, but I can't use that because the money is due next week."

"You mean the slaves don't belong to you?"

"No. As I said, they're leased. Greenfield hasn't

43

owned any slaves for years." She didn't mention that her father had given them all letters of manumission. Her father might have had a poor mind for business, but he'd been a kind man, in his own way. Freeing the slaves when there were no longer any fields for them to work, rather than selling them further south, had been an example of his thoughtful ways. Of course, it also meant that the slaves had been free to choose not to work in the mine, which most of them had done.

Nick nodded, glad for this bit of information. If the slaves didn't belong to Catherine, there was no reason for her to use them. "Using slaves to work your mine is something I want to discuss with you."

Catherine was about to ask what he meant when her attention was drawn to a small buggy traveling up the gravel road toward them. With a twinge of regret she recognized it as belonging to John Parker. Probably coming to check on his property, she thought, frowning at the idea. From all she'd heard, the slaves were better off working for her than in one of Parker's fields. Maybe part of her bitterness stemmed from the fact that those fields used to belong to the Brousseau family. They had since Paul Brousseau fled France in 1700 to settle the land south of the James River given to him by England's King William.

"Catherine! Mr. Colton!" Marie leaned out of the buggy, waving as John Parker brought the horse to a stop. "John came to the house to see you, Catherine, and I told him you were at the mine. He just insisted that I come along."

44

Watching Marie look down at Nicholas Colton expectantly before he reached up and lifted her from her seat, Catherine could well imagine who did the insisting. Well, she couldn't be bothered about her sister's flirtations now. Catherine had more important worries on her mind.

"What brings you over this way, John?" Catherine's smile never reached her eyes as she greeted the owner of Windy Hill, the plantation that neighbored what was left of her own.

"Why, I came to see you, Catherine." John Parker removed his hat and bowed over the hand Catherine offered him. "I didn't realize you'd be so busy." His gaze slid toward Nick.

"This is my new mine manager." Catherine's tone was even and Nick couldn't tell if she was sorry or glad about the fact. "John Parker, this is Nicholas Colton."

Nick reached out to shake hands with Catherine's neighbor, conscious of a sense of dislike that seemed to flow both ways. There was nothing objectionable about the man, certainly nothing to elicit the feelings Nick harbored. Parker was average height, perhaps a little on the thin side, with dark brown hair, slicked back and straight except for the crease his top hat had caused.

"You from around these parts, Mr. Colton?" John Parker studied Nick, making him wish he were wearing anything but the partially buttoned hard luck clothes of a miner.

"No sir, I'm not." Nick's succinct reply bordered on rudeness, but he noticed Catherine was quick to smooth over the breach.

"Mr. Colton is from New Castle."

John Parker let out a low whistle through his teeth. "You're bringing them all the way from England now?" He shook his head. "When are you going to realize, Catherine, that all the help you need is right here in your own back yard?"

A short while later Nick stood beside Marie, watching the dust spun up by the buggy wheels drift down and settle on the road. After Parker's remark about finding help, Catherine had been quick to suggest that she and Parker return to the house for a talk. Since the buggy held only two people with any amount of comfort, Marie volunteered to stay behind and walk home.

Nick glanced over at the woman's flounced gown and wondered in disgust if he was going to end up carrying her over the rough path.

"They look sweet together. Don't you think?"

"Who?" Nick slapped his hat once against his pants leg, dislodging a sprinkling of coal dust before finger combing his still damp hair and covering it with the hat.

"Why, my sister and Mr. Parker, silly." Marie touched his arm in mild rebuke and let her fingers linger.

Sweet? John Parker he didn't like, and as for Catherine . . . Well, Nick could think of several words to describe her—bold, bossy, even beautiful, he reluctantly admitted—but sweet? He wasn't about to admit any of this to Marie, so Nick mumbled something that she seemed to take as agreement.

A sudden premonition gripped Nick, and he stared

down into Marie's too-innocent blue eyes. "Is there any reason they should look sweet together?" Marie's face lit up and Nick knew he'd not only been maneuvered into asking the question, but that he wasn't going to like the answer.

"Of course," Marie cooed. "Didn't Catherine tell you? John Parker is her intended."

Chapter Three

The oak leave's serrated edges meshed like inter-twined fingers, all but blocking the star-sprinkled canopy of night from Nick's view. He leaned against the rough trunk of a loblolly pine, smoking a cheroot, thinking. Surrounded by the soft darkness, with only an occasional hoot owl or croaking frog to distract him, his mind was too active.

Suddenly annoyed by his train of thought Nick threw down the cigar stub grinding out the spark with the heel of his boot. What did he care if Catherine Brousseau was engaged to John Parker? Though he thought she could have used better judgment in choosing, it made no difference to him who she married. He just wished she'd told him, that's all.

Here he'd been worrying about her, thinking she needed his help, when all the time she had a rich neighbor to take care of her. Well, he'd given Catherine his advice, and that was all he could do— all he was being paid to do. She'd likely close the mine now anyway.

Nick shrugged his broad shoulders as he began walking along the path. It was late, but he was too restless to sleep. Shutting down the mine was probably the best thing to do. Maybe he'd suggest she sell it to Travis Fielding. From what Nick could tell, Greenfield Mine had rich coal deposits. With the financial support that Fielding could provide, the mine could easily be profitable.

Yes, that's what he'd do, Nick thought as he wandered along the trail. It would be his last act before returning to England. Funny how the thought of leaving didn't give him a thrill. Hell, he hadn't even wanted to come to America.

The border of trees widened, revealing a small grassy meadow awash in moonlight, and that's when Nick saw her. She wore a white, muslin nightdress that shone almost iridescent in the pale light. Her hair was unbound, and the thick auburn tresses waved beguilingly down her slender back. Catherine didn't see him as she stood staring off into the darkness, and Nick knew he should leave.

But he didn't. A force he couldn't control moved him forward until he inadvertently stepped upon a twig, heralding his presence.

Catherine turned, instantly aware that she wasn't alone. She saw Nicholas watching her and pulled her knitted shawl tighter around her shoulders. Something in the dark shadows of his eyes made her aware of the intimate nature of this encounter.

"You startled me." A foolish thing to say, Catherine thought, for he hadn't, but it was all that came to mind to break the tense silence that

50

enveloped them.

"I apologize." Nick moved closer, drawn by the moonlight and her. "I didn't expect to see you out here."

"I couldn't sleep." Catherine stared at a spot on the ground in front of Nick's boots. "It's been so hot this spring. The cooler night air feels good."

"Is that why you're wrapped in that shawl?"

Catherine's gaze rose and met Nick's. "What?"

"This." Nick traced the intricate knitted pattern with a long lazy finger. "The way you have yourself bundled up, I thought you must be cold."

Cold? How could she possibly be cold with his large body so close to her? Every time he came near her she felt her blood run hot. Catherine's hands tightened in the folds of the wrapper. "No, I'm not chilly. It's just that I—"

"Don't want me to see you." Nick finished the sentence for her, though he by no means thought it was what she'd planned to say. But it was the truth.

Nick had almost kissed her this morning, and all day at the most inopportune times he'd found himself thinking about it, wondering what it would have been like. After he'd learned about Parker, Nick had almost convinced himself that it was just as well he'd never know. Now, he knew he meant to find out.

She should have run as soon as she'd seen him. Catherine realized that. But it was too late, now. Maybe it had been too late then. Catherine held her breath and waited to see what Nick would do.

The hand that had tracked the weave of her shawl inched up her neck, soothing the fevered skin beneath her hair. His thumb moved forward, slowly, angling her chin, raising her lips to meet his. But he didn't kiss her. His mouth was but a whisper away, so close that his breath fanned her cheek, so close that the tiniest movement would bring them together. Yet, still he didn't kiss her.

Catherine throbbed with anticipation. She had wanted his kiss this morning, dreamed of it all day, and now she longed for it.

His first taste of her was light, fleeting. No more than a brief teasing of the senses. But it sent a jolt through his body. Nick's arms folded around her slim waist and his mouth pressed against hers, hard. The pressure forced her lips apart and at that moment Nick's tongue thrust into the honeyed depths of her mouth.

The sensation was like none Catherine had ever experienced. She wanted to wrap her arms around his neck, to touch the thick dark hair that curled at his nape, but she couldn't do that and clutch her shawl, too. Silently, the wool garment drifted to the grass at her feet.

The muslin of Catherine's nightgown was worn, thinned by numerous washings. Nick imagined it served her well on warm nights such as this. It served him well, also. He had no need for imagination as his hands roamed the feminine curves of her back and shoulders, as his chest crushed her full breasts. She wore nothing underneath. The very thought heightened his arousal till he felt his heart pounding against his ribs, and tearing his mouth away from hers was the only way he could breathe.

"Marie was right. You are sweet."

The words were mumbled into the softness of her

52

cheek and, at first Catherine didn't understand what he'd said. Then one word became painfully clear. Marie. Nick might be kissing her, but he was thinking of her sister. What had been in her mind to think he wanted her?

Catherine pushed knotted fists against his chest, ignoring the kisses he lavished on her neck as effectively as he ignored her lack of response. "Stop it! Mr. Colton, please stop!"

Nick raised his head, staring down into eyes that were no longer closed in ecstasy, but glaring angrily at him. "What's wrong?"

Catherine reached down, grabbed her shawl and violently shook it free of debris before tossing it around her. "Nothing's wrong, Mr. Colton, except I'm standing in a meadow in the middle of the night being pawed by the hired help."

Nick's eyes narrowed and his hands encircled her upper arms, pulling her hard against him. "Hired help I may be, but that didn't seem to bother you a minute ago."

The truth of what he said caused the heat to rise and stain Catherine's cheeks. He was right. She hadn't cared then that he was a miner in her employ, and she didn't care now. Fear that he'd know how much she'd wanted him, or that he'd realize even now she was tempted to melt back into his arms, strengthened her resolve. Catherine raised her chin. "Get your hands off me."

"Gladly." Nick let go of Catherine so quickly she almost lost her footing. He reached out to steady her, ashamed that he'd let his temper get the best of him, but she'd already turned and started stomping across the meadow behind the house.

Jamming his hands into the pockets of his trousers, Nick watched her progress. It was for the best. Even though her response to him had been passionate, a woman like Catherine Brousseau was not someone to toy with. No. He could imagine with Catherine it would be all or nothing. And in his case it would be nothing.

He kicked a clump of dried mud, then headed back to the path. Hell, why was he suddenly feeling so sorry for himself? That was one thing he never did. Twelve hour shifts in the mines hadn't done it to him, and he'd be damned if he'd let a bossy, green-eyed woman do it. On impulse, Nick yelled over his shoulder, "It was real nice knowing you, Miss Brousseau. First thing in the morning I'll be leaving. I'll be sure to give your regards to Travis Fielding."

Leaving! Catherine swirled around, forgetting to clutch her shawl in her haste to discover what he was talking about. "But, you can't go." Not after she'd forced herself to make a bargain with John Parker. Just the thought of her talk with her neighbor made Catherine shudder as she made her way back across the open field toward Nicholas.

John Parker had been more than willing to give her the extra time she needed to pay for the use of his slaves. Of course, Catherine knew he'd always been more than happy to extend her father extra time and money, too, for that matter. The extensions had lasted just long enough until her father had no recourse but to deed most of Greenfield over to Parker.

As much as she longed to, Catherine knew all the

blame couldn't be placed at John Parker's feet. Her father's habit of betting, and betting poorly, on just about anything that came along was the real cause of losing most of their land, but Parker hadn't helped. And Catherine was sure he'd known what he was doing all along. Just the way he probably knew what he was doing now, granting Catherine an extension. Because wasn't she doing the same thing her father had done—gambling?

Oh, the last thing Catherine would do was wager on whose filly crossed the finish line first, or the roll of a die. But wasn't she gambling just the same? Gambling on herself. Gambling on Greenfield Mine. And most of all, gambling on the man who stood at the edge of the clearing, staring at her.

"You can't leave," Catherine repeated softly when she reached him.

Nick had been surprised when she'd stopped her retreat, demanding that he not go. He was even more shocked now that she'd marched up to him. Her expression, what he could see of it in the dim light afforded by the waning moon, appeared almost desperate. And her words were no longer an order but a plea.

"The timbers will be here day after tomorrow." Catherine looked up into Nick's ruggedly handsome face, waiting for him to say something, anything. If he left, she'd have no idea how to place the supports in the mine.

Cocking his head to one side, Nick folded his arms loosely across his broad chest. "I thought you didn't have the money to buy timbers."

"I don't, I mean, I didn't." Catherine shook her

55

head and started over, annoyed that she became flustered whenever she was near Nicholas Colton. "Mr. Parker agreed to let me pay him later for the use of his slaves."

"How much later?" Nick didn't know why he bothered to ask that. Parker probably granted his fiancée an unlimited time to pay him. After all, it was going to be all in the family.

"He gave me one month." At Nick's incredulous expression, Catherine repeated. "One month."

Nick straightened. "It will take almost that long to shore the tunnel up. You won't be taking coal from that mine for a good twenty days, and that's if nothing goes wrong." Nick forced himself to calm down. So what if the little lady didn't meet her deadline? No doubt her loving neighbor would give her another one.

Catherine swallowed back panic. She hadn't thought it would take nearly that long to have the mine safe to work again. What was she going to do? John Parker wouldn't give her more time without demanding something in return, of that she was certain. But what would he seek in payment? Would it be the house, the mine—or her?

Nick didn't miss the look of desperation, though he was at a loss as to why she should feel that way. "Wait a minute." He'd been hit by a sudden inspiration. "Is the money you owe Parker advance payment?" At Catherine's nod, Nick went on. "Good. Don't pay him."

"What?"

Nick took a step toward Catherine. "Don't lease the slaves. I've been meaning to talk to you about

56

this. If you'd had experienced miners working for you they'd have known what Sam Stevens was doing. Hell, there isn't a miner I know who'd rob the pillars as was done in your shaft, no matter who told them to do it."

Catherine tossed a stray lock of auburn hair behind her shoulder. What Nick said sounded reasonable, but if she didn't have the slaves in the mine, who would she have? Greenfield Mine's reputation wasn't the best. There had been too many accidents in it over the years. Catherine had tried before to hire miners with little success. No one seemed anxious to work for her. But she didn't feel like telling Nicholas that, not now. Besides, now the important thing was to get the mine producing again. Then they could talk about who would mine it.

"I'll think about it, Mr. Colton. In the meantime, I would like you to work out plans to shore up the mine and make it safe." Catherine turned on her heel and started back across the meadow. She hardly broke stride when she heard his sarcastic, "Anything you say, Miss Brousseau." Catherine didn't need his tone to tell her she sounded ungrateful and authoritative. But she hadn't known what else to do. Standing there beside Nicholas Colton, with him showing such enthusiasm for his idea, she'd had a moment of fear. She couldn't afford to count on him too much. He'd be leaving soon and when he did, the running of Greenfield Mine would be solely her burden, just as before. Resignedly, Catherine trudged home, climbed the stairs, and slipped into her bed.

*　　*　　*

True to John Parker's word, the timbers had arrived two days later. Since then, Nick had been doing some supervising, but most of the time he'd been working right along with the men placing the supports at strategic intervals in the tunnel. There had been few problems, and the job, for all its unpredictability, had gone smoothly.

Nick's greatest fear had been that the weak coal pillars would collapse before the wooden braces could be placed, but now seventeen days later, that didn't seem likely. There was only a small section left to do, and Nick had checked that about ten minutes before, leaving a crew of eight men to finish the job while he came up to complete some paper work.

Nick wiped the sleeve of his canvas shirt across his damp brow. The unseasonable hot spell hadn't let up, and as he squinted into the noonday sun, Nick thought about going back into the mine, just to cool off. The constant temperature of about sixty-five degrees would be a welcome relief from the heat.

A rustling noise behind him caught Nick's attention and he turned to see Catherine emerging from the shadows of the path. Since the night they'd kissed in the meadow, their meetings had been brief and very formal. It hadn't been difficult to keep their distance. Nick had been working hard, and she'd stayed away from the mine almost entirely. They'd seen each other at dinner, but Marie and Catherine's grandmother did most of the talking then, and Nick had taken to excusing himself as soon as the meal was over. He did report the mine's progress to her in the mornings, but even those times were short and succinct.

Nick watched Catherine as she made her way towards him, sorry that he hadn't taken the time to clean himself up when he came above ground. He felt dirty and sweaty and he marveled, not for the first time, at how she always managed to look so fresh and cool. Even in her plain, dark dress, with her shining hair pulled back from her face, she looked inviting.

"Are you almost finished?"

Nick shook his head and grinned, his teeth flashing white against his coal dust covered face. No, 'How do you do?' for the boss lady, she got right down to business. "Almost," Nick said with some pride. He'd finished the job ahead of his own schedule, and realized he felt a satisfying sense of accomplishment. "We should be able to start taking coal out tomorrow, day after at the latest."

"Good." Catherine worried her bottom lip, trying to calculate how far behind production this delay had put her. Maybe if she were lucky, she'd still have time to earn the money to pay John Parker.

"Have you thought about what I said concerning hiring experienced miners to work the mine?" Nick wasn't certain this was the time to bring up this topic, but the longer the slaves worked the mine, the more money it was costing.

Catherine's gaze lifted to meet his. "I've thought about it."

"And?"

"I'm just not . . ." Catherine paused as an odd tingling sensation vibrated up her legs. "What's that?" She looked at Nick beseechingly, but he'd already started racing toward the mine entrance. Catherine snatched up her skirts and ran after him.

Nick barked orders to the miners who'd stayed above ground. In his worry over what was happening in the shaft, he'd forgotten all about Catherine till he felt someone tugging on his shirt. Turning to brush aside the pesky irritation, he looked down into her panic-stricken face.

"Get the hell out of here!" he yelled, his voice harsh with concern. But she didn't move. She just stood, as if rooted to the spot, staring at him, her green eyes wide with shock.

The ground beneath him trembled, and Nick grabbed Catherine's shoulders, shaking her till her eyelids fluttered shut, then opened. "Do you hear me? Get a—"

A rumbling roar escaped through the hole in the earth, followed by a monstrous cloud of black. Nick clutched Catherine to him and threw himself to the ground. He landed with a thud on the packed dirt, pain shooting from his elbow to his shoulder, as he rolled his body to cover hers. Another thunderous noise followed and Nick squeezed his eyes shut and held onto Catherine.

He waited. The silence now lay as heavy on the land as the spewn coal dust. It was so quiet Nick could hear the pounding of Catherine's heart as she lay beneath him. Slowly he opened his eyes and looked into hers. Her face was as black as his. "Are you all right?"

Catherine nodded, barely able to speak as the old fear overwhelmed her. "W-was it an explosion?"

"No." Nick rose, pulling Catherine to her feet. The deafening roar of an explosion was what he had waited for, dreaded. Thank God it hadn't come. "But some of the mine caved in."

"What are you going to do?" Nick had turned away from Catherine, yelling for someone to man the rope that lowered the basket into the tunnel.

Nick shrugged off the hand she'd placed on his arm. "I'm going down."

Catherine looked first at the mine entrance where black dust still hung thickly in the air, then back at Nick. "But—"

"There are men down in the shaft, Catherine."

Catherine's breath left her body on a rush of air. She'd just assumed since Nick was out of the mine that everybody was. "Are they dead?" The question was a tormented whisper.

"I don't know." Nick brushed a strand of hair off her face. His touch gentled and he let his hand linger over the soft swell of her dirt-covered cheek. "Can you get the doctor?" She seemed so fragile—as if a stiff breeze would blow her over—that Nick hated to ask her to do anything. But he'd seen people in shock before and the best thing was to keep them busy and their minds occupied.

Straightening her back, Catherine forced the nightmarish visions from her head. She would not think of her grandfather, her sweet, kind grandpere, lying on the rocky floor of the mine, struggling for every breath till there was no more air—

"Catherine!"

Her gaze flew to Nick's and she nodded. "The

61

doctor. I'll go for him." Catherine turned and started running along the path.

She burst through the front door startling Marie, and yelling for Betsy. "Go into the village and find Doctor Shelton. Tell him there's been an accident at the mine." Catherine heard her sister's cry of dismay, but ignored it as she climbed the stairs and began pulling linens from a carved chest. She didn't realize Marie had followed her till she turned, balancing a pile of sheets and blankets in her arms.

"Is Nicholas hurt?" Marie's wide, ruffled skirts filled the bedroom doorway.

"No." Catherine paused, waiting for Marie to move so she could take the bedding downstairs. "But there are others trapped in the mine."

"Oh, thank God," Marie said, moving out of Catherine's way, apparently oblivious to anything but the news that Nick was all right.

Catherine didn't give her sister a backward glance as she struggled down the steps. She hoped what she'd told Marie was true. Nicholas had been safe when she left him, but she knew he planned to go down in the tunnel. Catherine hurried her step, anxious to get back to the mine.

When she arrived, Nicholas was nowhere in sight, but three of the miners who'd been in the hole were sitting propped against the dressing room. Catherine rushed over, sinking to her knees in the black dust. "Has Doctor Shelton arrived yet?" she asked of no one in particular.

"No ma'am, he ain't come," a miner she recognized as Amos answered.

Catherine examined the cut on the side of his face, and started tearing a piece of the sheeting, while calling to another man to bring her some water. "What happened?" She dabbed at the bloody gash, wiping it free of dirt before wrapping a linen strip around his head and tying it behind his ear.

"We was puttin' up them timbers when all the sudden the ceiling just starts fallin' in. Jim, Boz and me," Amos waved his arm at the other men lying beside him, "We weren't so far back as the others, so when Mr. Nick and the others come down, he found us pretty quick."

"Is Mr. Colton down there now?" Catherine moved over to Boz, but found him suffering from only a few scratches.

"Yea, he ain't been up since it happened. There's about five men trapped down there, and Mr. Nick and the others is trying to dig them out."

By the time William Shelton arrived, Catherine had taken care of the three men's most obvious injuries. But she was still glad to have the doctor here. The men who'd been caught behind the slide were likely to be in worse shape. And of course, there were the men digging to free the miners who were trapped. There was always the chance that their rescue attempts would trigger another cave-in. Catherine tried not to think of that.

The afternoon faded into evening, and still the men worked. Often the signal was given, and the above ground crew, by the light of lanterns and torches placed around the shaft opening, would haul up the basket, with its cargo of hot, dirty men. They'd slump down, exhausted, in the shade of the lamp-room, and Catherine would move among them, handing out drinks and the fried chicken Betsy had brought. But Nick never came up. Catherine would watch for him each time the basket ascended, and each time she swallowed a lump of disappointment.

"Won't be long now." A rescue worker acknowledged with a nod the biscuit Catherine had just given him. "Mr. Nick, he got a hole open to them."

"Are they all right?" Catherine slid down beside him, more tired than she could remember ever being.

"I reckon so. They was talkin' up a storm when we broke through."

A few minutes later—Catherine had just closed her eyes to rest—a wild cheer rang through the air as the first of the rescued miners was brought to the surface. It wasn't till the last of them was safely above ground that Nick followed.

Catherine stood, absently brushing the dirt from her dress as she tried to catch a glimpse of him. It wasn't easy. The rescued miners pressed around Nick and the others. But he stood taller than most, and through the crowd she saw him. Though black coal dust clung to his face and rumpled hair, he appeared, in the flickering lantern light to be sound enough. White teeth flashed in a grin as he acknowledged a comment from a miner.

Finding her knees suddenly weak, Catherine backed up till she could lean against the rough boards of the shack. Through most of the afternoon and night she'd remained calm, at least outwardly so, but now Catherine could barely control the emotions that washed through her. It was only relief that all the men were safe she tried to tell herself. After all, as owner of the mine, they were her responsibility. That must be the reason for her racing heart and the legs that could barely support her. What else could it be? Then Nick turned. His eyes met hers, locked with hers, and Catherine felt the air rush from her body.

Chapter Four

"Why are you doing this?" Catherine wished the question back as soon as she voiced it. Why was unimportant. Besides, Catherine felt certain she knew the reason—the real reason—behind John Parker's refusal to allow her continued use of his slaves. He wouldn't be content until he'd acquired all of Greenfield. But it simply wasn't in Catherine's nature to accept defeat without a fight. So she questioned—and argued.

"Catherine dear, I tried to explain—"

"Yes, I know. Your concern for your slaves is admirable, John." Catherine could not keep sarcasm from tingeing her voice. "However, you have my assurance that the mine is perfectly safe now."

"Your assurance?"

"Mine and Mr. Colton's," Catherine amended. She hadn't actually been in the mine, but her manager, after closing off the small portion that had caved in, seemed convinced that the tunnels were adequately shored up.

"You put too much trust in that man, Catherine."

"John," Catherine sighed, sinking into the chair behind her desk. "He's my manager. He comes highly recommended, *and* even without that he's proven his worth since he's been here."

"Really?" John Parker leaned across the polished desk, his brown eyes intent on Catherine's face. "In the short time since his arrival, he's fired your bottom boss and caused a cave-in at your mine."

"He hardly caused the cave-in, John. And how did you know about Sam Stevens?"

"Word spreads, Catherine." He shrugged, straightened, then retreated to a chair across the room. "Besides, he came by Windy Hill asking for a job."

"And you gave it to him?"

John Parker crossed his legs, making certain the crease in his trousers remained straight. "Had no reason not to. My mining operation is not near as large as yours, but I can always use a good man."

"That *good man* is the reason you almost lost eight slaves." Catherine rose, moving toward the window. The air inside the library sweltered with late afternoon heat, and she longed to join Grandmere in the shaded cool of the garden. But first she had to try and persuade her neighbor to change his mind.

"If you're referring to the charge your new mine manager made about robbing the pillars, Sam told me all about that."

"And you still hired him?" Catherine asked incredulously.

"When he explained that the charges were trumped up by your Mr. Colton I did."

"Trumped up. Why would Mr. Colton do something like that?" Catherine had meant her question to be rhetorical, to show the absurdity of Sam Steven's claim, but John didn't seem to notice.

"How should I know," he answered. "He comes here and tries to take over. Fires a man who's worked for you since before your daddy died, interferes when your friends and neighbors try to help you."

"Help me?" Catherine spun away from the faint breeze drifting through the window and faced her neighbor, her green eyes bright with anger. "Is that what you call riding over here and telling me I can no longer lease slaves from you?"

"Now Catherine, I've known you near all your life. You must know I have your best interests at heart."

Catherine knew nothing of the sort, but she let him continue as she forced herself to calm down. She sank into the ladder back chair by the window as the scent of the lilac bush beside the porch wafted about her.

"If you'd only give up this foolish notion of running the mine by yourself," John continued, "We would all be a lot happier. There is no reason to put off our marriage any longer." John raised his fine-boned hand as if to ward off the protest he assumed would come. "Now I know you said you weren't ready, but it's what your daddy wanted. And it would make things easier for you, not to mention for your grandmother and sister. You aren't in a position to think of only yourself, Catherine."

As much as she hated to admit it, he was right. As Marie was fond of pointing out to her, Catherine's refusal to accept John Parker's proposal of marriage kept what was left of the Brousseaus in dire straights. With one word Catherine could assure that Grandmere lived her remaining days in comfort. She'd be cared for by more than one busy granddaughter and a middle-aged cook. Without the mine to worry about, Catherine could spend more time with her grandmother instead of sitting her under an elm tree—alone—with only the blue jays and sparrows to amuse her.

Then there was Marie. Perhaps if she had the pretty things she desired, she wouldn't be so . . . Catherine forced her thoughts away from her sister. Thinking of Marie's shortcomings would accomplish nothing. For no matter what her feelings might be, Marie was her responsibility.

Marry John Parker. That's all she'd have to do. Then why did it seem like such a sacrifice? Catherine rose. "I'm sorry John, but Grandmere has been alone in the garden too long. I really must see to her." It was a dismissal, pure and simple. She knew it, and by the stiff way in which John retrieved his hat and cane from the library table, she was certain he knew it also.

But she couldn't marry him. Even if she didn't blame him in part for the hard times that had befallen her family, she just couldn't do it. Not as long as there were any other options open to her. And right now, she was already considering the possibility of leasing slaves from other plantation owners in the area.

After a strained good-bye that hardly suggested they were a betrothed couple, Catherine walked around the side of the house toward the garden. The heat had nudged the blossoms open, and the spicy fragrance of arbutus mingled with the sweet lilacs. Catherine paused on the grassy path and leaned

70

against the weatherboard wall. Closing her eyes, she breathed deeply, letting the smells remind her of springs when she was young, and Momma, Pappa and Grandpere were still alive. They were so happy. On warm afternoons they'd all sit in the garden. Catherine and Marie would run around till they were hot and tired then flop onto the soft grass and make wreaths of clover. Grandmere had taught them to weave the stems, and she'd laugh as they placed the crowns of plump pink and white flowers on their heads and pretend to be fairy queens. The sound floated to her across the years, enhancing the memory. Her grandmother's laughter—what a precious sound.

Catherine opened her eyes as another wave of giggles drifted to her on the spring scented air. This was no memory. This was real and now, and so unexpected that Catherine paused before following the path to the garden, afraid of breaking the spell. But it was broken for her. Another laugh, this one rich, bold, and decidedly masculine, rang out. Nicholas Colton.

Hurrying around the house, Catherine stopped when she spotted them sitting in the dappled sunlight of the spreading elm. Grandmere, her frail legs bundled in a love-knot quilt, the one she'd stitched so diligently fifty years earlier, rested in the rocking chair Catherine had carried out for her. She leaned forward slightly when she spoke, but it was hardly necessary. Grandmere had Nicholas Colton's undivided attention.

They hadn't noticed her, and Catherine watched, fascinated as her rugged mine manager lounged on

71

the spring-bright grass at her grandmother's feet. He smiled, a genuine smile full of warmth—a smile that spoke of the boy he must have been. Catherine felt a fluttering in her breast. As elusive as the breeze that ruffled through his rumpled sun-kissed brown hair, the feeling nonetheless startled her.

She'd certainly seen him smile before. Marie with her fawning and simpering never failed to elicit a flirtatious grin that annoyed Catherine no end—more so because she suspected he knew it bothered her. And of course, the expression he used when speaking to Catherine always hinted at amusement. Except . . . Catherine shut her eyes, recalling how he'd looked at her when he'd come up from the mine after the cave-in. It was if he could see straight to her soul. The ensuing two days had done nothing to dim the memory.

"Catherine. Catherine dear, are you all right?"

Her grandmother's words jolted Catherine to the present. She started forward, hoping they wouldn't notice the blush she felt creeping up her neck. Nicholas Colton didn't rise when she approached. That didn't surprise her. What did was that she had a wild inclination to sink down beside him, lean against his sturdy canvas-clad chest and forget about her troubles.

She resisted the urge.

"I hope you don't mind my borrowing your Mr. Colton, dear," Grandmere said as Catherine brushed a kiss across her wrinkled brow. "He came up to the house to see you, but was sweet enough to stop and say hello to an old woman, and I'm afraid I've talked his ears off."

Sweet? Catherine would never have used that term to describe him, but apparently her grandmother thought so. As Nicholas Colton assured the older woman that he'd enjoyed their talk, and that his ears were still intact, Grandmere bent down and patted his cheek. Catherine bit back a smile, avoiding her mine manager's eyes.

"Are you ready for your nap now, Grandmere?" Catherine noticed the lines of fatigue etched more heavily on her grandmother's face.

"I am a little tired, dear. Perhaps if you could call Betsy. . . ."

"No need for that." Nick stood and reached down for the elderly lady. He'd seen Catherine and the black woman struggling to carry her around. "If you're not *too* heavy, I think I can handle you."

Grandmere laughed as he effortlessly scooped her up, quilt and all, and headed for the house. Catherine could only stare in disbelief. It had been a long time since she'd had any one to help her with grandmere except Betsy. Finally she lifted the rocker, muffling an oath when she knocked a runner against her leg. But before she could take a single step along the path Mr. Colton called over his shoulder.

"Leave the chair, Catherine. I'll get it later."

The way he said it—almost like an order—riled her, but she put the chair down. If he wanted to lug the cumbersome thing up to the house, fine. But she'd thank him to refer to her as Miss Brousseau. She didn't recall ever giving him permission to use her Christian name. A vivid memory of being held in his arms and kissed until she couldn't catch her breath flashed through Catherine's mind, but she pushed it aside. That had been an unfortunate mistake, and it certainly would never happen again.

Whether it was Catherine's worry over finding new miners or her grandmother's sudden desire to talk, getting her ready for a nap seemed to take forever.

"Your Mr. Colton is such a nice young man, dear. Don't you think?"

Catherine tugged the drapes together, blocking all but the staunchest sun rays from the back bedroom. "I suppose so," came her noncommittal answer.

"He reminds me so much of Henry. Do you see the resemblance?"

"Well, they are both coal miners." Catherine had long since given up speaking of her grandfather in the past tense.

"But it's more than that, dear. They both have a solid strength. And of course, they are both handsome devils."

"Grandmere!" Catherine feigned shock. "How you do talk." Catherine laughed as she adjusted the linen sheet around her grandmother's narrow shoulders.

"Don't think I'm too old to notice such things." Her cold hand rested on Catherine's for a moment. "But don't tell your grandfather I said that. He is frightfully jealous."

Catherine gently squeezed the frail hand. "I won't."

"I think he's sad, you know."

"Who?" Catherine brushed wispy white hair off her grandmother's forehead.

"Your Mr. Colton."

"Oh, I don't think—"

"But, he is, Catherine. You can tell by his eyes. Do you know what he told me?"

"No, what?" Catherine smiled. She'd noticed Nicholas Colton's eyes more times than she should, and she'd never thought they appeared sad. They could sparkle with silent amusement or flair steely bright with anger, or smolder with undisguised intensity that—

"He told me he never had a grandmother. Isn't that a shame?"

"It is." Catherine patted grandmere's wrinkled cheek. "Everyone should have a grandmother just like you. It's too bad Mr. Colton's grandmothers died before he got to know them."

"Oh, I don't think they died, dear. He never had any."

"But that's imposs—"

"Will Mr. Colton be at supper tonight?"

"I suppose."

"Good. I want Henry to meet him. And Catherine dear, you should talk to him more. He likes you, you know."

"Rest well, Grandmere." Brushing a quick kiss across her grandmother's cheek, Catherine backed out of the room. Poor Grandmere. She could get so confused. There was her insistent belief that her husband and children were still alive. Catherine had become accustomed to that. But now came her contention that Nicholas Colton was sad, and more, that he liked Catherine. She shook her head. Grandmere must not notice the way Mr. Colton smiled at Marie as she babbled at dinner.

"Is she asleep?"

Catherine closed the door softly and turned to where Nicholas Colton lounged in the chair by the window, his long legs stretched out before him. He certainly made himself at home in her library. "She will be soon."

He nodded and stood—a little late to be taken as a polite gesture. "She's a nice person."

"She says the same of you." The words were spoken before Catherine could stop herself.

Nick smiled in acknowledgement. He knew exactly what Catherine's grandmother had said. Not that he'd wanted to eavesdrop, but the door between the library and bedroom was ajar, and he could only concentrate on the open window so hard. He motioned toward the parlor. "I brought in the rocker, but I wasn't sure where to put it."

"That's fine." Catherine swallowed, and wiped her hands on her skirt, wondering why he made her so uncomfortable. She needed to stop thinking of that kiss, of the way he'd looked at her. "You wanted to see me, Mr. Colton?"

"Yes." Nick paused. "Miss Brousseau. I thought you'd like to know that your mine has started producing coal again. We sent the first load down the rails this morning."

"It shall possibly be our last."

"What?" His news hadn't gotten the reaction he'd hoped. When he'd hurried from the mine to tell her he'd hoped a smile of gratitude would light up her face.

Catherine sank into the chair behind her desk, pinching the bridge of her nose between her thumb and finger. "John Parker is refusing to lease me his

76

slaves for the next year."

"Is that what he was doing here?" Nick had been more annoyed than he cared to admit when he'd seen Catherine's fiancé's horse and buggy in front of the house.

Catherine closed her eyes and nodded, pressing her fingertips against her forehead. "Yes, he voiced great concern for his slaves. The cave-in, you know."

"Admirable."

The single word, the way he said it, made Catherine smile, despite herself. Opening her eyes, she began to explain what she planned to do, but he no longer sat in the chair across from her. She hadn't heard him move—didn't know where he'd gone till she felt his strong hands on her shoulders.

"Headache?"

His breath fanned against the back of her ear, fluttered a mahogany curl, and sent tingles down her spine. Catherine wanted to be indignant. The nerve of the man to sneak up behind her and touch her. "Mr. Colton, I—"

"I used to get them occasionally. From being down in the mines." Nick's fingers splayed across Catherine's back. He could feel her warmth through the worn cotton of her dress. "A friend of mine would do this for me. Usually helped."

"A friend?" Catherine couldn't picture anyone but a woman doing this for him. The movements were too sensual as his calloused thumbs traced the taut chords in her neck. The thought made her angrier still at his impertinence, but she couldn't form the words to make him stop.

"Hmmm." Nick wasn't about to tell her who he'd

77

learned this from, or how he'd usually repaid her kindness. "Helps to relieve tension and worry."

Catherine's head fell forward. "I suppose I am somewhat concerned about the mine."

And about your grandmother, and your sister, and what's left of your plantation, Nick finished for her silently. He brushed a burnished curl off her slender neck. He didn't like to see her trying to shoulder so much responsibility. Travis Fielding had told him to check out the mine as a possible acquisition. He hadn't actually said for Nick to make an offer, but . . . Nick gently squeezed the smooth skin at the base of her neck. He'd examined the mine. It had a lot of potential for producing coal. Maybe he'd offer a little more than it was worth. Help her out a bit.

"Catherine?"

"Mmmm?" He used her given name again, but somehow with his hands tracing sensual patterns on her shoulders, it didn't seem to matter.

"Maybe you should consider selling Greenfield?"

The pleasurable sensations ceased as Catherine's head snapped up. "I have no intention of selling the mine. If that's the best advice you can give me, perhaps you should return to England. I hear enough requests for me to sell without paying someone to do it."

"Who wants you to sell?" Nick moved around the desk, leaning his hip against its corner. The set of her small body precluded any further thoughts of massage.

"Marie for one," Catherine answered, surprised that her head didn't hurt anymore. She probably should thank him.

"Who else?"

He'd laid his hand across the thigh that rested on her desk. Large and scarred, it looked like a worker's hand—a miner's hand. She'd noticed that before, but she hadn't known then how gentle his hands could be. She could still feel the warmth of his touch. Her gaze traveled up till it met his. She didn't want to even talk about selling, but she guessed it would do no harm to answer him. Then they could move on to more important things, like leasing other slaves.

"John Parker wants me to sell."

"To him?"

"Yes, to him." Catherine rose and after retrieving a bonnet and pair of gloves off the library table, walked through the door to the outside. Nick fell in step beside her, settling his hat low to shade his eyes. "He's made me several offers."

"Why does he bother?"

"He wants the mine." Catherine stopped and faced her manager. His large form blocked the sun, and his face was hidden in shadows.

"Seems like it would just be easier to wait."

"For what?" Catherine wished she could see his expression. He sounded almost angry, but what had made him mad she couldn't imagine.

"For the wedding. Anything you own will belong to him then anyway."

No doubt about his anger now. His voice almost dripped with it. "Who told you Mr. Parker and I were to be married?"

Fool, Nick chastised himself. Why in the hell had he brought this subject up. He didn't give a damn who she married. Just help her get the mine running.

79

That's what he'd been sent here for.

"Who told you, Mr. Colton?" A bumblebee buzzed around Catherine's skirt, and she swished it away without taking her eyes off Nicholas.

"Your sister might have mentioned it." Nick couldn't remember ever feeling so foolish. The moment he found some miners to work the mine, he would sail for home—forget all about this hard-as-nails little lady who had a way of stirring up his insides with one look at her big green eyes.

"Well, it isn't true."

Damn. Nick cursed the relief that flowed through him like warm honey.

"He's asked a few times." Catherine couldn't imagine why she took the time to explain her relationship with John Parker to her mine manager—one of her employees. She started back along the brick path toward the stables. "But I have no intention of marrying him—or anyone," she added. "And I have no intention of s—"

"Selling the mine," Nick finished for her, feeling a smile spread across his face. "So what are we going to do now?"

What a strange man. First he seemed angry, for no apparent reason, and now, he wouldn't wipe that infectious grin off his face. Catherine entered the musty darkness of the stable, trying to ignore his expression. "*I* am going to visit some neighbors. *You* could probably be of some use at the mine."

"Visiting?" Nick cocked his head to the side. "That seems a little out of character." He chuckled as her chin shot up, and she glared at him with her spring-green eyes.

Catherine led one of her few remaining horses, a worn-out dapple gray that had seen better days, into the sunlight, and began hitching him to a small buggy. "I didn't say these were social calls, Mr. Colton. There's more than one plantation around here with slaves to lease. And I intend to find some workers."

"I still think you should look into hiring experienced miners. I'll bet we could—"

"Mr. Colton," Catherine interrupted, though she did accept his assistance into the buggy. "I've tried to hire workers before—with little success." She pulled a plain straw poke bonnet over her chignon and tied the ribbon quickly under her chin. Gathering up the reins, Catherine looked down into Nicholas' steel-gray eyes. "I do appreciate your suggestions, however, important decisions concerning the mine are—"

"To be made by you. I remember, but thanks for the reminder, Miss Brousseau." He still couldn't help grinning at the haughty expression she threw him as she flicked the reins over the dapple gray's broad back. When the buggy disappeared down the lane, kicking up dust in its wake, Nick turned and strode back to the mine. It wouldn't hurt to get as much coal out of the mine as he could before Parker reclaimed his slaves.

Catherine found herself smiling too as she turned the buggy toward Middleford, her closest neighbor other than John Parker, but she quickly stiffened her lips into a grimace. She had no time to play word games with Nicholas Colton. She had no time to even think of Nicholas Colton except in reference to the mine. Why then did the man keep invading her thoughts?

Urging the horse to greater speed, Catherine forced herself to concentrate on her visit to Middleford. Owned by the Milleau family since the early 1700's, the plantation, unlike Greenfield, had prospered over the years. George Milleau, the present owner, a burly, hard-working man, had been a friend of her father's until about two years before his death. At the time, Catherine had asked her father about the obvious cooling of their relationship, but had received no logical answer. Forced to draw her own conclusions, she'd decided it probably involved an unpaid gambling debt. Wasn't that the root of all her father's problems?

Still, George Milleau seemed a fair-minded man, and had never let any dislike he might have felt toward Catherine's father, extend to her. That's why as Catherine rode between the gray-barked beech trees that lined the lane she began to feel more hopeful. Well-kept fields of tobacco spread toward the James River, a sure sign that the Milleaus were not slave poor.

Catherine slowed the buggy as the main house, an H-shaped manor, came into view. Like Greenfield, it boasted large brick chimneys on either end and two front doors. Unlike her home, the siding shone sparkling white and freshly painted in the sun, and the outbuildings, including the circular brick slave dwellings showed no signs of neglect.

A smiling black man Catherine recognized as Isaac

hurried down the front steps as she pulled back on the reins in front of the house. "Afternoon, Miss Catherine. Haven't seen you about for some time."

"I haven't had much time for visiting, Isaac." Catherine accepted his hand and climbed down from the buggy. "How have you been?"

"Oh, can't complain, Miss Catherine."

Brushing some of the road dust off her skirts, Catherine smiled up at the old black man. "Is Mr. George around? I'd like to talk to him."

"I reckon he is. Let me go find him for you." Isaac led the way into the richly furnished parlor. "The ladies are out on the veranda enjoying the river breeze."

Catherine followed Isaac through the house, toward the gossamer-curtained French doors that opened onto the veranda. She had no desire to join the ladies, whom she assumed to mean George Milleau's three daughters, however it wouldn't do to appear rude, either.

"Well, will you look who's come visiting."

Her sister's acerbic tone drew Catherine's attention from the breathtaking view of spring-brushed gardens terracing toward the river. Catherine took a calming breath. "Hello, Marie. I didn't know you were here."

"Really?" Marie's pale brows lifted in disbelief. "John brought me over this morning. Sarah asked me to spend a few days with them. You don't mind, do you?"

"Not in the least." Catherine sat on one of the wooden chairs, angry that it bothered her how much nicer than she the other women were dressed. Marie's light blue silk was one of the gowns that had precipitated the last round of the continuing quarrel between the two sisters over spending money. Money we don't have, Catherine reminded herself as she looked at the layers of ecru lace that adorned the sleeves of Marie's dress.

"Marie has been telling us about your guest, Nicholas Colton."

Catherine's gaze left Marie to fix on Ester. The least attractive of the Milleau sisters, Catherine decided it would take a stranger a while to get past the layers of curls and ribbons to notice the sharp nose and pointy chin. "He isn't exactly a guest."

"Catherine has definitely put him to work," Marie added with a flip of her ivory fan.

"That is the reason I hired him, Marie."

"Is he as handsome as Marie says?" Eve, the youngest sister asked, as her brown eyes clouded over dreamily.

"Well, he's—"

"I'm quite certain Catherine hasn't noticed his appearance any more than she'd notice what . . . what old Isaac looks like. And it's a cinch he hasn't noticed hers." Marie's blue eyes raked Catherine's faded brown dress as she stood.

Feeling color flood her cheeks, Catherine turned to Sarah, who, perhaps because of her superior age was doing a better job of hiding her giggles than the other young women. "I've come to see your father. Do you suppose he's about?"

In her defense, Sarah quickly rose and linked her arm with Catherine's. "Let's go find him."

"She didn't mean anything by it you know."

Sarah's words broke the silence peppered only by their footfalls on the polished floorboards.

"It doesn't matter." Catherine tried to ignore the embarrassment she felt.

"You really are very pretty. Your hair . . . and eyes are just . . . well . . . And I'm sure Mr. Colton has noticed."

"Sarah." Catherine couldn't help smiling at the other woman's discomfort. It seemed greater than her own. "It really doesn't matter. My interest in Mr. Colton is purely business. He's my mine manager. What he thinks of my appearance makes absolutely no difference to me." That sounded convincing, Catherine thought, amazed by her ability to lie.

"I'm glad you feel that way, Catherine." Sarah rapped on the heavy mahogany door to her father's library.

George Milleau's booming voice bade them enter before Catherine could decide how to interpret Sarah's last remark.

"Catherine!" George stood and rounded his carved cherry desk, a bright welcoming smile on his ruddy face. "Isaac told me you were here. I was just about to join the ladies. How are you?"

"I'm fine, Mr. Milleau. You're looking fit."

George laughed and glanced down at the paunch his well-tailored waistcoat couldn't quite disguise. "You're a real charmer, Catherine. Would you like some tea, or perhaps a spot of wine."

"No." Catherine brushed his offer aside. "No thank you. Just a moment of your time, if you don't mind."

"Not at all. Please sit. Sarah?" George looked to

his daughter in invitation.

"I better get back to our other guest, Father." She turned to Catherine. "Join us when you're finished with Father. We'd love to have you stay for dinner."

"Thank you, but I can't today."

"Of course. Another time then." Sarah swept out of the room, her full skirt rustling.

George sat behind his desk, steeped his fingers and looked at his young neighbor. "Well, Catherine, what can I do for you?"

"Lease me twenty-five slaves." Catherine, never one to evade an issue, thought getting right to the point of her visit the best tack. She listened while George Milleau expelled air through the gap between his front teeth.

"Now Catherine, you know I'd like to help you in any way I can . . ."

"But?" Catherine voiced the word he'd let drift silently through the high-ceilinged room.

"I don't have twenty-five slaves to spare."

"How many do you have?" If need be she'd lease some from Middleford and the rest from other plantations.

George rubbed his sagging jaw. "I'll be honest with you, Catherine. To work in Greenfield Mine—none."

"But, why?" Catherine jumped up, resuming her seat only when George motioned for her to sit.

"Catherine, I know your father and I had our differences, however I've always admired you and—"

"Just tell me why."

"It's a poor risk." The leather creaked as George settled back in his seat. "Your mine has a history of

86

cave-ins, and this last one only strengthens my resolve. If you want my advice, you'll sell the mine and move into town. John Parker will make you a good offer."

"What do you know about John's offer?" This time his placating hand movement did not have her sitting down.·

"Now, Catherine."

"He's been over here talking to you hasn't he?" Catherine stalked to the window, glaring out at the deep-green velvet lawn through the open shutters, trying to control her anger."

"Catherine."

"What did he tell you George? Not to lease me slaves?"

"I make my own decision, young lady. But he did mention he'd almost lost a dozen slaves when your mine caved in."

"It was eight, not twelve, and the section that caved in has been blocked off. The rest has been shored up with timbers and is perfectly safe."

"I'm sorry, Catherine. I've just got too much money invested in my slaves to take chances."

"I see." His tone was easy to read—there would be no changing his mind. Catherine gathered up her hat and gloves and reached for the brass door knob. "Thank you for your time Mr. Milleau."

"The other slave owners feel pretty much the way I do, Catherine."

Looking over her shoulder, Catherine's gaze locked with his. "You've discussed my affairs with others?"

George stood and walked toward the door. "We all

want what's best for you, Catherine."

"I think I can decide that for myself." Catherine opened the door and left.

Searching through the late evening gloom, Nick spotted Catherine's buggy coming toward him along the road. Relief replaced the worry that had forced him out to look for her, and he urged his horse into a gallop. For two hours after the dinner Catherine didn't return for, he'd paced the parlor in the main house. He'd lied to Mrs. Brousseau telling her Catherine had mentioned she'd be late. He'd been thankful that the older woman didn't remember Catherine's promise to be home for dinner. Finally, Nick had suggested Catherine's grandmother go to bed, and he'd saddled a horse and gone looking for his wayward employer.

Catherine heard the steady drum of galloping hooves before she could pick out the horse and rider in the fading light. Panic spread through her until she was able to make out Nicholas Colton. Reining in her horse, she waited for him to stop. His stallion snorted and pranced as Nick looked down at her.

"Where in the hell have you been?"

"What?" Catherine didn't think she'd ever been more shocked.

"You heard me." Nick dismounted and walked the horse behind the buggy, tying him there. "I asked where you've been till this hour."

"I don't have to answer to you." Catherine twisted around to look at him, her words shrill with indignation.

"Well, you sure as hell need to answer to someone." Nick motioned her over, then climbed into the buggy beside her. The fit was tight, and his leg pressed against hers until she jerked away. "Do you know how worried your grandmother has been?"

"I . . ." How could she have forgotten about Grandmere? "I should have come home earlier, but I was three plantations away when I realized how late it had become." She had no business explaining herself to the hired help, but he was right about her actions. "Is Grandmere all right?"

"Yeah." With a flick of his wrist, Nick started the buggy rolling. "Betsy and I put her to bed."

"*You* put her to bed?"

"Well, someone sure as hell had to." Nick stared straight ahead, knowing she stared at him in amazement.

"Oh, I forgot, Marie isn't home. She's spending a few days at the Milleau's."

"I hadn't noticed." Nick felt a lot of his anger melting away now that Catherine sat safely beside him. "Did you lease some slaves?"

"No." She should have believed George Milleau when he'd told her all her neighbors would refuse her. It would certainly have saved her a lot of time. "No one is willing to take the risk with their slaves."

Minutes passed as they rode along in silence, the croaking of tree frogs and clip-clopping hooves the only sounds. "What are we going to do now?" Nick finally asked.

"What you've been suggesting from the beginning. I'm going to Richmond to hire miners."

89

Nick threaded the reins through his fingers and looked over at his companion. "When do we leave?"

"I'll be going on tomorrow's stage."

Catherine's head jerked back as Nick yanked the horse to a stop. "Let's get one thing straight, Cate. You're not going to Richmond by yourself."

Chapter Five

"Cheer up Miss Brousseau. You might even be glad you decided to bring me along."

Catherine interrupted her scrutiny of the lush spring landscape drifting by outside the stagecoach window to glare at her traveling companion. Nicholas Colton's choice of words was as audacious as he.

Decided, indeed. She had no more decided to bring him along today than she'd decided the sky should be blue. Yet there he sat, or rather lounged, grinning at her from his seat opposite hers on the Richmond-Lynchburg Stage. Catherine's green eyes iced over in an expression that had quailed more than one man before she again shifted her attention to the passing scenery.

Nick watched her back stiffen as he chuckled at her obvious dismissal. Apparently his employer had decided to pretend he didn't exist. Sliding down further in his seat, stretching his long legs to the side, Nick examined her through narrow eyes.

Little Miss Brousseau was too used to being boss—not that she didn't work hard to deserve the title. But she needed to become more accustomed to sharing some of the burden. Hell, wasn't that why he'd been sent to America? And for as long as he stayed, he was going to see she did just that.

With a satisfied smile, Nick closed his eyes. He might as well have kept them open, for his mind's eye did a mighty good job of conjuring up a picture of her. The way she'd looked this morning.

He'd thought from the first time he'd seen her, she was a handsome woman, but seeing her every day in her drab work dresses hadn't prepared him for today. Not that her gown could be called fancy. Actually, the lines were quite simple, yet they emphasized the tiny span of her waist and the fullness of her breasts. Remembering how her body, covered only in a thin nightrail, had felt pressed against him, Nick shifted uncomfortably in his seat. Opening his eyes, he caught a quick flash of green before Catherine jerked her gaze back to the window.

"Any thoughts about how you're going to go about hiring these miners?" It was time to get his mind off Miss Catherine Brousseau and onto his job.

Catherine feigned interest in the passing landscape a moment longer before turning her attention to Nicholas Colton. She felt certain he'd caught her studying him. "I intend to put an ad in the *Commercial Compiler*," she said referring to Richmond's daily newspaper devoted to local and industrial interests. When he only seemed to contemplate this piece of information, Catherine blurted out, "Do you have a better idea?"

Instead of answering her question, he asked one of his own. "You ever hire miners before, Miss Brousseau?"

"Once." Honesty forced her to add, "I attempted to, once."

"And?"

"I had a difficult time finding anyone." A sudden lurching movement of the stagecoach forced Catherine to grab the cushion.

"Any particular reason?"

All manner of lies flew into her head, but Catherine decided nothing would be gained by avoiding the truth. As much as she resented her mine manager's attitude, they were both after the same thing—getting Greenfield Mine running again. Besides the quicker they did that, the quicker Nicholas Colton would go back to England. Then she wouldn't have to fight this compulsion to just look at him anymore.

Catherine sighed, and clasped her gloved hands together in her lap. "Greenfield Mine does not have the best reputation for safety."

"I gathered as much."

"But it's safe now, isn't it?"

"We're talking about men going over two hundred feet beneath the earth with darkness, water and poisonous gasses the only sure things. But, yes, Greenfield is safe—for a mine."

Catherine nodded and turned back toward the window. "They also didn't like the idea of working for a woman."

Her words were spoken so quietly, Nick had to strain to hear them. "Not a very enlightened attitude," he quipped.

"Do you mind? Working for a woman, I mean?" Her wide green eyes searched his face, narrowing at his reply.

"I guess it would depend upon the woman."

With that ambiguous remark he closed his eyes again, and for all Catherine could tell, fell asleep. It took her a moment to realize he never had answered her question about how he'd go about hiring miners. Well, what had she expected? For as long as she could remember, she'd had the responsibility of running the mine. Why had she been tempted into thinking that would change? If she were honest with herself, Catherine wasn't even certain she wanted it to change.

The few times she could remember her father taking time away from his social pursuits to make decisions about the mining operations, it had taken her extra time and effort to rectify his mistakes. Not that her father hadn't tried—occasionally. He simply hadn't been a collier. "It has to be in your blood," her grandfather used to say.

"I guess it skipped a generation, Grandpere," Catherine whispered, embarrassed when Nicholas Colton's slate-gray eyes opened, piercing her with their intensity. Flustered, Catherine turned away. "We're crossing the James River," she said needlessly. The whir of wheels skimming over the wooden bridge rang in their ears. Below them the fall line churned the river over rocks and around small tree-dotted islands as the stage approached the city.

Catherine led the way to the Union Hotel. Passing by some men whose chairs leaned against the brick edifice, Catherine and Nick entered the building.

"Since I did not ask you to accompany me," Catherine pulled her employee aside to say, "I won't be paying for your room." With regret Catherine realized she should have told him that earlier. Maybe then he wouldn't have insisted upon coming along. Catherine tugged her bottom lip between her teeth, struggling with the guilt she felt. Needless as it was, he had come along with good intentions, and it wasn't as if she'd paid him anything, as yet. Perhaps he didn't have money to pay for a room. He was, after all, only a miner.

Catherine paused on the wool rug, touching his sleeve with her hand. "Mr. Colton, if you haven't the means to . . . Well, what I mean is, you needn't let circumstances—" Catherine stopped and started again when she noticed the slow grin begin to spread across his handsome face. "What I'm trying to say is—"

"Are you suggesting that we share a room?"

Nick watched the color drain from her face as her green eyes grew enormous. Twin dots of angry pink returned to brighten her cheeks.

"Certainly not." Catherine turned and flounced away, clenching her fists when she heard his low seductive chuckle follow her. How dare he say such a thing to her? And after she'd tried to make amends for refusing to pay for his room. That showed what being nice to Nicholas Colton got you.

The room the hotel clerk gave her was relatively clean, simply furnished with a spindle bed, cherry chest of drawers, washstand and wing chair—and it was directly across the hall from Nicholas' room.

Catherine tried not to think of that as she poured water into the chipped porcelain bowl and began washing the dust of the road off her hands and face.

It didn't matter to her where his room might be. She'd ignore him. With a smug smile, Catherine dried her face, tidied the strands of auburn hair that had escaped her chignon, replaced her bonnet, and left the room. She'd go to the *Compiler*'s office and place her ad—and the devil could take Nicholas Colton.

But the devil didn't take him, because when she descended the stairs into the lobby, she saw him, leaning his hip against the front desk. Engrossed in the newspaper he read, he didn't seem to notice her, but Catherine had no doubt he would if she tried to cross the spacious lobby to the front door. There seemed to be no way to avoid the man's interference. Well, what did it really matter? She'd have to put up with his arrogant attitude and snide sensual remarks, but she could do that. She could do anything she set her mind to—hopefully.

Still Catherine hesitated in the shadows by the bottom of the stairs, watching Nicholas Colton. Obviously amused by whatever he read, she could see the tiny lines around his eyes crinkle deeper in mirth. Just the way they had when he'd made that remark about sharing rooms. Of all the impudence. The thought of her sharing a room with anyone was ludicrous, but with a common miner?

Catherine's gaze drifted down his large body, wondering again about him. She couldn't help but think him a puzzle. He declared himself to be a miner. He looked the part—most of the time, though certainly not now. But she still couldn't help wondering. He spoke like a gentleman—except for his crude remarks to her. And at this moment anyone would be hard pressed to think him anything but a wealthy planter or collier visiting Richmond for the day.

Though his fawn colored trousers did little to hide the power of his long legs, they hardly resembled the coarse hard-luck pants he wore at the mine. His pleated front shirt of fine linen peeked from beneath a well-cut brown walking coat and a lawn cravat tied in a barrel knot. Catherine shook her head. How would a miner, even a mine manager, afford such clothes? Possibly he spent his entire salary in England—he certainly hadn't gotten any wage here—on clothing himself. Catherine shook her head again. He didn't seem the type, and even though his clothes were obviously expensive, they didn't approach looking dandified.

Nicholas turned a page of the newspaper, and Catherine's attention focused on his hands. Thick wristed and large, covered by callouses and scars, she couldn't help but think the long fingers made them appear almost genteel. And they could be so gentle. Catherine could still close her eyes and remember how they'd felt massaging her neck and shoulders.

Goodness! Catherine jerked her eyes open and glanced around, hoping no one had noticed her silly lapse. She had problems—grievous problems—that if she didn't solve quickly . . . Well, Catherine didn't like to even think about what might happen to Grandmere, Marie and herself, if she didn't start making a profit on the mine. She had no time to waste, and certainly no time to spend speculating on her mine manager. He'd been sent to help her—period.

With quick, efficient steps, Catherine crossed the carpeting toward Nicholas. "I'm going to place my ad in the *Compiler*," she stated without preamble as she passed him.

If Nicholas took exception to her abrupt manner, he gave no outward sign as he folded the paper and fell into step beside her. Odors from nearby pastures mingled with the sharp tang of tobacco drifting from the warehouses along the river assaulted Catherine as she walked out into the late afternoon sunshine.

Nick grabbed her elbow, silently compelling Catherine to wait till the mule-pulled wagon had passed rather than trying to dodge the conveyance that rattled down the brick paved street. "Getting yourself run down by a team of braying animals won't help your mine any, Miss Brousseau."

"I'm quite capable of sidestepping a few mules, Mr. Colton. However, I suppose I should have taken your abilities into consideration before proceeding." Catherine ignored the amused cock of his dark brow, and the accompanying deep chuckle as they walked along Main Street. Though hardly crowded, there were more people as they neared the shopping district between 14th and 18th Streets.

The office of the *Compiler* smelled of ink and hot, sweating bodies. Founded by Thomas Ritchie, the editor of *The Enquirer*, some fifteen years earlier, it issued daily copy, using most of its space for advertisements and announcements. In this way Ritchie could devote his considerable editorial

98

talents on *The Enquirer* to expounding the virtues of the Republican party.

Catherine pulled in her skirts as she brushed by an untidy pile of discarded newspapers and approached the desk. Almost as unkempt as the office itself, she nevertheless knew the editor ran an efficient newspaper. She cleared her throat, successfully gaining his attention.

"Mr. Gordon," Catherine began, "My name is—"

"Brousseau, isn't it?" Samuel Gordon studied her with watery blue eyes over the top of his spectacles. "You're one of James's daughters."

"Yes, I am. The oldest, Catherine."

"Of course." Samuel stood and rubbed the bald spot on his head. "I remember years ago seeing you girls with your parents. Come into town to watch a horse race if memory serves me."

"You have excellent recall, Mr. Gordon." Catherine smiled. She remembered the time he referred to. It was Marie's birthday. Her twelfth. And in honor of the occasion her father had suggested a visit to Richmond. Though she'd been to Richmond before, at fourteen, Catherine had been too excited to sit still in the coach as they'd approached the town. Crowds of people had packed the small town because of the horse races, but the Brousseau's had one of the best rooms in the fanciest hotel. She'd had so much fun studying the people and watching the horses sprint across the meadow. It had been grand and wonderful memory. And her father had lost a lot of money, as usual. Thus, her present circumstance.

Catherine looked at Mr. Gordon, noticed his speculative glance toward Nicholas, and introduced the two men. "I'd like to place an ad in the *Compiler*," Catherine began after comments were exchanged about the unusually warm spring.

"You going to offer your mine up for sale?" Samuel sat down and searched for a clean sheet of paper.

"No. What ever made you think that?"

Samuel shrugged, dipping his pen in the pewter inkwell on his desk. "No particular reason. Just most of the mines are having trouble with water and such, and well, you being a woman . . ." The rest of his thought drifted off on the sultry air.

Being a woman indeed. It wasn't as if she actually went into the mine and chipped away at the rock with a pick. "I would like to advertise for men to work the mine, Mr. Gordon."

Samuel shrugged again and began scrawling something across the page. When he'd finished, he looked up expectantly.

Realizing he waited for her to tell him what she wanted printed, Catherine began, "Miners wanted." She glanced over at Nicholas, who had surprisingly kept himself in the background, and amended, "Make that experienced miners wanted, would you, Mr. Gordon?" Catherine brushed an errant curl under her bonnet. "Please state that I will pay a competitive wage. Will supply living quarters and meals. And that they should apply to C. Brousseau at the Union Hotel."

Catherine turned toward Nicholas. "Can you think of anything else?"

"Not a thing."

100

She studied him a moment before giving her attention again to Mr. Gordon. Her mine manager was being entirely too cooperative. She'd never seen him when he didn't have an opinion. Maybe it was because she was finally doing what he'd told her to do in the first place. For some reason that thought annoyed her as she read over the ad the printer had written. "I suppose that's all then." Catherine payed fifty cents after being assured the ad would run tomorrow morning.

"Where to now?" Nick asked as they left the small printing shop.

"Back to the hotel, I guess. There really isn't anything we can do until morning."

"We could take a walk. See the sights." At her expression of pure astonishment, Nick questioned, "When was the last time you took a day off, Miss Brousseau?"

"Well, I—"

"Can't remember, can you?" Nick grinned pulling her unresisting hand through the crook in his arm.

"I have a lot of responsibilities." He acted so smug, Catherine felt obligated to remind him that her life could hardly be described as fun loving. "There's my grandmother."

"Safely at home with Betsy and your sister." He hoped. This morning when he'd come up to the main house to meet Catherine, Nick had overheard the last of an argument between Marie and her sister. Angry because Catherine had called her home from the Milleau's house to help care for their grandmother, Marie had used some surprisingly vile language for a lady—until he'd walked in. Then the blonde had become all sweet magnolias and apple blossoms.

"And the mine." His large, calloused hand resting on hers sent wild fluttering through her body.

"Which you yourself have stated you can do nothing about till morning. Come on, Cate, show me Richmond."

She couldn't resist the low, sensual timbre of his voice, the magnetic pull of his steel, gray eyes as he looked down at her. "Oh, I don't suppose it could do any harm to take the afternoon off."

"And evening." He smiled into her wide-eyed expression. "Dinner, Cate. You will join me for dinner, won't you?"

"Well, I—"

"You have to eat."

Was the man a wizard? She found him coarse and arrogant, and he worked for her. She didn't even care for his company. Just being around him kept her in constant turmoil. Then why did she accept his invitation to dinner?

She was only being polite, Catherine assured herself as they strolled along Main Street. Simply because she employed him gave her no right to treat him rudely. Yes, that was it. She should be gracious. After all, they ate together at Greenfield. Catherine almost had herself convinced that her response had nothing to do with the excited skipping of her heart whenever he came near her, when he pulled her over to a tiny shop window.

"I'd like your opinion of that hat."

102

Catherine looked through the ripply glass at the headpiece and tried to suppress a giggle. Large and covered with wild plumage, it struck her as quite funny.

"You don't care for it?"

He sounded surprised, but Catherine had learned to recognize the silvery glint in his eyes for what it was—his teasing manner. Suddenly she couldn't hold the mirth inside her. The giggle she'd repressed before came out in infectious laughter. "I think if the poor bird who lost his feathers to such a crazy creation ever finds the person wearing it, he shall attack. And rightly so."

She had dimples. Not in her cheeks where he'd seen them on other people, but at the corners of her pretty mouth. Nick stood spellbound, staring, wondering why he'd never noticed such a delightful trait before. Then it hit him. He'd never really seen her laugh. And what a shame, for Miss Catherine Brousseau looked beautiful when she laughed.

Nick forced his attention back to the window when he realized how much he wanted to take her in his arms—right there on the street—and kiss those elusive dimples. He scanned the hats displayed in the shop. She was right about the one he'd pointed out. It had caught his eyes because of its outlandish feathers. However, the milliner obviously had some talent, for there next to the plumed concoction sat a dainty little bonnet of dark green silk trimmed with tiny pink rosebuds that looked so real he could almost smell their sweet scent.

It had to be Cate's. The only thing that would

improve the hat would be for it to surround her pretty, dimpled face. Nick could almost see the way her green eyes and auburn hair would complement the bonnet. And it even matched her gown. But though he'd never bought a hat before, Nick had a feeling buying this one for Cate would not be easy.

"Do you like that one?" Idly, Nick pointed to the rose-trimmed hat, knowing her answer the moment she saw it. Her noncommittal words in no way matched the gleam of appreciation in her eyes.

"Why don't you try it on?" Nick took her hand, leading Catherine toward the door.

"Oh, no. I couldn't."

"Why, not?" Without using physical force, he couldn't move her any closer to the entrance.

"Mr. Colton." Her tone implied that she felt him dense to even question her reason. "I simply cannot afford such luxuries."

"But, I—" In a flash of insight Nick knew she'd never let him buy the hat for her. Well, she was going to have it, one way or another. "I have a friend, in England, who would love it, I think. If you'd just try it on, I could tell better. She has your coloring." Actually Nick had never seen anyone with hair so rich, skin so flawlessly fair and eyes so green.

It hurt. Catherine couldn't understand why, but knowing he had a woman friend in England made her very unhappy—and foolish. What did she expect? A man who looked like he did, even if he were a miner, probably had lots of women flocking after him. But that didn't mean she had to model hats for them. Of course, if she didn't he'd think she cared, which, of course, she didn't. She'd show Nicholas Colton how the damn hat should look. Then he could take it back to England and stick it on his lady's head for all she cared. Same coloring, indeed!

Nick watched the variations of emotions shadow Catherine's face before she smiled up at him sweetly—too sweetly—and agreed to model the hat.

It looked even better on her than he'd imagined, and he'd thought it would look great. Nick circled Catherine as she sat on a stool in front of a large chevron mirror. "I don't know," he hedged. "It doesn't look too bad. What do you think?" he asked the proprietor, a middle-aged woman who claimed she'd just returned from her native country of France with the latest styles.

"Oh, but madam is a vision in the chapeau. The shade of green makes her eyes dreamy, and the roses match the blush on her cheeks."

"The hat's not for me." Catherine glared at the woman just to be certain her eyes lost any dreamy appearance.

Nick hid a grin behind the hand that rubbed his jaw speculatively. If Catherine pursed her lips any tighter, they'd stay that way permanently. She was angry about trying on the hat for someone else. He had a wild urge to tell her the hat had obviously been made for her. He intended to buy it, and she damn well better wear it. Then reality set in. She'd never do it. Besides his other plan might be fun.

He walked around her again, trying not to notice the slender stem of her neck, the way the pink silk bow emphasized the soft curve of her chin. "It's nice," he informed the milliner. "But I don't think it's exactly what I'm looking for." Nick excused his little deceit and the crestfallen expression on the French woman's face by the fact that he'd send someone round to buy the hat as soon as he returned to the hotel.

Catherine had stripped down to her chemise and cotton pantaloons. She'd rather have a bath or at least a swim in the stream near Greenfield, however, washing herself out of the pitcher and bowl appeared to be the best she could do. She certainly didn't have the money to have a tub and water sent up to her room.

She felt hot and dusty, and no wonder. She and Nicholas Colton had explored Richmond from Church Hill on the east to Gambles Hill on the west. Together they'd walked to Capitol Square and examined the new parapet and porches that had been built onto the executive mansion the previous summer. They'd visited the Capitol and Nicholas had surprised her not only by knowing that Thomas Jefferson had designed it, but by knowing more details about the great Virginian's life than she did.

"I admire him—even his Declaration of Independence" he'd assured her with a wink. "And don't worry, I don't hold your little rebellion against old Thomas or you."

Catherine caught sight of her reflection in the mirror over the washstand and realized she was smiling at the memory. Oh, well, she might as well admit it. She'd enjoyed herself this afternoon. Except for the hat. It still galled her that he had her try it on for someone else, and then decided it didn't even look good enough to buy.

She had eyes. That hat had looked wonderful on her. It would look wonderful on anyone. If money weren't so tight, she might even go back and buy it for herself. Catherine lifted the thick fall of hair off her neck so she could wipe the cooling washcloth across it.

"Of course," Catherine mumbled to herself as the idea hit her. She didn't have the money for the hat—and he probably didn't either. After all, she certainly hadn't paid him, and how much money could a miner earn in England, even an experienced one like Nicholas Colton? He'd most likely discovered the price and realized he couldn't afford it for his lady friend. A shiver of annoyance rushed through her at this last thought, but Catherine ignored it and finished washing.

Deciding what to wear was simple. She'd only brought one gown. Catherine glanced at the dress she'd hung by the window in hopes of relaxing some of the wrinkles from the day. Aside from the serviceable dresses she wore at home, this was the only one she owned that even hinted at being in style. She'd had it made before she'd realized exactly how far in debt her father had left the family. Catherine brushed a fleck of dust off the gored skirt. It really was a pretty gown. The rich green, close-fitting bodice, decorated with lighter green piping boasted long-sloping shoulders.

Catherine fastened her corset, and slipped into the

107

gown. The neck line was low, and wide, falling straight across her shoulders. Picking up the lighter green tucker she used to cover her exposed flesh, Catherine draped it around her shoulders, then stopped. Studying the effect in the mirror she removed the tucker. The decolletage was low, but not dramatically so. Actually, Marie's daytime gowns were more revealing than this. Still, Catherine wasn't accustomed to showing this much skin. She nibbled her bottom lip, just for a moment studying her reflection as Nicholas would. Folding the tucker she dropped it on the bureau.

By the time she heard the firm knock on the paneled door, Catherine had parted her thick hair in the middle and twisted it into a neat knot atop her head.

Lady friend in England or not, Catherine knew she'd made the right decision concerning the tucker as soon as she saw the appreciative gleam in Nicholas' slate-gray eyes. There certainly could be no harm in being admired—just for one night.

Nick forgot what he'd been going to say. He'd had some glib teasing remark on the tip of his tongue, and then she'd opened the door and he'd seen her. She smiled, her dimples appeared, and then she noticed the box.

"What's that?"

Nick forced his gaze to follow hers. "A hat box."

She continued to stare at the round wooden container. "It's the hat you tried on this afternoon. I decided to buy it after all," Nick said, suddenly remembering the story he'd devised.

"Oh." What was she supposed to say?

"I'm sure . . . Josephine will love it." Damn he'd forgotten to think up a name for his fictitious lady friend. Where'd he come up with Josephine?

"Josephine?"

"My friend." Nick grinned. "But I've been thinking." He caught his eyes drifting down toward her breasts and jerked them back to her face. "It will be quite a while before I return to England. Hell, the bonnet might even be out of style by then."

"You could send it."

"Josephine travels a lot." Nick congratulated himself on his forethought in explaining why he couldn't send the hat by boat. "Anyway, it would be a shame to leave the hat sitting in a box all that time, so I thought you might agree to wear it."

"Oh no, I couldn't."

"Josephine wouldn't mind."

"However, I would."

Nick had anticipated this reaction, and he hoped he could counter it. He followed her into her room, kicking the door shut with his boot. Her back and shoulders looked creamy smooth and it took a force of will not to rub his knuckles across her skin. He snatched off the box top and held up the hat. It appeared delicate and feminine in his large hands. "Just as I thought."

"What?" Catherine couldn't remember ever being so angry. The nerve of him trying to get her to wear his ladyfriend's hat. And he hadn't even mentioned her dress.

"This hat is the exact shade of your gown." And

109

your eyes.

"I'm not wearing that hat."

"Have it your way, but I certainly hope it won't keep you from hiring miners."

"What could not wearing a hat have to do with hiring workers?" She should never have agreed to have dinner with him. She should never have written to Travis Fielding!

"Probably nothing. However . . . ," Nick let the word linger. "Miners like to think the owners of the mines they work for are prosperous. It makes them think the owners have the money to take care of them. It makes them feel safe."

"So?" What he said made sense, but she still didn't know what it had to do with the hat.

"So, with the hat, you'll look prosperous. Let's try it." Before she could stop him, Nick slipped the bonnet over her head, letting his fingers trail along the curve of her jaw a few extra moments after tying the pink ribbon under her chin. "There," he said, smiling down into her upturned face. "I'd work for that woman any day."

She couldn't seem to catch her breath. His hands on her face and now her shoulders made her knees feel like day old porridge. Catherine backed away, all but forgetting about the hat. If wearing it helped to hire miners, she'd do it. The sooner miners came to Greenfield, the sooner the mine would show a profit, the sooner Nicholas Colton could take his hat and return to England. And she could stop having these extremely unsettling feelings.

*   *   *

Two hours later, Catherine lifted her hand and Nicholas pulled her onto one of the flat rocks overlooking the James River. The May moon rode high in the sky illuminating the bubbling rapids. She should be back in her hotel room asleep. There was absolutely no reason to be wandering along the river's shore. Except when they'd finished dinner Nicholas had suggested another walk. And after such a pleasant day Catherine didn't want to go back to her stuffy hotel room. But she hadn't imagined them all alone in such a private and romantic setting either. It reminded her of the night in the meadow— the night he'd kissed her.

"Sit down." Nick shrugged off his coat and spread it on the rock.

"Oh, I shouldn't." She didn't want to get too close to him.

"I've been looking for an excuse to get out of that jacket all day." Nick untied his cravat, and unfastened the top button of his shirt.

Catherine had noticed he'd changed his shirt before coming to her room this evening. It shone white in the reflected moonlight. She decided to sit down for just a minute. It really was cooler here by the river. Bull frogs croaked in harmony with the gurgling water. "Is there a river like this near your home in England?"

"Something like this. Not quite so rocky, though." Nick tossed a pebble into the glistening black water.

"Did you play in it when you were a boy?"

"No, I don't believe I ever did."

"Were you afraid of water?" Catherine teased, thinking of all the grand times she'd had splashing

111

in the creek.

He flashed her a smile, his teeth as white in the moonlight. "I don't think so. Just never had time. My mother died when I was eight. I went to work in the mines a few years after that."

"But that's so young. How did you—"

"Lots of boys start working when I did." Why did he tell her that anyway? He should have kept his mouth shut, but she had a way of making him open up, tell her things that only he and Travis Fielding knew. "We should be getting back." He started to stand, but stopped when she looked around at him. Her eyes shone emerald bright in the silvery light, and her skin glowed pale as ivory.

"I'm sorry if I offended you." His hand caught hers before she could rise, pulling her toward him. And there was no way she could deny him. Her heart fluttered wildly, her breathing stopped almost entirely as his lips brushed across hers. Gently at first, then his hand left hers and untied the ribbons of her hat. When he'd removed it, lain it in the soft grass beside the rock, his fingers wove through her hair, bringing her face toward his for a kiss more passionate than tender.

She should stop him. Somewhere in the back of her head the warning swirled around like the eddies of the river. But she'd had her chance and she'd let it go. His first light kiss and the removal of her bonnet had given Catherine plenty of time to insist upon leaving—if that's what she'd wanted to do. His tongue traced the seam of her lips, nudging, till she opened her mouth. His moan of pleasure vibrated through her body.

This was idiocy. Nick angled Catherine's mouth more securely against his. He'd given into temptation once before and kissed her, and had his arrogance thrown back in his face. But he'd thought about that kiss, dreamed about it, every day since then, and he meant to find out if reality could match his memory.

It surpassed it. His lips left hers to trail down her slender neck. Her breasts, pale and full in the moonlight rose above her gown, and he pressed a kiss to the valley between them. She smelled sweeter than the honeysuckle that vined its way down the slope behind them, but Nick couldn't define the scent. He just knew that it belonged only to Catherine.

She'd forgone the tucker to entice him, Catherine knew that now. She'd hoped he'd look at her longingly, notice her in ways other than as his employer. But she hadn't wanted him to touch her. As Catherine leaned back across his arm she wondered why she hadn't wanted that, and then his palm cupped her breast, rubbed her nipple taut through the silk, and she couldn't think at all. Her body arched toward him, and she clutched the pleated front of his shirt.

His mouth moved up her neck, stopping to nibble the underside of her chin before pressing against hers. This time Catherine offered no resistance. Her lips opened, inviting his tongue to caress hers. He pressed her back against the firm rock, covered her body with the hard length of his. She wound her arms around his neck, dug her fingers through the thick

113

brown curls at his nape.

Catherine didn't hear anything until he stopped kissing her. Even then, she only knew something was wrong because he whispered in her ear. "Someone's coming." His voice sounded low and husky, and sent chills down her spine, but his words spurred her to action. She jumped off the rock as soon as he rolled off her.

"Who is it?" Catherine tugged at her bodice where his mouth had pushed it down. Heat rushed to her cheeks when she noticed the front of his shirt. Open to his trousers, she didn't have to wonder who had done that.

"I don't know, Cate." Nick straightened his clothes. "But I don't think they're close yet."

"For heaven's sake stop calling me that name." Catherine twisted her hair, trying to restore some semblance of order, but it was useless. Her pins had scattered everywhere when his fingers had combed through her hair, and in the darkness, she couldn't find them.

Catherine felt tears sting her eyes and she blinked them back. How could she have let this happen? What if someone saw her? The voices were getting louder. All she wanted to do was go back to the hotel, lock her door and try to forget this had ever happened. She didn't realize she'd started climbing the slope until Nicholas's hand on her arm stopped her. "Let go of me."

"Where do you think you're going?"

"Back to the hotel." Catherine jammed the hat on her head.

"Not without me you aren't."

"Fine. Just don't touch me again." She pulled her arm from his grasp.

"Fine." It didn't take a genius to know that the boss lady regretted her actions here tonight. Nick just wished he could feel the same.

Chapter Six

"It's your move."

Catherine glanced down at the hand-carved ivory figures, grimaced at the discrepancy between white and black men, and nudged her king a square to the right.

"You can't move into check." Nick pushed the piece back to its original space. "Now try again. Remember, you're still behind three games to one."

The grin that accompanied this reminder spurred Catherine to examine the board more closely. She tried to concentrate, but too much of her attention focused on the door. Standing ajar, awaiting applicants for her advertised jobs to knock on the wooden panels, it remained silent—as it had all day.

The sun had passed its pinnacle and the only person to enter her room had been Nicholas Colton. He'd crossed the hall early this morning. They'd sat and stared at each other a while, Catherine's mind replaying every detail of the previous night by the river, then he'd gone down to the lobby. He'd returned with some bread, cheese and apples, the chess set, and confirmation that the ad was in the *Compiler*. Until then Catherine had thought maybe the lack of response could be because no one knew about the jobs.

Catherine's fingers idly traced the elaborate carved headdress on her queen. "Do you think anyone will come to apply?"

Nick shrugged. "I don't know. Do you want that last hunk of cheese?"

"No." Catherine pushed the remaining cheese and bread toward him. Worry over her future certainly hadn't cramped *his* appetite, she thought with disgust. He'd eaten enough to feed a small army. Catherine sighed, realizing how unfair she was. Why shouldn't he eat? After all, he was a big man, and big men probably required a lot of food. And he had sat with her all morning—even letting her win a game of chess to keep her mind occupied.

Though certainly no chess master, Catherine had been taught enough by her grandfather to know when someone threw a game for her. Deciding that watching the door wouldn't help, Catherine again pulled her concentration back to the game. Her next move gained her an approving nod from her opponent.

"Where did you learn to play chess?" Catherine asked. It wasn't a game she associated with miners, yet he played very well.

"My employer taught me."

"Mr. Fielding?"

"Hmmm. Check."

Catherine had a feeling any thoughts of winning

this game were useless. Maybe she should lose gracefully—she'd had enough practice—then concentrate on the next game. "Does Mr. Fielding teach all his miners to play chess?" Catherine watched as he shook his head, never taking his eyes from the board. He seemed to always be a couple of moves ahead of her.

"I lived with him for a while. He sent me to school."

So that's where he'd learned to read and picked up the trappings of a gentleman. Nicholas Colton was apparently a much more complex man than she'd first thought. Catherine worried her bottom lip, and made her move, studying the man rather than the board.

"Cate, with one move I can have you in checkmate."

"Oh, go ahead and do it then. I'm tired of this game anyway." With a shrug, Nick toppled her king, then stood and walked toward the window. It looked out over a small courtyard. The waxen white blossoms of the magnolia tree growing close to the hotel kept most of the town odors at bay.

Fascinated, Catherine watched the fine linen of his shirt mold over sinew and muscles as he stretched. It reminded her again of last night—of the feel of his hard body pressed against hers—of the unkind things she'd said to him as she'd hurried back to the hotel. She'd tried to pretend everything had been his fault, when in reality she'd wanted him to kiss her, to touch her.

Catherine folded her hands, resting them in her lap. "Mr. Colton?" He turned, piercing her with his stormy gray eyes as if he could read her thoughts. "I'd like to apologize for my behavior last night."

His reply didn't miss a beat. "Before or after we heard people coming?"

Catherine swallowed, wishing he'd stop staring at her in that way. She glanced at the door, assuring herself it still remained open. Catherine wouldn't have felt safe alone with him behind a closed door. "My original intent was to apologize for *after* we heard the voices, however I believe I shall expand it to encompass the entire evening."

"I see." Nick crossed over to his chair and shrugged into his brown frockcoat.

"Where are you going?" Catherine felt certain she'd offended him, and why not? Her tone had been unbearably haughty, even to her own ears. What had begun as an apology, had ended up sounding like another condemnation. If only he hadn't made that remark about which part of the evening she regretted. A true gentleman would never have said that.

"I've developed a powerful thirst. There are some taverns down by the river."

"You're going *there?*" Catherine's tone bordered on incredulous. "What if someone comes for the mining jobs?"

"Oh, I imagine you can handle them, Miss Brousseau." With a mocking bow he left the room.

For long minutes Catherine stared at the closed door, the sounds drifting in her open window—carts rumbling along the street, shopkeepers voices, and the sharp twill of a mockingbird—her only companions. He'd walked out on her—left her to handle what needed to be done—just like her father had done.

Catherine pinched the bridge of her nose, dislodging that thought, wondering why it had ever popped into her head. Her father may have had no mind for business, but he hadn't forced her to take on the responsibilities of the mine, the family. She'd done that willingly, gladly. Hadn't she?

Catherine sank into the wing chair, untying the satin ribbons beneath her chin. She'd donned the hat Nicholas had bought for his friend in England because she thought he might be right about looking prosperous, but now . . . Well, the miners when they came—if they came—were going to have to hire on to work for her without the stupid bonnet.

Feeling a little better after making that decision, Catherine leaned her head back against the chair. She didn't need Mr. Nicholas Colton to help her employ workers anymore than she needed his damn hat. She'd been taking care of Greenfield for close to five years and she would continue to do so for many more. Catherine tried to ignore the nagging question of how she'd do that without miners to dig the coal. It was easier to dwell on her annoyance with her mine manager.

Angry. There was just no other way to describe how she felt about Nicholas walking out on her. Maybe she should be used to handling things alone, but . . . but she hadn't expected this from him. Catherine closed her eyes and sighed. What difference did it make? Men seemed to have their priorities— drinking, gambling . . .

Catherine blinked her eyes open. She'd almost fallen asleep, and that wouldn't do. It was because she hadn't slept much the night before. Strange bed,

Catherine told herself, even though she knew it had been memories of lying in Nicholas' arms that had kept her awake—that had haunted her dreams even after she had drifted into a restless slumber. She could close her eyes now and recall the feel of his hard body pressed to hers, the moist heat of his lips, the fire he ignited in her. . . .

Catherine's eyes flew open, trying to focus her surroundings through the murky veil of dusk. Heavy shadows camouflaged the bed and bureau, but she finally realized where she was, and what she'd done. She'd slept, and by the looks of it, slept a long time. "Oh." A tiny moan of pain escaped Catherine as she sat up. Twisting her head she tried to massage the stiffness out, wishing for an instant that Nicholas were there to rub her neck. Then she remembered why he wasn't.

Squaring her shoulders, ignoring the discomfort caused from sleeping sitting up, Catherine marched across the hall to Nicholas' room. Her pounding brought no response so she opened the door. The room with its bed, chair, washstand and bureau, mirrored her own, and it was empty.

"He's been out drinking all afternoon," Catherine muttered to herself as she hurried down the stairs. "I've been asleep, and he's been drinking. Hardly a productive day." Thoughts of the money they'd wasted on hotel rooms propelled her out the lobby door and toward the docks. She'd show Nicholas Colton about walking out on her. After all she did pay him—well, not yet, but she intended to—and those in her employ did not spend the afternoon drinking.

122

"Probably why he insisted on coming along in the first place," she mumbled, pausing when she noticed a man dressed in a dirty sailor's blouse and a weeks worth of whiskers darkening his pock-marked face watching her. Not watching, leering, she thought, as she hurried around the corner away from him.

The streets in this section of town were not lit nearly as well as those around the hotel. Only an occasional street lamp or the light spilling from a tavern fought the ominous shadows. Catherine swallowed and looked around her, suddenly realizing she had no idea where she was, or where Nicholas might be. Oh, she was near the docks. The smell of pitch and tobacco, strong and acrid, confirmed that. And there were taverns. Raucous laughter drifted to her from establishments whose yardarms sported their names. But which tavern had lured Nicholas?

Taking a deep breath, Catherine walked into the tavern closest to her. Ignoring the startled gazes of its patrons, she asked the man behind the bar if he'd seen anyone answering Nicholas Colton's description.

"I ain't snitchin' on no bloke trying to get away from his missus to have a little fun," he growled before spitting a stream of tobacco juice towards a nearby spittoon.

"But you don't understand. This man isn't my husband, he's—"

"Ain't interested in your affairs, lady. Now git."

He didn't have to tell her twice, though Catherine tried to exit with as much dignity as possible, ignoring several lewd invitations tossed her way. Once outside, Catherine pressed her hands to her hot cheeks. She should return to the hotel immediately.

Though she'd been around rough men, miners, since she could remember, they'd all shown her respect. Well, all except Nicholas Colton, she amended. But this was different. She was way out of her element. She'd go back to the hotel.

The unmistakable sound of laughter—feminine laughter—reached Catherine's ears as she began retracing her steps. This tavern must be different she decided as she realized the sound came from the building she'd just passed. She'd try one more time. After all, nothing had really happened to her in the last one. She'd feel much safer walking the streets if Nicholas were beside her. And besides, Catherine realized she didn't know exactly how to get to the hotel. If she couldn't find Nicholas in this establishment, she'd ask one of the ladies inside to direct her.

Feeling much more composed, Catherine opened the ornately carved door and felt her control shatter like dropped glass. There were ladies . . . women in this tavern, but by the cut of their clothes, and the suggestive way they draped themselves around some of the men in the room, Catherine could only conclude that they were—

"Looking for a job, honey?"

"Are you addressing me?" The last word squeaked out of Catherine's tight throat as she noticed the woman who'd spoken. Impossibly red hair—lots of red hair—curled and snaked its way around a face made bright by painted lips and cheeks. But garish as that might appear, it was the woman's breasts that caught Catherine's attention. Draped—barely—in red satin, they were as big as . . . Well, Catherine didn't know anyone could be that big.

"Beauties, aren't they?" the woman said while running a ringed finger across her decolletage. "The men really love 'em. But don't worry, honey. You've got a cute little figure. And believe it or not, some men prefer your type."

Catherine snapped her eyes back to the woman's face, and shut her mouth, thoroughly embarrassed by the realization that she had been staring—and at what.

"We'll have to get you some other clothes, and do something with this hair. Is this it's natural color?"

Catherine stepped back from the woman who'd been fingering a strand of Catherine's hair as she spoke. Finally able to find her voice, Catherine answered, "Of course, it's the natural color. How could it not be?"

The other woman simply placed her hands on her hips—a posture Catherine thought emphasized her voluptuous shape—and laughed. "You're a funny one, honey. Come on into my office and we'll talk about wages. I usually keep—"

"Wait." The woman was leading the way across the room, and there was no way Catherine intended to follow. "I'm not here about a job. I'm looking for a man."

"Aren't we all, honey?"

Catherine squared her shoulders and started again. "I'm looking for one of my employees that might have uh . . . been in your establishment."

"Well, we have lots of patrons, as you can see. You want to narrow it down for me a little bit?" The woman swept her hand toward the gaudily furnished room, obviously proud of her place.

"On second thought, Miss . . ."

"Belle."

Catherine smiled, weakly. "I think, Miss Belle that I've made a terrible mistake. My employee is not likely to have come here. Thank you for your time." Catherine turned, reaching for the doorknob, anxious to leave. Even the odors of the dock would be preferable to the overwhelming scent of perfume that permeated this place.

"What's your man's name?"

"Nicholas Colton." Catherine opened the door, poised to make her escape. Answering the woman's question was easier than explaining why she knew he hadn't come here. For all his rough ways, Catherine just couldn't imagine him here with a woman like—

"Oh, you mean Nick," the woman said with a husky laugh.

Nick? Catherine stopped in her tracks. She shut the door, and turned to face the woman, unable to hide the shock on her face. "You know him?"

"Sure." Belle smoothed a wrinkle of red satin over her abundant hips. "He came in here this afternoon, and we got to be good friends."

"I see." And the way the woman cooed the words "good friends," ending it with some disgusting smacking noise, Catherine did see. Leaning against the door, Catherine realized she suddenly felt sick. Of course, what Nicholas Colton did with his own time—and who he did it with—was certainly none of her concern, although she had given him credit for better taste. After all, only last night he'd held her in his arms, and . . . Catherine forced her thoughts

126

from the memory. The point was, her mine manager hadn't been on his time. He'd been on hers. And she had no intention of paying him to . . . to—

"Is he still here?" Catherine couldn't stop her eyes from straying toward the stairs. She felt heat rise to her cheeks when she noticed an immodestly dressed female and her gentleman friend climbing the steps.

Belle's husky laughter regained Catherine's attention. "If he were still here do you think I'd be wasting my time talking to you? You've got a lot to learn, honey. 'Course if you're looking for Nick, maybe you're not as naive as you seem."

Catherine ignored that comment. She knew why she was searching for Nicholas. She intended to fire him! Catherine mentally tabulated how much money she could scrape together. She'd sell what was left of her mother's jewels—not much she remembered—to get the funds to pay her mine manager off and send him packing back to England. She didn't need this aggravation in her life. I'll find some way to take care of Grandmere and Marie, she thought, even if it means marrying— Oh my, she didn't want to marry John Parker.

Catherine decided she'd worry about that later. Right now she needed to find Nicholas, so she could rid herself of him once and for all. "Do you happen to know where Mr. Colton . . . Nick went?"

"Sure, honey. When he left here, he went across the street. I should be angry because he took some of my customers with him."

By the tone of her coo, it was obvious to Catherine that whether Belle should be angry or not, she wasn't. How disgusting. Catherine opened the door again, feeling herself older and wiser for her little chat with Belle. And sadder. Why did she feel sadder?

Armoring herself in the stronger emotion of anger—Catherine could muster up enough for Belle and herself—Catherine marched across the dark street. The building she entered bore little resemblance to Belle's establishment. There were no other women in it for one thing. No gossamer material or plumed feathers softened the stark crudeness of its furnishings.

Catherine glanced around the small room, pleased that no one had noticed her, because Belle must have been mistaken. Either that or Nicholas had been here and gone. Or maybe Belle had lied and Nicholas had been hiding in her room the whole time Catherine had questioned her. Maybe this very moment he had his face buried in those huge soft bosoms.

For goodness sakes, Catherine chided herself as she scanned the tavern's patrons again. It was no wonder, no one had noticed her entrance. They were all bunched around something in the back corner. By the looks of their clothing, this was a rougher group than she'd encountered so far in her tavern travels. Even the language they yelled made her ears ring. Obviously some sort of contest took place inside the ring of men, for sprinkled amid the crude cheering, Catherine could hear an occasional wager offered and accepted.

Probably a cock fight, Catherine decided as she backed toward the door. What else could these disgusting men be watching? Just as her back hit the splintery surface of the door, one of the men, an obese fellow, nearly as wide as he was tall, moved away to refill his mug. Curiosity got the better of Catherine. She glanced toward the opening the man's absence provided. Her mouth flew open.

Nicholas? Catherine blinked, then looked again. No roosters pecked and spurred each other. Instead two men sat squared off across a rickety table, elbows pressed to the wood, hands clasped, and eyes boring holes through each other. And one of the arm wrestlers was Nicholas Colton.

Catherine's eyes riveted on him. No longer wearing his fashionable frock coat, he'd rolled up the sleeve of his once white linen shirt. Even then the fabric strained against the muscles and sinew that bulged, sweat slick, in his strong arm.

His shirt clung to his chest and back clearly delineating the powerful ridges and valleys of his body. Catherine sucked in her breath as she watched the intensity exude from him. He'd wrapped a cloth, she recognized as his cravat, around his forehead, but it fell short of its job of keeping sweat from his eyes. But he never blinked. Moisture beaded his brow, following a course down his tightly grimaced face to his neck where the tendons stood at attention.

The combatants were evenly matched. For all the obvious force Nicholas summoned, the straining forearms, the clenched hands moved very little.

Catherine pried her attention from Nicholas long enough to assess his opponent, and she barely suppressed a gasp. Burly, with a black beard that thankfully covered most of his homely face, he appeared to outweigh Nicholas by twenty pounds. He bared his teeth—those he had—and growled, obviously summoning his strength for a Herculean effort, but the arms remained locked in an upright position.

Catherine, who'd transferred her attention back to Nicholas, thought she noticed a slight grin tug at the corners of his tightly pulled lips as he acknowledged the extra effort, and held his ground. Time seemed to stand still as the combatants, taut as bow strings, labored against each others strength. The crowd cheered each fraction of an inch that the powerful arms moved, and Catherine's heart pounded in her chest as she wondered how much more punishment Nicholas's body could take.

"Well, will you look at that." The fat man had returned with his full mug and spotting Catherine had let out a hearty wail. Somehow through the din of noise, his voice was heard, for suddenly Catherine felt herself the center of attention. Not of everyone. The arm wrestlers continued to stare at each other.

Catherine shrank back against the door, the skirt of her gown catching against the splintery wood. Studiously ignoring the men whom she could feel leering at her, she kept her eyes trained on Nicholas. His muscles bulged, his face grimaced, and then for no reason she could discern, for she hadn't made a sound, his eyes flicked toward hers—and locked.

The thunderous thump of flesh pounding wood made her start as the bearded man, taking advantage of Nicholas's loss of concentration sent his arm crashing to the table. Nicholas seemed not to notice as he jumped to his feet, facing her, his steely eyes shooting angry flames.

"What the hell are you doing here?"

"I . . ." Now Catherine found herself with the

dubious honor of being the center of everyone's attention. She swallowed, wetting her suddenly dry lips, and then the absurdity of his question struck her. What was she doing here? The query should more be what was he doing. They'd come to Richmond to hire mine workers, and to that end nothing had been accomplished. Oh, she'd done her part—placing an ad in the *Compiler*, sitting by all day waiting for applicants to appear. But he . . . he had left her to cavort with a big-bossomed prostitute, and to play childish games.

And to think she'd been taken by the sight of him when she'd walked into this . . . this place. She'd even silently cheered his efforts, hoping for his victory over the giant he'd been foolish enough to arm wrestle. Well, she was glad he'd lost. Absolved herself of any blame. Certainly wouldn't endure his yelling at her. "I came looking for you," she said, her chin raised defiantly.

His eyes bore into her a moment angrily, then, inexplicably, his expression changed—softened. He started toward her, a smile tilting the corners of his chiseled mouth. "Isn't that just like a woman?" he asked the room at large, as he yanked the material from around his head and mopped his face with it. "Always sticking their pretty noses in where they don't belong."

The fact that he tweaked her nose as he spoke flustered Catherine enough to slow her first angry retort, but it was nothing compared to the shock of what he did next. For all the burly crowd in the tavern to witness, he draped his arm around her possessively, firmly. Before she could protest,

131

Catherine felt herself hauled against his hot sweaty body. She steeled herself to be repulsed, but to her surprise found she wasn't. To her annoyance, she actually found his musky odor intoxicating, but she couldn't say the same for the familiar way he bundled her toward the door.

"Mr. Colton, if you please."

"Hush up, Cate." He spoke softly, obviously for her ears alone as he grinned back at the tavern's patrons. "I'll expect to see all of you bright and early day after tomorrow at the mine."

"Whoa there, Nick." The burly, bearded giant stepped forward. "Thought the deal was that I'd come to work for you if you beat me arm wrestlin'."

"Damn, Sampson. Are you going to hold me to that? You know as well as I do that a couple more minutes and the victory would have been mine."

"But it weren't. And that's the truth of it."

"Well, hell." Nick moved back toward the center of the room, keeping a surprisingly quiet Cate plastered to his side. "Are we going to have to go at it again?"

"That weren't the deal neither," Sampson insisted. "One match. That's what we said."

"You going to blame me for taking my eyes off your ugly mug to look at this?" Nick glanced down at Catherine grinning at the color that stained her cheeks. She apparently had caught on enough to what was going on to keep her sharp tongue still, but that didn't mean there wouldn't be hell to pay later.

"Ain't my fault you can't handle your woman." Sampson nodded his grizzly head, glancing around at the others in the tavern.

Nick could feel his afternoon's work slipping

away—and all because Miss Catherine Brousseau hadn't stayed at the hotel where he'd left her. He tightened his arm around her shoulder, letting his hand slide down her arm suggestively. "Oh, I can handle her all right. I just like to do it in a more private setting." Response to his remark was as he expected. The men seemed to think it highly amusing, and Catherine did not. He thought if her body became any more rigid, she'd shatter.

"Hell, I guess I ain't got nothing else to do," the giant finally stopped laughing long enough to say. "Might as well earn some money working in your mine." He looked around the room. "What do you say boys?"

Nick would hardly call their response enthusiastic, but they had agreed to show up for work. Now if his other problems were so easily solved, he thought as he propelled Catherine along the dark street, out of earshot of the tavern. With morbid curiosity he wondered what she'd chastise him for first. He didn't have to wait long to find out.

"Your mine! You told those men Greenfield was your mine?" Nick had pulled her around a corner, and they stood in front of what appeared to be an empty warehouse.

"Now, Cate."

"Don't 'now Cate' me. And get your hands off me." Catherine just realized his arm still lay across her shoulders. He really was the most insufferable man. I trusted you to be a gentleman. I gave you a job. Brought you to Richmond. And where do I find you . . .

Nick let Catherine go on spilling her vinegar,

133

which she seemed to have in ample supply, until she came around to a remark that questioned his parentage. Grabbing her shoulders, he shook her just hard enough to gain her attention. Ignoring her dropped jaw, he hissed, "Listen here, Miss High and Mighty Brousseau. I've had about all this I'm going to take. You wanted miners. I got you miners. And believe me, it was no easy task. Most people in this town seem to think Greenfield Mine is about as desirable a place to be as the gates of Hell.

"If I had to do a little lying to get some men to take the job, it seems to me you should be grateful for the help instead of carrying on like a banshee."

"A banshee!" Catherine caught her breath enough to challenge his remark. He glared down at her and she tried to take a step backward, but his hands on her shoulders stopped her. He suddenly seemed very intimidating with his huge towering body and scowling face. Sweat had darkened his hair, and now the night made it seem almost black. His thick brows nearly touched over his steel-gray eyes, and Catherine knew a sudden fear. If he should attempt to hurt her there was nothing she could do, and no one was around to help.

Even in the darkness, he must have sensed her fear because he let his hands drop and his voice lowered. "Listen Cate, I didn't ask for this job, nor did I want it. But as long as I'm here, I intend to do my best to see that your mine gets going again and shows a profit. Those men weren't about to work for a woman. So, I let them think they'd be working for me. In a sense they will be."

"Is that why you didn't want this job? Because

you'd be working for a woman?" Catherine hadn't realized until now that he hadn't jumped at the opportunity to do anything his employer, Travis Fielding, asked of him.

Nick laughed, and shook his head. "I consider myself a little more enlightened than that." Taking her arm he started back along the street. As they reached the better part of town more street lamps lit the way, and Nick rolled down his sleeves.

"Why then?" Catherine couldn't help the almost personal affront she felt at his revelation.

Nick glanced down at her. For all that her hair had come loose of its pins and curled in unkempt disarray around her face, she was a pretty sight. A sight he'd do well not to grow too fond of. This was only a job. He had to remember that. He looked away and shrugged, trying to ignore the nagging thought that his involvement was more than it should be. "I wasn't crazy about leaving New Castle, I suppose."

"I see." Catherine took a deep breath. Now that she knew what he'd been doing, thoughts of her earlier outburst plagued her conscience. "Mr. Colton, I'm truly sorry for that comment I made about your . . . your . . ."

"My questionable parentage," Nick supplied, able to tell even in the scant light that she colored several shades darker.

"Yes." Catherine swallowed. "It was inexcusable of me to say that."

"Maybe you accidentally hit upon the truth."

Catherine's eyes met his, and for just a moment she felt an understanding grow between them. Perhaps he'd given her another puzzle piece to his complex

135

personality. But in an instant the feeling disappeared and he grinned at her in a way that made Catherine wonder if it had been there at all. He was probably teasing her again.

"How did you find me anyway?" Nick asked as they entered the Union Hotel.

"A friend of yours mentioned your whereabouts." Catherine gathered up her skirts and started up the stairs.

"A friend?" Nick rested his shoulder against Catherine's doorjamb. "Who?"

"I believe she gave her name as Belle."

"Ah." He grinned and even though the light from the square lamp hung midway in the hall offered little in the way of illumination, she noticed the twinkle in his eyes. "Wonderful woman, Belle."

"Yes, she did seem to have some outstanding attributes."

Nick cocked his brow and chuckled. "Really? I didn't notice. She did suggest several men who needed work."

"How thoughtful of her."

"I hired three of them."

"You have interesting methods, Mr. Colton, for hiring miners." Catherine knew she should close her door and see an end to this day. But though she fingered the smooth round knob, she remained, exchanging sallies with the man who lounged in her doorway. His shirt clung to his strong torso, the open buttons at the top and lack of neckcloth revealing the curling golden brown hair on his chest. His grin was crooked and infectious. The sight of it almost took

136

her breath away.

"I have interesting methods for a lot of things."

Was it her imagination, or did he move closer? She could swear the heady musk of his body drew her nearer. "So Belle implied. She asked me to convey to you her wish that you return and see her again—anytime."

"Do I detect a note of jealousy in your voice, Miss Brousseau?"

"Not at all." Catherine stepped back, tightening her grip on the doorknob. "Actually I'm quite fond of your friend, Belle. She did, after all, offer me employment."

Brushing his damp palm away from her breast she fingered the brass handle of his bureau, smiling when she caught the reflection of his dejected expression in the mirror.

"What's the matter," his voice whined.

Tracing the blonde curl that twined across her naked shoulder, she answered, "Maybe I just don't feel like playing."

"Well, what if I do?"

Shrugging daintily, she sat on the satin chaise, lifting her leg and slowly rolling down her stocking. She could hear his pathetic panting from across the room. She stripped off the other stocking. "I didn't say I wouldn't let you touch me. It's just . . . well, hard for me to feel romantic when I'm so worried." Her rosebud mouth pouted.

"About what?" He knelt beside the chaise.

"I simply can't understand why it's taking so long." She let him look his fill at her creamy white breast, even arching her back so that the pink nipples puckered prettily against the thin muslin of her chemise. But when his hand reached out, she sidled away.

"These things take time."

"You've been telling me that forever. I'm beginning to lose faith in you, John."

"No." He nearly shouted the word. Grabbing her hand, he held it to his heart. "She'll sell. You'll see. I've convinced all the planters here about to refuse to lease her mine workers. Without them she'll have to sell. And I'll be there to buy, then sell at a profit. Just as we planned."

She lowered her lashes. "I guess you haven't heard. Catherine went to Richmond to hire miners. She left yesterday."

"That won't do her any good. Word is that Greenfield isn't a healthy place to work."

"And did you spread that word?" She smiled showing even white teeth.

"Yes, I did," he preened. "I've taken care of everything."

"But, I thought you were going to marry her."

"She won't have me. I told you that." The angry tinge to his voice was unmistakable.

"That's just because she doesn't know you like I do." She trailed her finger down the front of his trousers, outlining the obvious bulge. "If she did, I know she'd jump at the chance to marry you."

"Your sister barely tolerates my presence. I doubt

138

she'd jump at the chance to join me in bed."

"We already know Catherine doesn't know what's good for her. Maybe you just need to force her a little." Marie curled her hand around his hardness.

"Do you mean rape?"

"Oh, John." She squeezed gently. "What an awful word. You know I wouldn't want you to do that. I just know you." She squeezed harder. "Your skill." She felt him jerk beneath her hand. "She might protest at first, but in the end she'd enjoy it—and be grateful."

John's breathing came hard and fast. "I still don't understand why you want me to marry her."

"To get control of the mine. So you can sell it." She smiled again. "And give me the money."

He reached for her again and this time she suffered his caress. "I don't know why you don't just marry me. I have enough money for you."

"I'm not the marrying kind, John. I told you that. But that doesn't mean we can't be together—like always." Marie faked a moan as his hand skimmed up her thigh.

"If you ask me, that English guy she brought over here is the real trouble maker. He messed up the little deal we had with Stevens."

"That was unfortunate. With Catherine scared to death to enter the mine, she'd never have suspected a thing—until it was too late, that is." Marie squirmed beneath him. "But don't worry about Nicholas Colton. I can take care of him."

"I don't want you around that man, Marie."

Throwing back her head, she laughed a high-pitched cackle that she usually tried to disguise. "John, John. Don't start being possessive. That's not a trait I admire." Her hand wriggled between their bodies, placating the hurt expression in his eyes. "You worry about Catherine," she cooed. "And let me attend to Nick Colton."

Chapter Seven

Closing the tally book with a pat of satisfaction, Catherine smiled. The mine had been back in operation but a fortnight, and already Greenfield was showing a profit. Not that there'd actually been any money yet. But there would be—soon.

She leaned back in the hard chair, idly rubbing the ink stain on her finger. By her calculations, when the load of coal heading for Richmond this very moment sold, there would be enough money to pay the men—including Nicholas Colton—their first months salary, put a healthy dent in some of the debt her father and Marie had run up, and see Greenfield in operation until the next load sold.

Resisting the urge to open her account book and read the figures—just to make sure—Catherine stood, stretching her arms above her head. Crossing to the open door in the back of the library, Catherine glanced in at her grandmother. The older woman slept soundly, and by the looks of it, would for some time. Covered to the tip of her chin in a blue and white quilt, her white hair hidden by a night cap, Grandmere's face appeared calm and content in slumber. More relaxed than Catherine had seen her in a long time.

"She probably senses through me that things are going better," Catherine murmured as she backed away from the door. Though she'd certainly tried to spare her grandmother the worries that had plagued her for so long, Catherine knew some of Greenfield's problems had troubled her. About the only person who hadn't been affected by the troubles was Marie. Catherine felt a pang of guilt for mentally chiding her younger sister. After all, Marie couldn't seem to help her penchant for beautiful clothes and society. And, Catherine admitted to herself, she felt partly responsible for Marie's carefree attitude.

After their father died, and Catherine realized the financial disaster he'd left, she'd tried to talk to Marie about it—with little success. Every time she broached the subject, Marie would fly into a rage, finally ending with the condemnation of their father for leaving the mine to Catherine. It became easier by far to simply try and handle the problems by herself, which is basically what she'd been doing for years— even before she'd realized the extent of their father's debt.

Even the one concession Catherine had asked of Marie, that she curb her spending, had fallen on deaf ears. That is until Catherine had been forced to cut off Marie's credit. Oh, she'd flown into a royal rage then, dancing around, threatening all sorts of dire results if Catherine didn't sell the mine. Catherine crossed to the window, memories of the day last year still fresh in her mind.

Shocked. She'd actually been shocked at the things Marie had said to her. Awful things about hate and revenge. Catherine shook her head, surprised that it still hurt so much. After all, Marie had apologized profusely after Catherine explained that if they sold the mine they'd have nothing—no home, no chance for any income to take care of Grandmere.

Resting her hands on the sill, Catherine leaned out the window. The afternoon sparkled brightly as only a day in late spring could. The hot spell that had enveloped the land at winter's end had broken, leaving the sky clear and the temperature mild. Too nice a day to be melancholy, Catherine told herself, especially when everything seemed to be working out. Catherine headed for the door. Maybe soon Marie would be able to buy more of the pretty clothes she craved. Maybe she'd buy some, too.

After all, she liked nice things. Catherine thought of the beautiful little bonnet that sat on top of her wardrobe—the one Nicholas had bought for his friend in England. He'd insisted she keep it for him, citing the fact that it would most likely get ruined in the cabin. She doubted his logic, however, she couldn't say she minded giving in to it. This way she could look at the hat anytime she wished. Sometimes, at night, when no one was there to see, she'd try it on. The annoying thing was that during those times, she'd find herself pretending he'd bought the hat for her.

"Silly, silly," Catherine chided herself as she walked toward the path to the creek. A pleasant breeze, alive with the fragrance of roses, rustled the

143

leaves of the huge spreading elm near the house. Robins had nested in that tree when she was a child. She'd always waited anxiously for the fat speckled babies to make their appearance. Catherine smiled sadly, wondering if the robins had made a family there this year. She hadn't had time to notice.

Catherine passed the cut-off to the mine, resisting the urge to stop by and check how things were progressing. Nicholas had been right about the miners. They would definitely resent any bossing she might try to do. So Catherine had stayed in the background, finding out about the operation through her mine manager's daily reports.

He was efficient and dependable. Catherine would certainly give him that. Every morning, without fail, he'd appear at the library door, felt hat in hand, to report the previous day's results. His reports were concise, as far as she could tell, accurate, and he never stayed a moment longer than necessary.

Not that she wanted him to, Catherine assured herself as she brushed her hand against the scaly bark of a hickory tree along the path. All she desired of Nicholas Colton was that he manage her mine well. Just as he was doing. She couldn't be more pleased that he'd stopped making his flirtatious comments or looking at her the way that made her feel warm all over. Theirs was a business relationship. As it should be. As she wanted it. Without even realizing what she did, Catherine shredded the bark she'd peeled from the tree.

It had just been so sudden. Catherine left the shade of the path, stepping into the sparkling sunlight that sprinkled the splashing creek with fairy dust. One minute Nicholas had stood in her doorway at the hotel in Richmond leaning toward her as if he intended to kiss her—and more. Catherine's breath caught now simply remembering the expression in his stormy gray eyes. It had mesmerized her.

She'd fought with herself, trying to decide what to do. A part of her, a part she hadn't even known existed until she'd met Nicholas, wanted nothing more than to melt into his arms and forget propriety. Of course her rational self advised strongly that she shut the door, lock it, and blot out the sight of his strong male body. And that's what she would have done, Catherine assured herself as she sat on a grassy knoll beside the rushing water, if it had been necessary. But it hadn't. Nicholas had straightened, a shuttered look hiding the intensity in his eyes, wished her a good night, his voice formal, and left. He'd spoken to her with the same reserved politeness ever since.

Shaking her head, Catherine forced her thoughts away from that night. She had more sense than to waste the first free time she'd had in ages thinking about a hired miner. She leaned back, smiling as she watched the cloud ghosts frolic across the azure sky. So intent was she on enjoying the warmth of the sun, the dancing tune of the bubbling stream that she didn't notice the sound of the approaching horse until it was very close.

Looking around, shading her eyes with her hand, Catherine hid a grimace as she saw John Parker dismount and head her way.

"Afternoon, Catherine."

"John." Catherine turned back to stare at the creek, wondering to what she owed this unexpected—

145

and unwelcomed—visit.

"You look relaxed."

"I am." *Was* would be closer to the truth, Catherine admitted silently, as her neighbor dropped to the ground beside her.

"This is the life you were meant for Catherine. Resting in the shade, no worries to wrinkle your brow. Now isn't this better than sitting in that office of yours?"

"This is pleasant," Catherine answered, deciding against pointing out to him that she sat in the sun, not the shade, and that she'd just left the library, where she'd toiled over figures all morning.

But apparently he knew that this lull in activity was not the norm, for he reached out and tidied a lock of auburn hair that had loosened from her chignon. "You could have this all the time if you would but marry me."

"John, I . . ." Catherine resisted the urge to draw away from him. She would not be his wife, but she had no real desire to hurt him. True she blamed him for taking advantage of her father's weakness, and stripping her of most of Greenfield. However, it was her father's choice, and if John hadn't lent him money Catherine knew her father would have found some other way to back his wagers.

"Catherine, you've kept me waiting long enough."

"John." Catherine did sidle away when he moved closer, his arm brushing against her breast. "I can't marry you. I thought you knew that."

"Can't, Catherine?" John lifted his light brown brow in a questioning scowl. "I see no reason why our marriage can't be accomplished."

He was right. There was no logical reason. He'd courted no one else that she knew of, and Lord knew she had no other suitors. Her father had wanted this match, and most people in the county expected it. John had money. He'd promised to see to her needs, her sister's needs, and even to take care of her grandmother.

"You haven't been toying with me all this time, have you, Catherine? I hadn't taken you for a tease."

"No, of course not." She'd only wanted to let him down easily—encourage him to turn elsewhere when his constant advances were ignored. Had she inadvertently led him on?

"I didn't think so." He leaned forward, his smile holding little warmth. "Now, when shall we wed? I had thought to do it as soon as possible, but I know how you women are with your planning, and—"

"You don't understand, John. I don't love you. I—"

John's laugh cut her off. "Catherine, dear, that will come after we're wed."

"No, John." Catherine angled her body away from his. "I feel certain I could never love you." Kindness kept her from adding that she could never even like him.

And then there was the mine. If she married John, he'd have control of it—of all of Greenfield. Her heritage, all that so many people had worked hard to build, would be swallowed up, gone forever.

Catherine turned back to tell him, to try to explain, but her words stuck in her throat when she saw the feral gleam in his brown eyes.

"I've tried to be patient with you, Catherine,

though I'm beginning to wonder why."

"I realize you don't understand—"

"You're right. I don't." He moved closer. His presence suddenly menacing. "But perhaps after this I won't have to."

"After what?" Catherine scurried to rise, not exactly frightened, but certainly uncomfortable with this side of John she'd never seen before. His hand, stronger than she would have imagined clamped on her shoulder, preventing her escape. "Stop it. You're hurting me."

"It won't hurt for long."

"Have you lost your mind?" Catherine knocked his hand away from her leg, and tried again to get up. The grass was slick and with his hands on her she couldn't manage. Then before she knew what his intentions were, John pushed her back, covering her with his body.

With all the force she could muster, she pushed against him. "Get off me, John. Stop this or I'll scream."

"Go ahead. There's no one to hear you." He jerked at her skirts, fumbling through her petticoats with demanding fingers.

Perhaps he was right and no one could hear her since they were too far from the house and the mine was too noisy, but that didn't stop Catherine from trying. She drew in a breath, ready to scream for help, but before she could make a sound John's sweaty palm clamped down on her mouth. Catherine, her eyes wide with apprehension, stared at John over his restraining hand. The fear that she'd kept a firm grip on, suddenly burst upon her and she wriggled and bucked, trying to escape John's groping hand.

Nick slung his jacket over his shoulder and turned his eyes away from the scene by the creek. When he'd come up the path earlier, on his way to pick up some equipment at his cabin, he'd noticed Catherine and John Parker sitting on the grassy hill. They'd been having a rather intimate conversation then. But now . . .

Against his will, Nick let his gaze stray to the two people lying by the water. From his angle, he couldn't see clearly, but there could be little doubt that the two were making love. Parker lay on top of Catherine, all but obliterating her from his view. Disgusted with himself, feeling like a voyeur, Nick forced himself to move along the path.

What did he care anyway? Catherine may have denied planning to marry her neighbor, but by the looks of things Marie had been right. Nick slapped a vine out of his way, cursing when a thorn tore into his flesh. Squinting down at his thumb, Nick tried to find the splinter. This served him right, Nick decided. He had no business thinking about Catherine Brousseau as anything but an employer. Hadn't he decided that for himself that last night in Richmond?

He'd looked at her then, standing in the doorway, and he'd wanted her. Not just wanted her, felt that he needed her. God, the feeling had almost overwhelmed him.

And it had scared the hell out of him.

His plans didn't include forming an attachment to a woman right now, especially a woman like

Catherine. She wasn't the kind you bedded and left—unless you were John Parker, Nick thought with derision. But then Parker wasn't going to leave her. Nick leaned against a rough pine tree, his thumb forgotten. Maybe he should have pressed his advantage in Richmond. He'd noticed the look in her eyes. She desired him as much as he had her. With a little sweet talking . . . But then that didn't go along with the decision he'd made that night. The decision to keep his distance from her.

And he'd succeeded, admirably, even taking his meals with the new miners. And where had that put Catherine? Sprawled on the ground under John Parker. Damn, he wished he hadn't seen that. And God, he wished he didn't care.

Disgustedly, Nick shoved his hand into his pocket, grimacing when the rough fabric rubbed against his cut skin, and started back toward the mine.

The first piercing scream halted him in his tracks. The second had him racing toward the creek.

John's hand slapped back across her mouth, but this time it blocked her nose, too. With most of her air cut off, Catherine's head began to spin and she felt her limbs grow weak. Oh, how foolish it had been to bite his hand. At the time it had seemed a flash of brilliance. He'd let go of her mouth for an instant, and she'd screamed. But now instead of raping her, he was going to kill her, because she couldn't breathe. With one last reserve of strength she freed her hand from between their bodies, ignoring John's plea to stop fighting so much, and clawed at the hand that denied her air.

Then she was free. Not only her mouth and nose, but her body was free from the terrible weight of her assailant. Gulping precious air into her burning lungs, Catherine looked up in time to see Nicholas twist John around and send his head jerking to the side with one powerful punch.

"Nick." Her voice sounded raspy to her ears, and she couldn't be certain Nicholas heard her until he knelt down beside her, cradling her head in his arms.

"Catherine. My God, Catherine, are you all right?"

Catherine tried to smile. He looked so concerned. "I . . . I just need to catch my breath. John . . . he tried—"

"I know. Don't try to talk." Nick glanced over his shoulder to where Parker lay in a rumpled unconscious heap. The instant he'd topped the small hill, and seen what that bastard was doing to Catherine, Nick had flown into an unholy rage. It had been a struggle not to wring his scrawny neck when he'd pulled him off Catherine. How could he have thought that she would voluntarily make love with that man?

"I'm all right." Catherine tried to sit up, but Nick continued to hold her against his chest. His heart pounded in her ear as if he'd run a race.

"Did he hurt you, Cate?" If he had Nick knew no power on earth could keep him from tearing Parker limb from limb.

"No." Nicholas' meaning was clear by the intensity in his gray eyes.

"Are you sure?" Nick's gaze traveled down to the white petticoats Catherine was nervously trying to pull down over her legs. "Tell me true, Cate. I swear I'll kill the bastard if he touched you."

"No." Catherine laid her hand against his chest. "He frightened me. That's all." Closing her eyes, Catherine endured the embarrassment of Nicholas lifting her petticoats to examine the tears in her stockings. Now that the shock had passed, Catherine found her relief turning to mortification that this man would see her in such a state.

"I'm really all right," Catherine repeated swatting at her skirts. Nicholas ignored her hands, and gently lowered them himself.

"You need to get cleaned up. I'll help you back to the house."

"I can manage." It was a good thing he ignored her. As Catherine stood, with Nicholas' help, she found her legs too shaky to support her weight.

A moan from John had them both looking toward his prone body. While they watched, he opened his eyes and rubbed his jaw, looking around as if he had forgotten where he was. One word from Nick snapped his head around. Recognition and fear flooded his expression.

"Get up, Parker." Nick repeated his free hand tightening into a fist.

"Please, Nick." Catherine touched his arm, before turning to face Parker. "I want you off my property, John. You are never to return again. Do you understand?"

"Answer the lady," Nick commanded after Parker's silence stretched longer than he could bear. Nick still had the strongest desire to decorate the man's face with more than the purple bruise that adorned his

152

swollen jaw.

"Don't worry, Catherine. I've no desire to visit Greenfield again." John swooped up his hat, brushing the grass from its brim. He kept his eyes carefully away from the mine manager. When he reached his horse, he mounted quickly, then turned. "All you needed to do was say no, Catherine."

"Let him go . . . please." Catherine's soft plea plus the pressure of her hand on his arm kept Nick from bolting after the horse. He glanced down at the woman by his side. Though she looked outwardly calm, Nick sensed she needed him more right now than she needed revenge. Besides, his path would cross Parker's again.

Catherine left the shelter of his arm, wanting to get back to her house. Absently running her fingers through her hair, she realized that she must look a disheveled sight. Long tangles woven with twigs and leaves streamed down her back. All the pins had scattered in the grass during John's attack. She could avoid Grandmere and Marie—Catherine had no idea where her sister was—but chances of Betsy seeing her were great.

"Don't you ever just wear your hair down?" Nick knelt beside the creek and wet his handkerchief. Though he wore his miner's clothes, and coal dust stained his pants and shirt, the handkerchief was clean.

Nicholas's words told Catherine he understood her dilemma. "I suppose so." Now that she'd stood and her skirt covered her petticoats, she didn't feel so rumpled.

"Here." Nick wiped the damp linen gently across

her cheek. "You have a scratch, but it doesn't look too bad."

Catherine winced when the cool water touched her scraped skin.

"Sorry."

"No, it's all right." Catherine shut her eyes as he continued to clean her face with soft, tender strokes. He smelled of coal dust and exertion, but she had the strongest desire to press against his broad chest, to wrap her arms around his strong neck and feel safe and loved. But that was silly. He had helped her, was still helping her, but he didn't love her—nor she him. He'd done his best to ignore her, for heaven's sake, and she'd been glad. Catherine decided this desire to be held stemmed from her experience with John Parker. She'd probably feel the same for anyone who'd helped her. Wouldn't she?

"There, now your face is clean." Nick stepped behind her and began sifting debris from her long auburn hair. He remained quiet for a moment, then his curiosity drove him to speak. He hadn't liked Parker from the beginning, but he hadn't thought him capable of forcing himself on a woman. "Why did he do this?"

"You mean, why didn't I say 'no'?"

Grabbing her shoulder, turning her around to him, Nick stared into her eyes, shimmering like dew-covered grass with unshed tears. "That's not what I meant, and you know it."

"I know. I'm sorry. It's just . . ." Catherine couldn't help thinking of the other time she'd lain beneath a man—Nicholas. She hadn't said no then, at least not until she'd allowed him to kiss her, to touch her, and he wondered if Nick remembered, too. But it had been so different. Catherine swallowed, looking down, unable to continue gazing into his eyes without leaning into him.

"I don't know why he did it." She walked away from him. Nicholas did nothing to stop her. "He seemed almost like someone else, someone I didn't know." Catherine gave a derisive laugh. "That's silly. I've known John Parker almost all my life."

"But you didn't like him."

Catherine swung around, surprised at Nicholas's insight. As far as she could remember, she'd never mentioned any dislike for John Parker to him. Shrugging, she picked her way down toward the creek. Water bugs skittered across the surface, deftly defying the hungry minnows beneath. "Greenfield used to be much larger. I told you that we owned the forests that now belong to Parker, but there was more, much more. Fields and meadows down to the river."

"What happened?" Nick propped his booted foot on a rock.

"My father had a penchant for gambling." She laughed again. "Unfortunately, he wasn't very good, or lucky, or whatever it is that makes a successful gambler. He also lived beyond his means." She paused. "I loved him very much." Catherine looked up at Nick afraid that her confession sounded too much like a condemnation of her father.

Nick nodded as if he could understand what it meant to love a father who had not taken the best care of you—he who had never known the care of a father at all.

155

"John Parker lent my father large sums of money using the land as collateral."

"And collected."

"Yes. He's offered to buy the rest of Greenfield."

"The mine."

"But I refused to sell. That's when he began proposing marriage again."

"Again?" Nick cocked his brow.

"My father and John had talked of it before he died."

"But you'd never agreed."

"No, never," Catherine answered. "And I wouldn't agree now." She brushed a curl behind her ear. "That's what our conversation was about. He demanded an answer, and I told him no. The funny thing is that I had the feeling he knew before that I wouldn't and had accepted it.

"Then why did he react so violently today?" Nick leaned his forearm across his knee and stared at Catherine.

"I don't know. I just don't know."

Catherine jerked awake, an uneasy feeling causing her heart to beat painfully in her chest. Only a dream she rationalized snuggling down further under the quilt. Who wouldn't have bad dreams after her experience with John Parker yesterday? But with sudden clarity, Catherine realized she'd been dreaming of Nicholas. And to her dismay, though they'd been lying together, it had not been the least unpleasant.

No it hadn't been a dream that had awakened

her . . . Catherine took several deep, calming breaths, but it didn't help. Flinging off her covers, she decided to check on her grandmother. The elderly woman had seemed better of late, more alert and happy; however, at her age, the possibility of a sudden illness couldn't be overlooked. A whiff of air blew in the open window. Odd, Catherine thought, it seemed too warm for anyone to need a fire, yet she definitely smelled . . . smoke.

Catherine's feet hit the wide pine floor planks on a run. Sticking her head out the window, she searched the darkness. What she saw made her gasp. Above the shadowy loblolly pines, clouds of smoke shaded a sky stained orange and red.

"My, God!" Catherine pulled away from the window, and fumbled in the darkness for her clothes. She couldn't tell exactly what was ablaze, but it came from the direction of the mine. Catherine's heart beat faster as she yanked her nightrail over her head. She couldn't figure why her chemise gave her so much trouble until she realized she'd put it on backwards.

"Damn." The curse escaped her when she stubbed her toe on the corner post of her bed. Stepping into her shoes, she grappled with her buttons, unconcerned whether or not she'd matched them to the correct hole.

She opened her bedroom door and flew down the stairs, her shoes barely touching the treads. At the bottom she swung around the newel deciding to go out through the parlor so she wouldn't disturb her grandmother. Her precaution was useless. As Catherine picked her way around the horsehair sofa, she heard Grandmere's voice.

157

"Catherine. Is that you?"

Retracing her steps, trying hard to catch her breath, Catherine stuck her head inside Grandmere's room. Even though Catherine's eyes had adjusted to the near darkness, Grandmere's bed appeared only as a deeper shadow against the darkness. "It's me, Grandmere. Go back to sleep."

"What's wrong, Catherine?"

"Just a little trouble at the mine. Nothing to concern you." Catherine felt ready to pop out of her skin with the need to get to the mine, but she didn't want to leave her grandmother to worry.

"In the middle of the night? It is the middle of the night, isn't it, Catherine."

"Yes. I don't know exactly what time it is." She hadn't looked at a clock. "But I told you we were running two shifts now. I better go see if they need me."

"All right, dear. Be careful."

"I shall." Catherine started to pull the door shut.

"Oh, Catherine?"

"Yes?" She hadn't been able to hide the anxiety and annoyance in her voice. Catherine had no idea what was happening at the mine while she stood calmly trying to talk with her grandmother.

"My Henry is safe, isn't he?"

"Oh, yes, Grandpere is fine." Catherine felt tears sting her eyes. Distractedly she brushed them away as she headed for the front door. She couldn't worry about her grandmother now. She'd done all she could. Now she needed to think about the mine and what the fire could mean. She hoped no one was hurt. "Oh please," she thought, as she grabbed up the lantern on the porch, "Don't let anyone be hurt."

At least she knew that Nicholas was safe. He'd left this morning to collect the money for the coal and wasn't due back until tomorrow morning. Catherine started down the path. The smell of smoke was stronger now, and Catherine quickened her pace even though she could scarcely see.

As she neared the clearing she could hear men yelling, hear the crackle of fire. Catherine gathered up her skirts and began to run, gulping in breaths of acrid air as each step brought her nearer the mine.

Intense heat hit her as she burst into the mine clearing. Catherine's arms shot up to protect her face and she squinted around her elbow at the blazing inferno before her.

Chapter Eight

"Sampson!" Spotting the burly miner silhouetted against the sheet of fire, Catherine rushed toward him, grabbing his arm. "What happened? Is anyone hurt?" she yelled up at his smoke blackened face.

"You better get out of here, Miss Brousseau. This ain't no place for a woman. Get back up to the house." He turned, dismissing her as he glared back at the flames.

"I asked," Catherine pushed herself in front of him, "if anyone was injured."

"No," he barked down at her, obviously annoyed by her persistence. "We got everyone out."

Catherine sighed with relief, then turned her mind to the next problem. "Why aren't you fighting the fire?" She could tell now that the blaze was confined to the barracks, the building that housed the miners when they weren't working. It was also obvious that though some attempt may have been made earlier to fight the flames, the miners now seemed content to stand by and watch.

"Ain't nothing we can do to save it."

Reluctantly, Catherine admitted the truth of his words. As he spoke, a section of tin roof crashed into the fiery skeleton of wood, sprinkling the night sky with a torrent of sparks. Like a shower of shimmering stars, they rained over the other buildings and surrounding trees.

Catherine grabbed Sampson's shirt, pulling the startled man's face to within inches of her own. "Well, there's something we can do to keep the fire from spreading! Get these men organized into a bucket brigade and wet down the storage shed and everything else that can burn. Now!"

Without even waiting to see if he followed her orders, Catherine hurled herself toward another miner she recognized from the tavern in Richmond. "Come with me," she ordered running into the storage shed. "Grab some of these shovels. We need to beat out the sparks before they catch the brush on fire."

When Catherine raced out of the shed, she noticed a human chain had formed to douse the area around the fire with water. She yanked two men off the line, commanding them to move the black powder down to the creek. Even though the explosives weren't in any immediate danger from the fire, she didn't want to take chances.

Clutching the handle of the shovel she'd dragged from the shed, Catherine hiked up her skirts and worked her way behind the blazing barracks. Several men had stationed themselves there to keep the fire from spreading into the brush. Another section of wall crumbled into the blaze and again the area was

162

littered with sparks. Catherine joined the men in stamping them out. She raised and lowered the heavy spade till her muscles burned nearly as hot as the fire, and all the time she kept wishing that Nicholas were here.

First you're glad he's out of harms way, then you want him by your side, Catherine chided herself as she leaned against the shovel handle, coughing, and watching for any new fires. But she couldn't help it. As much as she wanted him safe—and she refused to speculate why that had been her first concern—she knew he would have been a big help in organizing the men and fighting the fire. Who was she trying to fool? He would have had them working together before she'd even smelled the first whiff of smoke.

By the time the first pale streaks of dawn ribboned the eastern sky, the fire had burned itself out. Through tireless effort, the brush and buildings surrounding the mine had been spared. Only the barracks smoldered, a ruined heap of ashes and charred beams.

Exhausted, Catherine slid down to the ground, resting her head against a coal bin. The dirt beneath her had been worked into coal black mud by boot heels and water, but Catherine didn't care. She'd never wear her dress again, and a little more dirt wouldn't make any difference. Though she couldn't see her face, Catherine's arms and clothes were covered with black soot.

The men resting around her were equally filthy. Now that the crisis was over, Catherine noticed that some were dressed in their mining clothes, obviously the night shift workers, who'd been in the mine when the fire broke out, and the others wore only hastily donned trousers. They all looked as tired as she felt. Catherine sighed. Though the worst was over, the cleanup and rebuilding had yet to begin.

At least no one suffered more than minor burns, Catherine consoled herself as she thought of the job ahead. Since the men needed a place to live, they'd soon have to start building another barracks. But first they needed to clean up and get some nourishment and rest.

Pulling her protesting body up, Catherine faced the men. Again she wished Nicholas were here. She brushed a clump of dried mud off her skirt and began to speak. Finding her voice hoarse, she cleared her throat and started again. "I'm very grateful for what you men have done tonight. There will be a measure of my gratitude in your wages next week. Right now, I think you should—"

"What you doing down here, Miss Brousseau?"

Shocked, Catherine turned toward the man who'd interrupted her—Sampson. "I beg your pardon."

"You heard me." He stood, and though the effort obviously cost him, he now towered over Catherine. "You been giving orders all night, and I guess I was as quick to follow them as anyone here, but now I'd like to know why."

A low grumble of agreement accompanied his words, and Catherine's gaze drifted over the men who nodded their heads in accord. "I'm afraid I don't understand." Why shouldn't they obey her orders? She owned the mine. They worked for her.

"We hired on with Mr. Nick. We take our orders from him, and," he paused, "we don't like taking

164

them from no woman. They're bad luck."

Catherine resisted the urge to laugh at the absurdity of his last statement, opting instead to point out the obvious. "Well, Mr. Nick isn't here. So you can't take your direction from him."

Sampson shifted his weight, staring down at Catherine with eyes as black as the rest of his soot-covered face. "Heard tell when I was in Richmond about a hard-luck mine run by a woman. This wouldn't be it, would it?"

Catherine notched her chin higher, unable to shake an uneasy feeling that Nicholas had read these miners right when he'd told her they wouldn't like working for a woman. But there was no out but to tell the truth. "I own Greenfield Mine, but it's not a hard-luck mine as you describe."

Sampson gave a derisive snort. "Well, lady," he said, motioning his beefy arm toward the smoldering debris. "If this ain't hard luck, I don't know what is."

"It's nothing we can't handle if we all work together. After you men rest, I'm certain we can rebuild. Wait! Where are you going?" Sampson had started walking away and several other miners stood, following his lead.

"I ain't going to work for no woman. When we signed on, we thought Nick owned the mine." More miners pulled themselves up out of the muck and started after Sampson.

"Wait." Catherine twisted a handful of skirt fabric into a tight ball. She felt like crying. She felt like screaming. She felt like throttling that big lummox, Sampson. How dare he leave when she'd worked so hard to get him here. Wasn't the fact that she'd lost

165

valuable time and money in the fire enough? Did she have to have this problem, too?

Apparently so, for now all the men had joined Sampson as he walked away, ignoring her plea.

"Don't like the idea of working for no woman," one miner grumbled. "This here fire is the kind of stuff you get," another agreed.

"Oh, for heaven's sake," Catherine yelled. "Won't any of you listen to reason?"

Sampson stopped, and looked back at her. "We signed on thinking we was working for Nick."

"But you are," Catherine argued logically. "He gives the orders."

"Thought he owned the mine," Sampson growled as he started back down the path leading his crew of soot-covered miners.

"He does." Panic forced the words from Catherine before her mind could register what she said. "Or at least he will. When we're married." God! What had she said? And why had she blurted out such a lie? Desperation, Catherine conceded. Maybe no one heard her.

Sampson turned around, an expression of disbelief on his dirty face. "You're marrying Mr. Nick?"

Of course not. "Yes." It happened again. Her lying tongue seemed at odds with her mind.

"When?"

Never. "Soon."

"He never said nothing about it," Sampson said skeptically.

How could he? He didn't know. "It was a secret, but I guess there's no harm in you men knowing." Catherine bit her lip. The damage was already done.

She might as well see what good would come from it. Maybe the men would stay. She knew it would be only temporary—until they learned the truth.

She wet her dry lips. "What do you say? You aren't going to let Nick down are you? He'd be very disappointed."

Catherine paced the small cabin as she had for the last hour, measuring its cozy interior with her steps. A twig snapped outside, and she ran to the window, disappointed—or was it relieved—that it didn't herald Nicholas's return from Manchester.

"Probably a raccoon or possum," she mumbled as she again stalked the room. How had she gotten herself to this point, Catherine wondered? Clasping her hands together, Catherine reviewed last night's events. The fire, the miners attempt to leave—all of it came back to her with precise clarity. What she couldn't understand was what had possessed her to concoct that outrageous lie.

And it was a lie—a lie all the miners would discover as soon as Nicholas returned. What would they do then? Biting her bottom lip, Catherine admitted she knew the answer. They'd leave. Quick as a bug on a hot griddle they'd gather up their belongings—no, they had no possessions thanks to the fire—well, they'd head back to Richmond. To talk. Catherine leaned her arm against the fieldstone fireplace, and released a shattered breath. The miners were sure to spread the story of Miss Catherine pretending she was betrothed. To a miner, yet.

Shaking her head, Catherine renewed her pacing.

Why in the world, if she had to pick a pretend fiancé had she chosen Nicholas Colton, a miner? Brousseaus didn't marry miners. They married landed gentry like themselves. A shiver shook her form as she thought of John Parker, but she quickly dismissed him from her mind. Why Nicholas Colton? The question returned to torment her.

The miners respect him. That reason made sense, and satisfied her, kept her from delving further into her motivation. Instead she replayed the events since the fire burned itself out—since her lie. She'd awakened Betsy, and together they'd fried thick ham slices till they sizzled and filled the small kitchen with mouth-watering aromas. Betsy had brewed strong black coffee, and Catherine had spooned out bowls of corn mush.

They'd fed the miners who, to a man, had taken advantage of the soap she'd passed out, to clean themselves up in the creek. Then she'd given the men blankets, and sent them off to the clearing to get some rest. Of course they'd have to sleep out in the open since their barracks burned, but the day had dawned as pleasant as its predecessor, so that wasn't a problem.

No, the problem was that the miners thought she was going to marry Nicholas—Nick they called him—and she wasn't.

Grandmere might be able to help her solve this dilemma, Catherine thought, not for the first time. She'd been sorely tempted to take the elderly woman in her confidence this morning when Catherine had helped her dress. But she hadn't. It would only worry her, and that's something Catherine didn't wish to do. She had thought to seek Marie's advice, even willing to risk the chiding laughter Catherine knew would come, but Marie hadn't been in her room. Had she said she was staying with the Milleau sisters again? Catherine couldn't remember. She must remind Marie to make her whereabouts known. She'd do that as soon as—

"Catherine?"

Whirling around, her skirts swooshing softly around her ankles, Catherine faced Nicholas. She'd been so caught up in her worried musings, she hadn't heard his approach. Now he stood before her, leaning casually against the doorjamb, watching her, a puzzled expression marking his handsome face.

He'd been riding hard, she could tell by the way his white shirt, damp with sweat, molded to the powerful muscles of his arms and chest. His hair, the rich brown shot through with gold, tousled around his head in wind-swept disarray. Catching herself before she stepped forward, Catherine dropped the hand that longed to smooth down the jumbled curls. Instead she stood staring at him unable to speak, her eyes large.

"What is it, Catherine? What's the matter?" Nick tossed his leather saddlebags onto the table and started toward her. She seemed small and fragile standing before him, an expression he couldn't read shadowing her green eyes.

"I have to talk to you." Finally finding her voice, Catherine backed up until the rough stones of the fireplace dug into her back.

"All right." Pulling out a homemade chair, Nick

hooked a wooden leg with his boot, turned it around and straddled the seat. "Talk," he ordered softly.

Catherine sighed, dropping her gaze to the floor. Looking at Nicholas's blatant masculinity made it more difficult to express herself. His muscular thighs strained against the buckskin riding pants as his legs spread around the chair seat. And his thick arms, the sleeves of his shirt rolled to expose the curling golden hair that covered them, appeared strong even draped over the chair's bowed back. She swallowed. "There's been a problem. I—"

"Parker came back." Nick jerked out of the chair. He should have known better than to go off so soon after the incident with Parker.

"No." Catherine's eyes shot up, shocked by the force with which he'd spoken. "No, nothing like that. I don't think we have to worry about him anymore." Catherine didn't mention that the fear she'd seen in John's eyes—fear of Nicholas—would protect her as long as her mine manager stayed at Greenfield.

"Well, what is it?" Nick sank back onto the chair, wondering what problem could be so bad that she couldn't just tell him.

"There was a fire."

"At the mine?" Again he started to rise, but her hand on his arm stayed him.

"Yes, but—"

"The men?"

"They're all fine," Catherine assured him and paused. She didn't think she could possibly go through with this. "Where are you going?"

Nick shoved the chair back beneath the table. "To

170

the mine. It's obvious that's the only way I'll find out what happened."

"No wait." Catherine wet her dry lips. "I'll tell you." She watched as Nicholas cocked his brow and waited. "Last night the barracks caught on fire."

"How?"

"I don't know how." Funny but that had never occurred to her. First there had been the problem of the fire itself, and then her lie. . . . "One of the miners must have become careless with a lantern. Anyway, all of them escaped the building, and we kept the fire from spreading."

"But the barracks were destroyed?"

"Yes."

Nick raked fingers through his tousled hair. "It will cost some time and money to replace, but at least we have the means now." He nodded toward the saddlebags on the table. "In there's the payment for the first load of coal."

"The miners are resting now." Catherine sank into a chair by the table, wondering how she would ever broach the next subject—the one that had prayed on her mind all morning.

"Is something else wrong?" Nick studied her with narrowed eyes.

"No." Catherine's gaze shot up to meet his, afraid he'd read her mind. "I mean, yes." Catherine swallowed, disgusted with herself for being afraid to discuss this with him. After all, she owned the mine, and he was only a miner. But somehow, looking at his broad shoulders and ruggedly handsome face, she kept loosing track of that fact.

She took a deep breath and straightened her back.

"I have a proposition for you—a business proposition." There, she'd said it.

Raising his brow, Nick waited for her to continue. Catherine wished he'd sit back down. Leaning against the hearth, his arms folded across his chest, he seemed very formidable. But there was no turning back now. "I propose to deed over to you a portion of Greenfield Mine—one quarter of it, to be exact."

Air hissed out between Nick's clenched teeth. Never in his wildest imagination had he expected her to say that. He'd even given up all hope of buying the mine for Fielding, knowing how possessive she was of the thing. And now she offered him part of it on a silver platter. Of course, he'd rarely known of an offer that didn't have plenty of strings attached. That silver platter might turn out to be made of lead.

Catherine twisted her fingers together, wishing he would stop looking at her as if she'd lost her mind and say something. "I realize this must seem a surprise, but you have been very helpful with the miners, and—"

"What do you want from me, Cate?"

Suddenly finding the rugged fieldstone extremely interesting, Catherine traced the jagged edge with her finger. Her voice was barely above a whisper. "I want you to marry me."

"What?"

"I said, I want you to marry me." Catherine swirled around to face him, her eyes flashing green sparks. How dare he make her repeat herself. And couldn't he do something other than stare at her in disbelief? The anxiety she'd had was fast giving way to anger. "You needn't look so shocked, Mr. Colton.

172

I'm hardly asking a lifetime commitment from you."

His bark of laughter contained no humor. "How foolish of me to equate that with marriage." Nick ignored her scathing expression. "Now, I know you, Cate, and you've been fairly vocal about your feelings toward me. I doubt this proposal was spurred by undying love."

Choosing not to dignify his sarcastic remark with a reply, Catherine launched into her rehearsed reasons why this plan would benefit him. "As part owner you'd share in the profits—"

"And losses."

Oh, what an insufferable man! Catherine raised her chin. "Of course, I'd still continue to pay you a manager's salary." If he brought up the fact that he'd yet to receive a penny, Catherine swore to herself she'd leave the cabin, and forget this insanity. But he didn't. He simply stood before her, looking for all the world like a man in need of convincing.

"You would make the decisions—most of them," Catherine hedged. "And when you decided to return to England, I would make no claim on you. Once there you could seek divorce, or annulment." Catherine shook her head and more auburn curls escaped her chignon. "Whichever you choose. The fourth share of the mine would still be yours, would always be yours." Catherine allowed herself a slight smile. She'd certainly given a man with no prospect but to work his life away in the bowels of the earth good enough reason to accept her proposal.

When he still said nothing, Catherine felt her confidence slip but she kept her smile in place. "What more do you want?"

"The reason," came his succinct reply.

Damn the man anyway! Couldn't he leave her a modicum of pride? Did he have to know the whole embarrassing mess? She worried her bottom lip, pleading with her eyes. "Must that be part of the agreement?"

"Why, Cate?"

His tone allowed no hope of compromise as he leaned back against the fireplace. All during her speech, he'd been watching the woman more than listening to her words. They were immaterial. The salary she payed him—if she ever did pay him one—was paltry compared to the one he received from Travis Fielding. Profits from a quarter of Greenfield probably wouldn't come close to it either—especially since if he had his way most of the proceeds would be poured back into the mine to replace worn out equipment. No doubt about it, he'd lose money by marrying her. Travis Fielding was a benevolent and understanding employer, however he wouldn't continue to pay Nick if he owned a part of Greenfield Mine.

So why did he even bother to listen? Why worry about her motives? He'd done his job here. The mine was running again, and he'd determined that she wouldn't sell. Wouldn't his best course be to take the next boat back to England and forget all about Greenfield Mine and the woman who owned it?

Ah, but therein lay the rub, Nick thought, because he couldn't seem to do that. Ever since that night in Richmond, he'd been trying to get her out of his mind. Trying to pretend he hadn't liked the way she felt, warm and soft pressed against him. He may have

174

been shocked by her proposal of marriage, but that wasn't because the thought had never occurred to him. Well, maybe not marriage, Nick admitted to himself, but certainly the physical rewards that went with it. Even now, watching her pace back and forth in the cabin, he felt his loins tighten. He'd wanted her since she'd first looked up at him with those green eyes, and he wanted her now. Was this union she proposed such a high price for the desire he felt?

Desire, lust, call it what he might, his motives were clear. Hers, however remained a mystery—and he doubted they were the same as his. "Cate," he prodded, reminding her she'd yet to answer him.

"All right," she said whirling on him, her hands akimbo. "If you must know, you were right about the miners. They don't like taking orders from a woman. They don't even like working for one."

Nick suppressed a smile. "What happened?"

"During the fire I . . . I gave them some . . . suggestions of things they might do."

"Suggestions, Cate?" He'd been on the receiving end of her *suggestions* before so he could well imagine what she'd been like.

"Oh, all right, orders." She swiped a curl off her forehead. "I gave them orders. But, for heaven's sake, Nicholas, they were just standing there watching it burn, doing nothing to keep the fire from spreading, and the explosives . . ."

"Calm down." Three steps had him in front of her. Clasping her shoulders in his large hands, he looked down into her face. Agitation colored her cheeks a soft rose, and added sparkle to her moss-green eyes. "Wouldn't they listen to you?"

175

She knew it was silly, but his nearness made her feel better. He was so big and strong, solid. Someone to lean on, to help share the burden. Shaking her head, freeing herself from such foolish thoughts, Catherine explained, "They listened."

"Then I don't understand."

"They were fine during the fire. It was afterward, when the danger had passed, that they told me they couldn't work for a woman."

"So you . . . ?" Nick prodded again when he sensed she wished to halt her story.

"I told them the mine would belong to you as soon as we married." There, she'd said it, and if he'd wipe that stupid grin off his face and let go of her arms she could get back to the house and try to think of another solution to her problem. "Don't you dare laugh!" The grin had digressed into a chuckle.

"I'm not. I mean," Nick tried to sober his expression, "whatever possessed you to say such a thing?"

"I don't know." Catherine turned her face away, unable to meet his mirth-filled eyes. "They were leaving, and it just came out. Call it a moment of insanity." She twisted out of his grasp, a feeling of hopelessness overcoming her. "I'll leave you to pack now. I'm sure you'll want to be leaving too." Catherine backed toward the door. "Take your pay out of the saddlebags. I'll divide the rest among the men before they go."

Reaching behind her, Catherine grabbed the door latch, making herself move slowly. She didn't want this man to know how embarrassed she was—or how hopeless she felt. If she could just hold the tears at bay

176

a few minutes longer, perhaps she could manage to cry in solitude. "Thank you for everything. I'll . . . I'll write a letter to Mr. Fielding thanking him, and explaining how helpful you've been." She lifted the latch and turned to leave.

"Cate?"

"Yes." She looked back wishing he wouldn't prolong this. But then she guessed he had the right. After all she had tried to use him.

"When is it to be?"

"What?" Confusion wrinkled her brow.

"The wedding."

"You mean . . . you . . . you're actually going to do it, even after I explained what I'd done?"

Nick shrugged. "We've all said things in the passion of the moment—things we later regretted. That doesn't mean I can't see the advantages of your plan."

"Of course, the advantages." Annoyance accompanied Catherine's relief that he would marry her. Why should she care that he was influenced by the material things the marriage offered him? Hadn't she listed them for him? Hadn't she hoped they'd sway him toward her cause? Then why did she suddenly have this uncomfortable tightening around her heart? Certainly she hadn't expected him to want her.

Nick stood, leaning against the door frame, watching Catherine walk toward the house. He'd agreed to marry her this Sunday—agreed to marry her because of a lie she'd been desperate enough to tell. No, Nick admitted, the realization making him push away from the wooden jamb. He wasn't doing it because he wanted to protect her or save her mine.

He wasn't even doing it because she'd offered him his wages, then said the rest of her money would go to pay the miners, though his heart had gone out to her at that moment.

He wanted her, pure and simple—had never wanted anything more in his life. He wanted her enough to agree to a marriage she called a business proposition. Nick slapped the heel of his hand against the door as he entered the cabin. He only wished she wanted him.

"Have you lost your senses?"

Catherine stopped whipping the wooden spoon through the thick cake batter, and looked up at her sister. Blotting the moisture from her forehead with her sleeve, Catherine realized she was more surprised by Marie's appearance in the overheated kitchen than by her words. "I suppose it does seem ludicrous to be baking in this heat, but Grandmere has her mind set on a cake."

"You know I'm not talking about that." Marie's cheeks flushed with anger as she skirted the work table. "I came home as soon as I heard the news of this wedding." She nearly spit the last word. "What do you think you're doing?"

"I'm saving our family, Marie."

"By marrying this . . . this miner?" Marie snorted. "You're making us a laughing stock. Why the Milleau sisters could hardly believe it when I read them your note."

Catherine had assumed Marie would be unable to keep the news to herself. She'd even considered not sending for her sister because of it, and because of the very reaction she now witnessed. Catherine took a deep breath, wiping her floury hands on her apron. "I thought the Milleau sisters were intrigued by Mr. Colton."

"Is that it, Catherine? Does his overpowering maleness excite you?"

Catherine felt the color rising to her face. "Of course not. How could you say such a thing?"

"Don't be a prude, Catherine." Marie shook her head, sending her twisted blonde curls bouncing. "But don't be a fool either. If Mr. Colton interests you, indulge yourself. But for God's sake, don't marry the man."

"Marie!"

"Oh, don't play innocent with me. I've seen the way you look at Nick. You're not fooling anyone."

"Nor am I trying to. I'm marrying Mr. Colton so that I can keep the mine in operation. It is purely a business agreement."

"And he agreed to that?"

"Of course." Catherine felt disloyal disclosing her arrangement with Nicholas to her sister, but she didn't want Marie to think she lusted after her mine manager. Especially when deep down, in the most feminine part of her, Catherine feared her sister had hit upon a truth. She did think Nicholas attractive. She found herself remembering his kiss and longing to feel his strong body pressed against hers. She dreamed of him and woke up hungry for his touch. But that had nothing to do with her proposal—and more importantly, it would have nothing to do with their marriage.

Chapter Nine

"It's beautiful, but . . ." Catherine looked into the faded green of her grandmother's eyes—eyes that seemed lucid and full of purpose for the first time in months—and her protest died on her lips.

"I wore that gown the day I married my Henry. He loves it so. Says the rose color is most becoming."

"It is beautiful," Catherine repeated glancing down at the elaborate ball gown she wore. Its looped skirt draped over a petticoat of time-yellowed silk, heavily embroidered with pink flowers. The bodice, fit snugly about her slender waist, had sleeves that ended below the elbows in a cascade of frothy lace, and, to Catherine's dismay, dipped daringly low over her breasts.

The gown was beautiful, and very out of style, having been made near a half-century earlier. But that wasn't the reason Catherine hesitated to wear it. She cared little about such things.

She demurred because the dress was obviously meant for a special occasion, a celebration. And her wedding to Nicholas Colton certainly did not fall into that category. It was a business arrangement. She knew it. He knew it. But Grandmere did not.

The older woman had been absolutely ecstatic, more vibrant than Catherine had seen her in years, as soon as she'd learned of the upcoming wedding. Catherine had indulgently complied with all her grandmother's plans—to this point.

Grandmere wanted the wedding to take place at Greenfield, in the parlor, so she could attend. Catherine had readily agreed. The less fanfare, the better.

Grandmere had suggested the menu for the wedding dinner include a cake. Catherine hadn't planned on any festivities, but, they did have to eat, and cake was a common enough dessert.

But the gown, oh, what was she to do about the gown? Grandmere had saved this as a surprise till now, less than an hour before the minister was to arrive to perform the ceremony. Her grandmother had prevailed upon Betsy to search the attic, find the dress, and refurbish the lace, all in secrecy. And the two ladies had succeeded. If only she'd known of their plan earlier, Catherine thought, perhaps she could have done something, but now . . .

Catherine moved in front of the cheval mirror. Gnawing her bottom lip, she studied her reflection. She'd planned to wear her green traveling dress. That would have acknowledged the day as slightly out of the ordinary, without proclaiming it the event of a lifetime.

"You see," Grandmere observed. "I knew it would look lovely on you."

Catherine had to admit, her grandmother was right. The shimmering satin hue gave her ivory complexion just the right touch of blushing pink. And the fit was most becoming, if only it didn't rest so wantonly low on her breasts.

Deciding that unless she hurt her grandmother's feelings completely—something she had no wish to do—she must wear the gown, Catherine slipped her fingers inside the bodice and gave it an upward yank.

"Now stop that, Catherine," Grandmere chided from her rocking chair. "The gown is fine the way it is. Besides, your new husband will not be able to take his eyes from you."

"Grandmere, I . . . I—" How could she tell her grandmother that she had no desire to attract her bridegroom's attention? All she wanted was for him to run the mine.

"Now, don't get yourself flustered, dear. There is no reason to be embarrassed by the intimate part of marriage. Goodness, I should know. Henry and I have been together for almost sixty years. Of course, you want to appear desirable for your husband." Grandmere's expression clouded as if she relived moments from the past. Her head fell back against the padded headrest, and her hands, frail and blue-veined, dropped listlessly to her lap.

Catherine smiled indulgently, thinking it would be some time until her grandmother returned to the present when, with a start, Grandmere shook her head and impatiently brushed at her crocheted shawl. "Betsy," she called , her thin, reedy voice filled with determination.

"Betsy," Grandmere repeated when the black

woman came into the room. "How is everything coming?"

"All's about done, Miss Lillian. Dinner's most ready, and I put flowers in the parlor just like you asked."

"Good. Now would you please pick me a few more flowers—from the roses that climb the south wall?"

"The pink ones?"

"Yes." Grandmere observed Catherine with a speculative eye. "Don't you think some of those blossoms would look lovely woven through her hair?"

"Oh, I surely do, Miss Lillian. I'll go fetch some this minute."

"Wait," Catherine called, but Betsy had already disappeared out the door. Her hands spread in supplication, Catherine turned to her grandmother. "I really appreciate all you've done, but—"

"It's been my pleasure, dear."

"But," Catherine continued, "I really don't think I want flowers in my hair."

"Why ever not? I think they'd be most becoming."

"Maybe so, however . . ." Oh, how could she explain? "I just am not the type to wear such things."

"You used to, Catherine. Do you remember the crowns of flowers we made when you were younger?"

"Yes, of course, I remember." As Catherine sank down in front of her grandmother the wide skirt fanned out around her. Taking the withered hands between her own, Catherine kissed the enlarged knuckles that could no longer weave flower stems.

"You've always been very dear to me, Catherine."

Blinking back the tears that burned her eyes,

184

Catherine rested her head in the black silk folds of her grandmother's lap. She still smelled as sweet as a lavender sachet. Age could not change that anymore than time could dim the pleasant memories that that fragrance induced. A butterfly's touch caressed her hair, her cheek.

"You can't imagine how happy I was when you told me you were planning to marry Mr. Colton." Catherine closed her eyes and said nothing. What could she say? "I've worried so about you dear. I'm old and won't be around much longer. No. Don't protest. It is true, and we both know it."

"Henry, bless his heart, is older than I. And your mother and father . . ." Grandmere sighed. "Well, they don't seem to be around much anymore. But Mr. Colton is young and strong. He'll take care of you long after the rest of us are gone. He reminds me so much of Henry. I know they will become great friends. Don't you think so, Catherine?"

Lifting her head, Catherine stared into her grandmother's kind eyes, the same eyes that she'd looked to for love and guidance for as long as she could remember, and nodded. "Yes," she whispered, her heart gladdening with the smile that wrinkled Grandmere's face.

"He cares for you."

"Yes, I know." Catherine agreed. "And I've always loved Grandpere." Her grandmother's carefree laugh made Catherine sit back on her heels.

"Of course, your grandfather loves you, dear, but I was speaking of Mr. Colton."

"Nicholas?" Catherine couldn't hide her surprise.

"Yes, Catherine." Grandmere leaned her slumped

shoulders forward and touched the tip of her granddaughter's nose. "I've seen the way he looks at you when he thinks no one notices. He's truly smitten, but then why shouldn't he be? You're a wonderful person." Grandmere rested her head back wearily. "I'm so glad you've found someone who loves you, and someone for you to love."

"You're tired." Catherine stood and brushed her hand across the paper thin skin of her grandmother's brow. "Would you like me to help you into bed?"

"No, no." Grandmere opened her eyes. "I don't want to miss the wedding. I'll just sit here and rest for a moment."

"I'll come for you when Reverend Martin arrives." Catherine spread a knitted afghan across her grandmother's lap. A soft sigh was the only response as she tiptoed out of the room.

Lifting her skirts to climb the stairs to her own room, Catherine couldn't help thinking about what her grandmother had said. "He cares for you." A warm feeling had rushed through her body when she'd realized who her grandmother meant. Could Grandmere possibly have noticed a look, an expression of caring sent Catherine's way by Nicholas Colton?

Catherine chided herself for this delusion. How could she even entertain such a thought? Her mine manager was marrying her for one reason, and one reason only, to acquire part of the mine. That was as clear as the agreement they planned to sign as soon as the marriage was legal. If Grandmere thought she saw secretive expressions of love, Catherine had to remember that this woman also imagined her husband—dead and buried more than ten years—still lived with her.

Opening the door, entering her lonely room, Catherine felt an overwhelming sadness that life couldn't be the way Grandmere imagined it.

What in the hell was he doing? Nick kicked a stone that lay in his path—the path between his cabin and the main house. With a snort of disgust, he bent over and brushed the dusty mark off the toe of his boot. It shone with all the gloss his vigorous rubbing could give it. Why he'd taken the trouble, he didn't know. Hell, he didn't know why he was doing anything lately—most of all getting married.

How could he have agreed to such a plan? Somehow or other, when Catherine had told him her idea, it had sounded logical. Logical! It was ludicrous! Stupid! Idiotic! And he was more the fool for agreeing to it.

He kicked another rock, not bothering to wipe away the damage to his shiny boots. Thank goodness it wasn't too late. He'd go to the house, ask to see Catherine, and tell her he couldn't go through with this. He'd offer to buy the mine. Give her top dollar. Hell, he'd give her twice it's worth and suffer the consequences of Fielding's wrath later. With the money she could leave Greenfield, take care of her grandmother, and live happily ever after.

She could even give some money to Marie. At the thought of the younger Brousseau, Nick felt a pang of guilt—undeserved, he reminded himself. He certainly hadn't invited the comely blond to his cabin last night. God, the woman was a tease—just the opposite of her straitlaced sister.

Marie had pretended to stop by to wish him happiness in his marriage, but Nick had been around long enough to know that his happiness—at least with Catherine—was the farthest thing from her mind. She'd drifted around the room, letting her eyes stray now and then, ever so covertly, toward the open door where his bed could be plainly seen. She'd pranced and posed and smiled, and honest to goodness, he'd been tempted. Who wouldn't? She was a beautiful woman, and by all indications, a willing one. And it sure as hell had been a long time since he'd had either. And once he told Catherine he couldn't go through with this marriage—business proposal, she'd called it—it would be a lot longer.

But he'd sent Marie away, mindful of her suddenly peevish mood, and spent the rest of the night tossing and turning on his bed, unable to sleep. The trouble was, he didn't want to hurt Catherine. He didn't want anyone to laugh at her—and he didn't know why he should care so much.

That's what bothered him more than anything, Nick thought as he stopped and leaned his shoulder against a sycamore. He'd been sent here to pay off a gambling debt, for heaven's sake. He'd gotten the mine producing again, strengthened the shaft, even hired new miners. Was it his fault she'd alienated them?

Damn right it wasn't! In all honesty, he admitted, it wasn't hers either. Nick had had a long talk with Sampson and the others, and let them know how angry he was that she'd been forced to order them around.

Still she shouldn't have told them that stupid lie about the two of them getting married. Because he wasn't going to do it.

Then why are you dressed in your best suit? And why did you polish your boots till your arms ached? And why did you send Marie away? Nick pushed himself away from the tree trunk, not liking the only answer that came to mind.

Betsy answered his knock and the sprightly black woman gave him a toothless grin that sent his palms to sweating. "Do you suppose I could speak with Miss Brousseau? Catherine," he amended. The last thing he needed was to face Marie.

"Well, I reckon she's ready, but it ain't good luck to see the bride before the wedding."

"You may be right, but I need to see her for a minute." Nick smiled at the dubious expression on her wrinkled face. "Please," he added for good measure when she seemed uncertain what to do.

"Well, I'll tell her you're here, but don't be surprised if she don't come down yet. The preacher ain't even here."

Nick watched her scurry from the room, then sat on one of the straight arm chairs by the window. It looked as if the furniture had been moved from the center of the room, forming a small empty place near the end fireplace. And flowers. He'd never seen so many colorful blooms in one place. Their fragrance filled the air with the sweetness of an English garden. He leaned back and closed his eyes, letting the scent wash over him.

"You wished to see me?"

Nick opened his eyes, started to rise—then stopped. He'd long ago given up denying to himself that he enjoyed looking at Catherine. She had an arresting face, vibrant and expressive. But he'd never seen her look as beautiful as she did now. Realizing he stood bent at the waist, frozen in the act of rising, Nick finished the process, never taking his eyes from her.

She looked like something out of one of the portraits in Travis Fielding's long galley. Her dress was fashioned along the lines of gowns worn when the colonies had rebelled, totally outdated, but Nick didn't care. The things that it did to her body took his breath away. That night in Richmond, he'd caught a glimpse of what she looked like behind those washed-out work dresses she wore, but even that hadn't prepared him for this.

Her waist seemed small enough to span with his hands. He imagined doing it, then letting his fingers trail up the watered-silk, warm and pliant as it stretched across her ribs, till he reached the soft weight of her full breasts. They were white and creamy smooth and Nick rubbed his palms along his pants to soothe the itching.

"Mr. Colton?"

Her words drew his attention to her face, and Nick realized he'd been staring—and where. His mouth felt dry and he swallowed, deciding that her face looked different, too, because of her hair. Instead of being pulled back in a tight knot, it curled and waved gently, twining with pink roses to rest alluringly atop her head. The style emphasized the sweet line of her neck, the curve of her jaw.

Nick cleared his throat, speaking before the silence dragged on any further. "I wanted a word with you."

She cocked her head as if waiting for him to continue, and Nick knew a moment of panic. He imagined her leaving Greenfield, the home she loved, and couldn't go on. He'd never known a place to call home until Travis Fielding plucked him from the mine, and even that wasn't the same as having roots that spanned generations as she did. How could he expect her to sell and go off someplace? He couldn't. And he knew she wouldn't.

She'd stay here and face the shame of having the man she said was to marry her leave, and she'd find some way to run that mine with or without him— until it wore her out. She'd fight on until her green eyes lost their luster and she was forced by someone like John Parker to accept defeat.

Nick's blood surged at the thought, and he remembered then and there why he'd decided to marry her. He couldn't let anything happen to her. He just couldn't.

"I wondered if you had our agreement ready." Inwardly cringing at the flimsiness of his excuse, Nick watched her nod and turn toward the library door.

"It's in the desk." Catherine turned to cover her disappointment. For a moment she'd thought he'd say something about the way she looked. His stare had been bold and had made the pulse pound in her head. She'd felt certain by his expression that he'd liked what he saw. But he hadn't said a word, too interested in making sure she didn't renege on her part of the deal to even give her appearance a second thought.

Well, she was glad he hadn't. Hadn't she been afraid he'd notice the dress, her hair, and think she was going to a lot of trouble over a simple business agreement. "Here it is." Catherine closed the dovetail drawer with the heel of her hand, and passed a single sheet of paper to him.

Actually, the agreement protected her more than him, since all her property would automatically become his when they wed. The document he scanned, rather than giving him one fourth of Greenfield, stated that she would continue to own three quarters of the mine and all of the remaining property.

"Is everything to your satisfaction?"

Nick lifted his brows and grinned. He'd barely read the neat, precise handwriting, thinking instead about the woman standing before him. Because of that her question took on a more personal meaning than he imagined she meant. His gaze drifted lazily from the shining crown of auburn curls to the dainty tips of satin clad shoes. "I'd say everything is nearly perfect."

Betsy's announcement of the reverend's arrival interrupted any response Catherine might have made to his remark. And if truth were known, she didn't know what to say.

"Shall we sign this now?" Nick asked, his brow cocked.

"I suppose so." Catherine handed him a pen, and watched as he scrawled his name boldly across the bottom of the page. She added her name, then started toward the door. "I almost forgot Grandmere."

"I'll get her." Nick squeezed her hand. "You wouldn't want to mess up your pretty gown."

After only a perfunctory knock Reverend Martin walked into the parlor. Ever since Grandmere's health had deteriorated so that she couldn't attend the church, he'd been a weekly visitor. Seated on the horsehair sofa, accepting a cup of punch from Betsy, he looked up when Catherine opened the parlor door, allowing Nicholas to precede her into the room. He carried Grandmere high on his chest as if she weighed no more than a feather.

"Ah, so this is your young man, Catherine," he said after Nick had settled the older woman into a vacant rocking chair.

"Now don't tease, Reverend," Grandmere admonished, but her pale eyes shone bright among the folds of wrinkled skin.

After the introductions, and a few inquiries as to whether they should wait for anyone else—Marie had left this morning giving no indication that she would be back today—there seemed nothing left but to proceed with the ceremony.

Catherine stood, stealing covert glances at the tall man beside her, reminding herself that this was a simple business agreement rather than the soul-shattering experience it seemed. He took her hand, enfolding it in the work-hardened palm of his own, and her knees felt weak. Catherine tried to concentrate on Reverend Martin's soft Virginia drawl, but the words seemed to drone together. The feel of Nicholas Colton's hand on hers is what she knew, his smell, the warmth of his big body.

A pause captured her attention, and then Nicholas spoke in his deep whiskey-smooth voice. Another pause, and instinctively Catherine knew it was her turn.

The ring—she'd forgotten there would be a ring. But apparently Nicholas hadn't because he slid it on her finger. Catherine's mind registered a flash of mellow gold and the green twinkle of cut stone before his hand again engulfed hers.

And then it was over except for the kiss. Catherine wanted to turn to the minister and explain to him that this didn't qualify as a real wedding, thus they could forgo the kiss. But her husband . . . her husband had other ideas, and before she knew it he'd wrapped his arms around her, thick and strong as two steel bands and bent down to touch his lips to hers.

The kiss couldn't be called passionate, though it set Catherine's stomach to fluttering, but then this was hardly the time for passion, standing in the front parlor witnessed by Grandmere and Reverend Martin.

Catherine's hands flattened on Nicholas's chest as he lifted his head. There eyes met, locked, a spark of a promise, a memory of a vow, the moment more intimate than the kiss.

Behind them Reverend Martin coughed, then cleared his throat, and Catherine pulled away self-consciously. She twisted the ring on her finger, testing the unaccustomed weight. How had she ever thought she could pretend this wedding meant nothing more than her signature on a piece of paper? She'd committed her life to this man, and he to hers— no matter that the agreement stood only temporarily.

Catherine dragged the brush through her thick fall of hair feeling again the strange sense of loss, and unable to pinpoint the reason. Everything had gone according to her plan. She was married, and though the miners had received the day off because of her wedding, they'd be back at work in the morning. Then the coal could be mined, sent to Richmond, and Greenfield would be saved. Her life would go on as it had.

Sighing, Catherine laid the brush on her dresser and crossed to the silvery patch of moonlight by the window. The warm summer fragrance of roses and magnolias drifted through the open panes. Yes, the day had gone very well. Even after the wedding nothing had gone awry. The dinner was all Grandmere had hoped, and though she had grown tired, Catherine could tell she savored the day.

Of course, Grandmere hadn't been the only one to enjoy the dinner. Nicholas had seemed most relaxed and happy. And why not, Catherine thought. He'd managed, with very little effort, to gain one quarter of a mine, raise himself in society, and take up residence in the house. This evening he'd moved into the spare room at the end of the hall.

Catherine leaned out the window, admitting to

herself that her assessment wasn't fair. Mr. Colton had worked hard for the mine, and he could have left her in a terrible bind. A bind of your own making, a little voice reminded her.

Still . . . Catherine jerked inside the window, knocking her head on the sash, when she heard the door open. "What are *you* doing here?"

Nick's eyes narrowed. This wasn't exactly the greeting he'd imagined. Oh, he'd known better than to hope for open arms—at least in the beginning—but this. . . . "I'd have thought you would have expected a visit from me tonight."

Expected? Why ever would she. . . . Realization hit Catherine with a force that made her eyes tear open. How stupid of her not to think of this. Of course she thought of their marriage in purely business terms, but he apparently did not. She would simply have to explain. "Mr. Colton."

"Yes, Mrs. Colton."

His words unnerved her almost as much as the bold stare of his smoky gray eyes. Catherine glanced at her bed hoping to see her wrapper, but then remembered it still hung in her wardrobe. She'd feel silly retrieving it from there so she just had to face him in her nightrail. With its high-buttoned collar and flowing skirt, it certainly covered her adequately. She cleared her throat. "I don't think you understand."

"Oh, I understand perfectly, Cate." Nick stepped toward her. The moon shining in the window behind her rendered her gown near transparent. He could clearly see the outline of her rounded breasts,

196

the narrow waist and flared hips—the V between her legs.

"I . . . I don't think you do." Catherine found it difficult to speak, to even breathe. His presence in her room was overpowering. She swallowed nervously, trying to think of something to say that would stop his slow, steady advance on her. Trying not to notice his attire. Today at the wedding he'd been dressed impeccably in buff colored trousers and brown frock coat, and she'd found it impossible to ignore how handsome he was. But now he'd removed the jacket, untied his cravat, unbuttoned his flowing white shirt. He looked rakish and dangerous as he stalked closer.

"I never meant for this to be part of our agreement."

"Didn't you?"

He stood so close that Catherine had to tilt her head to look into his face. Moonlight gilded his tousled hair, the piercing eyes and square pugnacious chin, and his wide beautiful mouth. His masculine scent surrounded her and Catherine locked her knees to keep from falling toward him. "No, I—"

He silenced her words, her protest as his warm lips touched hers. Catherine reached out to push him away—to draw him nearer—and her hands tangled with the crisp golden brown curls on his chest. Her fingers fanned encountering warm skin and she felt his moan vibrate through the iron-hard muscles.

"Oh, Cate . . . Cate." Nick rasped his mouth along her jaw, nuzzling behind her ear, trying to gulp air into his lungs. He'd told himself to move slowly. She was his wife. His. Knowing that, certainly he wouldn't experience the wild burst of passion he'd felt the other times he'd touched her. But he had— did. Her innocent touch and one kiss, one closed-mouthed kiss, had exploded on his senses making him hard and aching. His hands slid down the thin linen of her night gown and clasped her rounded bottom pulling her against him.

Catherine's gasp made no sound as his mouth covered hers again. His tongue thrust inside with strong bold strokes. It grazed along her teeth. It caressed the inside of her cheek. It teased and beckoned her tongue. And it drove every thought but him from her mind.

Her hands surged around his neck digging into the thick curls at his nape. Instinctively, wantonly, her body rubbed against the rock-hard bulge pressing into her belly. Her tongue responded to his taunt and met his, forcing another moan from his broad chest.

"Oh God, Cate." Her breasts flattened against him, but he wanted to feel them in his palms, to stroke the nipples to prominence with his thumb. His hands dragged up her sides, testing the curve of her hips, the dip of her waist. Firm and perfectly formed, Nick outlined her flesh with his finger, feeling the blood rush, hot and savagely through his veins, just looking at her. He skimmed the fabric, molding it to her shape, and lifted the protruding tip of her breast toward his descending mouth.

"Nick." Her voice sounded husky, foreign to Catherine as moist heat surrounded her nipple. Her head fell back, and if not for the hands that now

198

clung to his broad shoulders, she would have fallen at his feet. He suckled and nipped at her breast through the clinging material, and then as if he feared his teeth may have hurt, soothed the torrid tip with his tongue. A breeze, fragrant with night blossoms, air-dried her gown as he shifted to lavish the same attention on her other breast.

Heat coiled through her, tight as a wound spring. It intensified with each movement of his mouth till her hands clutched at his shirt and her legs pressed together.

The moist heat left her breast and traveled lower. Catherine's eyes were shut too tightly to see, but she could feel. Tingles ran up her spine as his mouth left a slowly descending trail of damp fabric. Her breathing came in quick, excited gasps, and then as he buried his face between her legs, not at all. His tongue caressed her, the thin fabric of her nightrail only heightening her body's response. Her senses soared and her knees buckled sending her sliding toward the floor.

Strong arms scooped her up, carried her to the bed and stayed wrapped around her as his weight sent her deeper into the mattress.

"Oh Cate, how I want you."

Catherine looked up into passion-drugged eyes that she imagined matched her own. With a growl his mouth opened over her only to jerk away as he reached for the buttons of her gown. His large hands fumbled to work the tiny fastenings from the holes. Just when Catherine thought she couldn't stand the frustration of being separated from him a moment longer, she felt a yank and heard the sound of rending fabric. Cool air teased her flesh as he left the bed to tear out of his own clothes.

And then his mouth seared her naked breast and his hand assuaged the ache between her legs. Her body arched, writhing against him. She clutched his shoulders, loving the feel of his hot, moist skin. Scoring his skin with her fingernails as the spring inside her body wound tighter.

"Let it come, Cate." His tongue and his breath caressed her ear as his fingers continued to drive her past knowing anything but him.

"What?" The word squeezed past her painfully tightened throat. What could he mean? Was there something better than this fire that consumed her? And then she knew. Her body throbbed, and the room seemed to explode with brilliant lights. His pulsing shaft replaced his finger, and with one bold thrust he was inside her, slowly stretching her to accommodate his size.

Catherine gasped as the pain flashed through her. She opened her eyes to see him staring down at her, concern shadowing his gray eyes.

"I'm sorry. I tried not to hurt you." He rested his weight on his elbows, his lower body perfectly still. His hand brushed a strand of auburn hair off her cheek.

"It's all right." How could she tell him that the momentary pain meant nothing compared to the pleasure he'd given her—the pleasure he still gave her? Words failed her, but her body did not. Slowly she arched, taking him deeper. His eyes registered surprise and then glittered with passion. He moved, squeezing deeper into her body, sliding back till he almost left her, then slowly, so slowly filling her again.

Catherine met his motion, matched it, all the while feeling the spring tighten again. This time when her release came, when the sparks crashed about her head, he drove deep one last time, and with a hoarse shout collapsed on top of her.

Chapter Ten

Bright ribbons of sunshine danced across the room, teasing Catherine awake. She lay a moment, her eyes shut, wondering why she felt so different—so content. Familiar sounds lulled her, beckoned her mind to drift. The lisped song of the waxwing, the fussy chattering of scrapping blue jays, a low, tuneless whistle.

A whistle! Catherine's eyes flew open. Last night! How could she have forgotten about last night? Memory washed over her, flooding her senses as her gaze alighted on her husband's bare, broad back. He bent forward, rinsing shaving lather from his face, and Catherine watched the hills and valleys of his corded muscles knot, then relax as he reached for a linen towel.

She'd touched that back, clung to the wide expanse of golden skin, dug her nails into his flesh while he . . . Heat poured into Catherine's face as with vivid clarity she recalled all he'd done last night—all she'd allowed, nay wanted, him to do. What had she been thinking?

Nothing. He'd touched her, and she'd ceased to do anything but feel.

He draped the damp towel over the wooden bar on the washstand and stretched. Catherine felt the warmth that flushed her face slowly seep down her body. Sunlight caught the brown curls on his arms, as he extended them high above his head, turning them golden. And if she'd thought the muscles of his back powerful, well, his arms and shoulders were—

"You're awake."

Catherine scrunched her eyes shut the second she noticed him start to turn, but judging by his low devilish chuckle, she hadn't fooled him. The mattress dipped, and Catherine decided that feigning sleep was useless. Her lashes fluttered open and she stared into clear, gray eyes alive with mirth.

"You were quite the sleepyhead this morning, Cate." He leaned forward, fanning Catherine's tangle of hair across her pillow with his long, sun-bronzed fingers. "Not that I blame you. I woke much later than usual myself." His lazy grin and the brush of his thumb against her cheek, sent goosebumps down Catherine's legs. His face tightened and for an instant his eyes lost their laughter. She saw a flash of what had clouded them last night. Her breath caught, but before she could completely grasp its meaning, he straightened.

"I'm late." He sounded all business now. "We need to start moving coal out of that mine. Besides." He smiled again, and Catherine wished for just a moment that he didn't have to go. "The men will give me enough ribbing as it is."

He shrugged into his shirt, the one she'd yanked off him last night, and stepped into his boots. Catherine watched, unable to look away as he quickly finished dressing. He never glanced back her way, but did keep up a running monologue of his work plans for the day. Catherine barely heard what he said, her mind was still trying to comprehend all that had occurred, but she did notice a pause and that his eyes pinned her questioningly.

"Will you bring dinner down to me?"

The tone of his voice indicated it wasn't the first time he'd asked her. Catherine swallowed and nodded.

"Good." He reached for the doorknob, then stopped. In four long strides, he'd covered the distance to the bed. His lips brushed hers lightly, then skimmed lower to graze the crest of an exposed breast. Catherine tried to sit up, then realized the sheet only covered her to the waist. Reaching for the linen, Catherine knew it was too late to hide herself. Her bodies response to his caress was obvious.

Nick looked very pleased with himself as he stood. His voice husky, he said, "I'll see you later."

Catherine yanked the sheet up over her, then foolishly realized there was no one to hide from now. He'd gone. After a few calming breaths Catherine sat up and threw her feet over the side of the bed. It took her a minute to figure what tangled around her arms. When she twisted and noticed the torn remains of her nightrail, her face flared scarlet.

What had she gotten herself into? All she'd wanted was for the miners to stay and for someone to run her mine. It had seemed so simple. She'd never meant to share the intimacies of marriage with Nicholas Colton.

"Didn't you?" His words from last night drifted back to her. "No, I didn't," she told her reflection in the mirror. Now that she no longer had to see that broad shouldered body or look into those smoky gray eyes, Catherine felt more in control. And that's the way she liked it. Mr. Colton had known very well she hadn't expected him when he'd walked into her room last night. He'd also known precisely what to do to make her forget her objections, a small voice reminded.

"That's because I wasn't prepared," Catherine murmured as she combed the tangles from her hair. Next time she would be. What did she mean next time? There wouldn't be a next time. She'd have a talk with him today, when she took his dinner to the mine. Nicholas Colton *would* be made to understand that she wanted nothing from him except his expertise in mining. When he left her to return to England, she wanted no memories or longings to tie her to him—to break her heart.

Even late as she started it, the morning dragged. Grandmere sat in the garden barely uttering a word. Now that Catherine had time to spend with her, the elderly woman didn't seem to know Catherine occupied the chair next to her. Her reflective attitude was not what Catherine hoped for right now. She tried again to make conversation—anything to keep her from sitting in the shade and thinking about last night.

"It's another warm day, isn't it?"

Grandmere slowly turned her head. "What did you

say, dear?"

Catherine shooed away a pesky fly. "Nothing." She was being stupid to blame her grandmother for not taking Catherine's mind off last night. This was her problem. Catherine studied Grandmere with narrowed eyes, noticing the dark smudges above her cheeks, the lackluster eyes—things she'd been too self-absorbed to see earlier. "Are you feeling poorly?" Catherine tried to keep the worry from her voice.

"Just a little tired, dear. All the excitement wore me out."

"Oh, I should never have had the wedding." The words were out before Catherine had time to consider them.

"Nonsense, dear." Grandmere raised her hand and Catherine took it, sinking down to the ground at her feet. "I'm very happy I was able to see you married, and I wouldn't have given up one second of the planning. Mr. Colton is such a nice man."

Catherine wondered if her grandmother had any idea what that "nice man" had done to her granddaughter last night. Of course she did. Hadn't Grandmere tried to tell her about the marriage bed? But Catherine hadn't listened.

"Would you like me to help you back to bed?" Grandmother rarely took a morning nap, but she looked like she could use one now.

Her agreement had come quickly, Catherine thought some time later as she stared down at a row of figures in her tally book. Too quickly. Tiptoeing over to the open door of her grandmother's room and peeking in helped smooth the worried frown from Catherine's face. Her grandmother slept peacefully.

207

She probably is just tired, Catherine tried to convince herself. Yesterday had been more excitement than she was used to.

Catherine moved back to the desk and closed the ledger, resting her palm on it for a minute before heading to the kitchen.

"Miss Catherine. Didn't expect to see you in here today." Betsy paused while lifting a copper kettle out of the wide brick fireplace and smiled.

"I can't imagine why," Catherine teased, hoping Betsy wouldn't notice the blush she knew stained her cheeks. "Aren't married folks supposed to eat?"

"You're funnin' with me, Miss Catherine. I thought you'd be spending some time with that new husband of yours."

"He's down at the mine." Catherine retrieved a wicker basket from under the work table in the corner of the room.

"Lands sakes, you done pushed him off to work all ready."

"I didn't push him, Betsy. Besides, we need the money from the coal. You know that."

Catherine couldn't make out Betsy's grumble as she hung the kettle back on the iron hook. Obviously the black woman's idea of her marriage was almost as romantic—and unrealistic—as her grandmother's.

"Miss Lillian's sleeping so I don't think she'll want anything to eat for a while." Catherine cut thick slices of bread off a fresh loaf.

"She ain't ailing, is she?"

Even Betsy thought Grandmere seeking her bed in the morning unusual. "She says not." Catherine swiped hair off her forehead. "Just tired. But I'd appreciate it if you'd check on her now and then." Catherine turned to find the black woman studying her closely. "Was there any of that ham left from yesterday?"

"Sure. What you doing?"

"I'm packing a dinner for Mr. Colton." Catherine would have had to be blind not to notice the sudden gleam in Betsy's dark brown eyes. "He didn't wish to take the time to come to the house and eat," she finished lamely.

"Fixing a picnic, huh?"

"I am *not* fixing a picnic, I'm fixing a dinner, as I said." Catherine took the ham Betsy offered and sawed through it with the butcher knife. Honestly, maybe Betsy was worse than Grandmere.

Catherine wrapped the bread and ham in clean linen napkins and placed them in the gingham-lined basket. "What's that?" Catherine looked up to see Betsy add something to the woven basket.

"Some of your wedding cake, and a jug of apple cider, cool from the cellar." Betsy covered the food with a tablecloth and handed the basket to Catherine, grinning her wide, snaggle-toothed grin.

"Thank you." Catherine draped the container over her arm. "I'll be back soon."

"Oh, don't hurry none on my account, Miss Catherine."

Catherine slammed the door on Betsy's lewd laughter. "You'd think I was going off to some lover's tryst," Catherine told no one in particular as she headed down the path toward the mine. Nothing could be further from the truth.

Catherine had practiced her speech over and over

again in her mind as she'd gone about her morning tasks. She'd simply tell Nicholas that she hadn't planned on their marriage being one in the truest sense of the word. It was a business agreement. Catherine smiled as she skirted a fern whose fronds grew into the pathway. She'd explain that because men ofttimes are driven by their baser need, she would not mind if he sought relief elsewhere, as long as he managed it without embarrassing her.

A sudden vision of Nicholas doing the things they'd done last night with Belle, the prostitute from Richmond, appeared before her. All right, so she didn't like it, but what else could she do? Many more nights like the last one and she'd have a truly difficult time letting him go back to England. And that had been the agreement.

Her husband emerged from the washhouse as she stepped into the clearing. He'd pulled on clean work pants but the fresh shirt was slung across his bare shoulder. He looked up and smiled, and Catherine felt the now-familiar flutter in her stomach. She wanted to set the basket down and run, but, she reminded herself, Brousseaus weren't cowards. She'd just tell him and be done with it.

"Hello, I'd—" Catherine hardly got those words out before he grabbed her hand and started pulling her back along the path. Her face bloomed with color as she heard the loud guffaws of the men. Goodness, did everybody have the wrong idea about this meeting?

"Where . . . where are we going?"

Nick paused and grinned over his shoulder. "To a place I know. It isn't far." He noticed the basket that thumped against Catherine's leg with every step and transferred it to his arm. "Better?"

"Yes, but—" Again she was cut off by his movement as he pulled her further down the path. He swerved off before he reached the cabin, and headed through the underbrush toward the creek.

Catherine knew these woods as well as she knew her house, so it came as no surprise when they came upon a section of the creek that was dammed off to form a deep pool. Sunlight dappled through the poplar leaves, forming intricate patterns on the bubbling surface of the water.

Nick set the basket on a stretch of grass, and gave in to the desire that had hounded him since he'd risen this morning. He found Catherine's gasp of surprise as his arms wrapped around her endearing. She had the softest skin he'd ever felt, and with his lips he reacquainted himself with the curve of her jaw.

"Mr. Colton. I must talk to—" His mouth and the bold thrust of his tongue cut off her protest—if indeed that's what it would have been. At this moment, all thoughts of denying him fled her. Catherine's body melted toward him like warm honey.

"What do you want to talk about?" He lifted his head.

"Well, I . . ." Catherine tried to pull the fuzzy edges of her mind together, to no avail—till she noticed his grin. The devil knew exactly what he did to her, *and* he enjoyed every minute of it. Catherine cleared her throat. "About last night."

"What about last night?" The grin broadened.

"Well, I . . . I . . . I simply cannot talk to you while

211

you're doing that."

"What?"

Catherine scowled. He sounded so innocent. "That!" Her eyes flashed down.

"Oh . . . this." His smile became positively demonic as he squeezed and molded her breast to fit his large hand. "Do you want me to stop?"

What a stupid question. Of course she wanted him to stop, except that to say it would belie her body's response. Her nipple thrust toward his palm so greedily that its outline was visible beneath her dress. Catherine stood, not knowing what to say, fast losing the urge to say anything at all, and then his hand left her. He left her too, striding over to the edge of the water and plopping down on a rock.

"What are you doing now?" Catherine watched in disbelief as he yanked off one boot, then the other. Standing, he unfastened his work pants before deigning to answer.

"But . . . but, I thought you did that back at the washroom." Catherine admonished herself to look away as he stripped the trousers down his lean hips, but her eyes refused to obey. He peeled off his drawers, and Catherine caught a flash of firm white flank before he dove into the water.

"Washing in the washroom isn't the same as this." Nick surfaced, sputtering water, to grin at her again. "Now, what did you want to talk about?"

He'd tossed out this question just before leaning his head back into the water. Within seconds the rest of him floated to the surface, broad chest, long legs— everything. Sun and shade, light and dark, danced sensually across his muscular body. Catherine's mouth went dry.

"Well?"

He must have noticed the drawn out silence, for the way he said the word, it seemed as if he really did want to know what was on her mind. But the problem was, she couldn't possibly tell him. Granted, he no longer distracted her by his touch, but just looking at him affected her almost as much. "It's nothing," Catherine heard herself say.

"Good."

A splash of the blue-green water and Nicholas was on his feet, moving toward the shore. He looked like a god with droplets of moisture clinging to the hard planes and corded muscles of his body.

"Why don't you come in?"

"The water?" Catherine squeaked.

"Sure. It will cool you off." He scooped a handful of sparkling water and threw it across the bronzed expanse of his chest. It trickled through the tight, water-darkened curls.

"I'm not hot."

A crooked grin was his only answer.

Did he plan to force her into the pool? He stalked toward her like a giant cat. The water was shallower near the bank and the surface played around his upper thighs, exposing the rest of him to her view. There was no way she could resist him if he carried her into the creek. Catherine decided a compromise might be warranted.

"I suppose I could put my feet in." With precise movements Catherine unlaced her shoes and stripped her stockings. For a second it crossed her mind that she shouldn't expose her ankles to him, then she

213

raised her eyes to see his bare back and bottom as he swam across the pool, and she felt foolish. Besides, he'd seen a lot more than her feet last night.

The water felt cool, sending goosebumps up her legs and across her arms, even as the sun filtered through the willows and warmed her back. Catherine kicked, feeling like a child again as the liquid ran between her toes. Shading her eyes against the glare, Catherine scanned the shimmering ripples. What had become of him? When she'd climbed down to the smooth sandstone rock where she now sat, she'd seen Nicholas gliding across the surface, but now . . .

"Mr. Colton?" Catherine leaned forward. Any number of things could have happened to him. He could have hit his head or gotten a cramp. "Nicholas?" Her heart beat faster. Her voice rose higher. "Nick!"

"Here." He popped out of the water less than two feet from her, his hair dark and slicked back and droplets raining down his face.

Catherine's heart tightened, and she came close to jumping in to the creek to wrap her arms around him. He looked so incredibly handsome standing there, so utterly male with his strong body and his rugged face and grin. Grin! Anger rushed through her. He was grinning. She'd been scared—had almost jumped into the water, even though she wasn't entirely certain she could still swim—and he thought it funny.

"Why you—" For want of anything else that could defuse her anger, she kicked water on him—hardly a punishment since he couldn't get any wetter. "What's the idea of hiding from me?"

"Whoa." He caught her foot, wrapping his hand

214

around her ankle before she could splash him again. "I wasn't hiding."

"Let go of me." Catherine twisted her foot, but only managed to get the other one caught, too. "Then what were you doing?"

"Just exploring under water. There's a beaver dam up at that end." He motioned toward the turn in the creek with his chin. "What's the matter? Were you worried about me?"

"Certainly not." Catherine gasped when he pulled her ankles apart and stepped between them, dampening the hem of her dress.

"I think you were. I think that's why you're so angry."

Did the man ever do anything but grin? And now he was sliding her further down on the rock. "That's ridiculous. You startled me is all."

"If you say so." Nick slipped his hand over the curve of her arch, that smile still plastered to his face but now noticeably absent from his eyes. They had turned smoky gray. "You have nice feet, Catherine."

Funny how his saying something like that made her feel warm all over.

"Nice small ankles, and legs." His gaze dropped to her feet that now rested lightly against his hips, then raised to meet hers. "I noticed your legs last night."

Catherine sucked in a breath of air when she realized her lightheadedness came from lack of air. It helped—a little. He'd moved closer, spreading her legs, forcing the skirt to climb her thighs, pinning her against the rock with his hard body. He smelled of fresh water and sunshine and that distinctive fragrance that belonged to him alone.

215

"What . . . what are you doing?" Catherine could feel his cold hands, such a contrast to her suddenly hot skin, moving beneath her petticoats.

"Taking off your pantaloons."

"Oh." He'd said it in such a matter of fact fashion that Catherine felt powerless to protest. The cord snapped, he lifted her briefly, and then the white, ruffled cotton drifted down the creek.

Hiking up her skirts, Nick lifted her against the hard, hot part of him that yearned for her. Cool water lapped around his thighs, a sensual counterpoint to the fire that consumed his loins. Last night when they'd made love he'd known why he'd turned Marie away, why he hadn't been more than moderately tempted to slack his lust on any of the prostitutes in Richmond—why he'd married Catherine.

He wanted her, had since the first time she'd looked up at him with those bottomless green eyes, eyes that stared at him now with a mixture of wonder and anticipation. He'd known then that passion dwelled within her, though she did her best to keep it at bay with her straitlaced demeanor. But it was there—in the way she cared about her grandmother, the way she worked for the mine, in the way she responded to him.

"Put your arms around me, Cate." Nick murmured as her movement brought him closer to the naked lower part of her body. "Now kiss me." His voice was a breathy whisper that mingled with the gurgling creek, the chirping birds.

Catherine dug her fingers into his damp hair, and stared at his beautiful mouth. Like a magnet it drew

216

her, first to trace it with the tip of her tongue, then to nip at the corners. He smiled at her playfulness, but groaned, the sound vibrating against her breasts as she wrapped her bare legs around his hips.

His square jaw jutted toward her, reaching for the lips she kept just beyond his touch. His hands were busy elsewhere, clutching the roundness of her bottom, so she was at liberty to set the pace. And whatever imp had taken possession of her enjoyed the teasing play with him, especially since she knew he would allow it for only so long.

Her fingers trailed around his neck, its thick, corded muscles delineated in bold relief beneath the weather-tanned skin. She skimmed over the intriguing scar on his chin, and then returned to circle it.

"How did you get this?" Catherine said, her voice unsteady.

"I fell."

Catherine cocked her head. "Oh, where?"

"In a mine. Against an outcrop of flint. When I was a kid."

"How about your nose? Did you break that at the same time?" Catherine could feel his tightly restrained control nearing the breaking point. She anticipated the moment as much as he did. His hands gripped, then slipped forward to grasp her hip.

"No. I ran into something."

"Wh . . . what?"

"A fist."

Catherine's burst of laughter stopped abruptly when Nick's finger entered her. "Now," he growled. "Kiss me, Cate."

217

And she did, with an open-mouthed abandon she would have thought herself incapable of, if she could think at all. He shifted, lifting her higher, and then he filled her. There was no pain today, only a deep feeling of completion as he drove toward the core of her being.

Skirting the rock, Nick sloshed through the water, collapsing on the sloped, moss-covered shore. Rolling her under him, he plunged again, each thrust bolder than the last, until her cry of release blended with his.

For long, peaceful minutes, Nick lay on top of Catherine, his head nestled on her breasts, listening to the slow, steadying of her heartbeat. He couldn't remember when he'd felt happier, more at peace. His feet and lower legs rested in the water, in the creek that ran down past his mine. Maybe he only owned one quarter of it, but he still liked the feeling.

Ownership. He'd never known it before. Never knew how much it would mean to him. He belonged here—to this place, to this woman.

Stretching, Nick moved up her body, resting his elbows in the springy green moss on either side of her head. God, she was beautiful, with the sun finding the red in her hair and turning it to flame. Her eyes seemed enormous, two deep pools of liquid emeralds, surrounded by fine-as-china skin.

She'd surprised him, too—would have knocked his pants off, if he'd had any on—when she'd teased and played with him before their lovemaking.

But turnabout was fair play. His hand drifted down to her breast, and his tongue scraped across her cheek, then sunk into the sweetness of her mouth. He lifted his head, his lips still grazing her, and asked, "Do you know what I want to do?"

It was a question fraught with sensual overtones, and Catherine felt heat return to parts of her body she'd thought were surely satiated. "What?" The tip of his tongue punctuated the word.

Nick raised his head further, his eyes dancing with laughter. "Eat," came his succinct reply. "I'm starved."

"Oh, you. . . ." Realization and embarrassment hit Catherine at the same time.

"Now, Catie. . . . Watch where you're grabbing. Don't you think I owed you one?" Nick rolled her on top of him and laughed up into her eyes, his bright with promise.

"Tonight, Cate," was all he said, but Catherine felt her face flame.

"And, now." Nick stood and waded into the water. With deft movements, he untangled her pantaloons from a gnarled branch sticking out of the water. "What's for dinner? I really am hungry." After spreading the feminine underclothes on the ground to dry, with apparently no more concern than if it had been a handkerchief, he yanked on his trousers.

"Mmm, ham." Nick sat cross-legged beside the wicker container, rummaging through its contents. "Aren't you going to eat?"

Catherine stood, brushing sand and dirt off her skirt, and started at him. "My dress is dirty."

Nick glanced up, munching on a slice of bread. "I suggested you take it off."

219

She couldn't fault him there. He had. What had happened? She'd brought him his dinner, hoping to have a quiet conversation with him—to tell him there would be no more intimacies between them. And instead she'd made love to him. In the water! In the daylight! And it had been wonderful, so wonderful that she'd been eager to do it again. So wonderful that she couldn't help thinking of the coming night.

Catherine turned and flailed at her skirt to hide her blush.

"Come here." Nick reached out and grabbed the dark cotton material, turning her so he could inspect the back of her skirt. "Looks like the stain will come out, but you need some new clothes anyway."

"There's no money." Catherine sank down on the ground beside him, deciding the damage was already done—to her dress and to her no lovemaking plan.

"I have some."

"Some what?" Catherine paused from sipping cider and glanced up.

"Money. I have enough to pay for some improvements around here, starting with your wardrobe." Travis Fielding had not only paid him extremely well, he'd offered suggestions about how to invest some of the money—chief among them was Fielding Mining, a very lucrative enterprise.

Catherine's jaw dropped open. "Oh, Mr. Colton, I couldn't ask you to do that."

"Why not? You're my wife, aren't you?"

"Yes, but—"

"And don't you think you should call me something other than Mr. Colton?" Nick grinned. "You did last night."

She didn't need *that* spelled out for her. "Be that as it may, I can't let you spend your money on Greenfield . . . or me. That wasn't part of our bargain." And neither was sleeping with you.

Nick reached for the jug and took a healthy swig, backhanding the moisture from his mouth. "I guess I'll just have to buy some presents then. You wouldn't object to that, would you, Cate?"

"Well, I—"

"You can start with that hat?"

"The flowered bonnet? But what about your friend in England?"

Nick reached for his shirt, shrugging it over his muscular shoulders. "There is no friend in England. Least ways not one I wanted the hat for. I bought it for you."

"But, I . . ." Heavens, what was she to say? But he didn't give her a chance to say anything. With one smooth motion he rolled to his feet.

"I better get back to the mine and make sure everyone's working. Thanks for bringing my uh . . . dinner."

"Anytime." Catherine shaded her eyes and looked up at him, feeling herself blush again when she noticed his wink.

"I'll hold you to that. See you later."

For a long time after he disappeared through the underbrush of wild blackberries and honeysuckle, Catherine sat staring. This marriage wasn't turning out anything like she'd planned.

Not that he hadn't kept his end of the bargain, he

had. The men were back at work and so was he. She'd just never expected the other things—the kissing and lovemaking that made her feel warm all over, the niceness. Imagine him wanting to spend his money on her. He couldn't have much. Of course, she'd never let him do it. His money was his. But the thought had been sweet.

Catherine gathered up the remains of dinner and stuffed them into the basket. She'd started up the path when a flash of white on green caught her eye. Her pantaloons! My heavens. What if she'd forgotten them? Quickly, looking over her shoulder, even though she knew there was no one there, Catherine grabbed the damp garment and stuffed it in her basket.

She supposed there was no way she could stop her husband from making love to her, and if she were truthful she'd admit she didn't want to stop him. But it was going to make it so much harder when he left her to return to England. And he would leave. That had been part of the agreement. He'd leave, get a divorce, and she'd be left with a broken heart.

"Did you have a good time?"

Betsy's question and lecherous grin greeted her when she stepped into the hot interior of the kitchen.

"It was very nice," Catherine answered haughtily. Goodness, wouldn't the black woman have a grand time teasing her if she knew what had really happened? "Thank you for helping with the dinner." Catherine set the basket on the wooden work table. "I think I'll check on Grandmere." Turning back toward the door, Catherine had almost reached it when Betsy's voice stopped her.

"Oh, Miss Catherine."

"Yes." Catherine looked over her shoulder, her face burning crimson when she saw what Betsy held between two gnarled brown fingers.

"You forgot your drawers."

Chapter Eleven

"Are you sure you saw someone?"

Sampson pulled his hand down across his scruffy black beard, and seemed to ponder for a moment. Leaning back against the wooden spindles of his chair, he shook his head. "Well, now Mr. Nick, I guess I ain't exactly sure. But pretty damn close to it."

Nick folded his arms across his clean work shirt, and studied his bottom boss for a long moment. "But you couldn't tell who it was?"

"Didn't see nothing but a shadow." Sampson snorted. "Whoever it was ran away fast enough when I yelled out."

"I wish you would have come up to the house to get me."

Sampson balanced his chair on two legs. "Didn't see no need. No way we could've found nobody in that dark. And I thought we was just supposed to keep people away from the mine."

"You're right." Nick steepled his fingers. That was the order he'd given after the fire. More to the point, after he'd talked with the men about the fire, and discovered that no one had left a lantern burning. No one could think of any reason for the blaze to start—no one until Jones, a short dark haired fellow recently immigrated from Wales, mentioned the noise he'd heard when he'd gone outside to relieve himself.

"Didn't think much of it at the time," Jones had said. "Thought maybe I'd startled an animal, raccoon or something. But now that I think about it, was mighty loud for anything like that."

"How long after that until the fire broke out," Nick had asked.

"Don't rightly know for sure. But I was still awake. Good thing, too, 'cause we might have all burned to a crisp if I hadn't smelled the smoke."

Nick scanned the front room of the cabin he'd lived in before his marriage, thinking about that conversation, wondering if it had any connection with what Sampson had seen last night. Maybe he was being overly cautious, but he couldn't help believing it did. "Sampson, I want you to put two men on guard every night."

"That means taking men away from the mine. They have to sleep sometime."

"I know that. But I'd rather take this little precaution than run the risk of rebuilding those new barracks—or burying someone."

"You think someone set that fire—is trying to set another?" Sampson's chair flopped forward, and he leaned his elbows onto the table.

Nick shrugged. "I don't know. But I'm going to be prepared if they do."

"Who would do something like that?"

"I don't know that either." Nick stood and paced the room he now used as an office. He turned back to face Sampson. "But I do know that this operation has been plagued with problems for about a year now, and I'm starting to wonder if some of them aren't man made."

"You could be right. All I know is that this here mine sure has a godawful reputation for safety. Fellow would have to be crazy to work here."

Nick's bark of laughter echoed through the cabin. It cut through the tension he'd felt since coming down here this morning and seeing Sampson waiting by the door. "What are *you* doing here then?"

"Maybe I'm crazy. Or maybe I decided that I could work for anyone who beat me arm wrestling." He flexed his arm, showing off the corded muscles and tendons that bulged against the restraints of his canvas shirt.

"I didn't win if you recall."

"Aw hell, we both know I took advantage of you when your missus walked in that tavern. If it hadn't been for that." He shrugged. "Who knows."

Nick chuckled and slouched back into his chair. After a moment his expression sobered. "Did you tell anyone else about last night?"

"Not a soul, boss."

"Good." Nick rested his hands on a pile of papers. Catherine still took care of most of the bookkeeping, but he'd started working with the orders. "I'd like to keep it that way for now."

"They're going to wonder why we're increasing

the guard duty."

"Just tell them to see me if they have any questions." Nick had no idea what he'd tell them, but he'd think of something. He stood again. "Thanks for being so alert last night, Sampson. I appreciate it."

"Sure thing, Mr. Nick. I'll be getting back now."

Nick clasped the burly man on the shoulder. "I'll be down soon."

After Sampson left, Nick sat down and started sorting through the papers on the table he used as a desk, but his mind was on what Sampson had told him. Was it possible that someone was sabotaging the mine? The notion was hard to accept. He could envision someone making a comfortable living off the coal in the mine, but from what he'd been able to see, they wouldn't get rich. It hardly seemed the type of property that people went to the trouble of fussing over.

And that brought up another point. Who would care enough to cause trouble? Sam Stevens came to mind. He'd been responsible for the robbed pillars and he'd been pretty bitter when Nick fired him. But according to Parker, he had another job now, and it didn't seem likely he'd jeopardize that to seek revenge.

Of course, there was Parker himself—certainly no love lost between himself and the owner of Windy Hill. But Greenfield's troubles had been going on for about a year, like he'd told Sampson, and Parker had been a friend of Catherine's until recently. Hell, he was even engaged to her. At least Parker thought he was. Why would Parker do anything to mess up a

228

nine that would eventually belong to him?

Nick rubbed his chin. It didn't make sense. But if not Parker or Stevens, then who? If Catherine had any other enemies, he sure didn't know about them. Maybe he'd talk to her, try to discover if someone else had it in for her or her family. For damn sure, though, he wasn't going to let her in on his suspicions. She'd been almost carefree these last two weeks since their wedding, and he wasn't going to have her worrying about this. If anything was amiss—and now that he reasoned it out, he doubted there was—he'd take care of it.

Leaning back on his chair, Nick stacked his booted feet on the table. Being married to Catherine was even more pleasurable than he'd imagined. She was one sharp woman, but that didn't keep her from being soft and sweet, too. Nick chuckled. She was still throwing a fit about going to Richmond to buy some clothes for herself, but Nick was determined to get her there if he had to tie and gag her.

Not that he minded the clothes she wore. Now that he'd seen the beautiful body that lay beneath, he could just use his memory when she appeared before him in one of her prim gowns. Nick chuckled again, thinking how angry Catherine would be if she knew what he was thinking. She'd probably—

"Mr. Nick!"

Nick's feet hit the ground as Sampson pounded through the open door. "What in the hell's wrong?"

"I checked out the supplies . . . ," Sampson paused to catch his breath, "like you told me earlier. And there is something missing."

"What?" The expression on Sampson's face told him it wasn't a couple of pick axes.

"Black powder."

Nick trudged up the path toward the house. As had become his habit since marrying Catherine, he'd bathed in the creek and changed into clean clothes before heading home. Home. He liked the sound of that. Greenfield had begun to feel like home to him. That was one of the reasons he didn't want to see anything happen to it.

"Damn," he swore under his breath, causing a robin to take wing and flutter across the path. He'd spent one hell of a frustrating day trying to find that missing powder—and trying to keep the rest of the men from knowing what he and Sampson were doing. First he'd checked purchase receipts against usage entries in the storage shed to make sure he wasn't chasing ghosts where none existed. Then, because his numbers didn't match, he'd inventoried the storage shed. Sampson was right. There was black powder—powder they used when they needed to blast away rock—missing.

"Where'd you see that person last night?" Nick had asked Sampson when they'd confirmed the loss.

"By the door to the storage shed. I figured I scared him away before he done any harm, but maybe not."

Nick replaced his worried frown with a smile as he followed the path out of the woods and saw Catherine sitting in the garden. "All alone?"

Catherine looked up from the shirt she was

mending and her face brightened. It happened every time she saw him. And every time the fear of what she would do when he left to return to England grew stronger.

"Where's Grandmere?" Coming upon the two ladies sitting under the elm tree was another thing he looked forward to at the end of the day. He didn't even mind when Marie was with them, though thankfully, that wasn't often. Though they'd never spoken of it, he found it hard to overlook her visit to his cabin the night before he wed her sister.

"She's in bed. Oh, Nick." Catherine laid down her sewing, unable to keep the concern from quivering her voice. "She didn't get up at all today."

"Is she sick?"

Catherine moved her skirts so her husband could sit beside her on the bench. "She says not. Only complains of being tired."

"How about the doctor? Has he seen her?" In his time at Greenfield, Nick had come to care for the old woman as if she were his own grandmother.

Catherine nodded. "I sent Betsy around for him today." She sighed. "He says she's old."

Nick cocked his brow. "Hardly a profound diagnosis."

"Oh, Nick, I'm scared. She hasn't been the same for days now. She rarely gets up, and all she does is talk about Grandpere and Papa."

"She did that before," Nick pointed out logically, but he placed a comforting arm around his wife.

Catherine shook her head. "It's not the same. I know she mentioned them before, but now it's constant. She doesn't seem to know I'm even there. And when Marie stopped in to see her today, she didn't know her."

"Marie's here?"

"She came after supper last night. You had gone back to the mine to check on the second shift. I must have forgotten to tell you." Catherine rested her head back against Nick's arm. "It's such a relief having her home, especially with Grandmere ill."

Nick seriously questioned the wisdom of Catherine's sentiment, but he said nothing. In England, after Mr. Fielding had taken him from the mines and given him the trappings of a gentleman, he'd met his share of women like Marie. Self-centered and manipulative, he'd done his best to stay clear of them. He doubted it would be that easy in this case. Marie apparently came and went as the urge struck her, and for now, at least, she would be here.

Supper that evening seemed strained to Nick. Catherine spoke very little, and he knew her mind centered on the vacant chair at the foot of the long mahogany table. Grandmere had declined to come to the table and judging from the tray Nick had seen Catherine carry from her room, had eaten very little.

Marie on the other hand, appeared unaffected by her grandmother's ill health.

"Whatever is wrong with everyone? Here I cut short my visit at the Milleaus to come home and you act positively morose. Catherine, I thought marriage would perk you up a little, but here you are acting as much like a backward mouse as ever."

Nick noticed a sudden spark of anger flash in

Catherine's green eyes, but she quickly smothered it. "We're glad to have you home, Marie, however, certainly you can understand how concerned I am about Grandmere."

"Oh, pish posh, Catherine, if we all pulled long faces like you every time Grandmere stayed in her bed, this would be a dreary place indeed. Marie took a dainty forkful of chicken. "Isn't that right, Mr. Colton?"

Nick looked into sky blue eyes that stared at him guilelessly. "I don't think my wife's solicitude is misplaced."

"Well, of course it isn't." Marie smiled sweetly. "We all want to see Grandmere up and about, her old self again. I just meant, well, it isn't helping her if we all sit here and mope like Catherine, now is it?"

"If you'll excuse me, I'm not very hungry." Catherine pushed out her chair and rose before Nick could offer his assistance.

"Cate." Nick's voice cut across the room as she reached for the door knob.

"Please finish your meal. I'm only going to see if Grandmere needs anything."

"Catherine always has been such a dutiful little granddaughter."

"She's worried." Nick attacked his chicken with a vengeance.

"And you think I'm not? You wound me Mr. Colton . . . or may I call you Nick now that you're my brother-in-marriage."

"As I recall, you called me Nick before." Nick didn't look up, but he could feel her smile.

"Well, so I did . . . Nick." Marie sipped her wine. "Tell me, Nick. Is Catherine as dutiful a wife as she is granddaughter?"

This time Nick did look up. He met her eyes, till she turned away, then balling his linen napkin, he stood. "If you'll excuse me, I believe I'll see if I can be of any assistance to Catherine."

Nick strode toward the door, pausing only when he heard Marie's laugh. "You really don't need to answer that, Nick. I think I know my sister well enough to guess what your response would be if you dared voice it."

"Bitch." Nick mumbled the word under his breath as he slammed the dining room door. He was immediately sorry—not for the sentiment, Lord knew he didn't regret calling a spade a spade—but for letting her get to him. And for letting her know it. Besides if Grandmere had been asleep, his slamming the door was sure to wake her.

As if to prove his point, Catherine met him outside the older lady's room, her head tilted questioningly. "What happened?"

"Nothing."

"Nick?"

"All right, damnit. Your sister made me angry, and I slammed the door. I didn't wake your grandmother, did I?"

"No." Catherine turned back to enter the room. "She didn't even flinch."

Grabbing her arm, Nick swung Catherine back around toward him. "Why do you let her talk to you that way?"

"Marie?"

"Hell, yes, Marie. Who else would I mean?"

"Please keep your voice down."

Nick cupped Catherine's shoulders with his hands. He was fast losing his patience. "If slamming the door didn't wake her, my talking won't either. Now answer my question."

"I don't know. That's just the way she is. She doesn't mean any harm." She felt his arms tighten. "Well, she doesn't."

"I don't like it."

"You don't like it. Listen to me Nicholas Colton. Marie may not be the kindest person, but she is my sister." Catherine raised her chin, ignoring the heat she felt from his hands on her. "I've tolerated her tongue for years, and I will continue to long after you leave." How dare he worry her with his minor scuffle with Marie, when she had more important things on her mind. Besides, he liked Marie. She knew he did. Was this an act for her benefit?

"When I leave?" Nick repeated. What in the hell did she mean by that? He asked her, not in the calmest tone.

"I mean that my relationship with Marie is none of your business. Now if you will excuse me, I'll get back to my grandmother?" She twisted out of his hands, and marched through the door, shutting it in his face.

Damn woman. Nick tramped out of the house, swinging the door open wide, but in deference to Grandmere—and no one else, he emphasized to himself—shutting it quietly. Leaning against the

235

mottled trunk of a sycamore, Nick lit a cheroot and stared up at the night sky.

What did she mean it wasn't his business? He was her husband, wasn't he? Didn't that make it his business? And what the hell did she mean about him leaving? Had he given any indication he planned to leave? Hell, no! He'd even written to Travers Fielding informing him that he'd married Catherine. He'd mentioned that he and his wife would be visiting him as soon as everything was settled here.

"Humph," Nick snorted and watched the red tip of his cheroot arch toward him. Maybe he should have talked to Catherine before sending that post. She sounded like she was ready for him to leave. Well, hell, he'd done what she wanted. The miners were working and the coal was rolling out of the black hole. Why wouldn't she want him gone? Obviously he read more into two weeks of lovemaking and sweet talk than he should have. For all he knew Marie and Catherine were cut from the same cloth. His wife just excelled at subtlety.

"Tsk, tsk. Does Catherine make you leave the house to smoke?"

Nick narrowed his eyes, watching the pale pink clad figure float toward him. "What do you want, Marie?"

"My, my, you are in a grouchy mood." She traced her finger down his waistcoat buttons. "Just like a big, bad bear."

Nick's hand snaked out, capturing her wrists before she could continue her exploration southward. "I asked what you wanted."

"Not a thing." Marie swayed closer, ignoring his

grip on her. "I just saw you out here all by yourself, and thought you might want some company."

"Well, I don't." Nick tossed aside her wrist with the same contempt he threw down his half-smoked cheroot. He ground the spark with his heel.

Marie smiled, her blond curls pale in the meager light. "You don't fool me, Nick. You're too much of a man to be content with my sister's limpid loving." She shrugged her bare shoulders. "If she allows you that. There will come a time when you'll want a real woman. And maybe . . . just maybe I'll let you have a taste."

Nick watched her walk away her ruffled skirts swaying provocatively in the moonlight, and felt . . . disgust. What kind of woman would so blatantly try to seduce her sister's husband? And how could Catherine defend her?

But then Catherine didn't know this side of her sister's personality—probably wouldn't know . . . unless he told her. What if she didn't believe him? What if Marie claimed the seduction came from his quarter?

Nick slapped at the tree bark with the palm of his hand. It had been one hell of a day. First the trouble at the mine with the missing black powder, then Grandmere's illness, and now Marie. Well, there was nothing he could do about Catherine's grandmother, but he intended to find out who took those explosives—and he intended to give Marie Brousseau a wide berth.

But right now he was going to bed. Nick rolled his head to one side and then the other, trying to relieve the tension in his muscles, as he climbed the stairs. Catherine wasn't in their room, but then he hadn't expected her to be. With swift movements he shed his clothes, then climbed into bed—alone. Lacing his fingers behind his head, aiming his elbows at opposite walls, Nick stared at the quivering flicker of candlelight dance across the ceiling.

Damn if he didn't miss Catherine snuggling up beside him. Disgusted with himself, Nick stretched across the pillow and blew out the taper.

Catherine had let him know where he stood. After her grandmother. Nick had no problem with that considering the poor old lady's health. But did she have to rate him after her male sniffing, seductress of a sister? Nick pounded his fist into the feather pillow and shut his eyes. Well, what had he expected? She'd played her cards square right from the beginning. A business arrangement she'd called it. It wasn't her fault he'd started thinking of their marriage in other terms. Perhaps he should write Travis Fielding another letter—one that explained the first had been a joke, and that he was returning to England on the next ship. With that thought firm in his mind, he fell asleep.

The moon topped the trees when Nick woke. He'd been dreaming of Catherine—damn his weak flesh—and had rolled over to wrap his arm around her waist. But she wasn't there. Rubbing his hand over his face, Nick glanced around the room. Shadowy outlines of furniture—a wardrobe, a washstand, the turned spindles of his bed—stood in silent watch, but no Catherine.

"Fool woman, has probably been up all night," Nick mumbled as he yanked on his trousers. It would serve her right if he just left her there, he thought, pulling on his boots. He jammed his arms into a shirt, not bothering to button it, then fumbled in the darkness for the doorknob.

He cursed his wife, the darkness, and his own stupidity for forgetting to bring a candle when he bumped his head at the top of the box stairwell. A feeble wedge of light, escaping through the open bedroom door, shone across the wide planks of the library floor. Nick followed the glow. By the flickering flame of a gutted candle, he spotted Catherine, and all of his anger evaporated. Curled up in Grandmere's rocker, her head folded down against the arm, she appeared delicate and vulnerable—and very uncomfortable.

"Cate." Dropping to his knee in front of the chair, Nick whispered her name. "Catie, love."

One small hand came up to rub her nose, then Catherine's eyes opened slowly. "Nick. Oh, Nick." In that no-man's land between sleep and wakefulness, Catherine didn't bother to think that Nick had married her for a share of the mine or that the only other thing he wanted from her was sex. Her arms wove around his neck and she buried her face in the silky hair of his chest. His skin was warm and smooth and smelled wonderfully of him. She could hear his heart beat, strong, steady, like him. She needed that strength. She needed him.

Their earlier argument had played around in her mind all evening as she'd sat by her grandmother's bed. She'd been stupid to defend Marie to him. She knew what Marie was like, had known for years, but as she'd told him, that was Marie. There was no changing her. And she was her sister—if something

239

happened to Grandmere, the only family she'd have left. Catherine snuggled closer in the shelter of the arms Nick had wrapped around her. No matter that Nick was real and strong and solid now, she knew he would leave in the end, and she'd be alone.

"Cate, honey, let me take you up to bed."

His words tickled her ear, vibrated through her cheek that was pressed to his chest. They were soothing, but . . . "I can't. Grandmere—"

"She's asleep, Cate."

"No, but there's something wrong. Listen to her breathing."

Nick shifted his gaze to the older woman, watching and listening to the shallow motion of her slowly rising and falling chest beneath the thin quilt. The noise was low and feeble, but definitely there—a bone-dry rattle. With each breath she drew, the air seemed to roll around painfully inside her before escaping. Nick looked back at Catherine and their eyes locked.

"And she's been waking up frequently and calling for my grandfather," Catherine continued. She could tell Nick recognized the seriousness of the situation.

"But you're not helping anything by wearing yourself down, maybe even getting sick. Let me take you to bed. You need some rest."

Catherine pushed away from the arms that began to scoop her up. "I can't leave her alone."

"You won't be." Nick stood cradling Catherine's resisting body against his.

"But—"

"As soon as I take you upstairs, I'll come back and sit with her."

"But—"

"I've had some sleep, so I'll be able to stay awake."

"Bu—"

"And I'll call you if there's any change. Now are you satisfied?" Nick shifted her in his arms.

"Do you promise?"

"Cate . . ."

"All right. All right. But put me down. I can walk. And then she won't have to be alone at all." Catherine would have much preferred to stay snuggled against her husband's hard chest, but she was truly worried about Grandmere. As soon as her feet touched the floor, Catherine leaned over her grandmother. She looked sunken, more frail than she'd ever seen her, hardly more than a shadow of her old self. And it had happened so quickly. Catherine sighed, reaching out but stopping short of touching the hollow cheek.

Nick lit another candle and handed it to Catherine. "Take this with you and get some rest." He brushed his lips across her forehead. "And don't worry."

Catherine paused outside the doorway and looked back in the room. Nick had already settled into the rocking chair, his long legs propped up on a stool. It should be Marie sitting there at her grandmother's bedside. But, of course, she hadn't offered, and Nick had. A man she'd known less than two months, a man who had married her for a share of Greenfield Mine, was the one who cared enough to help her.

She was dying. Nick wasn't certain how he knew, but he knew all the same. He cleared his throat to chase away the burning behind his eyelids. She'd been kind to him, and he hated to see anything

241

happen to her. Sitting there in the darkness, Nick let his gaze drift over the tiny figure while his mind imagined what his own grandmothers might have been like—could still be like, for all he knew.

His mother's mother was dead, at least he was fairly confident of that. Searching the cloudy recesses of his brain, he couldn't remember his mother ever speaking of her parents. Of course, he'd only been eight when she'd died, but he'd assumed if her parents had been living they would have taken him, and, for sure, no one had.

Certainly not his father. Nick leaned his head back, trying to fight the angry feeling that overtook him whenever he thought of the man who'd fathered him—and then disappeared. He could remember his mother speaking of him. She used to say he was rich and wonderfully handsome. She'd thought of him almost like a knight in shining armor. Nick hadn't been too small to know that she'd loved him, too, till the day she died, cold and hungry with no one but a young son she worried about leaving.

But Nick had hated him—still hated him. God. Nick shook his head. Why was he lancing old wounds. His father couldn't hurt him by his absence anymore. Nick was a grown man. He didn't even have to worry about going hungry anymore, thanks to Travis Fielding. Hell, he even owned part of a mine.

"Catherine?"

The crackly voice cut through Nick's thoughts and he leaned forward in the rocking chair. "She's in bed. I can get her for you."

"Mr. Colton, is that you?"

"Yes ma'am." Nick dragged the chair closer to the bed. His knee brushed the wedding-ring pattern on the quilt. Grandmere lifted a narrow, reed-thin hand and reached toward Nick. Without thinking he enfolded it in his. It felt terribly cold.

"I'm so glad you married Catherine."

"I'm glad, too. Now maybe you should try to sleep some more."

"She can be stubborn, my Catherine. She gets that from her grandfather, my husband." She paused, closing her eyes, and Nick thought she'd taken his advice about getting more sleep. That's why her next words were all the more unsettling. "He's dead, you know. Died in a cave-in, many, many years ago. Died in his mine. Henry loved that mine. Catherine gets that from him, too."

Nick realized he was squeezing her hand and loosened his grip. He did nothing about the dampness that blurred his vision.

"She's like him in so many ways, but then, so are you. I knew that the first time I saw you. Strong. You'll take care of her. I don't need to worry."

"No, Grandmere. You don't need to worry." She smiled a weak, faint smile, at his words.

"Would you be a good boy and fetch my granddaughter. I think I should like to see her now."

Nick couldn't remember leaving the bedroom to get Catherine, but he must have hurried, because he had another bump on his head from running into the low ceiling at the top of the steps. He knew he hadn't taken the candle. He hadn't wanted Grandmere to be alone in the dark.

He glanced down at Catherine. She was clutching

her grandmother's hand much as he had done moments earlier. And she was crying. Nick brushed the thick hair off her neck and rested his hand along her shoulder.

"I want you to be happy, Catherine, please, don't mourn me."

"Grandmere, don't. . . ." Catherine paused, trying to stifle a sob. "Please, Grandmere. Don't leave me all alone."

"You're not alone, dear. You have—"

"Would someone tell me what's going on?" Marie demanded as she walked through the door, carrying a lantern. "There's so much noise I can't sleep."

Nick jerked around, ready to carry her out of the room if necessary, but she must have realized what was happening for her manner seemed to mellow. "What is it?" she whispered to him.

"Your grandmother is dying." Nick would have softened the words had he thought she cared.

"Are you sure?"

Nick didn't even respond to that as he turned back to his wife. She had knelt beside the bed, and was calling her grandmother's name over and over again.

"Catherine."

"She won't answer me," Catherine sobbed. "She just called Henry, and now she won't answer me."

"Move, sweetheart." Nick lifted her aside, then bent his head down to listen to the old woman's chest. Nothing. "She . . . she's gone, Catherine."

"No. Oh, no, Nick."

Catherine looked up at him with disbelieving eyes in a pale, tear-stained face. He felt an ache in the region of his heart, a sense of loss, and he needed to touch his wife—hoped she needed to feel him close.

"Come here, Cate." He opened his arms and they moved together, hugging, trying to ease the pain.

Nick closed his eyes, resting his cheek in the fragrant softness of his wife's hair so he didn't see Marie's face. An expression of undisguised hatred marred her beauty as she looked at the embracing figures of her sister and brother-in-law.

Chapter Twelve

"I've been looking for you."

Catherine glanced up, shading her eyes against the filtered sun shining through the elm, and made out the outline of her husband. Of course, she'd known it was him as soon as she heard his voice. "I'm sorry. Did you want something?" Catherine started to rise, but Nick's hand stayed her, and when he sat down on the lush green grass, she sank down again too.

"No." Nick leaned back and filled his lungs with the sweet fragrance of late afternoon. "I just wondered where you were." That wasn't entirely true. He'd had a pretty good idea where he could find her.

"I see." Picking a clover, Catherine began methodically stripping its leaves.

"It's peaceful here." He'd been up on this grassy knoll behind the garden before, on the day of the funeral, but hadn't visited the small family cemetary since. He glanced around, noting the neat rows of graves. What had she told him? Ah, yes, seven generations of Brousseaus were buried here. Seven generations made for a lot of graves. The newest one, its mantle of dirt still freshly piled in a slight mound, was directly behind them. Someone, Nick assumed Catherine, had placed a bouquet of roses near the headstone.

"It is nice." Catherine brushed the torn leaves off her skirt. "I never came up here much—before. Grandmere spoke so often about my grandfather, even my parents, as if they were alive, somehow it just felt strange to face the proof that they weren't."

Nick nodded, stretching out his long legs and crossing them at the ankles. "She knew, though."

"Knew what?"

"That they were dead . . . at least your grandfather."

"Whatever makes you think that?" Catherine turned, her gaze finding Nick's and holding.

"She told me. The night she died."

"But she always insisted he was alive . . . down at the mine . . . or off to Richmond for something."

Shrugging, Nick broke the stare. "Maybe so, but she told me he was dead. Even mentioned how it happened."

"In the mine." Catherine plucked more clover, shredding it onto her lap. "There was a cave-in. But that's not what killed him. It was the gasses."

A warm breeze, laden with the fragrance of magnolia, trilled the loose curls around Catherine's face, further mussed Nick's hair.

Catherine twisted around, facing Nick again. "What else did she tell you? You didn't mention that she'd spoken to you that night."

"Not much." Nick watched a redheaded wood-pecker, drill the elm bark, looking for dinner, before he met his wife's eyes. His smile, when he gave it, was sad. "You didn't ask. And I haven't seen you much lately."

"I . . ." What could she say? She had been keeping to herself. Often, she managed to be away at supper time, and at night . . . well, she'd either be asleep by the time Nick came to bed, or at least convince him that she was. And the funny part of it was, she didn't know why. "I'm sorry."

"I didn't ask for an apology." Nick stood, reaching down his hand for Catherine. "You ready to go back to the house? Betsy is frying up some chicken for dinner."

Catherine looked at that hand, that large, firm-as-a-rock hand, with its work-hardened palm open toward her. What could she do but reach for it? He pulled her up in one smooth motion, but he didn't move. Catherine found herself pressed against his length, felt his arms wrap around her neck. Calloused thumbs tilted her face up toward his.

"It's all right to be sad, but your grandmother wouldn't want this." Nick cocked his head toward the tombstones.

Tears welled in Catherine's eyes. "I loved her so much. She'd always taken care of me. Even when my parents were alive . . ." She shook her head. "They were gone a lot. Grandmere was always there."

"I know." Nick's hand curved around Catherine's scalp, pressing her damp cheek against his chest. "She loved you too, and she wouldn't have wanted you to be this unhappy."

Catherine sniffed. "You're right. It's just . . . I feel so alone."

"Cate." Nick's arms tightened. "I'm here."

Catherine clutched handfuls of Nick's jacket. He'd said the same thing the night her grandmother had died. "I'm here." Simple words—words meant to comfort, but words that wouldn't last forever.

He'd be gone soon. She *had* kept track of the tally book in the two weeks since her grandmother's death and knew that things at the mine were running smoothly. Before long Greenfield Mine wouldn't need the services of Nicholas Colton. And then what would she do? Find another way to make him stay, to make him be here? She'd made an agreement. She couldn't break it.

"Cate?" Nick cupped her shoulders, holding her at arms's length, looking deep into her green eyes. The tears had stopped. "Are you ready to go back now?"

Catherine nodded, a tentative smile curling her lips. "I suppose I do need to get back to living. Thank you."

Dinner wasn't exactly festive, but Catherine forced herself to enter the conversation as often as she could. Of course, with Nick constantly asking her opinion, and encouraging her by flashing his devilish grin at her, she hadn't much choice. He had a way about him that made her want to smile just looking at him.

"Catherine." Marie laid down her fork, and ran her finger along the golden curls that twisted down the front of her shoulder. "I'm surprised to see you at the table. Nick and I were getting used to dining alone."

"Oh." Catherine blotted her mouth with the

napkin, daring a quick look at Nick. He seemed to take a sudden interest in his turnips. "I'm glad you were here to keep him company, Marie."

"So am I, sister dear. So am I."

Catherine swallowed, trying not to notice the boldly appreciative expression on Marie's face as her eyes lingered on Nick. His stare was still centered on his plate, but then he knew, his wife watched him also.

"Well, I'd like to play some whist," Marie announced when they'd finished eating. "How about you, Nick . . . and of course, you too, Catherine?"

"It was nice of you to ask, but I think I'll go to my room. I'm tired."

"That's too bad, Catherine. We'll see you in the morning, won't we Nick?"

"I'm tired, too." Without glancing Marie's way— he didn't have to visualize the angry expression on her face—he held out his arm for Catherine. "Shall we?"

"I didn't mean to take you from your cards," Catherine said when they'd entered the privacy of their room. Then why did she feel this tiny surge of victory that he had chosen coming with her over staying with Marie?

"I'm not interested in playing games, Catherine."

The deep timbre of his voice played along her spine, sending tingles of anticipation rushing through Catherine's body. Her heart beat faster, and her pulse raced. Turning, she walked towards the window, trying to stop her knees from wobbling. "What does interest you?"

"I think you know."

Catherine gripped the edge of the sill when his hands clutched her shoulders. Lips warm and heady with promise moistened the side of her neck.

"I want you, Cate." Catherine's body wilted against him. "But I won't force you, never that. If it's too soon, I—"

"No." Catherine twisted her face around, brushed her lips across the roughness of his cheek, sought purchase with his mouth. "It's not too soon."

His kiss made her weak. Catherine tried to turn into his arms, but he wouldn't let her. His hands played along the front of her body, cupping her breast, following the lines of her corset to her waist, then lower to press the heel of his palm against the V between her legs.

"Cate." He nipped her earlobe, ran his tongue down the side of her neck. "You taste so good." His fingers fumbled with the buttons down the front of her dress, unfastening a few, then reaching down to press her against the hard bulge she could feel through her skirt and petticoats. How could this much desire for her build in only two weeks? Nick didn't know but he felt like a randy youth eager to experience love for the first time.

Not even realizing what she was doing, Catherine rubbed against him. His groan of desire bordered on impatience, and she found herself helping him with the buttons. Her gown slipped from her shoulders, and Nick pressed kisses to the soft skin between her chemise straps.

"You have a lovely back," he said as his mouth

252

skimmed across it, his hands now pulling the pins from her hair, then pushing down the linen of her shift. "So straight, strong with pride."

"Nick." Catherine felt her knees buckle, and it was only the strong arms surrounding her that kept her upright.

Nick bent and lifted her, carrying her to the bed. Feverishly he shed his clothes, then started on what remained of hers. "I should never touch you until we are both naked. It's too damn frustrating."

A bubble of laughter caught in Catherine's throat when she heard his lament. She stared up at him, trying to suppress her mirth. Not that he appeared humorous—far from it. His broad chest gleamed hard-hewn and bronze in the dim light of dusk. Golden brown curls wedged between his shoulders then arrowed down to the throbbing proof of his desire—proof that caused the ache in Catherine to intensify, but that didn't squelch her levity.

He must have noticed something—perhaps the trembling of her chest as she tried to smother any sound from escaping. His rugged jaw, sporting a dark bristle of beard, angled toward her. Eyelids narrowed speculatively over dark-as-slate eyes.

"Cate?"

"What?" A giggle surrounded the word.

"Is something funny?" His hands stopped wrestling with her stay laces as he studied her.

"No." Catherine squeaked, and then the dam burst. She laughed, the first true sound of joy she'd made in two weeks. She clutched her sides and rolled back and forth, barely able to catch her breath until she saw his face. "It's not you . . . it's . . . naked . . . you said we should get naked first." Catherine sobered with difficulty, biting her bottom lip to keep a chortle in. "I'm sorry." Catherine sensed he wasn't exactly pleased with her reaction. "It just struck me as . . . as . . . funny." Oh no, she was laughing again—hysterically.

Nick stared down at her a moment in disbelief. Granted, his experience with women was varied, but he'd never—never—gotten this reaction before. She looked wildly erotic. Her auburn hair, fired with red highlights splashed across the bed in untamed disarray. A breast that he'd managed to free from the confines of her chemise, thrust toward him, the nipple, pink and puckered. She looked wanton and desirable and as ready for him as he was for her— except she couldn't stop laughing. And suddenly, feeling the release of his own pent-up sorrow, neither could he.

Nick sprawled across the bed, his arm thrown across his eyes and joined her. When he'd laughed so much that tears gathered in the corners of his eyes, Nick rolled over toward Catherine.

One final giggle escaped her as she threw her arms around his neck. "Oh, that felt so good." She looked deep into his gray eyes, willing him to understand, knowing that he had.

"Your laughter . . ." Nick paused and touched the dimples on either side of Catherine's mouth. "Grandmere would approve."

*   *   *

She hadn't been a very good wife.

Catherine opened her eyes the next morning with that thought in her mind. She glanced around the room, found it as empty as her husband's side of the bed and stretched. Grabbing the spindles of the headboard, Catherine lay still for a moment, thinking. No matter how she looked at it, the fact remained. She hadn't been a very good wife. And Nick had been a good husband.

He had! Catherine sat up, impatiently tossing hair behind her shoulder as she realized the truth of her discovery. In the four weeks they'd been married, he'd been supportive, kind, thoughtful, helpful, certainly loving—Catherine's cheeks burned crimson as she remembered last night and the truth of that. In short, Nick was everything she could want from a husband.

Of course their marriage was a business arrangement, but he didn't act as if it were. From the very first day, when he'd let her know that intimacy would be a large part of the arrangement, to yesterday when he'd helped pull her from her melancholy, he'd treated this marriage as if it were real—as if he intended to stay with her.

"I'm here," he'd said. Catherine pulled on her wrapper, and slid out of bed. She liked having him here, liked being married to him, but would he stay? There had been a time, last night, when she'd wrapped her legs around him to draw him deeper inside her, that she'd thought he might.

Certainly he couldn't make love to her as he had, and not feel something for her. And if he cared for her, couldn't he be persuaded to stay at Greenfield?

She could offer him the mine, what was left of the plantation—

Catherine broke off in mid thought and moved to the mirror. Brushing back her hair she studied her face. True he'd agreed to marry her after she'd offered him a portion of the mine, but were those the types of things that would persuade a man like Nicholas Colton to stay? Were possessions what he craved? Or could she believe what he'd said last night as he'd reached for her a second time.

"You, Catherine," he'd said his voice husky with desire. "I want you."

Catherine felt her face flush and glanced at her reflection to see that thoughts of Nick had indeed colored her cheeks. But more, it had brought a sparkle to her eyes and a smile to her lips. She looked undeniably pretty.

Was this what Nick saw when he told her how beautiful she was? If so, he was going to see more of it.

Grabbing a brush, Catherine worked it through her hair. She wanted Nick to stay, to forget about the agreement and stay married to her. And she was going to do her best to see that he did. She hadn't been a good wife—but that was about to change. Catherine tied a ribbon around her curls, forgoing her usual prim chignon, and opened the wardrobe door.

If he liked her to wear pretty clothes, she'd do it. Well, she'd wear the prettiest thing she had, Catherine amended as she riffled through the gowns. There wasn't much to choose from, but she finally decided on a sprigged lawn gown covered with pink and blue roses. Marie had ordered the gown made, then refused to wear it because she thought the neckline unbecoming. Somehow it had been given to Catherine, though she'd never worn it either. But she would today.

And she'd pack Nicholas a dinner and take it to the mine. Perhaps they could have a picnic like the one they had the day after their wedding. Catherine felt a fluttering in her stomach at the thought.

Catherine placed her hand over her heart and stared back into the mirror. Yes, she'd surprise Nick, and she'd be a good wife.

"You sure this is going to work, boss?"

Nick removed his hat, checked the Davy lamp, and wiped the sweat off his forehead with his sleeve. A black stain marred the already dirty fabric. "It's been proven to do the job in several other mines."

"Yea, but I don't know. I've always been of the opinion that fire and mines don't mix," Sampson said as he leaned on the handle of his pick ax.

"You've got a point, but we have to do something about this methane gas." Nick peered into the furnace they'd dug at the base of a new shaft.

"The air shafts—"

"Aren't doing a damn bit of good, and you know it. Now hand me that ax." Nick took the tool from his bottom boss, already regretting the tone he'd used. Sampson was scared. Nick could see it in his stance, in the tight way he held his mouth. He could sense it. And why shouldn't he be? Hell, Nick was scared. The

257

temperature below ground was a comfortable sixty-five to seventy degrees, but Nick could feel the sweat running down his back.

Nick wedged himself into the opening where they'd already installed an air-tight door. "I read about this before I left England, and since I've been here I've spoken to some miners who've used this method." Nick wasn't sure if he talked to help relieve Sampson's fear, or his own.

"It's pretty simple really. Follows one of nature's laws."

"Yea, well, the only one of nature's laws I know is methane and fire make a big boom."

Chuckling, Nick tested the door. "You should be a scientist, Sampson." It fit tight. "Seriously though, there's no need for you to stay down here. I can handle the rest myself."

"Hell, Mr. Nick, am I the bottom boss or not?"

"You are."

"And are we at the bottom of this damn mine?"

"We are that." Nick tried to ignore the hiss of methane gas escaping from the coal.

"Then I guess I've got as much right to be down here as you."

Nick looked over at the man he'd come to like and admire in the short time he'd known him. He intended to stay. And though Nick might prefer he not take the risk, he knew there was nothing he could do about it. "Well, I just don't want to hear any lip if this doesn't work."

"Hell, if this don't work, neither of us are going to be hearing anything but harps and angels batting their wings together."

"Mighty sure of where you're going to end up, aren't you?" Nick squeezed out of the opening and stood as straight as he could in the low-ceilinged tunnel.

"I figure I've lived my life in hell holes like this, God's going to send me to Heaven when I die just to give me a change of pace."

"Irreverent, bastard." Nick checked his Davy lamp again. You could never be too sure. "Guess it's time to say your prayers, if you know any."

"Wait." Sampson's hand stayed Nick's arm as he reached for the match. "Tell me again how this works. If I'm going to be blown to kingdom come and back, I at least want to make sure I know why."

Shale flicked off the wall clattering to the floor as Nick hunched down. Dampness seeped through his clothing and boots, mingled with his nervous sweat. He was damned uncomfortable, wanting nothing more than to get this over with—one way or the other, but Sampson had volunteered to come down in the mine with him. He owed him a few extra minutes—an explanation—if that's what he wanted.

"When we start the fire . . . what's wrong?"

Sampson grimaced. "Just have a hard time listening to you say that word. Go ahead."

"When we . . . you know . . . at the bottom of this exhaust shaft, the heated air from the smoldering fire will create a vacuum. Then we'll open this door, and fresh air will be sucked down the other shaft and along the tunnel. It will pull the gassy air with it, through the furnace and out the exhaust shaft."

"Sounds simple enough."

"It is. And it's been proven to work. Now do you think we can get on with it?"

Bent nearly double at the waist, Sampson nodded. "Guess we better."

"Good." Nick reached for his match.

"Does the missus know you're doing this?"

"What?" He paused, looking back over his shoulder.

"You heard me. Does Miss Catherine know you're down here risking yourself on this here mine."

"No. No, she doesn't. But I'm certain she would agree with what I'm doing." After all, it was for the good of the mine. And wasn't that the main thing she cared about? With trembling fingers, Nick lit the match.

Once he began and the earth didn't shatter around him, sending tons of rock tumbling about his head, Nick found he worked more confidently. Opening the door to the furnace, he motioned for Sampson to follow him along the tunnel. Nick's Davy lamp cast rainbow shadows on the black coal as they walked along the underground tracks between the giant timbers. They passed cars loaded with coal, mules waiting to be led toward the shaft. And they noticed the draft as the furnace forced fresh air along the tunnel.

Watching the ever enlarging circle of light overhead, Nick and Sampson rode to the surface. "It's close to noon," Nick said as he vaulted out of the basket. "Take a break till after dinner. I'm going to get cleaned up and then do some work in my office."

"It worked, didn't it, boss?"

Nick clamped Sampson's shoulder. "You bet it did."

Nick dove beneath the crystal clear pool then swam for the shore. His arms sliced through the water till he reached the point where he could stand, then he strode toward the sun dappled grass. It was so pleasant here, he could stay forever. Memories of the time Catherine had brought his dinner sent tightness through his groin.

"Damn." He better get dressed and back to work before he found himself back at the house, dragging his wife to their bedroom. Sluicing water off his face with two hands, Nick glanced under the willow tree. Nothing. He squinted, then looked again.

"Lose something, Nick?"

Nick jerked his head around in time to see Marie emerge from behind a clump of hollies. "What do you want?"

"Not a very nice greeting, Nick, for someone who has your clothes." She pulled a shirt and trousers from behind her back.

"Toss them over here, Marie."

"And miss the fun?"

Cool water lapped Nick's thighs, a startling contrast to the slow burn of his temper. "There's no fun, Marie. Now just hand over my clothes and run along home."

"No fun?" Marie cocked her head, then deliberately began unbuttoning her dress. "Watching you swim is fun. And I'm sure we could find several other things to do in the water that would be equally amusing."

"What does it take to convince you I'm not interested?"

Marie giggled. "A good enough reason why you shouldn't be."

"Catherine."

Marie's laugh was brittle. Her fingers stopped their downward journey on her gown. "I won't tell your wife, if that's what worries you."

"It isn't."

"Well?" Marie shrugged.

Catherine glanced around the mine sight. Everyone seemed to be busy, and no one noticed her. Men worked the lift, urging the mules to pull the coal-filled cowe to the surface. Still others waited to unload the coal and sort it by size before it was loaded on wagons and taken to the Chesterfield Railroad. From there gravity would propel the coal-laden train to Manchester on the James River.

Yes, everything on the surface seemed to be running smoothly. She was sure it was the same down in the labyrinth of tunnels beneath the earth where diggers and mule drivers toiled. But, Nick was nowhere to be seen.

Catherine scanned the area again, after all, most of the men were nearly unrecognizable beneath the sooty coal dust. But that wouldn't hide Nick's height, the way he moved. With a feeling of disappointment, Catherine realized he just wasn't here.

"Hey, Missus Colton. You looking for the boss?" Sampson stepped out of the wash-house, drying his face on a linen towel.

"Yes." Catherine brushed back a strand of hair, conscious of the new way she'd fixed it, conscious also of the basket she clutched in her hands. The last time she'd brought Nick his dinner there had been snickers and insinuations from the miners—and she hadn't planned to do anything but talk to her husband. How much worse would it be this time. Could Sampson tell she had seduction on her mind?

Catherine gave herself an inward shrug. So what if he did? Nick was her husband. She had a right to seduce him if she liked. "I'm sorry . . . I wasn't listening."

"I said, the boss went to get cleaned up and then to do some work in his office."

"Oh. Thank you." Catherine turned toward the path.

"He sure is something, that man of yours."

"I beg your pardon?" Catherine stopped and looked back at Sampson who was chuckling and walking toward her.

"Cool as a cucumber he was this morning. Me, I was scared, and I don't mind telling you."

"Scared of what, Sampson? I don't understand."

"Aw, hell . . . begging your pardon ma'am . . . I'll bet I wasn't suppose to say nothing to you about it."

Fear inched its icy fingers down Catherine's spine. What had happened? If there had been an accident surely someone would have let her know, and the colliers worked so complacently so nothing could be wrong. But what did Sampson mean about being scared? Catherine sucked in a breath. "What happened?"

"Well, maybe I shouldn't—"

"Sampson. Tell me." Catherine clutched the basket handle till her knuckles were white.

Shifting his weight, Sampson stared at his boss' wife a second, then shrugged. "We put a furnace in the mine this morning."

"A furnace. Whatever for?"

"Boss said it would help circulate the air, help get rid of the methane build-up. And I think it's working," he added with a grin.

"That's good." Catherine smiled back. She wished Nick would have mentioned it to her first, but . . . "Why were you frightened?"

"Hell, lady . . . begging your pardon ma'am . . . but you start building a fire in a mine and well . . .

Catherine's eyes flew open. "That could be dangerous."

"You got that right."

"And you say my husband was there with you?" How dare he expose himself to such danger and not even tell her.

"Hell, he's the one that done it." Sampson didn't bother to beg her pardon this time, but Catherine didn't notice. She was already heading along the path to the old cabin.

Nicholas Colton had a lot of nerve risking his life

like that—and in her mine. Did he stop for one moment to think about how she'd feel if something happened to him? Probably not. Hadn't she lost enough people she loved lately without his going off and pulling some dumb stunt?

Catherine stopped dead in her tracks. What had she been thinking? It had been about people she loved and she had put Nicholas Colton in that category. "It must have been the shock of learning what he'd done," Catherine mumbled, then shook her head.

Catherine sank down on a fallen log along the path, not even noticing the squirrel she inadvertently chased away from his dinner. No, that wasn't it. She loved him, honest to goodness loved him. That explained why she'd resolved this morning to be a good wife to him—why she'd dressed up, and kept her hair down and packed his favorite foods in the basket. A smile tilted the corners of her mouth.

She loved him. Catherine wasn't certain how it had happened, but here was no denying it. She worried her bottom lip. But how did he feel about her? Standing up, brushing the chipped bark from the back of her skirt, Catherine decided she'd just have to find out.

"I'm telling you for the last time to toss my clothes over here and be on your way, Marie."

"Oh, you sound so tough. Are you tough, Nick? What are you going to do to little old me?"

Nick didn't dignify her silly chatter with an

answer. He simply strode out of the water, and advanced on her. He saw the first hint of doubt shadow her blue eyes—the first inkling that he wasn't playing games. She covered it quickly, yet her voice wasn't as lightly flirtatious when she again spoke.

"Now wait a minute, Nick." Marie took a step backward, brushing into a blackberry bramble as he approached her. "You'll get me all wet. Wait till I take my clothes off."

"You're not taking your clothes off, Marie. You're giving me mine." With a none too gentle motion he yanked the shirt and pants from her grasp. "Now get out of here." Turning in disgust, Nick shook the hand she placed on his arm away. Damn, wouldn't the woman ever learn?

Jerking around, Nick grabbed her shoulders with his hands. He loomed over her. He frightened her. And he was glad. He'd never hurt a woman before, but with this one he was tempted to make an exception. "Now you listen and you listen good, Marie, because I'm only going to say this once." His words were low, a mere angry hiss, so the smile that brightened her face surprised him.

He realized she wasn't looking at him, but to the side, a split second before he heard her syrupy sweet voice call out a greeting.

"Hello, Catherine."

Nick twisted around, the air leaving his body as if he'd been pole-axed. His gaze met green eyes, open wide, staring at him as if the punch in the gut that hit him had landed a blow against her. He had no idea how long they stood there, him naked as a jaybird,

266

and her clutching a wicker basket, until she whirled around and started back the path. But her movement spurred him to action.

"Cate," he yelled, starting across the clearing. "Would you come back here and listen to me?" But his only answer was the wind rustling through the pines.

Chapter Thirteen

"Cate! Will you wait a damn minute?"

Catherine ignored the yelled request, as well as the healthy dose of cursing that punctuated it as she hurried back toward the cabin, and the path toward the house. The wicker basket bounced against her knee with each step, a painful reminder of the scene she'd just witnessed. She almost threw the stupid thing into the ferns and brambles, but decided *he* would find it. Then he'd know how upset she was.

"Don't think about it," Catherine chastised herself. "Just don't. . . ." But it was too late. Her mind was already reliving the moment she'd come into the clearing. The moment she'd seen Nick with her sister.

Trudging through the underbrush, Catherine took a shortcut, yanking at her skirt when it caught on a blackberry bush. "Well what had you expected?" she mumbled, "Undying love?" Catherine blinked back tears.

She'd known from the beginning Nicholas Colton

liked Marie. Hadn't she noticed the very first time she saw him the way he smiled and flirted with—

"Damnit, I asked you to wait." Nick's hand caught Catherine's arm, swinging her around to face him.

"I don't want to wait." Catherine jerked on her arm, but couldn't dislodge Nick's grip.

"Well, you're going to have to now, aren't you?"

Catherine twisted her arm again, gritting her teeth, but there was no getting free of his grasp. "Let me go," she hissed.

"No. Not until we talk about what you thought you saw back there." Nick wasn't proud of using his superior strength, but he knew the moment he let her go, she'd high-tail it back to the house.

"I don't *think* I saw anything."

"Aw, come on, Cate. You don't honestly think I . . . She's your sister for chrisakes!"

Catherine raised her chin, however she let her eyes travel slowly, disdainfully, down his entire length. "I would prefer to conduct this conversation after you've put on your clothes."

Nick glanced down at himself, embarrassed when he felt a flush creep up his face. Bending over he tried to straighten out the pants he still held. "Hell, Catherine, you ran away so fast, I didn't have—"

"I did not run away."

A lift of his brow told her he thought otherwise.

"I simply saw no reason to stay when you were obviously occupied."

"But I wasn't . . ." Nick hopped on one foot as he tried to step into his pants. "Ouch! Damn brambles. Listen, Cate, if I let go of you will you promise not to run?"

"I didn't run!"

"Walk, then! Will you promise to stay here and listen to me?" He felt like a bumbling idiot trying to pull on his pants with one hand while he held onto his wife with the other.

"There really is nothing for us to talk about." Her chin climbed another notch. Why did he have to draw this out? All she wanted to do was go hide somewhere before she began to cry hysterically.

"Your choice, Cate. Either promise to stay while I pull on my clothes, or I say my peace *au naturel.*"

"I'll stay."

Nick loosened his grip, felt her stiffen. "You're not going to run, are you?"

"I said I'd stay." Catherine jerked away, crossing her arms over her chest and stared at him with what she hoped was utter contempt. She wished she could find his body repugnant, but even after all that had happened, she couldn't. Why did he have to look so good naked?

Nick fastened his pants and shrugged into his shirt. "Damn, there are a lot of thorns around here. Wish I'd have brought my boots."

Catherine glanced down at his feet. They definitely had run into their share of sharp thorns and thistles. No wonder he'd been cursing so much when he'd chased her. The soles, she noticed when he lifted each to inspect them, were covered with bruises, and were bleeding from several places. She firmly stifled her inclination to pity him.

After all, she hadn't asked him to chase her. And she certainly hadn't requested that he have an affair with her sister. But apparently he had, and she would

271

never let him know how much it hurt her. She had her pride. For the moment that was all she had.

"Listen, Cate. . . ." Nick looked up at her his eyes imploring. What in the hell was he supposed to say? I didn't do anything. Your sister, whom you usually refuse to hear anything bad about, followed me to the creek and tried to seduce me. That didn't ring true to his own ears . . . and he knew it was.

Besides, even if she did believe Marie had initiated the encounter, how could he convince her that he hadn't wanted any part of it? Hell, before he met Catherine, he'd have jumped at a chance to have an attractive, willing woman in his arms. He feared she'd never understand why that had changed— damn if he understood it himself. But he had to try.

"Cate, I—"

"There really is no need for explanations, Nick." For goodness sake. She'd watched the play of emotions cross his face as he'd tried to think one up.

"What?" Nick studied her incredulously. Her tone had mellowed, and her scowl softened. Was she simply going to take his word for it? He couldn't understand his good fortune.

"I said you needn't bother making excuses."

"Well, I wasn't going to make any excuses." Why should he when he'd done nothing wrong?

"I'm glad we understand each other." Catherine gave a curt nod and started for the path.

"Hey, wait a minute!" Nick wondered if his roar could be heard down at the mine. "You gave your word to stay till I had my say."

Catherine stopped. He had his nerve, yelling at her when by all rights, she should be screaming and crying, pummeling his chest and tearing his hair out. But then he'd know how upset she was—and how much she cared. Well, if he thought no more of her than to have her own sister as his mistress, then she'd never let him know her true feelings.

Straightening her back, she faced him, trying to keep her voice calm. "I thought you were finished."

"Well, I wasn't."

"Fine."

Nick combed his fingers through his damp hair. What was wrong with her. Why wasn't she angry? Hell, why wasn't she crying? She simply stood there looking at him as if he were a fly on the wall that annoyed her. Where was the hurt he'd seen in her eyes when she'd first seen him and Marie? Nick took a deep breath. "What did you mean when you said I didn't have to make excuses?"

"Simply that." Catherine felt the pressure growing in her, knew she had to get away from him before her true feelings burst forth. "You don't owe me any explanations. That wasn't part of our agreement."

Nick's jaw dropped. "Our agreement! For God's sake, Catherine, you found me with your sister, and your talking about our agreement?"

What did he want her to talk about, that she felt as if someone had pierced her heart with an arrow? Never! "That *is* the basis of our relationship."

"The basis of our . . ." Again Nick raked his fingers through his hair, jerking his head away to stare unseeing into the underbrush, then looked back at his wife. "I can't believe this . . . you."

Catherine fought the impulse to reach out to him when she saw the hurt in the depths of his gray eyes.

How dare he act the injured party. He who blatantly flaunted his affairs before her—his affairs with her own sister! It probably insulted his ego that he didn't have both sisters madly in love with him. The rogue! Catherine tamped down her anger. Showing that would prove her as vulnerable as showing sadness. "I really see no reason to discuss this further."

He couldn't believe it. All this time he'd thought she cared for him. Oh, he'd known she didn't love him, but he'd thought she had some feelings for him. But she didn't. She didn't care at all. And Nick couldn't imagine why that hurt so damn much. "You're a hard woman, Cate. I knew you were strong, but I never expected this . . ." Nick made a sweeping motion with his hand, then let it fall to his side.

Catherine almost laughed. Somehow she'd convinced him of her toughness when she felt like a quivering mass on the inside. Perhaps she should go to Richmond and join an acting company.

Well, she'd certainly convinced him she didn't care about his affair with Marie. She could at least take pride in that—then why did the look of disdain he gave her hurt nearly as much as his betrayal. For goodness sakes, the man was a devil. If she continued staring into those multifaceted gray eyes of his, she'd forget what she'd seen and beg him not to think ill of her. Catherine turned away, noting with a pang of regret that he did nothing to stop her.

Taking a deep breath, holding it, Catherine clutched the basket handle, driving a frayed piece of wicker into her thumb. "Under the circumstances, I would appreciate you removing your belongings from my room."

"It will be my pleasure, Catherine."

Catherine felt the air rush out of her, silently cursed the tears that stung her eyelids. "The room at the back of the hall is still vacant."

"I prefer the cabin."

Catherine nodded and started off through the underbrush toward the house, thanking God that Nick couldn't see the tears streaming down her face.

"Damn woman," Nick muttered, watching her go. "Damn cold-hearted woman." He kicked at a tree stump remembering too late that he was bare foot. "Damn!" Nick grabbbed his foot cursing everything from trees to women, ending with a blistering assessment of one in particular.

When he'd finished, he felt a little better, even if his foot did not. Catherine didn't care about their marriage—fine. He could handle that. After all, this entire farce sure as hell hadn't been his idea. He'd planned to call the wedding off, would have called it off if he hadn't felt sorry for her. Well, that should teach him to mind his own business.

From now on he'd stick with one of the first lessons he learned in the mines. He'd take care of himself and let others take care of themselves. And that included Miss Catherine Brousseau. Hell, she wasn't Catherine Brousseau, she was Catherine Colton. Well, divorce had been part of her damn agreement too, and he'd take care of that soon enough.

Nick picked his way back toward the creek, careful to avoid stepping on any thistles or prickly vines. What a fool he'd been to go running after her like that. He'd only done it because he thought she was upset. Ha! What a joke. She probably thanked this excuse to get him out of her room. "Fine with me."

"What's fine with you, Nick?"

Nick stopped in his tracks. He'd reentered the clearing by the creek, spotted his boots, and was heading toward them when the voice brought back the reason all the trouble had started. Marie. How could he have forgotten about Marie?

Ignoring her, Nick grabbed up his boots, then plopped down beside the water to pull on his socks.

"Did you catch up with Catherine?"

Nick grimaced when the wool sock caught on some torn skin, but he kept his eyes and his mind on the task at hand.

"What's the matter, Nick, couldn't you explain away what she saw with her own eyes?"

Nick stood, stomping into his boots. With easy strides, he headed for the mine.

"Nick?" Marie caught up with him and reached for his arm.

Nick jerked away from her. "Don't touch me. I don't want to feel you. I don't want to see you." His eyes narrowed and the words hissed through clinched teeth. "If I were you, Marie, I'd get out of my sight before I forget the gentlemanly behavior I learned from Travis Fielding, and revert to acting like a miner from the slums of New Castle."

Thankfully, Marie didn't press the issue. He didn't want to think about, much less repeat, some of the things he'd seen done to women, and men, too, when he was growing up. But for Marie, he'd have dredged it up. But there was no need, because she glared at him with undisguised hatred, her blue eyes as cold as horefrost. She turned on her heel, and headed off toward the house.

Nick snorted. She probably planned to fabricate some scathing lies about him to tell Catherine. It was almost funny, and Nick might have laughed if he didn't feel like his gut was on fire. Marie would be wasting her breath, because nothing she could say would matter to Catherine. She just didn't give a damn.

Nick trudged back to the mine, grabbed up his Davy lamp and headed for the supply shed.

"Hey, boss, what took you so long? Must have been some lunch your wife had in that basket."

Nick glared at Sampson. "Anybody ever tell you to mind your own damn business?" he growled at the black-haired giant, before slamming shut the shed door.

"Guess it ain't none of my business, but I never know'd Mr. Nick to pass up fried chicken."

Catherine stopped her hasty exit from the kitchen and glanced back at Betsy. She was bent over the work table, unloading the picnic basket that Catherine had unceremoniously flung on a chair when she'd rushed into the room. Betsy looked up and gave her young mistress a knowing wink.

Betsy's incorrect assumption brought on a fresh flood of tears, and Catherine jerked her head around before the servant could see them. "I don't think he was hungry," she mumbled before lifting the skirts of her flower covered gown and racing toward the house.

Betsy dropped the drumstick she'd lifted from the basket and rushed to the open doorway. She stood there staring after Catherine and rubbing her chin when Marie stormed around the side of the white-washed building. "What you in such a dither—"

"Have you seen Catherine?" Marie interrupted.

"Sure I has. She left here, heading toward the main house. What's wrong?"

"Nothing that I can't handle." Following the garden path to the main house, Marie paused only a moment when she heard Betsy's warning.

"You be nice to her now, Miss Marie. Poor Miss Catherine looked plenty upset."

Marie bared her teeth in a facsimile of a smile. "Of course I'll be nice to her. Isn't that what sisters are for?" Marie looked around sweetly. "It's husbands that need watching."

"What are you talking about, Miss Marie?"

Marie sighed. "I'm afraid Mr. Colton isn't the man we thought he was."

"Did he do something to Miss Catherine?" Betsy's black eyes narrowed.

Marie lowered her head demurely. "I really shouldn't gossip with the servants," she shook her blond curls, "but I know how fond of Catherine you are."

"What'd that man do to her?"

Marie sniffed and brought her hand up to cover her quivering lip. "Catherine would never forgive me if I told anyone. But I don't think Nicholas Colton will

278

be around to cause trouble very much longer."

Betsy gasped. "He's leaving her?"

"Or she's getting rid of him . . . I'm not certain which." Her curls bobbed again. "I really better go to her."

"Oh, sure, Miss Marie. No good you standing around talking to me when your sister needs you." She turned and walked back into the kitchen, muttering to herself. "Imagine that. Mr. Nick treating Miss Catherine bad. Miss Lillian so sure he's the answer to our prayers. You just never can tell."

Marie hurried into the house and up the stairs. She never hesitated when she reached Catherine's door, lifting her hand and rapping on it.

Catherine buried her head further in her pillow, ignoring the sound.

"Catherine, I know you're in there, so you might as well open the door."

Catherine moaned at the sound of her sister's voice. When she'd first heard the knock, she'd assumed it to be Nick, but she didn't want to see Marie any more than her husband. She impatiently scrubbed at her damp eyes. "Please go away, I'm resting."

"Oh, fiddle dee. We both know you're in there crying your eyes out. That's what I want to talk to you about."

"Go away, Marie."

"I won't. Not until you let me in so I can explain. Oh, Catherine, I couldn't stand it if you hated me."

Catherine flopped onto her back, throwing her arm across her aching eyes. "I don't hate you."

"I won't believe you unless you open this door."

Catching her breath on a sob, Catherine brushed a wet strand of hair away from her face. "Marie, please."

"I'm leaving Greenfield, Catherine. I need to talk to you."

Getting out of the bed, brushing the wrinkles from her dress, Catherine went to the door. She sighed, sensing she was making a mistake, but unable to help herself. With a click she turned the key in the lock, and opened the door. Marie rushed into the room.

"Are you all right? I've been so worried."

"I'm fine, Marie. Now what did you mean about leaving?"

"Well, you don't look fine. Your eyes are all red and your cheeks are flushed."

"Marie. You mentioned leaving." Catherine chanced a glance toward her mirror, realizing Marie's assessment wasn't far from the truth.

"I can't stay here. Not as long as *he* remains. What if he tries to force himself on me again?"

Catherine walked to the window, looking out into the garden below. The trees still swayed softly in the breeze, the flowers still leaned toward the sun. Everything seemed exactly the same—except her. She faced Marie. "Excuse me for saying this, but my hus—Nick didn't appear to be using force."

"Oh, Catherine." Marie rushed forward, taking Catherine's hands in hers. "That's what I was afraid you'd think. And maybe you're right. He wasn't using force—this time."

"Th . . . this time?"

"Catherine, I hate to have to tell you this. Actually,

280

I thought you knew, but then you up and married him."

"Knew what?" Catherine pulled her hands away from Marie's and grabbed her sister's shoulders. "Knew what?"

"That Nick has been after me since he first arrived here. I tried to resist him. I really did, but . . ."

Catherine turned away, staring again into the tranquil garden. She didn't want to believe what Marie told her. When she'd seen the two of them together—her husband and sister—Catherine had thought them equally guilty. She had no false beliefs about Marie. But Nick hadn't even bothered to deny his guilt. And now Marie spoke words that were too easy to believe.

How often had Catherine replayed the scene in her mind when she saw Nick for the first time? He'd looked at Marie then as only a man looks at a woman when he desires her.

And he was good at seduction. Catherine, to her misfortune, could attest to that. She'd planned for their marriage to be in name only, but he'd worked his magic about her, till she couldn't help wanting him. She'd even convinced herself that she loved him. He was impossible to resist. Could she blame Marie for succumbing to the same sensual spell?

Catherine glanced at her sister who'd plucked a handkerchief from her sleeve and dabbed at her eyes with it. "Don't cry."

"B . . . but you can never forgive me."

Catherine sighed. "Yes I can."

Marie tried a tentative smile. "Then you'll send

him away?"

"Send him away?" Even after all she knew of him, that thought tightened her throat. But it made no difference. "I can't do that."

Marie's hands dropped to her side. "Why ever not? We could send him away, then sell this place and start a new life. Grandmere is gone, and—"

"I can't send him away, and I can't sell Greenfield, even if I wanted to, which I don't. Nick owns one fourth of the mine."

"What?"

It amazed Catherine how quickly her sister's mood could change from despair to anger. "He owns . . . ," Catherine began, then gripped the window sill and leaned out. "What difference does it make? I told you we had a business agreement."

"But I thought you paid him to marry you."

Catherine's laugh was derisive. "With what? The mine wasn't producing enough coal to make sufficient money to pay the debts we had, let alone take on a new one." The long silence that followed her disclosure began to make Catherine uncomfortable. She turned back to her sister in time to see an expression of hatred on Marie's face. Unconsciously Catherine stepped back until the window sill pushed into her back.

"You had to make it complicated, didn't you Catherine?" Marie's voice sounded harsh. "Why couldn't you just sell the mine like any normal person? Or John. If you wanted to marry so badly, why didn't you marry him?" Marie advanced on her sister. "But no. That was too easy. And Catherine always has to show how good she is at finding unusual ways to handle problems."

"Marie, I—"

"Oh, shut up, Catherine. I don't want to hear any of your excuses. We both know that's how you got Daddy to leave everything to you. You were always helping out with the mine and taking care of things. Grandmere and Grandpere's little helper," she sneered. "Daddy's little helper. Even Momma, who should have loved me best because I was pretty, thought you were wonderful."

Catherine's hand fluttered to her throat, and she stared at her sister with uncomprehending eyes. She could barely believe what she heard. As far as she could remember, neither her parents nor her grandparents had ever shown any preference for her over Marie.

True, Grandpere and she had shared a common interest in the mine, and she had taken over much of her father's work. But that was only because he didn't do it himself, and someone had to do it. However, she'd never tried to curry favor, nor did she think she had. Papa had left the mine to her because he knew she could take care of it—and take care of Marie. Her sister had to understand that.

"Marie, with the money from the coal we sell, I can provide for you. And you don't have to worry about Nick. I'll talk to him, tell him to stay away from you." Marie's shrill cackle made the hair at Catherine's nape stand on end.

"Do you honestly think I care about that?" Marie gathered her skirts and turned toward the door.

"Nick loves me, Catherine." She smiled. "That's right, look surprised, but it's true. He told me so. Your husband, that you bought and paid for, loves me." She ran her fingers over the door handle. "But you can have him back, because I'm going away."

"Where?" The word squeezed through Catherine's tight throat.

"Away from here—away from you." Marie slammed the door as she left.

Catherine sank down into the nearest chair, her head spinning. She'd guessed before that her sister felt animosity toward her, but she'd never imagined it ran this deep. Marie's words, her actions, had seemed, had seemed . . . Catherine couldn't admit, even to herself that her sister had acted deranged.

"No," Catherine whispered. "She was only upset." But it hit Catherine suddenly that she, not her sister, had a right to be upset. Catherine was the wronged party, the jilted wife. Burying her face in her hands, Catherine prepared herself for tears that would not come. She was all cried out. First Grandmere, then Marie, and then Nick. All the people she'd loved. All people who'd left her.

Standing up, brushing hair from her face, Catherine walked to the washstand. Well, maybe they were gone, but she still had herself, and she refused to sit around feeling sorry for herself. Catherine poured water into the basin, and splashed it onto her tear-stained face.

So Nick loved Marie, did he? Well, he could have her. They could have each other. Catherine tried to ignore the painful sensation around her heart. She could forget about Nicholas Colton. She could! All she had to do was set her mind to it.

The mine seemed to be running efficiently, and when he left, she'd hire someone else to run it. After all, Marie had been right about one thing. Nick was bought and paid for. She could do the same thing again, only this time there would be no marriage vows or emotional involvement.

After brushing her hair into a bun at the back of her head, Catherine changed her dress and descended the stairs to the library. She still had time to go over some figures before supper. She only hoped she could eat. There was a knot in her stomach, and her throat ached with unshed tears.

Catherine leaned her head back against the chair, all her fine intentions crumbling about her. Tears ran unchecked down her cheeks. "Damn you, Nicholas Colton," she sighed.

"I don't know about this, Marie."

Turning abruptly, her ruffled skirts swaying about her, Marie looked across the parlor at Windy Hill. John Parker paced back and forth in front of the marble fireplace. "Are you saying I can't stay here?"

"Well, not exactly. . . ."

"John, she threw me out . . . my own sister. She's just so insanely jealous of her husband—as if I'd want him." Marie moved toward John when she saw him stiffen. "I've no place else to go. Besides." She smiled up at him. "I thought you'd be pleased to see me."

"I am." John reached for her hands, but she pulled them away.

"Well, you don't seem like it."

"It's just that people might talk if you stay here."

"What do I care what people say?" Marie pulled a lace-trimmed handkerchief from her flounced sleeve. "I've had such a terrible day. First Nick Colton tried to force himself on me—"

"That bastard!"

"Then Catherine. She was awful—yelling and screaming such terrible things." Marie paused, then looked up at John imploringly. "She'll never let me have my share of the mine—never."

John put his arm around Marie's rounded shoulders. "I don't know what else we can do. I've had Stevens down there causing trouble, stealing powder and—"

"Oh, Stevens has no imagination, and I'm beginning to wonder if you do either."

"But, Marie, what else can we do? The fire didn't work, and obviously marrying Catherine is out, thanks to that damn Colton. I'd love to get my hands on him. I'd—"

"Shush, John. We all know you had your chance with Nick and came out on the short end. Now don't take offense. I know it wasn't your fault, but we can't go off letting our emotions rule us. What we need is a plan."

John poured wine from the decanter for himself, silently offering Marie a glass. "Maybe we should forget the whole thing. Sure I'd love to see something bad happen to Colton, but we don't seem to be getting anyplace. You can stay here, we can marry, and—"

"What kind of man are you?" Marie rushed to his

side. "Colton beats you up, threatens you, and you're willing to forgive and forget?" She clutched his arm. "And what about me? I deserve part of Greenfield. It's mine and I want it. I can't just ignore what they've done to me. Nick and Catherine have to pay, and pay dearly."

Tongues, tongues... the smooth pull of its mate
glided, until... Catherine's arms wound around her

and blue roses. Marie had ordered ... made, then refused to ... because ... the

Chapter Fourteen

"Is there anything else?" Nick asked staring at his wife. He wished he didn't have an almost uncontrollable urge to leap across the desk and shake her till she responded to him in some way—in any way. She simply listened to his mining report, not meeting his eyes, rarely showing any emotion. No anger, no hate, no desire. Nothing. He cleared his throat, reminding her that he'd asked a question. She seemed to have forgotten he sat in the library with her.

"What? Oh, yes. There is one more thing." Catherine hesitated to question him about the discrepancy she'd found. Hearing his explanation would mean that he'd stay in her presence longer, and Catherine didn't know if she could stand that. It took all of her self-control to resist breaking down in front of him. How many times during these weeks since she'd seen him and Marie by the creek, had she been tempted to throw herself into his arms and beg him for an explanation? But then her memory would spring to life. She'd see him again, standing naked in the sunshine, his large hands cupping Marie's shoulders, and she'd have a hard time controlling her tears.

"Well . . . ?" Why was she dragging this out? Wasn't it bad enough that she'd forced him out of her life, did she have to torment him, too?

Catherine took a calming breath. "There's black powder missing."

Nick's gaze shot up and met hers. "How do you know that?"

"Do you deny it?"

"No I don't deny it." Nick pushed back his chair and stood, leaning forward to brace his hands on the edge of her desk. "I just asked how you knew." He'd asked Sampson to keep quiet about the robbery, and Nick sure as hell hadn't told her.

Catherine rose, feeling at a distinct disadvantage with him looming over her. "If you must know, I noticed a discrepancy in the inventory of supplies. But that is hardly the point."

Nick shrugged. "What is?"

Oh, he was so infuriating. Catherine clinched her teeth and angled herself across the desk, meeting his stare with her own. "What happened to the explosives? I always keep careful account of them."

"Meaning, I don't?"

"Meaning, what happened to the powder?"

"Someone stole it." Damn, he hadn't meant to tell her that. There was no reason for her to worry about this. But she'd made him so angry with her bossy ways.

"Stole it?" Catherine felt the air rush out of her as she sank back into the chair. Her hands gripped the wooden arms. "Who?"

Nick dropped back into his chair. "I don't know." He raked long fingers through his hair. A few people came to mind when it first happened, but . . ." Shaking his head, Nick continued. "I don't have any proof."

Leaning forward in her chair, Catherine searched his face. "But there are those you suspect. Any of the men?"

"No. We all work together pretty well. I trust them."

Catherine didn't stop to analyze why, if Nick trusted them, then so did she. She simply knew there was no more reason to pursue that course. "Then who?"

Lounging back, studying her with narrowed eyes, Nick decided there was no reason not to tell her. After all, they were just hunches. "It crossed my mind that Stevens might have something to do with it. I'm probably not high on his list of favorite people right now." Nick hesitated. He didn't know how she'd take his next idea. "Or John Parker. Thought it might be him."

"I don't know." Catherine bit her bottom lip. "I can't see John doing something like that. Besides he has access to all the powder he needs. And he certainly doesn't want for money."

"That's true. But I'm not sure whoever broke into the storage shed really wanted what they took. Could have just been trying to harass us, spook the miners so they'd quit." He paused. "And as for Parker, seems to me we can't be sure what he'd do." Nick's eyes snared Catherine's, wouldn't release them. They were both thinking about the time John had attacked Catherine, the time Nick had saved her, but neither said a thing.

When Catherine could stand the tension no longer, she tore her gaze away. "You might be right, but as you said, we have no proof. Besides I think Stevens seems more likely."

"He still working for Parker?"

"As far as I know." Rising, crossing to the window, Catherine traced the edge of the lacy curtain. "Marie is staying at Windy Hill with John."

"Is she?" What in the hell was Catherine trying to do? Nick had been aware Marie was gone. He didn't know where she was, and he didn't care. Well, if Catherine thought to get some rise out of him with that information, she would be disappointed.

Why in the world had she said that? It had nothing to do with the subject at hand. And what did she think he'd do when she told him where his lover was? Whatever if was, he hadn't done it. He still sat, looking at her with those cool gray eyes, showing no sign of surprise or anticipation.

He probably already knew. The thought struck her like a mule kick. Marie had said he loved her, and Nicholas Colton certainly had enough intelligence and initiative to find Marie if he wanted her.

Catherine jerked her head around, finding it less distressing to stare at the yard, anyplace but at her husband. By bringing up Marie, she'd shown that she cared about what happened.

Silence stretched between them, and Nick shifted in his seat. "I suppose I better get back to the mine. I'll let you know if we have any more trouble."

Catherine nodded, not looking around. "Why didn't you tell me about this before?"

"I didn't want you to worry." The truth slipped out before Nick could stop it. His words brought her lustrous green eyes back to lock with his. He felt the force of her stare through his body.

"Why would you care if I worried about something?"

He cared. Even now, when he knew she didn't, he cared. "I—"

The pounding at the door caused Catherine to jump, had Nick bounding to his feet. "What the—" Nick whipped open the door before Catherine could reach it. One look at Jones's face and he knew something was wrong. "What is it?" Catherine grabbed his arm, and Nick could feel her fingers biting his flesh through his shirt.

Jones bent double to catch his breath. "There's trouble. One of the mules bolted and the cart broke loose. Overturned and dumped coal everywhere. Saw it coming, but weren't nothing we could do."

"The men?" Nick grabbed his shoulders. "Was anybody hurt?"

Jones nodded. "Wilson, Creighton, maybe more." He shook his head. "Sampson sent me out of the mine to get you, so I ain't sure."

Nick started down the porch steps. "How about Doc Shelton?"

"Already sent for."

"Good." Nick started off the porch. "Cate?" Nick glanced around but his wife had disappeared.

"I'm here, Nick." Catherine stuck her head out an upstairs window. "I'm getting some linens. Go on to

293

the mine, I'll be there as soon as I can."

By the time Catherine ran the distance to the mine, the clearing was nearly empty. Only the men operating the lift were about.

"Where's Mr. Colton," she asked, clutching the linens to her chest.

"Down there." One of the men motioned toward the mine entrance with his thumb. "Everyone's down there. Needed them to lift the cowe."

Catherine nodded. The cowes were large wooden boxes that sat on wagons. Heavy by themselves, they would be even more so filled with coal.

"Ready . . . heave." The muscles in Nick's back and arms burned with effort. He braced his legs against the underground railroad ties and pulled on the cowe, trying to right it, till the tendons on his neck stood ridged.

"Ain't no use, boss, it's still too heavy." Sampson wiped sweat from his brow with the back of his sleeve.

"Get the shovels in here." Nick grabbed one and started heaving coal out of the cowe. "Take it easy Creighton. We'll have this thing off you in no time."

"Hurry boss. I can't feel my legs anymore."

Nick could hear the panic in the digger's voice. "Calm down now. It will just be a minute." Nick dug his shovel into the black coal. "You doing all right, Wilson?" Only the rhythmic scraping of steel against coal and the sporadic hiss of escaping methane accompanied the grunts of his men as they worked. "Wilson?"

"He ain't saying nothing, boss. He ain't moving."

Each word Creighton said got louder and higher pitched.

"Calm down, Creighton. He probably just passed out. Let's try this again." Nick jammed his shovel in a pile of coal. This time when the men pulled, he could feel the cowe give. "Just a little more," he gritted through his teeth. The wooden box groaned as they righted it.

"Careful now." Nick crawled over the coal toward the two men who'd been trapped beneath the overturned box. They were covered by coal, black with soot. Now that the cowe was moved, Creighton's whimpers grew stronger, but Wilson, who'd taken the brunt of the blow against his upper body lay silent.

Fear gnawed at Nick as he gently brushed bits of coal and shale away from the unconscious man. His own breath stilled as he bent over, listening at Wilson's chest for signs of life.

"Boss?" Sampson's question rang through the underground cavern.

Nick barely moved his head in a negative gesture, yet he knew the message carried. A pall fell over the men who moments ago worked feverishly to free the two trapped men.

"Is he . . . is he . . ." Creighton pushed up on his elbows, his face a mask of pain.

"You're going to be all right." Nick shifted his body till he faced Creighton. The cowe had landed on his right leg, and Nick could see blood and torn flesh through the rips in his wool pants.

"He saw it coming." Creighton squeezed his eyes shut and tears escaped out the corners, tracing wrinkles down his blackened cheeks. "We were digging, just digging, and laughing. He was telling me about this fellow he knew who . . . Then he yelled."

"Get some boards over here—now." Nick motioned for some men to take Wilson up, then helped position Creighton on the make-shift stretcher.

"They're signalling to come up!"

Catherine jumped off the bench beside the shed, rushing toward the pit opening. The miners operating the lift nudged the donkey into motion and the ropes groaned against the pulley, lifting the basket slowly up the shaft.

Doctor Shelton left his seat in the shade of an elm tree and joined Catherine. It took him only a quick look at the first miner brought to the surface to know that nothing could be done for him.

"Are you certain?" Catherine's eyes pleaded, but the grizzled doctor only shook his head.

"Crushed chest, Miss Catherine. He's met his maker."

Grabbing one of the linens she'd brought from the house, Catherine covered the body. Her eyes burned with unshed tears as she glanced back at the lift. They were bringing up another load. How many more would reach the surface never to see the sun again?

"Careful now. Lower him down easy."

Catherine stood out of the way as miners stretched a hurt man on the ground. From what she could see, he appeared to be unconscious, but at least, the doctor worked on him, so she supposed he was alive.

"How's he doing?"

Catherine hadn't noticed Nick come up from the mine, so his low voiced question startled her. She shook her head. "I don't know." Her eyes searched his face noting the film of black coal dust that covered his features. "Are there any more hurt?"

"No."

"Are you all right?"

Nick's gaze met hers. "I'm fine."

"Wilson." Catherine motioned to where he lay covered by the snow-white sheet. "He's dead." Her voice quivered.

"I know."

"This one's going to make it." Doc Shelton struggled to his feet, dusting off the knees of his black pants. "Fixed him up best as I could here. I want to take him back to my house so I can keep an eye on him."

"Jones and Franklin," Nick signalled to two of the men forming a tight circle around the doctor and his patient. "Hitch up a mule to the wagon and fix a comfortable place for Creighton in the back." Nick fell into step beside the doctor as he gathered his jacket from under the tree. "You sure Creighton's going to be all right?"

"Don't see no reason why not. He has a broken leg, some cuts. Should heal up pretty good. What happened down there anyway? Your wife here said something about a coal cart breaking loose."

"That's it, near as I can figure. What I don't know is why." They'd walked back and joined Catherine on the fringe of the group of miners. Instinctively, Nick draped his arm around her, remembering when he felt her stiffen that they were barely on speaking terms.

"Well, don't be so hard on yourself, son. Accidents happen."

"Yeah." Nick glanced toward the long sheet-covered

form. "That's not much consolation to Wilson, is it?"

Doc Shelton just shook his head, and climbed into the wagon beside Jones. "Send someone round tomorrow and I'll have a better idea how long I need to keep this one."

As the wagon pulled away, Catherine slipped from under Nick's arm. She'd allowed him to touch her because she sensed he needed the nearness of someone—as did she—but she couldn't forget how things were between them. Apparently he remembered too because he stepped away from her awkwardly, letting his arm fall to his side.

Nick shifted his weight from one foot to the other, suddenly realizing how he must look to her all covered with coal dust and sweat. "You might as well go back to the house. There isn't anything else you can do here."

Catherine nodded and for a moment wished she hadn't moved away from him. He seemed so sad, so in need of comforting. If only she were the one he needed. "What are you going to do about . . . about . . . ?" Her eyes strayed to Wilson, laying alone now by the lift, but she couldn't finish the words.

"He has no family, at least none that any of us know about, so I suppose we'll call the preacher up to bury him."

Again, Catherine had an almost overwhelming desire to sway toward him, offer him the comfort of another grieving human being. But she didn't. Instead she moved further from him, trying to break the pull. "Let me know . . . when."

Watching her walk away, up the tree-lined path

toward the house, Nick felt a deluge of desire. Not the physical kind, though Catherine could easily conjure that up in him. But he longed for the companionship they'd shared before he realized she didn't care.

Rubbing dirty hands across his face, Nick called himself the fool he was, then turned when he heard Sampson calling him.

"Gotta talk to you a minute, boss. Alone."

The emphasis his bottom boss put on the last word made Nick's brow raise questioningly, but he reined his curiosity until they'd walked almost half way between the mine and his cabin. "What's this all about Sampson? And what's in that bag?"

Glancing around quickly, Sampson tossed the burlap bag he'd clutched at his side toward Nick. "Take a gander in there."

"Looks like part of the harness, the traces." Nick pulled the leather strips from the bag.

"They're off that mule that bolted. Thought you want to see them."

"I do. I—" Nick's eyes shot up to clash with Sampson's. "They've been cut."

"Looked like that to me, too." Sampson spit a stream of tobacco juice onto the carpet of pine needles.

Nick fingered the leather, his thumb skimming across the smoothly sliced sections, catching on the jagged ends where the traces had torn. His anger fueled by Wilson's needless death, Creighton's injury, surged forward. Gripping the leather, twisting it with the force of fury, Nick growled, "We're going to get the bastards who did this."

299

He paced forward, Sampson keeping up with his long-legged stride. "Pull the men off guard duty. Starting tonight I don't want to keep prowlers away. I want to welcome them." Nick kicked open the cabin door, slamming it back on its leather hinges.

"But—"

"And this is what I intend to use." Searching through his saddle bags Nick yanked out a flint lock pistol. Holding it up he watched the sunlight trace the brass trimmed handle.

Sampson's eyes darted from the gun to his employer's face, the air leaving his body in quick ragged gasps as if he'd run from the mine. "You know whoever it is might not come back tonight."

"Then I'll wait until they do. No one is going to get away with this."

A week later Nick lay on his stomach on the small rise to the south of the mine clearing. From his vantage he could see it all. Thanks to the low hanging moon, startling white against a sky of obsidian velvet, Nick could make out the buildings of the mine site.

He shifted quietly, barely moving the nest of grass beneath him, and scanned the area. A gust of wind whistled through the sentinel pines overhead, sending the rope hanging from the pulley banging against the lift basket. The motion reminded Nick that he wanted to look into ordering a steam engine to replace the mules to take the men in and out of the mine. But not now. Not until he'd caught the person responsible for Wilson's death.

They'd buried the young miner the day after he died. There hadn't been much of a service. Reverend

Martin had prayed over the grave, and Nick had said a few words, and Catherine— Nick rubbed his hand over his bristly jaw remembering how his wife had brought a bouquet of flowers, daylilies and primrose and some others he hadn't recognized, and placed them on the freshly dug grave.

Silently blowing air through his teeth, Nick rested his chin on the curve of his arm, spreading the tall grasses so he'd have an open view of the clearing. He hadn't seen Catherine since that day. Sampson had taken to giving her the daily reports so Nick could catch some sleep after his nightly vigils. If the change in routine bothered her, she didn't say anything about it, at least not anything Sampson had told him.

He guessed she didn't care who gave her the information as long as she knew what happened at the mine. But she didn't know everything, that was for damn sure. Nick had seen no reason to tell her about the cut traces, or what he did every night. No need, and no opportunity. It sure as hell wasn't like he could tell her over supper or when they went to bed.

She also hadn't found out that he'd cut out the night shift, though he knew he couldn't keep that from her much longer. Mining only one shift was losing them money from lost coal production. And he should do something about it. And he would. As soon as he'd caught Wilson's killer. Nick figured chances of the man coming around were better if he thought everyone was asleep.

Nick studied the buildings again, watching, listening. Some cicadas joined a chorus of tree frogs but nothing else sounded nearby. In the distance though, Nick could hear the rumble of thunder. There would be a storm before this night was done.

Nick groaned deep in his chest. He'd stayed out during storms for the last three nights, and had gotten nothing more for his trouble but a gut full of mud. He toyed with the idea of calling it a night as it started to rain. Surely no one would skulk around in this kind of weather. Only the memory of Wilson's crushed body kept him still when the thunder and lightning moved closer and the first fat raindrops splattered on the leaves overhead.

"Damn," Nick muttered under cover of another loud peal, and reached around to raise the collar over his neck. The effort didn't help much, and he squirmed as the rain ran down his back. He'd suffer, but he guarded the gun, slipping it under his body to protect it from the elements. Now that's where Catherine belonged, he thought with a wry smile.

Shaking his head, Nick blew out air in disgust. The last thing he should be thinking about was having his wife under him. Just forget it, Colton, he warned himself. It wasn't meant to be. Besides, what do you want with some woman who doesn't even care if you make love to her own sister? Nothing, that's what. Then how come you can't stop thinking about her?

Lightning zig zagged across the sky, illuminating the landscape with its white hot light. Nick burrowed down further into the underbrush feeling like a woodland animal trying to protect itself from the drumming downpour.

Damn, Catherine anyway. If it weren't for her he'd be in England, safe and snug in his townhouse library reading a good book. Or, more likely, snuggled into bed with one of his lady friends. Yes, that's what he'd be doing. Nick peered through the wall of water trying to remember what one of them, any of them looked like, and couldn't. Damn you, Catherine.

Lightning flashed again, closer, and Nick used the moment to search the murky mine clearing. His eyes panned the buildings, the dormitory, the storage shed, the— Nick jerked his gaze back to the shed. What had he seen? He slushed water from his eyes, pinning them to the shadowy blur at the corner of the shed.

It moved—a shadow emerging from shadows. Nick stiffened, his body alert. Forgotten was the rain, the uncomfortable damp and mud, as he watched the dark clad figure slide around to the front of the building. Nick longed for another splash of lightning or even a lessening of the torrent of rain so he could tell who the late night visitor was.

Slowly, moving as quietly as he could, Nick stood and started toward the camp. Mud sucked at his boots, hampering his progress as he made his way down the incline. Now he was glad for the rain that formed a liquid curtain about him as he approached the building where the mine crew kept their supplies—the shovels and pick axes, and Davy lamps, the harnesses, and the black powder.

By the time he reached the shed the door hung open, swinging with gusts of driving rain. Someone was inside. Nick could hear them moving around, sliding wooden crates along the packed dirt floor. Instinctively he tightened his grip on the pistol he'd jammed under his shirt, hoping the heavy canvas had kept the powder dry.

His footsteps on the porch floor as he approached the door, sounded like cannon shots, but by this time Nick didn't care if the intruder heard him. There was only one way out of the shed, and he blocked it. Nick's eyes swept the room, but the interior was darker than even the outside so he could make out only a shadow on the far side of the room. Nick could tell by the stillness of the form that he knew he'd been caught.

Nick aimed the gun toward the figure. "Who's in here?" Nick waited but there was no reply. The click of the pistol's hammer echoed through the shed, was followed by an audible intake of breath by the intruder, but still he didn't answer. Nick felt dampness dot his brow, but this time it wasn't rain, but nervous sweat. Minutes seemed like hours, measured by the beat of the rain on the tin roof, as he faced the unknown man.

"Answer or I'll shoot," Nick demanded.

"Shoot and we'll both be blown to hell, along with all your men. I'm holding a barrel of black powder."

Nick strained his eyes but couldn't prove or disprove the man's boast. But he couldn't deny the possibility. And who was it that had made the threat? That voice. Where had he heard that voice before? Nick tried to remember, but before he did, a streak of lightning lit up the shed's interior. The blaze of light disappeared in an instant, but not before Nick saw whom he faced.

"Put the powder down, Stevens."

"And let you shoot me?" His laugh was harsh.

"What kind of fool do you take me for, Colton?"

"No one's going to shoot you. I caught you snooping around on my property. The law can handle this." Nick cursed the circumstances that forced him to say that, then hoped he could keep his word when he finally got the bastard away from the powder.

Again Steven's laugh slithered around the shed, raising the hackles on Nick's neck. "You still take me for a fool, don't you? We're talking about more than trespassing here and we both know it. Heard you lost a man last week because you use worn out equipment."

Nick's finger caressed the smooth trigger, longing to pull it—knowing he couldn't. "What do you know about our equipment, Stevens?"

"You seem to forget I worked here a long time."

"And you seem to forget I fired you."

"Oh, that's something I'll never forget, Colton."

Suddenly, the barrel came crashing at Nick's body. Sensing its approach, Nick ducked, but the edge of the staves slammed into his arm, knocking the pistol from his hand. Before Nick could recover Stevens plowed into him as he made for the door. Nick grabbed for Stevens, caught hold of his coat, but couldn't keep his grip. In the darkness his prey slipped away.

Rushing into the rain, Nick searched the area, seeing nothing until lightning silhouetted Stevens racing across the clearing, heading for the woods beyond the lift. Cursing the mire that dragged his steps, Nick ran, dove for Steven's legs, tackling him around his muddy boots. Stevens rolled and kicked, fighting desperately to break Nick's hold.

But he couldn't. Using the strength of his arms, Nick dragged the struggling man toward him, jerking out of the way of the knee Stevens tried to plant in his groin.

Plop! Nick's fist hit slippery, rain-soaked skin. Raspy breathing sounded in Nick's ear, but he couldn't be sure if it was Stevens's or his own. Nick tried to punch Stevens again, but he slipped in the mud and his fist passed harmlessly by Stevens's face.

Slipping, sliming, Stevens squirmed from beneath him, frantic for a foothold, but slithering back down to his knees. Nick threw himself at his foe, but Stevens twisted, and the next moment his body straddled Nick. Mud caked hands surrounded Nick's neck, pushing his head into the opening of the mine shaft.

Handmade bricks, lining of the vertical mine shaft, dug into Nick's neck. Lightning split the mica-black sky, and Nick saw the savage expression of the man trying to push him to his death. Rain pelted his face, but Nick gritted his teeth and using all his remaining strength, shoved Stevens off him.

Again Stevens tried to run, but he slipped in the mire, falling sideways toward the yawning hole. Nick rolled over and grabbed as Stevens's momentum carried him over the edge of the shaft. Catching hold of sodden material, Nick could feel the tearing, and in desperation Stevens's hand found Nick's just as Nick released his grip on the ripped shirt sleeve. Stevens's mud-slicked hand was all that stood between life and eternity.

Nick inched toward the abyss, thrusting his other

hand into the black hole, groping for another handhold. Nothing. He could feel Stevens wriggling, trying to reach something solid. But there was nothing. "Be still," Nick growled. "And hang on."

The muscles in Nick's arm burned. He twisted his head, yelling into the rainy night. "Sampson! Sampson!"

Stevens jerked and Nick could feel the slimy hand slipping from his grasp. He squirmed closer to the mine shaft, trying again to grab hold of the dangling man with his other hand, but he couldn't reach. Then suddenly, Stevens was gone.

Lights bobbed overhead, and when Nick rolled over he could make out Sampson and some of the other men leaning over him, carrying lanterns.

"Mr. Nick, is that you?" Sampson reached down and yanked Nick to his feet. "Didn't recognize you all covered with mud like that. What's all the noise about?"

Taking one of the lanterns, Nick bent over the mine shaft, but he could see nothing.

"Boss, what is it? Did you catch someone messing around the place?"

"Yea, I caught him."

"Who was it?" Water ran off his black beard as he looked around the clearing. "Where is he?"

Without answering Nick pointed into the mine's black mouth, and watched Sampson's gape open.

Chapter Fifteen

"Expected you up some earlier." Betsy looked up from kneading bread on the work table when Catherine walked into the kitchen.

Stifling a yawn, Catherine gave the black woman a baleful look. It was later than she usually awoke. Apparently, judging from the expression on Betsy's face, she still harbored the belief that Nick slept in the house—in Catherine's bed. She probably thinks he kept me up all night—and the truth was, he did. But not the way Betsy thought.

There had been no wild passionate love making, except in Catherine's dreams. She felt color flood her face just remembering some of the nighttime visions that had kept her tossing, waking up aching amid twisted bed linens. And then the thunderstorm, with its loud crashing and blinding light. No wonder she felt as washed out as an old rag.

Betsy motioned toward the pot hanging over the fireplace. "Water's hot if you want some tea." Brushing the back of her hand across her face, Betsy left a streak of white flour across her walnut brown cheek. "Guess that husband of yours kept you awake talking about the big excitement."

Here it comes, Catherine thought, more dreams of happy ever a— "What excitement?" It suddenly registered with her that Betsy wasn't referring to intimate husband-wife things.

Betsy's hands froze in the dough, her arms akimbo. "You mean you ain't heard?" Her voice registered disbelief. "Thought sure Mr. Nick would have told you all about it."

"I haven't seen Nick this morning." There, let her think what she might. "Now tell me what happened."

"You ain't heard?"

"Oh, for heaven's sake, I just told you that. Now please tell me." Catherine forced herself not to grab Betsy's arms and shake the information from her. Blood pounded through her veins and she could feel her heart racing as she asked another question. "Nick . . . he's all right isn't he?"

"Well, sure. I guess so." Catherine's breath left her in a whoosh. "But from what I hear tell, he's lucky to be alive."

"Lucky to be . . ." Catherine's knees gave out and she thanked the fate that had positioned the chair under her as she plopped into it.

"Well, don't know how much stock I put in what Mason says. You remember him, he's one of the men Mr. Nick brought back from Richmond?" At Catherine's nod she continued. "Well, he stopped in the kitchen this morning. According to him, Mr. Nick caught the man who had cut the harness."

Catherine held up her hand. "What harness?"

"The one that was on the mule the day poor Mr. Wilson got killed. How's Mr. Creighton doing, by the way?"

"Fine." Catherine waved the answer aside. "You mean it wasn't an accident?"

"No sirree. Not according to Mason. Course nobody knew it at the time, 'cept Mr. Nick, of course. So he set out to catch him in the act."

Catherine leaned forward, resting her elbows on the table. She could hardly believe what she heard. "But that was almost a week ago. How did Nick know the person responsible would return last night?"

"Didn't. He's been laying out there every night, just waiting. You sure you didn't know nothing about this?"

Ignoring the question, Catherine jumped to her feet. She knew there was no hurrying Betsy when she had a juicy story to tell, especially when she had an avid audience, but she wished the black woman would hurry. Catherine wanted to hear the part about Nick.

"So anyway, last night he come again."

Catherine resisted asking who, so she wouldn't break Betsy's momentum. But her ploy didn't work.

"Don't you want to know who's been doing stuff to the mine?"

Of course, she wanted to know, but she wanted to hear the part about Nick almost getting hurt first. Catherine sighed. "Who?"

"Sam Stevens, that's who. Never did cotton to that man. Why I remember one time when your daddy was still alive, and he—"

"Betsy!"

The woman's eyes grew as large as saucers in her dark face. She snorted and punched the forgotten dough.

Feeling sorry she'd yelled, Catherine draped an arm around Betsy's slight form. "Please, just tell me what happened last night."

Ten minutes later, Catherine slammed the kitchen door and set off with determined steps toward the cabin her great grandfather had built. She'd finally managed to squeeze all the information she could out of Betsy, and she was angry.

"No, not angry—furious. I'm furious," she mumbled, swatting at a bee buzzing around her head. Last night's storm had twisted branches off some trees and uprooted others, but Catherine didn't notice that any more than the earthy smell that permeated the air. Her attention focused on her husband—and his secrets.

How dare he not tell her that Wilson's death wasn't an accident, and his plans to catch Stevens—didn't he think she might have some stake in them? Catherine recalled Betsy's description of Nick almost being pushed to his death down the mine, and her step quickened. He'd almost died last night and he didn't have the decency to tell her. Had he forgotten who owned most of Greenfield? Had he forgotten she was his wife?

Layered dogwood branches drooped lazily in the midmorning sun, surrounding the cabin in a cozy cloak. Catherine opened the door without knocking and gave the main room a quick perusal. The table her grandmother had served countless meals on now stood, covered with neat piles of papers, close to the back wall. Nick obviously used it as a desk. But he wasn't there. Nor was he anyplace else in the room.

A sound, muffled and sleepy, coming from the bedroom, caught Catherine's attention. She turned and marched through the door. There he lay, his long body sprawled on the bed, covered minimally with the corner of a sheet. He seemed totally at ease, as if he hadn't almost been killed less than twelve hours ago.

Catherine opened her mouth to rouse him, but stopped, her eyes caught up in examining him. He really was a fascinating man to view, she thought. His brown hair, tousled at best, now lay in complete disarray around his head. Gold tipped lashes lay in a tight semicircle beneath his eyes. Sleep relaxed his jaw, and even with the days growth of whiskers, a shade darker than his hair, he looked innocent—like a sweet little boy.

But his body was not that of a boy. Broad shoulders, powerful arms and chest. Catherine felt her own body respond just looking at him. Her gaze wandered across the triangle of golden brown curls on his chest, then caught and followed the arrow of hair that disappeared beneath the sheet. Covered, but hardly hidden, the male part of him bulged beneath the linen. Catherine lost all the moisture in her mouth. Licking her lips didn't help, but she tried anyway. Yes, he had one beautiful body—and he'd shared it with her sister.

That thought, boiling up from the recesses of her mind, stiffened Catherine's spine. Angrily she

313

pushed at his bare leg, trying to ignore the warmth of his skin, and the tingle of crisp hair. Nothing happened. She nudged him again, and he threw an arm across his eyes, exposing one very hairy, very male arm pit. The third time she poked him, his forearm slid slightly, uncovering one eye which he slowly opened, focusing a sleepy gray stare on her.

Catherine propped fists on her hips. "Just what do you think you're doing?"

"I *was* sleeping." Nick grinned at the sight of her. It was almost like a continuation of his dream. Though in the dream she hadn't been wearing a scowl, she hadn't been wearing anything.

"I don't mean now. Last night. Who told you to try to catch Stevens?"

"Let's get this straight, Cate." Nick raised up on his elbows, yanking at the sheet when he noticed her gaze drawn to the slipping fabric. "Nobody told me to do it. Nobody has to tell me. Have you forgotten who's the mine manager?"

Oh, of all the arrogance. Catherine forced her eyes to lock with his. How did he manage to be nude during every argument they had? "And are you forgetting who owns three fourths of the mine?"

"I could hardly do that." Nick swung his legs over the side of the bed. "Not with you reminding me all the time."

"I don't—" So angry she couldn't face him another second, Catherine whirled around, her skirts twisting about her legs. Staring out the window she folded her arms across her chest. "I simply think you should have told me about the harness being cut, and . . . and what you planned to do."

"Why, so you could have ordered me not to do it?" Nick grabbed for his pants, and thrust a leg inside. He was in no mood for "Miss Boss Lady." It seemed as if he'd just gotten to sleep. And last night on top of a sennight of little sleep was taking its toll on his temper.

"Maybe!" Catherine glared at him over her shoulder, jerking her head around when she noticed the sheet had completely disappeared. "I would have at least suggested you forget the hero act and get some men to help you."

Hero act! Nick gritted his teeth and clinched his fists to keep from throttling her. And to think, minutes ago his dream mind had her writhing beneath him in ecstasy. Ha! She worried too much about being boss of her mine to succumb to carnal delights. Flashes of memory of the real Catherine wrapped in his arms proved his assessment wrong. She's a great one to talk of acts, he thought.

Dredging up a reserve of calm, Nick explained, "I didn't rely on others because I wasn't certain who could be trusted."

"You thought I might be involved?" Catherine swirled around, thankful he'd finished pulling on his pants.

"Don't be silly. I meant the men. You're the one that suggested one of them could be involved with the missing powder. I didn't tell you because . . ." There was no way he was going to tell her the truth, that he hadn't wanted her to worry. "Because, you didn't need to know."

Angry color stained Catherine's cheeks. "I didn't need . . . What if something had happened? What if

315

you'd been killed?"

"Then you could have hired someone to take my place."

Tears stung Catherine's eyelids and she turned away from Nick so he wouldn't notice. How could he think he could ever be replaced? "But you're my husband."

Nick's barked laugh made Catherine bite her bottom lip. "We both know how untrue that is, Cate. It takes more than someone saying a few words over people to make them married, and we don't have it. So don't pretend you care what happens to me."

Tears streamed down Catherine's face but she glared at him over her shoulder anyway. "Oh, you stupid, insensitive . . ." Whatever else she intended to call him dissolved in a sob as she ran from the cabin.

"Wait a minute, Cate. Catherine, get back here! Damn, woman." Nick tore out of the cabin, overtaking her before she left the clearing. Grabbing her shoulders, he forced her around, prodding up her chin with his thumb. "Why are you crying?"

"I'm not," Catherine insisted, ignoring all the evidence to the contrary.

"Are you trying to say you do care what happens to me?"

"I'm not trying to say anything." She attempted to twist her head away, but his hand now cupped her chin, holding it firmly.

"Cate?" Nick's voice quieted, the deep timbre sending chills down her spine. "Do you care—have feelings for me?"

Catherine stared into his crystal-clear gray eyes.

Eyes that held questions in their depths, and something more. Could it be hope? Regardless, she couldn't lie to him. Even if he threw her feelings back in her face, she couldn't lie. "Yes." The word barely drifted across the space that separated them but she knew he heard, for he folded her in his arms so tightly she could barely breathe. Catherine rested her cheek against the warm flesh of his chest, listening to his steady heartbeat and savoring the smell of his body.

"Cate." Too soon he pushed her away, holding her at arm's length and piercing her again with those intense eyes. "I never touched Marie."

At the sound of her sister's name, the reminder of what had happened, Catherine squirmed in his hands, refusing to meet his stare.

"Now wait. You're going to listen. I didn't touch her. I didn't want to."

"But I saw—"

"You saw me getting out of the creek, trying to get the clothes she'd taken." Nick let go of Catherine to run a frustrated hand through his hair. "Damnit, Cate. I was as surprised to see her there as you were."

Catherine swallowed, looking into Nick's face, searching for any signs of deceit. She wanted to believe him, needed to, but her sister's words flashed back to her. Would Marie make up all those awful things she said? What reason would she have to lie? Catherine's gaze dropped to Nick's chest.

"Catherine, look at me." When she did he touched the side of her face. "There was never anything between Marie and me—never."

A blue jay squawked overhead, protecting his territory from intruders. Catherine wanted to believe

Nick, but she couldn't deny that doubts still remained. Her eyes beseeched. "Why didn't you tell me this earlier . . . that day by the creek?"

"I tried." Letting go of Catherine, Nick turned to stare at the cabin. Sunlight bronzed the breadth of his shoulders, and Catherine longed to run her hands across the muscular ridges. Nick looked back at her. "Don't you think I knew how bad it looked? Hell, Cate, I didn't have a stitch on!"

Nick paced to the edge of the clearing and dropped to the grassy ground, leaning back against a rough-barked pine. Looking up at the sun filtering through the fan of needles, he shook his head. "I can't even explain it now—not to prove what happened. All I know is that when I tried before, and you told me not to bother, and brought up that damned agreement. I . . . I don't know, I just didn't think it mattered."

Catherine didn't know what to say, didn't know what to think. She watched him close his eyes, wondered if he waited for her to speak. He seemed so different, not like the cocky miner who'd exploded into her life and stole her heart. Now he appeared vulnerable and alone and she wanted to reach out to him. She wet her lips. "I would have believed you— at least I would have tried." Catherine wiped her hands across her skirt. "I wanted you to tell me it wasn't true."

His gaze leveled on her. "But you said—"

"I believed what I saw. When you had no ready explanation, what else could I think?" She cocked her head to the side. "And I didn't want you to know how much it hurt me . . . how much I cared."

"Cate."

"What?" She watched him sitting in the dappled shade of the trees, saw his hand reach out to her.

"Come here."

She walked to him, her skirt brushing against the grass and wild flowers, releasing their sweet fragrance into the morning air. Her hand touched his, tentatively at first, then as his strong fingers folded over hers, more firmly. He looked up at her, saying nothing, yet his eyes spoke volumes. Catherine felt him tug gently, knowing he could use his strength to pull her down to him, but knowing too, that he left the choice to her. To believe him or not.

Slowly she sank into the cradle of his body. He grinned then, that crooked, cocky grin that showed some measure of his arrogance had returned. Catherine smiled, unable to help herself. She loved the feel of his arms around her.

"It's good to see them again."

Catherine nestled more comfortably in his lap and looked up at him. "What?"

"Your dimples. I've missed seeing them."

"I don't have dimples."

"Sure you do. Here." Nick's calloused finger touched the indentation beside her mouth. "And here."

"They're not dimples," she giggled. "They're—" Catherine's breath caught, silencing her words, as his lips traced the path of his finger.

"Dimples," was all he said before his mouth covered hers, making any further argument impossible.

What started as the barest of touches, more a mingling of breath, a flirting of flesh, soon deepened.

319

Tongues, long denied the smooth pull of its mate, glided, aroused. Catherine's arms wound around his neck, her fingers folded into the thick hair at his nape. She arched toward him as his hands touched her body, gently at first, then with an urgency that seemed to burn through her gown.

"Cate." He shifted, rolling her down, and now the hardness that had seared her hip pressed into her soft belly. "I want you." His words were muffled against her neck. "Now."

"Here?" Catherine's breath came in heated gasps as his mouth traveled lower, joining his hands in caressing her breasts.

"Yes." His passion-dark eyes stripped away her inhibitions. "Here. Now."

Queen Anne's lace swayed, bowing their fragile heads as Nick unbuttoned Catherine's gown. Pressing his mouth to her shoulders, Nick exposed her breasts to the sunshine and to his admiring eyes. He took her hand, dragging it between their bodies. "Touch me," he commanded, moaning with pleasure when she wrapped her fingers around the bulge in his trousers. She squeezed and his open mouth came down on hers, his tongue probing, his teeth nipping.

Clothes no longer could be endured. Catherine groped at his buttons, yanking away the fabric and filling her hand with his heat. And Nick stripped away her gown, all the trappings of civilized womanhood, in his primitive desire to become one with her.

His first plunge filled her, sent her legs wrapping about his hips. Nick closed his eyes, resting his forehead against hers, trying to control the desire to take her hard and fast. He felt ready to explode inside her, around her.

"Nick?" Catherine's lashes fluttered open.

"Shh, Cate." His eyes locked with her, he pulled out, then stroked deep, loving the feel of her tight body surrounding him. Nothing felt as good as being inside his Cate. His pace quickened. Her body arched to meet each stretching thrust, again and again, until there was no thought, only fluid movement, uncontrollable movement.

The world whirled around—summer green trees swayed, meshing with blue sky, cotton clouds, and all glittered and shone with the sparkling golden sun. A kaleidoscope of vivid colors swirled then receded, slowly. Catherine opened her eyes, and discovered the sparkle remained. The trees, the grass, the honey brown head that rested on her breast, everything shone with a new, rainwashed brightness.

She lifted her hand from his shoulder, letting it drift through his hair. "Nick?"

"Hmmm?"

Catherine smiled at the sleepy sound. Where was her tiger of moments before? "Don't you think we should get up?"

"No. Can't move."

His breath tickled her nipple. "But what if someone should happen by?"

Nick raised his head, propping it on his hand, contradicting his earlier statement. "A fine time to be thinking about that," he teased, a grin playing on his sensual lips.

"I thought about it before," she insisted, though her tone matched the lightness of his.

"Oh, really?" His arched brow spoke of skepticism.

"Really," Catherine said, but honesty forced her to add, "at first."

"And what did you think of after that?" His thumb idly traced the curve of her breast as if to remind her.

Catherine rolled her eyes at his conceit, laughing with him as he let his hand glide down to pat her hip. "Seriously, Nick, maybe I didn't worry about it earlier, when I was . . . distracted, but someone could come this way."

"All right." Nick pushed himself up, groaning at the effort. "I doubt it because I gave the men the day off, but if it will make you happy, we can go inside. I need to get some more sleep." He reached down his hand for Catherine.

Suddenly, feeling foolishly shy, Catherine hesitated, bundling her gown and using it as a shield. He seemed too tired to notice. "I know you were up most of the night, so if I could just dress in the cabin, I'll go back to the house."

"Oh, no you don't." His outburst surprised her after the languorous attitude he'd exhibited since they made love. Long, sturdy fingers locked on her wrist, gently, but in a way she knew would hold her if need be. "You're not going anywhere. From now on where I sleep, you sleep."

"But . . ." Catherine wanted to explain to him that midmorning had arrived, and she rarely napped, but he started toward the cabin, with her in tow. Besides her own sleep last night had been sporadic, at best. And even if she felt fully rested, the idea of lying next to him, watching him sleep, had great appeal.

Nick dropped his pants to the bedroom floor, invited her to do the same with her hastily gathered clothes, and climbed into bed. The rope springs protested the sudden weight. Holding back the top sheet, he looked up at Catherine expectantly. With a slight shrug she brushed the clinging grass from her backside and feet, and followed him. Sighing contentedly, Nick gathered her close, smiling when she cuddled up to him. "We need to talk," he whispered into her hair.

He was so right. There were a hundred things she wanted to know, about him, about his feelings for her, but she hesitated to ask. Instead she decided to stay on relatively safe ground. The mine. He could begin by telling what had happened last night, then, maybe, they could progress to a more personal level. "Were you surprised when the thief turned out to be Stevens?" Catherine waited a moment, allowing him time to ponder her question. When he didn't respond she touched his shoulder. "Nick?"

His only response was a slow, sonorous snore. Catherine shifted, looking at him through a veil of hair that had come down during their lovemaking. Smiling she pushed her curls aside and lay back down. Poor thing must be exhausted, she thought. She'd watch over him while he slept, but he was right, later they had to talk—and not just about the mine. Her eyes lovingly caressed him, and she decided he had the most handsome profile she'd ever seen, pugnacious nose and all. That was her last thought as she drifted off to sleep.

"I thought I was the one who needed rest."

Catherine slowly opened her eyes, reluctant to

release her lovely dream. Seeing Nick smiling down at her, his tousled head propped on his hand, made her realize her sleep induced illusions hadn't been entirely fantasy. She smiled, reaching up to cup his cheek with her hand. "Good morning."

Nick laughed at that, softening the sting by turning his head and kissing her palm. "Catie girl, I'm afraid it's long past morn."

Glancing toward the window, noting the dusky darkness shrouding the view, Catherine's eyes widened. "What time is it?"

"Not sure." Nick picked up a strand of long auburn hair and let it sift through his fingers. It felt like silk. "By the looks of the sky, I'd guess it to be close to eight o'clock."

"At night?" Catherine tried to sit, but Nick's hand on her shoulder stayed her. "I've been gone all day. Betsy will be beside herself."

"She's not." Nick's hand drifted down her arm.

"What makes you think that?" Catherine tried to ignore the sensual stirrings his calloused fingertips caused.

"She's the one who woke me." Deciding the sheet covered too much, Nick inched it down.

"Betsy was here?" Catherine shot up, twisting to the side and staring at her husband. Nick decided not to stop her from sitting, since the sheet now pooled around her hips, exposing her creamy, rose-tipped breasts.

"Hmmm." Leaning over, Nick traced his tongue along the gentle ridge of a rib, watching in delight as Catherine's nipples tightened. "She nearly scared ten years off me, too. Have you ever awakened looking into a face like that?"

In spite of herself, Catherine smiled. "So she saw us . . . like this?"

"Well, not exactly." Nick shifted. "We were asleep—and covered."

Catherine could feel the rasp of his grin against her stomach. It sent chills of longing racing through her body. Her fingers played in his soft brown hair.

"Betsy left a basket of food in the other room, if you're interested." His mouth trailed northward, caressing the underside of her breast, nipping, soothing with his tongue.

"I'm not," came Catherine's breathy whisper as she leaned back on her arms.

"Not what, Cate?"

Moist heat surrounded her nipple. "Interested in food." Catherine tried to swallow. She arched her body toward him. "Do you know what you do to me?"

Looking up, Nick caught Catherine's eye. His grin was wicked. "I think I have a pretty good idea."

Pulling her down beneath him, Nick proceeded to show her just how aware he was.

Hunger, a gnawing sensation deep in her belly, woke Catherine. Moonlight streamed through the window, liming the homemade bureau, the bed, the man lying on his side next to her. Smiling, she wriggled from beneath the arm he'd flung across her waist, surprised when his hand tightened around her wrist. She thought him asleep, but his sleep roughened question proved otherwise.

"Where you going?"

"To see what's in the basket Betsy brought."

"Bring it in here, would you? I'm starved." As if to prove his point, he rubbed his hand across his flat stomach.

Catherine forced her eyes not to follow the movement—or to move lower. Turning her head, she sat on the edge of the bed, wondering how she could cover herself before walking across the room. When she thought him asleep, there was no problem. But now, with him propped on bent arm, watching her, that devilish grin flashing in the silvery moonlight . . .

Sensing her unease, amused by it—she'd hardly seemed shy earlier—Nick rolled to the other side of the bed. Picking up her chemise, he draped it over her head, kissing the tip of her nose when her head reappeared through the linen.

Catherine found the covered basket on Nick's desk. By the time she carried it back into the bedroom, Nick had pulled on his pants. He'd fastened all but the last few buttons. The trousers rode low over his narrow hips. Dragging it off the bed, Nick spread the quilt on the floor in the puddle of moonbeams spilling through the open window.

When he noticed her standing in the doorway, watching him, a hesitant smile curved his lips. "Midnight picnic," he said.

Betsy had outdone herself, packing chicken, cheese, and pears from the tree behind the house, and fresh bread. Probably from the loaves I saw her making this morning, Catherine thought. It hardly seemed possible that it had only been earlier today that Catherine had gone to the kitchen. So much had happened since then, but more importantly, her attitude had changed so drastically—toward her husband, toward life in general.

"What are you smiling about?" Nick reached over and wiped some pear juice from the corner of Catherine's mouth.

"Am I smiling?" Catherine asked, knowing full well her face mirrored his. "Maybe it's because I'm happy."

"So am I."

Catherine lowered her eyes, suddenly finding the crust of a blackberry tart fascinating. "Do you think there will be any trouble because of Stevens? Betsy told me he was dead."

"No." Nick hid his surprise at the change of topics. He'd thought they were talking about something more personal. However, he supposed taking a life, even if it was in self-defense was rather personal. "I already talked with the sheriff last night."

Catherine nodded, flaking off a smidgen of crust. "I suppose running the mine will be easier now that he's gone."

"Probably. He's caused us a lot of trouble lately." Leaning back against the side of the bed, Nick drank some of the wine Betsy had left. "If I were a betting man, I'd wager some of the so-called accidents, Greenfield Mine has had could be traced to him."

"Why would he do such a thing?"

"Since I fired him, I'd say his motives were simple enough. Before that." Nick shrugged. "I don't know. We probably never will."

Crickets sawed their legs, calling their mates,

softening the silence inside the cabin. Nick rested his head against the mattress, turning it to stare at Catherine. "Is that why you're happy, Cate? Because you don't have to worry about Stevens anymore?"

She met his gaze, reluctantly. "No. But it probably does change things."

"Like what?"

"Our agreement." Catherine ignored the gust of air Nick let through his teeth. "You said you'd stay until the mine was running well."

"Is that it, Cate? You want me to go?"

"No!" The word burst forth with embarrassing zeal. "No, I don't," she repeated more softly. "But I want you to know that I remember our agreement, and I won't try to stop you if you want to leave." Catherine held her breath as he stared at her, his gray eyes narrowed as if searching her for clues. As if trying to decide what to say.

"I don't want to go, Cate." Catherine started to breathe again. "My life in England was a good one. There are people I will miss." Nick thought of Travis Fielding, wondering if he might persuade the older man to visit America. "But this is where I belong."

Standing, striding to the window, Nick stared out at the night. "I never realized until I came here, how much I missed having a home, a place I could call my own—a family." He glanced over his shoulder. "You've given me a lot, Cate."

Touched by his admission, Catherine smiled at him. "You've given me a lot, too. I'd have nothing, if you wouldn't have helped me with the mine, hiring miners, and all the other things you've done." His shrug seemed to dismiss his accomplishments as nothing. "You helped make Grandmere's last days good for her. I don't know if you knew, but she was very fond of you. She," Catherine hesitated, "we both were happy when you gave me your name."

Nick snorted, resting his forehead on the cool window pane. "Hell, Cate, it's not even my real name."

Chapter Sixteen

"I . . . I don't understand." Catherine's arms hugged her waist, molding the loose fitting shift to her body as she stared at her husband. Silhouetted by the moonlight, he turned. She couldn't see his face or his expression, yet she knew he studied her, and she knew those eyes shone intense.

"I'm a bastard." His gaze never wavered, and he noticed with something akin to relief that neither did hers. Laughter, sounding cynical to his own ears, escaped him. "You called me that once, and I took exception to it. I shouldn't have."

"But, I never meant . . ." Catherine started forward, thought better of it and stopped. He seemed so distant.

"For it to be taken literally? I know." Nick leaned his hip against the sill, crossing his arms.

"Do you know who your father is?"

"You mean, do I know my real name?" Nick shrugged. "I've no idea. Colton is a name my mother made up to hide her shame." Nick laughed again. "It means 'from coal town.' That's me. Nick 'from coal town.'"

"Nick." Catherine crossed to him then, picking her way barefooted between the remnants of their moonlight picnic. She stopped when she was close enough to feel the warmth of his skin, to catch the masculine scent of his body. He looked down at her, towering, even in his relaxed pose, and her hand touched his bare arm. "Tell me about it, Nick—your childhood, your mother."

Nick hesitated. Catherine's eyes—her whole body—spoke of understanding, but would that remain if he told her the truth? She'd known hardships, at least, she thought she did, but he was sure she knew nothing of the seamy side of life. She'd lived her life at Greenfield, propped up by generations of ancestors who'd dug their roots so deep into the rich soil of Virginia that there was no way to dislodge them.

"Nick, please." Her fingers tightened, reassured.

"We lived in a tavern." Nick's glance skittered away, then returned. "It wasn't really a tavern, though you could buy anything you wanted to drink there. But that's not why the men came." He stopped and sucked in a ragged breath. "They came to buy what the women were selling—what my mother was selling."

Nick glanced away, unable to meet Catherine's eyes now that she knew, torturing himself because he wanted to look at her, to read her thoughts in her expression. "I'll never forget the smells of that place," he continued. "Stale smells of spilled liquor, unwashed bodies and . . . sex."

Looking out the window at the night-darkened landscape, Nick took a deep breath of woodsy scented air, reminding himself that he wasn't back there. He wasn't Lizzy Colton's little bastard any more, considered by everyone but her to be forever underfoot. Memories of how she'd protected him, often in the process earning the wrath of old Simon Webster, the brothel owner, softened Nick's discomfort. He'd painted an ugly picture—a true picture—but it wasn't entirely a fair one. Not to his mother.

"She wasn't always a prostitute."

Nick's voice startled Catherine, who'd been watching him turn away, pull inside of himself. Catherine had feared she'd opened a Pandora's box, only to have Nick pulled inside, and the door forever closed. But he was stronger than that. As he turned back to Catherine, Nick began telling her about his mother.

"She'd been raised in a small shire to the north of New Castle. My mother used to tell me stories about her family, and about his." Nick fell short of calling the man who'd sired him, Father. "Her father had been a smithy." Nick lifted a shoulder self-consciously. "At least, that's what she told me. At the time, living as I did, I thought being the offspring of a smithy sounded most honorable. I couldn't understand why my mother said it wasn't good enough—not for the lord's son."

"Was he your father . . . the lord's son?"

Nick combed his fingers through his tousled curls. "According to my mother, yes."

"What happened to him?"

"He left." Nick shook his head. "And never returned."

"Didn't your mother ever try to find him? Maybe he just needed a reminder. And you, surely he would have done something if he'd known about you."

"She didn't want him to come back to her because of me. If he didn't want her for herself, she didn't want him. I thought about trying to find him, after she died, when I was older, but she'd never really given me anything to go on—no name, not even the shire where she'd been born. So . . ."

"There was nothing you could do?"

"No. Most of the other girls who lived in the house didn't believe my mother. They thought she was fantasizing about this rich, handsome man who was going to rescue us from the brothel. But I believed her. Until the day she died, alone, diseased, and lying on filthy sheets, I thought he'd come for her." Nick's eyes sought Catherine's. "I believed her."

"But you don't anymore?" Catherine felt tears welling up, but blinked them back. She sensed that Nick didn't want her pity—he needed her understanding.

He shrugged again and swallowed. Catherine could see his Adam's apple quiver with the effort of controlling his emotions. "I don't know. Maybe it was all a story, mind games she played to help her cope with life. Or maybe she thought I'd feel better thinking my father was rich and powerful and had once loved her, rather than thinking he was one of the miners who visited her."

"Do you?" Catherine cocked her head, searching what she could see of his face.

"Maybe. But I've lived with this for as long as I can remember. The question is, do *you* think it matters?"

"I might have . . . at one time," Catherine admitted honestly after a slight hesitation. "But it doesn't now, not to me." Catherine smiled up at him happy to know that she spoke the truth. Before she'd met Nick, she might have been silly enough to think who a person's parents were was important. Now she knew it was the person himself that mattered. Her hand inched down toward his. "I think it still bothers you, though."

Nick felt her fingers entwine with his. "I guess it does . . . sometimes. The trouble is, I want to believe that she told me the truth. That she didn't lie to me." His thumb rubbed against something hard and he lifted their braided hands, turning them until the silvery light from the window reflected off the dull gold and emerald ring on Catherine's finger.

"This was hers." He twisted the ring around her finger, sending a spark of green across the room. "She told me he'd given it to her."

"It's beautiful. He must have loved her very much."

Nick arched his brow cynically, but his eyes were gentle as he lifted her hand to his lips and pressed a kiss to the ringed finger. "Don't tell me we have another believer?"

Catherine's chin rose a notch, and she kept her back straight, fighting the urge to melt into him. "Yes, I believe it." She wanted to, for him. "But it's something you're going to have to accept on faith. I don't suppose you'll ever know for sure."

Pushing himself away from the window sill, Nick stretched, his hands high above his head. "One thing I do know is that if I don't get some sleep, I'll be no good in the mine come morning." He draped his arm around Catherine's shoulders.

"You slept all day." Catherine's tone teased as she retraced her steps toward the bed, but in her heart she was sorry that he'd put an end to their discussion. There was so much more she wanted to know about him.

"If you recall, I didn't sleep *all* day." His grin made her blush. "But regardless, I have a lot of lost sleep to make up for."

Together they cleaned up what was left of the food. Catherine took the basket into the other room while Nick stepped outside to shake the quilt. Back in the bedroom, he shucked off his trousers and lay down. Catherine stood beside the bed, biting her lip in indecision. Finally, gripping her shift by the hem, she slipped it over her head and climbed in beside Nick. His arm wrapped around her, and they fell asleep.

"Nick?" Catherine blinked her eyes open, brushing a thick veil of hair off her face. She awakened moments earlier to the unmistakable feel of a lonely bed.

"Right here." He ambled over to the bed biting into a pear leftover from last night. "I tried not to wake you."

"You didn't." Catherine smiled up at him. He'd dressed in a pair of thick wool pants and a canvas shirt. Heavy work boots covered his feet. He looked ready to get back to the mine.

He set the pear on the small bedside table, licked the juice from his fingers and leaned over the bed. "You're looking mighty good this morning." His large hands cradled her shoulders as he nuzzled her neck. "I'd say good enough to eat," he laughed, his words muffled by thick auburn hair as he took a make-believe bite out of her shoulder. "We didn't leave much food last night."

"Ah, don't tell me one little pear isn't enough for you for breakfast," Catherine giggled.

"Well, actually, I ate a badly crumbled blackberry tart, too." He sat up, giving her that grin that never failed to set her stomach aflutter.

"If you're still hungry, you can stop at the house. I'm sure Betsy will feed you."

"Don't have time." Nick stood, turning toward the door. "Besides, if I did." He looked back at her, his stormy gray eyes raking her quilt shrouded form. "I wouldn't waste it eating."

Heat spread through Catherine's body, and she came close to telling him to forget the damn mine.

"Catherine?"

"Hmmm?" She thought he'd gone, but he stood in the doorway, his hands stretched over his head, grasping the frame above it. He swung himself forward slightly on the balls of his feet, appearing rather ill at ease.

"Do you think we could stay here awhile? Just for a few days."

"Here? You mean in the cabin?"

"Yeah." He dropped his arms, moving his head to survey the bedroom. "I know it's not what you're used to. But it's not too bad. And," he smiled sheepishly, "I know this is stupid, but it feels more like it's mine and I'd like you to share it with me."

Touched more than she could say, Catherine held

out her arms, closing them around his broad shoulders when he sat on the edge of the bed.

"If you don't want to, I'll understand. And I'll move back into the house, if you want me."

If she wanted him? Catherine couldn't believe he had to ask. She did want him back in the house, but first they'd stay in the cabin, for as long as he wanted. She told him so, and received a lingering good morning kiss in response.

"I guess I better go." Nick's eyes slid down to Catherine's creamy breasts, and he itched to shed his clothes and join her in bed.

"I guess so." Catherine saw the indecision creep across his face and would have laughed if her own body didn't burn so warm just feeling him near.

"The men will be waiting." The hand he rested on the pillow nudged over, brushing against the side of her breast. He watched, fascinated, as the nipple tightened. He tore his eyes away. They locked with hers. "What was I saying?"

"The men," Catherine's voice sounded breathy, "are waiting."

"Yeah." Nick stood up, rubbing his palms down his thighs. "You know, I'm going to be awful hungry," his gaze swept her, "by dinner time since I didn't have any breakfast."

"Would you like me to bring your dinner to you?"

"Yes." Nick swallowed.

"To the mine?"

"No, the pool. Bring it there, and I'll be waiting."

Catherine lay watching the doorway long after he'd disappeared through it. It had only been twenty-four hours since she'd stormed into the cabin, convinced she hated the man who'd just left. She'd thought him capable of lying and infidelity and of trying to take control of the mine from her. Now . . .

Throwing her legs over the side of the bed, Catherine straightened her shoulders, and tried to figure out how she felt about him now. She loved him, of course. Even when she'd hated him most, when she'd seen him down by the creek with her sister, she'd been hard pressed to deny the love she felt.

But did she trust him, believe what he said about Marie? Catherine rested her elbows on her knee, trying to imagine the scene she saw happening the way Nick described it. Possible, she admitted to herself. Knowing her sister, even probable. But could she ever be certain?

Something she'd said to Nick last night came rushing back to her. You'll never know for sure, she'd told him, concerning his mother's truthfulness. You'll just have to accept her word on faith. Catherine dug her fingers into the mattress. That's what she must do. Accept him on faith. There was no other way, if she wanted him. And she did.

He'd never mentioned love, yet she sensed he was happy here. He told her how nice it was to have a home, a family. After what she'd heard of his early years, she could well imagine why.

Jumping to her feet, scooping up her shift and jerking it over her head, Catherine made a decision. He wanted a home? She'd give him one. He wanted her? She'd gladly give him that, too. She could make him happy. She knew that she could.

And he could make her happy. She loved him.

That in itself would be enough. But he also took care of her, and the mine. And he did a fine job of it.

"Yes, Catherine decided, buttoning her dress. She and Nicholas Colton were made for each other. Her grandmother, rest her soul, had known it from the start. Now Catherine knew it, and before she was finished Nick would know it, too.

Grabbing up the basket, giving one last inventory taking look around the cabin, Catherine started back toward the house.

"Well, there you are," Betsy said as Catherine entered the kitchen.

"Yes, here I am," Catherine answered, unable to erase the smile from her face. Even the servant's teasing couldn't bother her today. "How would you like to visit your son in Manchester?"

Doubt shaded the black woman's wrinkled face. "You ain't thinking of pushing me aside, is you, Miss Catherine? I was only funning with you."

Taking back by Betsy's words and her fearful expression, it took Catherine a moment to figure the reason for her strange behavior. When she did, Catherine couldn't help laughing. "I only meant for a few days. You couldn't possibly think I could get along without you for any longer than that."

Betsy's face brightened. "Then how come you want me to visit Thomas?"

"I just thought you might like to. You're always talking about him, and well, I know you hardly ever get to see him." Catherine knew that Betsy was understandably proud of her son. A freed man, he worked at the coal yard across the river from Richmond.

Catherine emptied the basket. "I'm moving down to the cabin for a few days, so there really won't be much for you to do. Of course, you can stay here if you like, but—"

"What are you going down to that old cabin for?"

"Nick asked me to, and I thought . . ." Catherine shook her head, realizing when she felt the swaying weight that she'd forgotten to pin up her hair. "It's too complicated to explain. I just am. If you want to go to Manchester, I can find you a ride."

"But you want me back?"

"Of course, I want you back." Catherine threw her arm around Betsy's shoulders. "You're part of the family." Betsy had been offered papers of manumission by Catherine's father when Thomas and the other slaves that had worked Greenfield had received theirs, but she'd refused them. This was her home, she'd said.

"You go ahead and get ready." Catherine leaned down and untied the calico apron at Betsy's waist. "I'll talk to Nick at dinner time. He probably has a wagon going out this afternoon that you can catch a ride on."

"You sure you won't be needing me none?" Betsy moved to the back of the kitchen, toward the little room where she slept.

"No, you go ahead." Catherine flashed her a confident smile that turned to a frown as soon as the old woman had closed her door. Since most of the servants were gone, Catherine had helped in the kitchen often. Betsy had even taught her how to cook. But she'd never done it completely by herself.

Well, there was only one way to handle this, and

that was to jump right in. Catherine spent the rest of the morning packing up foodstuffs and taking them to the cabin. She also moved some of her clothing and brought down clean linens. Later, as the sun climbed close to its zenith, Catherine surveyed the cabin, smiling at what she'd accomplished.

Her silver brush and mirror lay on the bureau next to Nick's straight razor and strap. She'd tidied up his clothes, hanging them from the pegs lined neatly along the walls. Glazed crocks, overflowing with wildflowers from the meadow, scented the air. Bluets and chicory, jopeyeweed and blazing stars, she'd gathered them in bunches, wanting nature's help in decorating the rooms.

With a satisfied nod, Catherine picked up the basket she'd packed with dinner and headed for the creek, anticipation thrumming through her veins.

Nick pushed open the door of the washhouse and lifted his face to the buttercup sun. Buried beneath tons of earth in the dark confines of the mine tunnels, morning had seemed to last forever. More than once he'd been tempted to head for the shaft and have the basket take him to the surface. But he'd stuck it out, knowing the heady feel of anticipation would only help to fuel his desire when he saw his wife. Not that his desire needed any help. Being in her arms, burying himself deep inside of her, had been all he'd thought of this morning.

Nick spotted Sampson talking with a group of men by the tripple. "I'll be working on orders this afternoon. Send someone up to the cabin if there's any problem."

"Can't imagine why there would be, Stevens being dead."

Sampson had a point there. Nick noticed the loss of a sizable amount of stress himself now that Stevens's private vendetta against Greenfield Mine was over. Nick just wished Stevens hadn't fallen into the mine. He'd have loved to force a reason out of him for why he'd done it. Nick wanted something to scratch away the niggling doubt that remained with him no matter how hard he tried to reason it away. Nick shook his head and started up the path. This was stupid. He'd caught Stevens red-handed.

The blue and white quilt splashed across green grass in the clearing next to the dammed-up pool. Nick sank to one knee and peeked in the basket, unleashing the aroma of fresh baked bread. Turning his head, he glanced around for some sign of Catherine. He spotted it on a tree branch not far from the creek. Her dress and petticoats flapped in the breeze like a banner.

Grinning, Nick reached for his shirt buttons as he rose and strode to the water's edge. He saw her then, her long, dark hair trailing behind her like the picture of a mermaid he'd seen once in a book.

"Cate," he called when he realized she hadn't noticed him. She looked up, shading her eyes against the bright sun, and smiled. Water droplets sparkled on her arms as she waved. "What you doing?"

"Swimming." Catherine splashed and ducked under the surface, wiping water from her eyes when her head reappeared.

"How's the water?"

Catherine stood, walking toward him, and even from this distance she could hear his gasp of breath. "Why don't you come in and see for yourself?"

What had become of his shy little wife? She appeared before him now like a fantasy. Nick couldn't take his eyes off her as she came toward him, the swirl of water slowing her step seductively. Hair glistening dark and smooth down her back caught the sunlight, reflecting the barest hint of fiery highlights. Sleek and ivory-toned, the gentle curve of her shoulders molded into the swell of full, rose-tipped breasts. Puckered by the cool water, or, he hoped, thoughts of him, her nipples tempted his hand and his suddenly dry mouth, as they swayed beguilingly with each motion she made.

Closer she came, and Nick could do nothing but unconsciously rub the palm of his hand against his prickly wool pants and watch the lapping water dip lower, creating the illusion of a slow, sultry unveiling. He saw her navel, the drop of water nestled in its recesses shining like a flawless diamond. Then the water played about her hips, and lower. Wet curls glistened and Nick heard the harsh rasp of his own breathing.

She stopped, trailing her fingers through the water, before reaching toward him. Cocking her head to one side, smiling at him in a way that made his body throb, she gestured in invitation. "Come on in, Nick."

Her voice further entangled him in the web she wove, yet it allowed him to act. Slowly, not taking his eyes off her, Nick leaned against the rock and tugged at his boots.

His shirt was next, and as Catherine watched the gradual exposure of his body she felt the same stirrings she'd seen in Nick's eyes as he'd watched her. His shoulders were broad and thick with corded muscles, his chest wide, bronzed by the sun, softened by whirls of golden brown hair. His hair curled around his hard flat nipples, then narrowed, arrowing its way down.

He lowered his trousers, unhooking them from the part of his body that strained swollen and hard from its darker brown nest. Without missing a beat Nick stepped into the water. Its coolness washed around his legs, but did nothing to temper the heat inside him.

Catherine wondered if she could survive till he came to her. Her entire body sang with anticipation. The tiny ripples of water his movements caused brushed against her thighs as intimately as a kiss.

He stopped just short of touching her. His large body cast a shadow across her. But the shade wasn't what caused her to shiver. He lifted her and the golden nimbus of hair on his chest grazed her breasts with each breath they took. Her breasts filled, the nipples distended, reaching out to him.

How long they stood there, the water sizzling around them, their bodies burning with barely suppressed desires, Catherine didn't know. His eyes reflected light like a thousand shining prisms, promising delights beyond compare. Dampness spread at the apex of her legs that had nothing to do with the water nudging her thighs.

Nick bent forward, brushing his lips across hers, lightly at first, and then with more urgency as jolts of desire ricocheted through his body. The next instant his arms wrapped around her, crushing her slick body to him. Catherine clutched his neck, meeting his open mouth in kind. She wriggled against his long, hard length, locking her legs around him when he lifted her, moaning a sigh of satisfaction when he thrust deep inside.

Wet and wild, he took her. There was no need for gentle caresses, their eyes had done that. Now as they moved breathlessly toward the final release, Nick's fingers bit into Catherine's soft derriere, hers into the firm muscles of his shoulders. Their movements became frenzied. Exploding inside of her, Nick growled deep in his chest as her body convulsed around him, squeezing the last nuances of passion from him.

Nick's breath came in jerky rasps, as he clung to her there in the thigh deep water. Catherine's hair stuck to his shoulder as she lifted her head from his neck. She looked at him, an expression of total amazement on her face.

"That was something, wasn't it?" Nick still hadn't steadied his breathing.

Catherine nodded, afraid to trust her voice. His eyes, before they'd touched, had promised her the stars, and he'd delivered the entire universe.

Later, after they'd swam and splashed in the pool, they sat on the quilt, eating the dinner Catherine had prepared.

"This is good," Nick said around a bite of meat pie.

Catherine bent forward and brushed a piece of crust from his chin, tracing the small scar there with her fingertip before straightening. "Betsy taught me how to make it years ago."

"She did a good job." Grinning at her expression, Nick winked and pulled her closer. "So did you."

Catherine laughed at his teasing manner and leaned back in his arms. "The way you are eating, you must have been pretty busy this morning."

"Did you ever consider that you're the one that saps my strength?" He squeezed her under the breasts, chuckling at the narrowed look she threw over her shoulder. "Seriously, we were pretty busy this morning. One of the veins of coal we're digging is getting wider."

Catherine sat up. "Why that's wonderful."

Nick nodded, his mouth full of fruit, but he didn't seem as excited as Catherine thought he should be.

"Isn't it?"

Nick swallowed, tossing the plum pit behind him. "Well, it is, and it isn't. The coal looks good." He shrugged his shoulders. "And plentiful. But it's heading straight east—toward the river."

"You're afraid of flooding?"

"That thought crossed my mind."

"What are you going to do?"

Sitting up, leaning against the willow tree that umbrellaed them, Nick couldn't help but be pleased by her question. She wanted to know what *he* intended to do about the problem. He almost wished he could come up with an easy solution—one that she would accept. But as far as he knew, there was none. Not unless she was willing to let go. And even though she'd put more faith in him, he didn't think she was ready for his suggestion.

Nick cleared his throat, hating to risk spoiling the companionship they'd found by proposing his idea. She watched him expectantly, and Nick picked a blade of grass, keeping his eyes on it as he twirled it between his fingers. "What we need is a steam engine. It could lift water from the mine. We could hook it up to the lift, too."

"We can't afford to buy a steam engine. You know that." Catherine wasn't sure what she'd expected him to say, but it wasn't that.

Nick shrugged, pulling his knees up, and resting his chin on them. His eyes met hers. "I don't see any other way to mine that vein."

"But a steam engine. Do you know how much they cost?"

"I've a pretty good idea."

Rising, Catherine began pacing the perimeter of the blanket. The back of her shift, where her wet hair hung, clung damply to her body. She plucked leaves from the arching willow branches, then turned to face Nick. "I have too many debts to pay off to even consider such a purchase."

"I have some money."

Catherine's expression softened. "Thank you for the offer, but believe me, it wouldn't be enough."

"We could always look for some backers." Now he'd done it. Nick watched the look of shock cover her face.

"You mean sell part of the mine?"

"You wouldn't have to sell it outright. Just interest some investors in it. I could probably find someone who—"

"In exchange for what?" Catherine demanded

though she knew the answer.

"Shares in the mine." Nick kept his voice calm and steady, a stark contrast to hers.

Catherine's stare was intense, meant to make him look away in defeat. When he didn't, she did. "I can't." Resisting the urge to drop her head in her hands, Catherine continued. "I would just be finishing what my father started—chipping away at Greenfield. Soon there'd be nothing left." Her gaze met his. "I'd have nothing."

Nick tried not to let her admission bother him, but it did. Did she really feel that Greenfield Mine, a glorified hole in the ground, was the only thing she had? Sighing, Nick tilted his head, studying the threads of sunbeams spinning through the narrow leaves. "You gave me a share."

"That was different." Catherine dropped to her knees. "You're my husband."

"And you had no choice," Nick added cynically. Had he actually thought because they enjoyed each other sexually that Catherine would come to realize life was more than a mine?

She had the good sense to lower her eyes. But they jerked up fast enough after she'd analyzed what he said. "Are you telling me, I have no choice now?"

"Not and mine the new vein." Nick crossed his arms over his raised knees and peered at her over folded, thick wrists. "I won't risk the men in a tunnel that isn't properly drained. And there's no way we can do that without a steam engine."

"So, we'll have to—"

"Close up the new tunnel," Nick finished for her.

"But there's still enough coal, isn't there?"

"Sure." Nick stood shaking crumbs from his shirt, and pulled it over his head. "There's still enough to keep us busy." Bending over, Nick stuck his stocking feet into his boots.

"Where are you going?" Catherine watched him dress, wondering about his reaction to her decision. He didn't act angry, yet she sensed withdrawal.

"Back to the mine." Nick tucked in his shirt and reached for his hat. "Thanks for the dinner."

"But I thought you were going to work on orders this afternoon . . . in the cabin." Catherine stood, slipping her dress over her head.

"I was." Nick watched her button her gown over her breasts, wishing he didn't feel betrayed. He'd been fairly confident she wouldn't accept his idea when he'd suggested it. So why now did he feel her rejection of his plan was tantamount to a rejection of him? "But I think there are some other things that need my attention more."

"I see." After moving the basket, Catherine shook the quilt, folding it neatly and draping it across her arm. "Well, I guess you know best." His reaction to her ill-advised words was a raised brow. Hadn't she just let him know, at least to her way of thinking, that he didn't know best.

Dropping the quilt, Catherine went to Nick where he stood, so tall and straight, under the tree. Taking his hands she looked up at him. "I'm sorry about the engine. I know you're angry about the investors, and—"

"I'm not." Nick shook his head, giving her a tentative smile. "I'm not angry. You've made it very clear from the beginning who has final say about this mine, and I accept that." He squeezed her hands, before pulling his away. "I'll see you tonight."

When he walked away, Catherine had to bite her lip to keep from calling him back. But he stopped without her saying a word.

"Hey, Cate." Nick waited until she looked up. "I really did enjoy the dinner." He grinned. "And the swim." He chuckled when her face blossomed red. He liked the way she could boldly seduce him one minute, then blush about it the next.

He started toward the path and Catherine waved, surprised when he paused again.

"And tell Betsy I'll have the coal wagon wait at the end of the lane for her at about two o'clock. It will deliver her right to her son's door."

With that he strode away, disappearing behind a stand of pine trees. Catherine was left alone to wonder if she'd done the right thing—refusing to sell shares of Greenfield Mine.

outline ... tongue, Nick shifted his weight, clamping ... around her leg when she tried to take her hand and later He felt ready some time beside her around her

Chapter Seventeen

Trubue's Tavern on Buckingham Pike, a weatherboard building shaded by a giant sycamore tree, was a stopping point for the Richmond-Roanoke Stage. It was also where Catherine picked up her mail.

"Whoa." Catherine pulled back on the reins, stopping horse and buggy next to the hitching post in front of the tavern. Gathering her full skirt in one hand, she jumped, landing on the sandy roadway with a soft plop.

A bluebird, hidden by waxy green magnolia leaves, warbled melodiously, momentarily drawing Catherine's attention from the two elderly men sitting on the tavern porch. Impeccably dressed in white linen suits enough alike to have been cut from the same cloth, they sipped mint juleps and watched Catherine climb the steps.

"Afternoon, Miss Catherine. Fine day to be out for a ride. Come to collect your mail, did you? The post just got here not more than an hour ago."

"I'd say it was more like an hour and a quarter."

Before Catherine could answer, the second man spoke up, dragging a pocket watch across his stomach.

"Makes no difference, right Miss Catherine?"

"Well, I . . ." Catherine backed toward the door to the tavern, not wishing to involve herself in a controversy between the two cousins. Edger Howe and Elmer Marshall were, like Catherine, lifetime residents of the area who could trace their families back generations. They lived with Miss Alice Howe, Edger's sister, Elmer's cousin, on the family plantation by the river, but they spent most of their time right here—sitting on the porch of Trubue's Tavern. They gossiped with the patrons and argued with each other, though not always in that order.

"Well, I should think it does make a difference what time the stage comes in, especially if you want to catch a ride to Richmond on it. Isn't that right, Miss Catherine?"

"Well—"

"Miss Catherine's not here to catch the stage, Elmer, only to pick up her mail. And the truth of it is that the post has already arrived."

"Humph."

Catherine hid a grin as Elmer leaned back in his chair. Batting the mint sprig out of the way with an age-spotted hand, he took a self-satisfied sip.

"How are things going down at your mine, Miss Catherine?" Edger, obviously feeling he got the better of that disagreement, asked with only a slight smirk thrown his cousin's way.

"Just fine, Mr. Howe. We're sending loads down the river on a regular basis now."

"Heard what happened out your way last week. Real shame about Mr. Stevens. But it seems like he deserved what he got."

Catherine nodded, hoping for the day when her old bottom boss's death wasn't the main topic of conversation.

"That husband of yours must be able to take care of himself pretty good. Why I was just telling Elmer, couldn't have been three days before it happened, that you found yourself a real good man."

"I don't recall you saying anything of the sort," intoned Elmer petulantly.

"Why sure I did. It was last Wednesday, no Thursday. I recall because it was the day Miss Marie came by with John Parker to pick up a package that come from Richmond. Must have ordered a hat or something. Didn't you think it looked like a hat box, Elmer?"

Rubbing a finger down his long nose, Elmer wrinkled his brow. "Yes, if I had to say, I'd go with it being a hat box."

"Well, anyhow." Edger nodded with satisfaction. "You're husband was in the night before and had shared some time with us. We mentioned it to your sister. And that's when I said what a fine fellow he seemed to be." Edger gave Elmer a pointed look.

"And what did she say?" Catherine couldn't resist asking, after she'd allowed enough of a pause for Edger Howe to continue his story without prompting. Why did he have to grow reticent now? Ever since he'd mentioned Marie, Catherine had felt a lump of anxiety growing in her stomach.

"Oh, she agreed wholeheartedly. Said she dearly

loved her new brother-in-law. Mentioned how she was visiting with neighbors to give you and your new husband some time alone, but that she was coming home soon. 'Just couldn't wait to be one happy family again.' Isn't that how she said it, Elmer?"

"Now that you mention it, I do remember talking about Mr. Colton, but are you sure it wasn't Friday? I just don't think—"

"No, no, not Friday. Don't you recall we stayed home with sister on Friday? Besides . . ."

The quarrelsome voices faded as Catherine mumbled a quick farewell and entered the interior of the tavern. Smiling a greeting at the proprietor she collected Greenfield's mail and hurried back outside. Elmer and Edger were still debating what day they'd seen Marie, and seemed to barely notice her as she climbed into the buggy and headed home.

Home. Greenfield was home to her, and to Nick . . . and to Marie. There was no denying that. Catherine let the dapple gray trot slowly down the tree-canopied lane as she thought about the possibility of Marie coming back. Catherine couldn't help that the idea made her uneasy, and that in itself upset her.

Marie was her sister. But it had been so pleasant without her. Catherine shook her head. "It's Nick," she whispered, her voice mingling with the rattling sound of the cicadas.

She believed Nick never seduced Marie. She did. But that didn't mean Catherine thought it hadn't crossed her husband's mind. He was only human. Though he seemed to enjoy their marriage for what it was, he had eyes and a lusty nature that couldn't help being drawn to Marie. It would be different if he loved me, Catherine thought. But, he never mentioned the word she longed to hear—not even in the throes of passion.

Catherine realized the horse had slowed its pace to almost a walk and gave the reins a flick. There was nothing she could do about Marie. If she wanted to come home, Catherine wouldn't stop her. And if Nick . . . Catherine swallowed, refusing to think about the possibility of his wanting her sister.

Later that afternoon, Catherine finally glanced at the mail she'd tossed on her desk in the library. A bill from a seamstress in Richmond caught her eye, and she started to put it aside, deciding that would be the next debt she'd pay upon receiving more money. Wondering if John Parker was paying for Marie's gowns now, Catherine opened the post, just to assure herself that nothing new had been added to the account.

The other letter wasn't addressed to her but to Nick. Since he served as agent, selling Greenfield's coal throughout the coastal region, this wasn't unusual. However, there was something about the letter Catherine found unusual, and she didn't even know why.

As far as Catherine knew, Nick hadn't received any correspondence from England. She looked at the letter again, wondering if it could be from Travis Fielding. Nick had told her he'd written to his former employer, telling him about his marriage. Could this be a letter demanding Nick return to New Castle? And if it was, what would Nick do?

Opening a drawer, Catherine sifted through

papers until she found the letter of recommendation Mr. Fielding had sent with Nick. The handwriting didn't match the new letter. Catherine's sigh of relief was tempered by self-rebuke. What was wrong with her? First she worried about Marie taking Nick from her, and now it was Travis Fielding. Catherine shut her eyes. This was ridiculous.

This last week had been wonderful. They'd moved back into Catherine's bedroom in the main house after deciding to keep the cabin as a place where they could meet occasionally. At first, after their disagreement about the steam engine, Catherine wondered if Nick would hold her decision against her, but he hadn't.

He'd only mentioned the incident once, and that had been last night when they were getting ready for bed. Catherine had been brushing her hair when Nick bent down and touched the tip of his tongue to her ear lobe. The memory of how it felt sent shivers up Catherine's spine even now.

His eyes had met hers in the mirror issuing a silent plea to hurry. But when she'd joined him in bed, he'd been staring at the ceiling, his hands stacked beneath his head. "Nick," she'd said, pulling him back from his musings.

He'd been apologetic, but from the way he reacted when she spoke his name, he hadn't even known she'd climbed into bed. She'd questioned him about his thoughts and had been surprised when he had looked at her, his eyes serious, and he'd said, "If we keep Greenfield a family operation, we aren't going to be able to keep up."

"Nick, I—"

"I know . . . you don't need to tell me." His fingers had touched her lips. "You don't want to sell or bring in investors. But I think it only fair to warn you, we're fighting a losing battle financially.

"The competition from mines in Maryland and Pennsylvania is getting stiffer. And even some of the local miners are looking into incorporating so they can afford steam engines and the extra labor force they need." He'd rolled over, resting his head on the crook of his arm. His impassioned eyes never wavered from hers. "But there's more to it than that. Our new ventilation system is working pretty well. But it's not foolproof. We need better ventilating doors and stoppings—thicker, more airtight. They should be at least three inches thick with iron reinforcements." His hand trailed along the curve of her jaw. "Keeping the mine safe and staying competitive is simply going to require more money than we have."

"But—"

"I know." Nick had rolled over onto his back, blowing air out between his teeth. When he'd turned his head back toward her, his expression had softened, and his smile was sensual. "We'll see how it goes."

Now, Catherine leaned back against the library chair. Was she being uncompromising, insisting that Greenfield Mine be kept in the Brousseau family? She certainly didn't want any of the miners injured. Pinching the bridge of her nose, Catherine closed her eyes. She wished her grandfather were still alive. He could advise her. Or even Grandmere. But they were gone. And she was alone, except for Nick—

and he wanted her to bring in investors.

"Hi, pretty lady. Does your head hurt? Maybe you need your neck rubbed."

Catherine's smile was in place before she glanced over to the open library window where a grinning Nick had poked in his head. She hadn't expected him home from the mine yet, but the sight of him gave her a warm feeling. "My head doesn't hurt, but I wouldn't mind a neck rub. I was just thinking."

"About me?" Nick asked before leaving the window and coming in the door.

"Now why should I waste my time doing that?" Catherine quipped as he pulled her out of the chair and into his arms.

"Oh, I don't know." Nick's words were muffled by Catherine's hair as he nuzzled a particularly sensitive spot on her neck. "Maybe because I've spent most of the day thinking of you."

"You have?" Pulling away, Catherine searched his face for indications that he was teasing, and found none. Did his mind truly linger on thoughts of her, the way hers did of him? She couldn't resist asking. "What about me?"

"For one thing." Nick hesitated. "The way you smell."

"What? Oh, so I smell, do I?"

"Hmmm" Nick took a deep breath. "Better than an English garden." He nipped at her shoulders, laughing when she did. "I thought about your mouth, too." His tone sobered.

"My mouth? What about it?" Catherine felt her pulse quicken and the familiar weakening of her knees as his gaze seemed to scorch her lips.

"I kept remembering last night, and that little trick you did with it." His voice was husky, and his hands that had rested lightly on her hips now slid down to cup her bottom. "Wondered if you might want to try it again."

Catherine didn't have to answer. The wanton way she responded to his kiss spoke as eloquently as the hard heat that pressed into her stomach.

It was much later when Nick stretched his arms above his head, grabbing the rungs of the spool bed. "Do you know what Betsy fixed for dinner?"

Catherine opened her eyes. "Is food all you ever think about?"

"No." Nick pulled her on top of him, smoothing back the fall of auburn hair. "Sometimes I think about the way your mouth feels around—"

Catherine's hand flew up to still his words, and she felt heat flood her face. "You're shameless."

"Entirely." Nick nibbled on her fingers. "And starved. You take a lot out of me, woman."

It wasn't until they were sitting at the dining room table that Catherine remembered the letter she'd picked up earlier.

"Probably just an order from Norfolk," Nick said when she told him. "I wrote to the shipyard down there about supplying them with our coal."

But after supper Nick joined Catherine in the parlor, letter in hand, a puzzled frown forming a line between his brows. "Do you know a solicitor in Richmond named Berringer, Matthew Berringer?"

Closing a volume of poems and looking up, Catherine thought for a moment. "I don't think so. Why?"

"He wants to see me. That's who the letter is from. Says it is imperative that we meet as soon as possible."

"What for?"

Nick studied the parchment again in the light of the argon lamp. "He doesn't say. Just emphasizes that he has some important information for me." Nick folded the letter, putting it into the breast pocket of his jacket. "Well, I suppose we should go to Richmond."

"We?" Catherine bunched her skirts to make room for Nick to sit beside her on the horsehair sofa.

"Sure. We could stay overnight at the Union Hotel." His finger touched the tip of her nose. "And if you're good I'll even let you share my room."

Laughing, Catherine bit at his finger. "Do you think we should both leave the mine?"

"It's only for a couple days, and Sampson can handle it. Besides, this will give you someplace to wear your new hat."

How could she resist a few days alone with Nick and a chance to wear the pretty little bonnet that he'd bought for her, Catherine thought the next morning as she straightened the flowered hat over her curls. She peered into the looking glass smiling at her reflection. Her eyes were bright green and shining, her cheeks a becoming rosy hue. She appeared to be what Nick had called her yesterday, a pretty lady. The thought brought a smile to her lips, brightened her mood. She looked different . . . happier. And there was little doubt Nicholas Colton was the reason. Perhaps Grandmere had been right about him.

Her gaze dropped to the cut glass perfume bottle that had been her grandmother's. Lovingly she traced the sparkling grooves with her finger. She missed Grandmere, terribly, but realized the older woman hadn't left her alone. She had Nick.

And he was right about the mine. She wouldn't allow her pride to interfere with its operation any longer. If Nick thought they needed more money to insure the miner's safety, then they'd just have to get it . . . from investors. After all, as Nick had pointed out to her, she had given him a share. And even though he was part of her family now, she was also part of his. She wasn't Catherine Brousseau, but Catherine Colton. Catherine "of coal town."

Nodding at her reflection, confident she'd made the right decision, Catherine decided to wait until they returned from Richmond to tell Nick. She didn't even want to think about the mine on their little trip. Except maybe she'd ask the lawyer, if she managed to see him alone, if he knew any investors who might be interested in the mine.

"Ready yet?"

Catherine swirled around to see Nick leaning against the door jamb, his arms folded across his chest. He pushed away, walking toward her, his eyes never leaving her face.

"You're beautiful." A single finger under her chin raised her lips to meet his.

When he pulled away, Catherine had to grasp his arm to keep from arching forward. To cover up the motion, she laughed and brushed an imaginary fleck of lint from his handsome chocolate-colored jacket. "This hat certainly does—"

"It's not the bonnet, Cate. It's you." Nick's lips

363

brushed against her cheek, and he felt the stirrings of desire sprout within him. Shaking his head at his poor timing, Nick straightened and took his wife's hand. "We better go," he advised before leading her downstairs.

This constant hunger for her was something he'd never experienced with any other woman. Before, whenever he'd been with a woman for any length of time, he'd find his appetite for her steadily decreasing, until even the lust that had attracted him in the first place was dry as dust. But with Catherine, it seemed to feed upon itself. The more he had her, the more he wanted her.

Maybe being married to her had something to do with it, he thought, as he admired the swell of her gown from the tiny waist while helping her into the buggy. Possible, but he didn't think so. There was more to it than that.

He liked her appearance, had from the first time she'd looked up at him, but if he were honest, Nick had to admit he'd tired of women who were more classically beautiful.

He admired her courage and the tenacious way she stood by her beliefs—though at times, like her refusal to discuss investors for the mine, that trait could border on bullheadedness. But even that he understood. He who had never had anything, could sympathize with her need to hold on to her heritage. But he was certain that she'd change her mind as soon as she realized how important it was to the miner's safety that they improve the ventilation system, because something else he liked about her was her kindness and caring for others. Oh, yes,

Nick leaned back against the stage seat, closing his eyes. She'd see reason soon.

"Are you certain you want me to come along? I could stay in the hotel room and—"

"There's no need of that," Nick interrupted, shrugging into his jacket. "Whatever this solicitor wants to see me about shouldn't take long. Then we can take a walk down by the river, or . . . ," he planted a kiss on the side of her neck, "shop for hats."

They found Matthew Berringer, Esquire's office on the ground level of a narrow brick house on Main Street. A young man with lank blond hair showed them into an ornately decorated office as soon as Nick gave his name.

"Ah, Mr. Colton." A man of about fifty with pale hazel eyes that seemed to bulge over his spectacles held out his hand to Nick. "I'm Matthew Berringer, and this must be Mrs. Colton. Very charming. Please, please be seated. May I get you something? Some tea perhaps, Mrs. Colton, or something stronger for you?" he asked Nick.

"Nothing for me, thank you. Cate?"

"No, thank you. I'm fine." Catherine sat in the red velvet chair Mr. Berringer offered.

"Well," the attorney began after seating himself behind a huge mahogany desk. "I imagine you're wondering why I asked to see you."

"The question has crossed my mind." Nick leaned back in his seat and studied the solicitor through narrowed eyes.

"I've always been of the impression that when you

have bad news to impart, it's best for all involved to get right to the point."

"And you have bad news for me?"

"I'm afraid so." Matthew Berringer removed his glasses, polishing the lenses with a handkerchief as he spoke. "I regret to inform you that Travis Fielding is dead."

"Dead?" Nick jerked forward. "I don't believe it?"

But from the seat beside him, Catherine could tell he did. He grabbed the arms of his chair, and Catherine reached out to cover his large white-knuckled hand with her own. His hand turned, enveloping hers in an impassioned grip. His expression never changed, yet Catherine knew his pain and welcomed the chance to share it with him.

"Unfortunately it's true. There was a hunting accident. Let me see." Matthew replaced the spectacles on the end of his long, narrow nose and shuffled through some papers on his desk. "Ah, here is the letter. Steadwell. That was the name of his hunting lodge."

"Yes, Steadwell." Nick had been there often, accompanying his employer to the place he enjoyed far more than the busy city of New Castle. It reminded him of the place where he'd grown up, Travis had often said. Quiet, country, and peaceful. Nick tore his thoughts from the memory and focused on reality—Matthew Berringer's words.

"I'm afraid I don't have any more details. I am truly sorry to be the bearer of such unfortunate tidings."

"Certainly not your fault." Nick heard his own voice though it sounded like that of a stranger, someone who didn't feel like a mule had just kicked him in the stomach. He glanced over at Catherine, saw the tears swimming in eyes green as spring grass and felt an odd stinging behind his own. Standing, he pulled Catherine up with him.

"Thank you for your time Mr. Berringer." Nick knew he should offer his hand, but to do so he'd have to let go of his wife, and at the moment, he just couldn't seem to do that. Besides, the sooner he left this office with its bright red drapes and chair coverings, the better off he'd be.

"Wait! Mr. Colton, please wait."

Nick was almost to the door before what Matthew Berringer said registered in his mind. He stopped, catching Catherine's shoulder when she bumped into him.

"That was only part of what I needed to see you about. There's more, much more."

Nick couldn't imagine there could be anything else, but he retraced his steps. He continued to hold Catherine's hand.

Matthew Berringer appeared flustered as he straightened his jacket and removed his glasses before resetting behind his desk. "I realize you are upset; however, what I have to tell you may help to ease your loss."

Nick came close to telling him that nothing he could say would do that, but he realized any remark he made would only prolong this interview—something Nick didn't wish to do.

"Since you worked for Mr. Fielding, I'm certain you have some idea of his tremendous wealth—"

"I had terminated my employment."

"Yes, yes, the letter stated as much." He smiled at Catherine, and she had the feeling he was noticing her for the first time since she walked in the room. "You informed Mr. Fielding of your marriage to Miss Brousseau, but apparently he didn't consider that sufficient reason to break your ties."

"I don't understand. What is it you're not telling me?"

"Simply this. According to his will you are Travis Fielding's primary heir. He left money to people on his staff, long-time retainers, but the bulk of his estate, mines, homes, and sizable monies are yours."

"He what?" Nick was out of his chair, leaning over the desk before Catherine could stop him, before she could even absorb what she just heard. "There must be some mistake. What about his family? I know he has a brother. They weren't close, but surely he should be the heir."

Matthew Berringer folded his hands. "As far as I can tell, there was no mention of a brother. As I have already stated, his extensive holdings were left to you."

Combing his fingers through his hair, Nick realized how menacing he must appear and sat back down. "I just don't understand why he'd do this." Of course this wasn't the first thing the man had done that left Nick wondering. There entire relationship had been a series of question marks that Travis had never seen fit to answer.

Why had he been chosen to leave the mine and live in the big house and to receive a formal education? Travis had told him it was because he had shown promise, and he liked to reward those who could help themselves. And Nick had accepted that answer because he wanted to believe it. But deep down he'd known that there were plenty more deserving than he. Perhaps he had survived on his own, even bettered himself, as much as a miner could, but that hardly warranted the kind of recognition he'd gotten from Travis. And now this. . . .

"Of course, I'm hardly privy to Mr. Fielding's thoughts, however he must have wanted you to have his worldly possessions, for he did, indeed, will them to you. You are a very wealthy man, Mr. Colton. I can give you an accounting of exactly how wealthy if you like."

Nick's hand flew out in a gesture of dismissal.

"I understand," Matthew said as he rose. "I've overwhelmed you with the news as it is. Perhaps later, when you've had a chance to digest everything I've said, we can discuss this matter. In the meantime, here is a bank draft made out to you. It should easily cover your trip and any other expenses you might incur. If not, let me know. You have access to almost unlimited funds."

Catherine sat staring at her husband, trying as she knew he was, to fathom what had happened. One thing that had registered with her was the word trip. She gnawed her bottom lip. It wasn't her place to ask, but she wanted so badly to know. Luckily, Nick must have noticed the word also.

"What trip?" he asked.

"To England . . . New Castle. That was Mr. Fielding's request, that you make a visit home. Perhaps you will find some answers to your questions there. In the meantime I think it fair to assume that

369

your benefactor took a liking to you. And according to the letter, you were very good at your job. It states that he sent you to America to acquire a mine for him, and you certainly succeeded there."

Again the lawyers smile beamed toward Catherine but this time it faded when he saw the look of shock on her face. Ignoring Matthew Berringer, Catherine gaped at Nick. Admittedly he was upset and overcome by the news he'd heard, but surely he would set the attorney straight. He hadn't come to Virginia to acquire Greenfield Mine for Mr. Fielding, he'd come to help her get it working again. Hadn't he?

But he said nothing to contradict what Berringer said or to allay Catherine's fears about Nick's motives in their relationship. He merely accepted the bank draft from Matthew Berringer, and without even glancing at the amount, stuck it in his jacket pocket.

Neither Catherine nor Nick spoke on the way back to the hotel. Catherine was torn between offering her sympathies again, and asking him to explain exactly why he did come to America. But when she tilted her head to glance up at him, Nick seemed so involved in his own thoughts that he appeared not to notice she walked beside him. She remained quiet, thinking.

She felt badly for her husband's obvious pain, yet she couldn't stop wondering about the details surrounding Travis Fielding's death—more precisely, his will. "You're a very wealthy man," Mr. Berringer had said to Nick. A wealthy man who no longer needed a marriage that provided him with one fourth of a barely profitable mine.

Catherine turned her head, fighting tears, and concentrated on the swirls and curlicues of wrought iron that bordered the well-kept yards they passed. But she couldn't keep her mind from accepting the truth. Nicholas Colton didn't need her anymore, possibly never had, except as a means to obtain Greenfield for his employer. Mr. Berringer had said Nick was good at what he did. Did that mean he would go to any length to do his job? Did the end justify the means to him? Enough to lie to a plain country girl, marry her . . . make her fall in love with him?

Well, she'd known from the beginning that it wouldn't last. Hadn't she offered Nick an out before he ever agreed to the marriage? Now he could take it.

Nick stopped in the hotel lobby only long enough to order a bottle of whiskey sent to their room. It fleetingly passed his mind that he could afford anything else he wanted, but he stuck with the whiskey. He was in no mood to celebrate his new wealth.

By the time he reached the room, Nick felt ready to burst from keeping his grief bottled up. Flinging himself down in the chair he buried his face in his hands.

"Nick?" Catherine stood by the door, unable to keep herself from being affected by his obvious pain. When he looked up at her, tears shimmered his eyes to silver, and she rushed toward him, clutching his neck when he yanked her down on his lap. Taking a quivering breath, fighting her own tears she cradled his head. He may have deceived her and was probably leaving her, but he had helped her through her own grief when Grandmere died. She could do no less for him.

Dampness seeped through her bodice as she dug her fingers through his thick hair, knowing all the while the agony of having her own heart break. She loved him so much, longed for him to feel the same about her, yet knew it wasn't to be. He sobbed and she made soft comforting sounds, wishing she could do more.

How long they sat like that, Catherine had no idea. Someone had knocked on the door with the bottle Nick had ordered, but she called for them to leave it outside. She could feel Nick calming, knew when he inched her away and turned his head, that he was embarrassed by his display of emotion. She wanted to tell him not to be, that she understood completely, but something about the way he rose and went to the washstand, keeping his back to her, stopped her. She'd served her purpose.

Nick splashed water on his face, shaking his head at what he'd just done. He hadn't cried since his mother had died and left him alone. But he'd only been eight then and had an excuse. Now at twenty-nine, he did not. But news of Travis Fielding's death had made him feel like a kid again—vulnerable.

He'd rarely thought about his feelings for the older man, but he supposed he must have loved him. He would have to, to be so upset by what had happened. Travis Fielding had treated him like a son. And Nick had to admit, there were times he'd thought of the older man as the father he'd never had. But, of course Travis had been far superior to the scum who'd deserted his mother and him.

Drying his face on the linen towel, Nick caught Catherine's eye in the mirror. She really had been very understanding through all this. "I better go down to the docks and see about passage for England."

This was it. He planned to leave right away. Catherine bit her lower lip, trying to tell herself it was better this way. But as much as she tried, Catherine could not get her voice to work. She merely nodded her agreement.

"When I get back, we'll do some shopping for some dresses and hats." Nick hoped outfitting Catherine for the trip would keep his mind off his pain. If anyone could, it was Cate.

"You don't need to buy me things before you go." The last thing Catherine wanted was a pay off.

"Cate." Nick folded the towel, then hung it over the wooden bar. He didn't want to argue with her over spending money on clothes. What had Matthew Berringer said? "Nearly unlimited funds." Certainly this old bugaboo about money should be laid to rest. "You need new clothes."

"I don't." Catherine pulled herself up to her full height. She thought she looked very smart in her green traveling dress and new hat to match, but apparently now that Nick was wealthy, this wasn't good enough for him. So much for him telling her that she looked beautiful. Wounded pride tilted her chin. "You go on and see about your passage. I'll take the stage back to Greenfield." Catherine ignored the force of his stare as he abruptly turned to face her. "Thank you for all you've done for the mine, and I wish you good luck in your new life."

"My new life? What in the hell is that supposed to mean?"

Chapter Eighteen

"I hardly think that needs an explanation." Catherine hoped her voice would remain steady. She felt as if her heart was breaking. "I am very grateful to you and—"

"Cut the drivel, Cate. I don't recall ever asking for your gratitude, and I don't want it now. What in the hell did you mean with that remark about my new life? What's wrong with the old one?"

Why was he doing this? He stood, hands on narrow hips, glaring at her with such force that his thick brows nearly met. Couldn't he simply leave without making a scene, or did he think she would make one now that she knew him to be wealthy? Perhaps he expected her to demand more of him, maybe that was the reason he'd suggested the shopping, to forestall her requests. Well, she'd show Nicholas Colton that she was a woman of her word.

Catherine forced her gaze to meet his. "We had an agreement, Nick. You fulfilled your part, and I intend to fulfill mine."

Nick whipped his fingers through his hair, staring into space for a moment, then back at Catherine. "The agreement? Is that what all of this is about?"

"It is the basis of our relationship."

"If you think that, lady, we don't have a relationship." Shaking his head, Nick made his way to the window, leaning his hip against the sill and lifting the curtain to look at the scene below.

What did he mean by that, and why was he trying to make her seem like the one who wanted out of their marriage. *He* was the one who'd lied to her about his reason for being here. And *he* was the one who was leaving. Catherine clenched her hands around clumps of skirt fabric to keep them from trembling. "I suppose we don't at that," she said, studying the medallion design of the carpet. "However, I am a woman of my word. I shan't fight any divorce proceedings you might initiate, nor shall I ask for any more than we agreed upon. And of course one fourth of Greenfield Mine is still yours."

Nick's eyes tore back at her. He'd known she was strong, hell, that was one of the things he liked about her, but he'd never suspected her of being hard. Yet, there she stood, as calm and cool as you please, saying she wanted him out of her life. Tossing his love aside and paying him off with part of Greenfield.

Nick could feel the anger boil up in him, restlessly, uncontrollably. He tried to tamp it down, but his voice defied his attempts. "I don't want one fourth of that damn mine!"

"Well, I won't let you have all of it. You may have fooled me once, but now that I know, you won't get any more of it. Never! Do you hear me?"

"People in the lobby can hear you, Cate. My question is, do they understand you any better than I do, because I sure as hell don't know what you're talking about."

Catherine lowered her voice. She'd hoped to handle this so he wouldn't know how upset she was, but, as usual, she'd gotten caught up with her emotions. If he could stand there, unaffected by their upcoming separation, then so could she.

Taking a calming breath, Catherine began to explain to him in a rational tone. "You needn't try to pretend anymore, Nick. I heard what Mr. Berringer said, as I'm sure you did."

Trying to make sense of her words, Nick rubbed his hand across his eyes. "Mr. Berringer said a lot of things. You want to refresh my memory? Give me some clue as to what you're referring to."

"The reason you came here," Catherine said, tired of the cat and mouse games they were playing.

"To help with your mine?" Nick felt genuinely perplexed.

"To *acquire* my mine." Catherine raised her chin. "Did you think the solicitor's little slip would go unnoticed by me?"

"Cate, I—"

"Don't try to deny it. I heard him."

"I wasn't going to deny it!" Hell, now she had him yelling. "Travis did mention that I was to look into the advisability of purchasing Greenfield."

"Ahaa!" Catherine tossed her head, auburn curls escaping her chignon.

"What the hell does that mean? Ahaa!" Nick mimicked her motions.

"It means, I knew it. You tried to cheat me."

"Cheat?" Nick advanced on Catherine till he stood close enough to see the gold flecks in her green eyes. "I never cheated you."

"You pretended to help me."

"I *did* help you."

"You took one fourth of my mine." Catherine's head tilted back at an uncomfortable angle, but she refused to evade his eye.

"You gave me one fourth of your mine. It was part of our agreement." The last word was said with such vehemence that Catherine took an involuntary step back.

Catherine was honest enough to acknowledge that, still . . . "You tried to get more."

"The hell I did!"

"Don't try to deny it, Nick. I'm not the innocent country girl you took me for." As Catherine turned her head, the hat ribbon brushed against her cheek. With jerky motions, she untied the bow and flung the bonnet onto the bed. Nick watched it land before turning back to his wife. "Do you think I can't remember all those times you pressed me to bring in outside investors?"

"My advice to you had nothing to do with getting control of the mine."

"Oh, really?" Catherine's expression was smug, as if daring him to prove otherwise. He didn't even dignify her question with a response. He shrugged, walking away and again looking through the window down at the street. This only further infuriated Catherine. She marched toward him. "And I suppose you deny that Travis Fielding's

378

name wouldn't have been the first to cross your lips if I had agreed to sell off shares."

"I don't deny anything, Cate." Nick's voice was as level as the look he gave her. "I also don't think this is a good time to be having this discussion."

"What's the matter, Nick? Can't you think of any lies to tell me?" Catherine knew she was saying more than she should, more than she believed. But somehow it was easier to place the blame on Nick, to think that he'd deceived her, rather than to admit that he was leaving simply because he didn't need her anymore—didn't love her.

Nick glared at Catherine, his nostrils flaring in anger. But beneath the steely gray fire of his eyes there was a sadness that touched Catherine, or would have if she hadn't been so wrapped up in her own pain. With a great deal of difficulty, Nick reigned-in his temper. "I'm going down to the docks. We'll discuss this when I return. In the meantime, I suggest you try thinking things through rationally."

"Rationally!" The cool uninvolved way her husband stated his intentions incensed Catherine. It was all fine and good for him to speak in reasonable tones and of rational thought. He wasn't the one being left behind. It wasn't his heart that was breaking.

"Yes, rationally." Nick paused, his hand surrounding the brass doorknob. "This hasn't been the best day I can remember. Travis Fielding is dead, and though that apparently means nothing to you, I was very fond of the man. And now this." Nick waved his hand in a way that seemed to encompass Catherine, the room, their entire conversation. "Whatever wrongs you think have been perpetrated against you are all in your imagination—just like your suspicions of Marie and me."

Reminding his wife of that in the middle of a disagreement was not the smartest thing he ever did, Nick realized as he saw the green fire spring to her eyes. He left the door, and advanced on her to make amends. He really did feel bone weary, and didn't wish to argue.

"Don't come near me." Catherine backed toward the bed, away from Nick. Feeling tears sting her eyelids, Catherine blinked. She couldn't let him see how much he'd hurt her. Now that she knew the real reason Nick had come to Virginia, she was beginning to doubt all he'd said to her. He'd assured her there was nothing between Marie and himself, but wouldn't someone who was trying to deceive her into selling the mine do almost anything? Lying to an unsuspecting wife would be easy for someone like that.

"Cate." Nick continued, advancing on her. The expression on her face made him wonder exactly what she was thinking. "Let's stop this nonsense." He reached out and touched her shoulder, anger flaring in him when she jerked away. Again he tried to tamp his reaction. His hand dropped. "We're both upset. We need some time to cool off. When I return—"

"I won't be here." There was no way Catherine was going to prolong this discussion. He intended to leave her, so let him, but let him do it quickly. As far as Catherine could discern, they had nothing more to talk about.

"What?" Nick gripped her shoulders without realizing he'd even moved.

"You heard me. I'm taking the next stage back to Greenfield."

"What about England?"

"I think you can board a vessel for your home without my help."

Nick stared down at her in disbelief. She wasn't going with him to England. His home, she had called England. And there was certainly no doubt what she considered her home—her precious Greenfield. "So that's the way it's to be? The end of our agreement?"

Catherine nodded, unable to trust her voice. His fingers dug into the sensitive flesh of her upper arms, but the pain was nothing compared to the tightening around her heart.

"Answer me, Cate. I want to hear you say it. Tell me our agreement—everything—has ended." He shook her, spilling more auburn curls around her shoulders. "Say it," he demanded again.

"It's over." Catherine's words burst forth. "When you leave this room, it's all over. The agreement, everything."

Nick felt as if she'd hit him in the gut. All these weeks he'd thought he meant something to her and he hadn't. She hadn't cared for him at all, only for what he could give her—workers for her mine, management for her mine, always the mine. Nick paused, staring down into her wide green eyes.

There had been something else between them. Sex. He'd always thought of it as more than that, but apparently she hadn't. But she'd liked the intimate aspect of marriage. That enjoyment had been one thing they'd shared—apparently the only thing. Heated desire shot through Nick's body, and with one swift motion he yanked Catherine against him. The feel of her softness mingling with his hurt and anger made a potent aphrodisiac.

"What are you doing?" Shock tinged Catherine's question as she squirmed beneath his hands.

"Just collecting final payment on our agreement." Nick's mouth ground down over hers, forcing her lips open with the pressure of his.

"Don't." Catherine wrenched her face away from his onslaught, but he was not to be deterred. His hot, lusty mouth traveled down the stem of her neck, pausing often to nip the tender skin with his teeth, then soothe it with his tongue. "Please stop." Tears choked her words.

"What's the matter, Catherine? Don't you want to give your loving husband something to remember you by? Forever is a long time to be separated."

"No." Catherine tried to pull away when he roughly pulled the tucker from the bodice of her gown, exposing the tops of her creamy breasts to his gaze and mouth. "You don't really want to do this."

"Oh, that's where you're wrong, my dear Cate." Nick thrust his hips forward, proving beyond question the truth of his words. His hardness pressed against her. Even through her skirts, fiery tongues of desire shot through her body. Desperately Catherine tried to twist away from the contact before he could feel her traitorous body's reaction.

"Hold still, Cate." Nick's hand locked over her jaw. "You wouldn't want to renege on our agreement, would you?" His tongue plunged into the hot depths of her mouth, forcing her head back.

"This was never part of our agreement," Catherine said when Nick pulled away so they both could breathe.

"That would be hard to prove, Cate, since we set the precedent on our wedding night." His body forced hers back on the bed. "And most every night since."

Catherine landed on the mattress, the quilt-covered feathers pillowing around her. Before she could twist away, Nick followed her down, trapping her between the softness beneath her and the steely strength of his hard body. Skirts and petticoats bunched between them, his trousers and frock coat still covered him, but Catherine could feel the heat—could feel herself melting before it.

He moved, finding a more satisfactory spot between her legs, and Catherine's body softened in accommodation. When he moved again, rubbing his manhood against her stomach, Catherine couldn't resist arching toward him.

It was a slight stirring, but Catherine knew he'd felt it. Raising himself on his elbows, Nick searched her face. "You want this as much as I do."

"No!" Catherine tried to avoid his eyes, but again his hand anchored her jaw, forcing her to look at him.

"You're lying." Nick's breathing came in short, shallow gasps. "I can read desire in your eyes." His gaze left hers to travel down the rumpled neckline of her gown to where her nipples thrust against the green silk. Resisting the urge to trace the tempting outline with his tongue, Nick shifted his weight, clamping his hand around her leg when she tried to squirm away.

"You don't really want to do that." He growled the words in her ear as his hand riffled through the layers of petticoats.

"Yes, I do. Let me up."

"You're lying again, Cate. And I can prove it." His fingers found and cupped the core of her femininity. Through the cotton of her pantaloons her moist heat dewed his hand. Even without that confirmation, the low moan of desire Catherine made was proof enough. Her arms, which up to this point had fought a losing battle to push him away, now clutched the back of Nick's jacket.

Her response to him was sensual and complete, all he could have hoped for, and his body acknowledged it with a throbbing urgency that left him breathless. But he wanted more. Even as he yanked open the ribbon, baring her flesh to his probing hand, Nick knew this wasn't enough. He'd wanted her loyalty, her heart, and she gave him her body—and only that until he left.

She'd tried so to match his demeanor of indifference, and failed. Failed miserably. Nick touched her and she melted. Resolve disappeared. Common sense disappeared. The painful truth of his leaving disappeared. All that remained was his hand inflaming her passions, the splendid weight of his body pressed to hers, his raspy breathing that matched her own, his masculine smell, his taste.

There was no demurring this time when his lips met hers. Open mouthed she greeted him, taking the length of his tongue, sliding her own along the sleek surface. The rhythm matched that of his finger as it skimmed across the center of her sensuality. This was no planned cadence, for rational thought escaped them both, but it was the pulsing beat of life handed down from the beginning of time.

Catherine's flattened palms molded over the bunched muscles of his back, the fine wool broadcloth a poor substitute for the smooth warm skin she knew lay beneath. Seeking his flesh, she explored the strong column of his neck, lacing her fingers in the thick curls. The slow steady embers he ignited burst into flame, convulsing her body with uncontrollable spasms. Catherine clutched Nick's head, digging her fingers into his hair, fusing his mouth to hers.

Reality faded and she floated, separate from her mortal body, yet in tune to every nuance of sensual delight. How long she existed in this limbo, Catherine wasn't certain, but just as she thought it would end, as the trembling of her body ceased, he filled her.

His possession of her, hers of him, had never felt so achingly sweet—bittersweet. *The last time.* She pulled him in completely. *The last time.* He plunged, trying to reach her very soul.

Her skirts were bunched around her waist, his trousers about his knees. But for their hungry mouths, all was covered but the place where their union was complete. Hair meshed as Catherine arched to meet his every forceful thrust.

She tightened around him. The tiny vibrations that played themselves out in his memory, in his most erotic dreams of her, began tingling along his flesh.

"Cate." He wasn't sure he'd called her name on

this plane until she opened her passion-drugged eyes and stared into his. Heavy lidded and shining with sultry rapture, they drew him in, as surely as her body welcomed his. Release exploded through him, sparing no quarter as it racked his body completely.

Until the last he watched her, watching him, knowing they both gained pleasure from giving it. But too soon the tremors faded, the eyes that had mirrored his passion closed. Nick collapsed on the bed, throwing his arm across his face. He resisted the strong desire to pull her into his arms. What was the use?

She didn't want him in her life. And though he'd proved that he could still control her passions, the lesson had been hard won. For he'd also shown himself to be completely vulnerable to her. And his vulnerability ran deeper than the carnal pleasures they could give each other. He'd started trying to teach her a lesson and ended making love to her.

Rolling off the bed, Nick straightened his pants. Though he tried not to, he couldn't resist glancing toward Catherine. She lay on the pink quilt in a rumpled heap. Wrinkled and disheveled, her gown exposed shapely legs partly covered by torn ruffled cotton, though she had pushed down her skirts enough to cover herself. For long minutes he looked at her, hoping she'd return his stare. But her face remained firmly turned toward the wall. All he could see was a tumble of sun-shot auburn hair.

Finally, not knowing what else to do, Nick picked up his carpet bag, thankful that he hadn't taken the time earlier to unpack it, and started toward the door. He paused, reached in his pocket, and laid the bank draft on the desk before leaving the room.

Catherine jerked, reacting to the sound of the closing door as if she'd been shot. She released her breath on a sob, and new tears joined the silent ones she'd been unable to check.

"He's gone."

Marie opened her eyes, turning her head to stare at John from the daybed where she'd been napping. "Who's gone?" Her voice hinted at the annoyance she felt at being awakened.

"Nicholas Colton," John said, obviously pleased to impart this news.

Leaning up on one arm, Marie brushed golden hair from her eyes. "Where did he go. And for how long."

John smiled, pulling a chair beside the chaise before he answered. "To England. For good, as I understand it. At least Edger Howe seemed to think it was a permanent move."

"I knew it." Marie sat up, swinging her legs off the satin chaise. "I knew she'd never be able to keep him here. Not even with the mine." Her blue eyes shone bright as she looked at her lover. "When did he go?"

"Last week. According to Edger, he and your sister went to Richmond. She returned. He didn't." John clamped his hand between Marie's stockinged thighs.

"Stop it, John. It's the middle of the day." Marie tried to push his hand away and stand, but he held tight.

"Time never stopped you before, Marie. Besides,

the way I figure it, we have something to celebrate."

Marie sighed as his fingers pried open her legs. "Can't you ever think of anything but rutting like a damn bull?"

Anger flashed in John's eyes before he stood, pushing Marie back onto the daybed. "I suppose not." He yanked the top of her chemise, rending the delicate material. "Of course, you've always led me to believe you liked my *rutting*."

At least he was quick, Marie thought later as she stepped into her gown and waited for the servant to fasten it.

"What are you going to do?" John watched her from the corner of the room.

"Why, I'm going home. Poor, sweet Catherine is probably lonely now that her husband has left her." Marie smiled. "She's probably distraught, needing a sisterly shoulder to cry upon."

"And you'll offer her that?"

"Well, of course, John. What are sisters for?"

Chapter Nineteen

Candlelight prismed by the crystal chandeliers gave a soft glow to silk and satin evening clothes as the dancers swirled around the ballroom at Hawhorn Manor. Strains of a waltz, played by the string quartet at one end of the room, drifted through air laden with rich perfumes. Heavily brocaded drapes, framing floor to ceiling windows, yawned open to admit cooling autumn breezes. For even though the room was as large as it was grand, it seemed overflowing with life. Leaning against the watered silk wall near the wide double doors opening onto a large hallway, Nick watched the dancers dispassionately.

His eyes met those of a pretty young lady whose silvery blonde curls bobbed beguilingly on her bare shoulders as she glided by in the arms of a gentleman.

She smiled. Nick didn't.

"Not interested in the ladies tonight, Nick? Or is it just that particular one that lacks appeal?"

Nick straightened, pulling himself away from the

wall, at the sound of his host's voice. "I assure you my lack of interest is no reflection on the lady in particular, for she is lovely." Nick doubted he could pick her out again if she paraded in front of him, but he had no desire to offend. And for all he knew, the lady who'd smiled at him could be Lord Hawthorn' daughter. "I fear my mind is occupied elsewhere."

"Ah yes. How did you state it in the letter? The mystery of your inheritance, I believe were your exact words."

Nick grinned. "It does pray on my mind." Though it hadn't at this moment. Not until Lord Hawthorn mentioned it. At least that wasn't what Nick had been thinking about earlier. But he doubted Lord Hawthorn was interested in the laments of a spurned husband. Nor would he care that Nick had been imagining Catherine covered from head to dainty toes in silks and jewels, dancing in his arms.

"You really should enjoy yourself, Nick. Live for today. Keep the past behind you—where it belongs."

Nick stared at his host, noting again the similarities between his lordship and his late brother, Travis Fielding. He first noticed how much they favored one another this morning when Nick had arrived at Hawthorn Manor. Both brothers were tall and solidly built, nearly as large as Nick. Lord Hawthorn's hair, though mostly gray, still held hints of its original dark brown.

"Do you know why your brother willed his wealth to me?" Nick could contain the question no longer. He'd wanted to ask it as soon as he'd arrived this morning, but Lord Hawthorn had been occupied then. His house, as now, overflowing with guests.

had required his attention. Though Nick realized he should have waited for a more suitable time to ask, a time when he could get Lord Hawthorn alone, he'd pushed ahead anyway.

Lord Hawthorn didn't seem at all taken aback by Nick's blunt manner. Instead he appeared lost in thought before answering. "I'm afraid Travis was the only one who could answer that with absolute certainty."

"But your letter . . . I thought," Nick began. He'd written to Lord Hawthorn when all other avenues of discovering the truth had proved fruitless. When he'd received an answer, inviting him to come to Hawthorn Manor, Nick had assumed he would soon learn of Travis Fielding's motives.

Lord Hawthorn held up his hand. "I said I couldn't answer you with absolute certainty. And that's true. But when I responded to your post I had a theory. Now that I've seen you, little doubt remains."

The last musical chords floated through the air and the dancers separated. Several men, their ladies clinging to their arm, approached Lord Hawthorn and Nick. Noticing them, Nick resisted the urge to leave. He had no desire to engage in inconsequential chatter, not with Lord Hawthorn's promise of a theory still ringing in his ears. Still, he must be polite and—

"We can continue this conversation in my study." Lord Hawthorn motioned toward the hall. "Unless you've a wish to meet Lord Brathway. But let me warn you, he's terribly dull."

Nick's deep chuckle blended with the sound of their heels striking the polished marble floor of the entranceway as they made their escape. Lord Hawthorn led the way through a deeply paneled oak door to his study. "I really shouldn't speak of Brathway as I do, and mind you," he pointed a long aristocratic finger at Nick, "if you ever so much as breath a word that I did, I shall deny it."

Nick shook his head, realizing Travis and his brother were alike in more than their looks. Even though he'd been a tough employer, expecting nothing but the best from Nick and everyone else that worked for him, Travis had never shied away from a good laugh. The brothers were so much alike that Nick wondered again why they had never seemed to get along.

Accepting the snifter of brandy Lord Hawthorn offered, Nick settled into the soft confines of the leather chair his host indicated. He leaned back, deciding Lord Hawthorn would continue their conversation when he was ready. Nick had tried for nearly a month now, ever since he'd arrived in England—to no avail—to find the answer to why Travis had made him his beneficiary. A few more minutes would make no difference, though he wished the older man would stop watching the firelight reflect through the amber liquid in his glass and get on with explaining his theory.

"How long did you know Travis?"

Expecting answers, not questions Nick sat forward. He placed his glass on the inlaid table beside his chair and met Lord Hawthorn's eyes. "I've known of him since I was ten. Approximately nineteen years. I worked in one of his mines as a pit boy."

"But you didn't actually know him then, did you?"

"No. The first time I met your brother, I was sixteen. The bottom boss ordered me to go up to the big house." Nick shook his head, remembering that day years ago. "I thought I was going to be fired. There didn't seem to be any other explanation for why the mine owner wanted to see me."

"Were you still a pit boy?" Lord Hawthorn swirled the brandy in his glass.

"By that time I was a digger, sometimes a gas man. I was large for my age," Nick said when he noticed Lord Hawthorn's surprised glance.

"You still are." Lord Hawthorn raised his glass. "As am I, as was my brother," he mumbled into his glass as he took a sip of the warming liquid. "But tell me, what happened when you met Travis. I take it he didn't terminate your employment."

"To the contrary." Nick was tired of answering questions, wished to ask some of his own, but sensed Lord Hawthorn would only start giving answers when his own curiosity had been satisfied. "He took me into his house and gave me an education."

"And did he give you any explanation for his benevolence?"

"No."

"But given your penchant for ferreting out explanations, I assume you asked."

"I did."

"And?"

Nick leaned back, crossing his ankles. "And I was told he enjoyed rewarding those who could help themselves."

"But you didn't accept that explanation, did you?"

"Not entirely."

393

"Yet you continued to allow Travis to treat you as a son."

Nick stood, suddenly annoyed by the turn of the conversation. He began to doubt that Lord Hawthorn knew anything about the will. Perhaps he even resented that Nick had received the bulk of the inheritance rather than someone more likely— himself.

"Wait. Where are you going?" Lord Hawthorn stood.

"I've kept you from your other guests too long. It's time I allow you to return."

"I think I can be the judge of that, Nick. Have you lost interest in the reason for your sudden wealth?"

"Hardly." Nick leaned against the marble mantel. "I'm simply beginning to wonder if you intend to tell me your theory."

"Maybe, Travis simply took a liking to you. Though your manners leave something to be desired." Lord Hawthorn motioned toward the chair Nick had vacated, and reluctantly Nick sat down. "You are an engaging enough young man."

"I'm flattered," Nick responded wryly. "However I hardly think that sufficient cause."

"Nor do I. Nor do I." Lord Hawthorn resumed his seat. "Tell me about your mother. Before you object, let me assure you that it is important that I am familiar with your background before I tell you what I know. You will simply have to trust me on this point.

"But I think you should also be very certain that you wish to open this Pandora's Box. Sometimes it is better to simply accept what is," Lord Hawthorn prophesied.

"And do you think this is one of those times?"

"Perhaps. Though I can tell by your expression that what I think makes little difference to you."

"I want to know," Nick stated succinctly before telling Lord Hawthorn all he remembered about his mother. When he'd finished, the older man stared into his brandy for long minutes before facing Nick.

"I don't think there's any question in my mind now. I still don't know if I should be the one to tell you. It should have been Travis."

"Travis is dead."

"Ah yes." Lord Hawthorn raised his glass as if to toast his dead brother. "So the task is left to me." He settled back in his chair. "Let me begin at the beginning.

"Travis is . . . was my younger brother, by a score of years, so we never were what you would call close, though I did love him—in my way. By the time he was old enough to do more than drool his mush, I was being groomed to become what I am," Lord Hawthorn arched his arm in a broad sweep, "a wealthy earl. I took my training seriously." He shook his head. "I took myself seriously. Something I rarely do anymore. But that's a different tale.

"My family's lands were extensive, still are. And not just here. We own land in several shires."

Nick thought the family history interesting, however he couldn't understand what any of this had to do with his inheritance. He found his mind wandering, as it had so often since he'd left her, to Catherine. What was she doing now? Did she miss him at all? Did she ever think of him?

". . . and that's when Travis first met her."

Nick only caught the end of what Lord Hawthorn

said, but something, maybe it was the tone of his voice, convinced Nick that this was important. "I'm sorry. Whom did you say he met?"

Lord Hawthorn looked at him as if trying to decide whether to continue explaining to such a poor listener. But in the end, he relented. Lifting his glass again in a mock salute he answered. "His one true love. The love of his life. The woman that made him complete." Lord Hawthorn's words were derisive, however Nick couldn't tell who was the butt of his ridicule.

"Of course, he didn't realize it then. Or, then again, maybe he did. But rest assured, I didn't.

"A case of lust is what I put it down to. An ailment that could be cured by a quick roll behind the barn." Lord Hawthorn set down his glass and laced his fingers across his still lean stomach. "But Travis didn't see it that way. He wanted to marry the girl.

"Being the older brother, I explained to him that things like that simply were not done. But Travis persisted." Lord Hawthorn stared into the flames dancing in the fireplace. "There was nothing left for me to do but contact our father. I knew he'd be able to put a stop to Travis' foolishness. And he did."

"How?" Nick urged. He could feel Lord Hawthorn's regret as a tangible presence in the paneled study.

"He called Travis back here, to Hawthorn Manor, using the excuse of needing him. Of course, Travis, being somewhat naive, didn't see the summons for what it was. He saw it as a chance to plead his case. But then he didn't know our father as I did. Father wouldn't allow anything to stand in the way of his

396

pride or his station in life . . . and that included a smithy's daughter."

Nick sat forward, forearms resting on his thighs. His mother had said her father was a blacksmith. "What happened to the girl?" Nick demanded, startling Lord Hawthorn with the emotion in his voice. He had an uncomfortable feeling that this story was very closely related to him.

"She vanished—without a trace. At least, that's what Travis thought. By the time he figured out that father was interfering in his affairs, it was too late. Travis returned looking for her, but she'd gone."

"Where?"

Though Lord Hawthorn's face remained grim, the hint of a smile played at the corners of his mouth. "Ah, you are more perceptive than Travis was. You guessed I knew the girl's whereabouts. He never did. At least not until I told him—and then it really was too late."

Lord Hawthorn straightened. His voice became more firm. "In answer to your question she was in New Castle. You see the girl, hardly more than a child herself, was soon to bear one. And having been abandoned by her lover—"

"A fact I'm certain you were quick to point out." Nick could feel nausea grip him. There was no need to tell him who the girl was, or what kind of anguish she felt over her abandonment. Clutching the cushioned arms of his chair, Nick resisted the urge to bash Lord Hawthorn's face in—at least until he heard the rest of the story about his mother and father.

"Ah, yes. You see Lizzy trusted me. She even gave

397

me a letter to deliver to Travis." Lord Hawthorn met Nick's accusing glare. "You're quite right. I never did."

"I did find her a dwelling, and as time grew near for her delivery, I saw that some money was forwarded to her."

"To ease your conscience?" Nick spit the words as if he thought the possibility of the older man having such a thing out of the question.

Lord Hawthorn apparently chose to take the comment on face value. "Yes, I suppose that was the reason. Though I had nothing against Lizzy personally, actually I found her a charming girl, I thought I was doing the best for my brother—for my entire family."

"When did you realize you hadn't?"

Lord Hawthorn stood and walked to the window. Pulling back the drapes he stared into the darkness. "When Travis wouldn't—couldn't let it go—that's when I knew. He'd given up the search. There was no place left to look, and of course, he had no idea about New Castle. But he still couldn't let it go."

"But you knew—about New Castle, I mean."

"Yes, I did," Lord Hawthorn agreed. "Before you give in to temptation and use that fist to flatten my nose," Nick looked down at his hand and forced his fingers to relax, "let me tell you that I did go to New Castle, and I did try to find your mother. But she no longer lived in the small house I'd found for her. I searched for a time but could find no clue as to her whereabouts. And I decided the whole mess would blow over sooner or later. All Travis needed was time."

"But it didn't."

"No. And finally, whether to soothe my conscience or perhaps share the guilt, I went to Travis. When I told him my part in the scheme, he did use his fist. And then he never spoke to me again."

Something in the way Lord Hawthorn said the last part told Nick that the older man had already been punished far more than Nick could ever do. He rose, determined to leave this house before another hour passed.

"At least after I told him, he knew about you." Lord Hawthorn's words stopped Nick at the door. "I kept tabs on Travis, discovering that he shifted the impetus of his search from your mother to you. Maybe he just discovered that she had died. Apparently, he found you." Lord Hawthorn's eyes met Nick's.

"Why he never told you who you were, I can't tell you. Maybe he felt partly responsible for the death of your mother." He shook his head. "Though Lord knows he shouldn't have. But anyway, I'm certain now, that's the reason he left you his estate. You are his son."

A son who never knew the man he loved was his father. Nick stared at Lord Hawthorn, his uncle. Though he doubtless regretted his part in the deception, Nick couldn't erase the vision of his mother, forced to lead a life repulsive to her sweet nature, forced because of the actions of this man. Nick left the room without a backward glance.

It took Nick three days of hard riding to reach New Castle. Rains turned the roads to a muddy quagmire. Nick was almost glad for the concentration it took to guide his horse. It gave him little time to think.

However, now, dry and toasted warm by the hearth of his own fire in New Castle, he could not seem to do anything but think. Images of the past and present mingled in his mind with unrelenting clarity. He saw his mother suffering, slowly dying from living in poverty and shame and the loss of her love. He saw Travis as he must have looked doggedly searching for the woman, later the son, who could make his life whole. And he saw Catherine, sweet Catherine, as she'd been when he'd left her.

Regret. Regret over what had been, over what should have been, filled his mind.

"Will there be anything else, sir?"

Nick's chin lifted from his chest, and he looked up at Seymore, his butler, an outward sign of the wealth he now possessed. "No, nothing, thank you." Nick sent the man away.

Wealth had its advantages, its creature comforts, but it had never bought Travis happiness. And if Nick's last glimpse of Lord Hawthorn was any indication, it hadn't made him feel any less regret. And what of himself? Nick stretched his long legs before him, catching his boot on the fireplace fender. Green eyes and an elusive dimpled smile branded his mind. Was he happy now that he'd joined the elite ranks of the wealthy? Or was he also riddled with regret?

"You're white as a ghost!"

"I feel fine," Catherine lied, trying to make her step livelier as she entered the kitchen.

"You are not fine and I know it even if you don't. Now you go right back up to your room and lie down."

Catherine plopped down on a hard kitchen chair. "Lying down doesn't help. I told you that." Catherine regretted her tone and smiled at the black woman who hovered over her. It certainly wasn't Betsy's fault that the floor seemed to swing from side to side.

"Here." Betsy shoved a piece of toasted bread and a cup of tea in front of Catherine. "If you're going to insist on getting up, this should help."

"Thank you." Catherine took a hesitant nibble of bread, then another, aware of Betsy's brown-eyed stare.

"You write him yet?"

Catherine sighed. "No. And as I told you yesterday, and the day before, I have no intention of doing so."

"You best let him know, girl."

Instead of answering Catherine took a sip of tea. As far as she was concerned Nicholas Colton had lost all his rights—except those spelled out in their agreement—when he'd boarded the packet for England.

"Mr. Nick aughta' be told about this baby," Betsy insisted.

"What baby?" Marie swept into the kitchen, her ruffled satin skirt brushing the door jamb. Her blue eyes narrowed, pinning Betsy with a disapproving look. "I've been sitting in the dining room nearly a quarter of an hour, waiting for my breakfast, and here you are, gossiping about someone's baby."

"I'm sorry, Miss Marie. I'll bring your meal to you right away."

"Oh, never mind. I might as well eat it here. It's easier than walking back outside. The weather grew chilly last night." Marie sat at the table opposite Catherine, draping her shawl around her shoulders. "I wanted to talk to you anyway, Catherine. And since you always seem to be busy—or occupied in here—" Her scowl again found Betsy. "We might as well do it in the kitchen."

Catherine forced a smile to her lips and wrapped her fingers around the warm teacup. She had no desire to talk at length with her sister, but right now, she was just thankful that Marie hadn't pursued the topic of the baby. Catherine knew she couldn't keep the secret much longer—already she'd had to loosen her stays—but the longer she could keep her secret from Marie, the better.

Catherine would have been happy to keep her precious news all to herself. She hadn't told Betsy. The older woman had simply guessed the truth the first time she'd seen Catherine run from the kitchen and lose her breakfast behind the lilac bush.

Since then Betsy had nagged her incessantly about contacting Nick. But, of course, Betsy didn't know the entire circumstances of Nick's going to England. As much as Catherine missed him and wished that he would come back, she knew it would never happen. And she refused to use the baby as bait. If he didn't come back for her, she didn't want him at all.

". . . well, what do you think?"

Catherine's eyes focused on her sister. "I'm sorry . . . I didn't hear."

Marie pursed her lips. "Were you listening to me at all? Oh, never mind. I said that when I was in

Richmond last week I stayed at the Baldwin's. You remember Sissy Baldwin, don't you, Catherine? She visited the Milleau sisters last spring. Maybe you never met her, but you must have heard me mention her."

Catherine nodded, forcing herself to pay attention. The sooner she listened to Marie's chatter about this ball gown or that hat, the sooner she'd leave, and Catherine was beginning to feel queasy again.

"Well, while I was there, I was introduced to this perfectly delightful man. He's from England. And you'll never guess why he's in from Virginia."

Catherine caught Betsy's eyes, and the older woman rolled hers heavenward as Marie continued with her story.

"He's here meeting with representatives of the local mine owners, looking for mines to buy. I told him about ours, and he was very interested."

"Well, I'm not." Catherine stood, trying to ignore the nausea.

"You're just being stubborn, Catherine. You don't even know what he has to say."

"I know I'm not interested in selling the mine."

"You're impossible!" Marie flounced around on her seat.

"Marie." Catherine strove to keep her voice calm, though she was sorely tired of explaining this to her sister over and over again. "If we sell the mine, we will have nothing left."

"And what do we have now?" Marie stood, hands on her hips, her eyes hard with hatred. "We barely make enough money to keep this old house going. And look at you. You worry so much about this stupid mine, you can't even keep a husband."

Marie's words cut like the jagged edge of a sharp rock, but Catherine tried to conceal her hurt. "Marie, I wish you'd try to understand. I—"

"You're the one who needs to understand, Catherine." Marie stood, balancing her hands against the table, and leaning forward to glare at her sister.

"Don't you go yelling at Miss Catherine now. Not in her condition."

"How dare you question anything I say or do you old—" Marie's gaze swung from Betsy to Catherine. "What condition is she talking about?"

Under her sudden scrutiny Catherine paled. She knew Betsy was only looking out for her good, but at this moment she would gladly do without a champion. Why hadn't she let Betsy know that she preferred her condition be kept secret as long as possible?

"What is she talking about, Catherine? Are you ill?"

"No, I'm—"

"She's in the family way. And I don't think it's a good idea for you to upset her."

"She's . . ." Marie's eyes widened as they again switched from Betsy to Catherine. "You're pregnant?" A humorless laugh escaped her lips. "I don't believe it."

Catherine's back stiffened and she raised her chin a notch. "I am going to have a child, yes."

"And no husband," Marie smirked.

"She's got herself a husband. He's just—"

"Betsy, please. I don't need you to defend me." Catherine turned to her sister. "The situation

404

etween Nick and me is my own business, as is the
ct that we are having a baby."

"That's where you're wrong, Catherine." Marie
rapped her stole around her shoulders. "I know
ou. If you have someone to save this place for, you'll
ever sell."

"I never intended to anyway," Catherine began,
ut before she finished, Marie had disappeared out
ne door. Catherine's gaze dropped to the twisted
nen napkin caught between her fingers.

"That girl ain't no good." Betsy clanged a brass
an against the bricks as she grabbed it off a hook.

"Betsy," Catherine sighed.

"I know. You don't have to tell me. You don't like
ne talking about your sister that way, but I'm going
o say it anyway. She just ain't got one ounce of
uman kindness in her whole body."

Catherine thought about what Betsy had said later
s she went over the ledger book. *Tried* to go over
eemed more like it. Too many other things cluttered
er mind to concentrate on how many tons of coal
Greenfield produced last week. Enough, was all she
ared at this point.

At least she didn't have to be concerned with the
vorkings of the mine. Sampson and the other miners
ad stayed after Nick left. This had surprised
Catherine at first until Sampson told her about the
etter he'd received from Nick. Apparently Nick had
vritten it before leaving Virginia. In it he'd asked
ampson to take over managing the mine until he
eturned.

Catherine leaned back and rubbed her temple. She
vondered how long it would be until Sampson and

the others realized Nick wasn't going to return. Well, she couldn't worry about that now. And she wasn't going to think any more about Marie.

If Marie wanted to be ugly about the baby that was her business. Though Catherine hoped that wouldn't be the case. Ever since Marie returned to Greenfield, asking Catherine's forgiveness for the way she'd left, they had gotten on reasonably well. And Catherine had enjoyed having her company ... any company since Nick was gone. Catherine shut her eyes trying to close out the sadness she felt about Nick. She knew it had to be. She'd known it from the beginning. But that didn't stop it from hurting.

"Think about the baby," she told herself. "Think about how wonderful it will be to have a precious young life." But nothing could erase the fact that she had not created that life alone. She and Nick had forged its creation. But he would not be a part of their child's life, any more than he was part of hers.

Tears squeezed past her eyelids, and impatiently Catherine brushed them aside.

That's when she heard the pounding of hooves on the packed dirt road. Rising, Catherine walked to the window. Lifting the curtains she stared out at the winter-gilded landscape. The hand that flew to her mouth stifled her gasp of surprise.

Chapter Twenty

"Nick." The word escaped, defying Catherine's best efforts. Nor could she stop herself from rushing to the door. Swinging it open, she squinted into the weak afternoon sun. He'd ridden closer, near enough for her to know for certain that no apparition brought on by wishful thinking galloped up her lane.

She could hear the clip clop of hooves, the heavy breathing of a hard-ridden horse, almost smell the mingled scent of man and beast. And she could see. Like a starving creature she feasted on the sight of him, tall and proud, his great coat-cape flying from broad shoulders.

Though still too distant to make out eyes shadowed by the low, flopping brim of his hat, she knew he stared at her. Icy-fingered, wintry wind billowed her skirt; yet Catherine found her lungs suddenly devoid of air. Why had he returned? And what did it mean to her—to them?

With a flare of nostrils and sideways jerk of his

head, the stallion stopped, stomping the packed earth in front of the porch. Throwing his leg over the broad back, Nick slid to the ground. For seven weeks, since he'd made the decision to return, he'd imagined his reception at Greenfield. Like a schoolboy learning his lessons he'd practiced what he would say when he first saw Catherine. He'd been sublime, he'd waxed poetic. Yet now, seeing her, the perfect oval face pale, her body trembling, he could remember none of it.

"You're cold," he said climbing the steps to stand before her. Gently he took her frigid fingers in his hand and led her inside.

Had he expected to be met with hugs and kisses? That had been one scenario his mind had conjured up, Nick admitted to himself. Since he'd found that one the most appealing, he'd fantasized it often, and now he succumbed to disappointment as reality set in. She didn't throw herself into his arms, but merely stared, wide-eyed, and disbelieving.

Flashes of her lying on the hotel bed in Richmond, refusing to look at him as he left shot through his memory. Had she wanted him to leave, or had they both been ruled by misunderstanding and pride?

Nick walked to the fireplace, stretching his hands toward the fledgling fire. The room suddenly seemed as chilled as the outside. "I hadn't expected it to be this cold."

Catherine didn't know if he referred to the weather or to his reception. The questioning look he threw over his shoulder revived her voice. She couldn't simply stare at him forever. "It's been unseasonably cold. Of course, so much of the discomfort is caused

408

by the dampness. I wish it would go on and rain as it's threatened to do for days. Though perhaps it's better if it doesn't, for I fear we might have sleet." Catherine realized she rambled, and about something as silly as the weather, and stopped.

Moving to her desk she straightened an already neat pile of papers. "How did you find England?"

"Nearly the same as when I left it."

"Oh." Catherine sat in one of the hard-backed chairs. He didn't seem willing to elaborate on his trip, nor did he seem ready to say why he'd returned.

"How have you been? You look tired."

Catherine's head jerked around. She had a sudden vision of Betsy writing to Nick, telling him about the baby, begging him to come back to Virginia. But Nick's expression revealed nothing more than mild inquiry. "I'm fine," she answered knowing that she would have to tell him—but only if she were certain he planned to stay.

"And the mine?" Nick hadn't a clue why he asked that. The mine was the least of his concerns. But she acted so distant. Suddenly his coming back seemed less than the splendid idea he'd convinced himself it was.

Was that why he'd come back? For the mine? But that didn't make sense if he'd inherited all that money. Why would he need her mine? "It's running very well. Sampson has done an admirable job." She didn't mention she knew Nick had written to the miner. They both knew he'd made no effort to contact her. "I'm sure he'll be glad to see you."

Well, that will make one person, Nick thought. "Maybe I'll walk down to the mine and see him."

Don't send me out in the cold again.

"That sounds like a good idea." *Don't leave me so soon.*

But with only a nod of his head, he did.

By supper time, Catherine had become more accustomed to Nick being back, though, of course, she still had no idea why he'd returned, or for how long.

Still, she couldn't help the excitement that flowed through her. She dressed in her best green gown, thankful that the waist still fit, and spent much longer than usual fixing her hair. After brushing it till the thick fall nearly crackled with life, she piled it softly atop her head.

Betsy noticed her appearance the moment she walked into the kitchen.

"Where you off to Miss Catherine? And here I fixed a nice stew for your supper."

"I'm not going anyplace. We have a guest." Surprised that Betsy didn't know of Nick's return, Catherine assumed his long stay at the mine had something to do with it. He'd yet to return to the house.

"Nick is back," Catherine answered Betsy's silent inquiry.

"Hallelujah! I knew that boy wouldn't stay away. Always knew he had sense—more than most folks around here." Her brown eyes met Catherine's.

"I don't know if he plans to stay." Catherine felt the need to defend herself.

"Of course he'll stay. He come back didn't he? And with the baby. What did he say about it?"

Silence hung in the air as thickly as the savory scent of rabbit stew.

410

"You didn't tell him. Lord, child what's wrong with you?"

"I told you I don't know if he's staying." Catherine stopped, realizing her argument meant nothing to Betsy. "I just came to tell you we'd have one more for dinner." With that she left the kitchen, ignoring, or trying to, Betsy's grumbling about some folks not knowing what was good for them.

But Betsy was wrong. Catherine did know what was good for her. Nick. She'd known for a long time. But what if he didn't feel the same? She would not force him to stay if he didn't want to. And telling him about the baby—knowing how he felt about his own fatherless childhood—was tantamount to coercion.

Later, Catherine realized her mistake when Marie entered the dining room where she and Nick sat. She should have gone straight to her sister as soon as Nick had gone to the mine. Marie didn't like surprises, and walking into a room and seeing Nick was a big one. Catherine could tell by the look of shock on her face. Of course the expression vanished quickly, replaced by a smile that could light up a room.

"Well, Nicholas," Marie drawled in a voice soft enough to simulate magnolia blossoms and smooth sheets, "I didn't expect to see you again."

"I can't imagine why not." Nick's eyes swept to Catherine's then back to Marie.

"Catherine told me you'd returned to England." Her full skirts flounced to the side as she sat. "For good."

Again Nick's gaze searched for Catherine's but she seemed intent on folding and refolding the napkin in

411

her lap. He wished he hadn't gone to the mine, wished cowardliness hadn't kept him there all afternoon. They needed to talk. Nick had told himself they could do it at supper—and later. But he hadn't taken Marie into account. He stared at his sister-in-law with a decided lack of warmth. "When did you move back?"

Marie must have noticed the hostility in his tone—she'd have been hard pressed not to—for her expression changed again, and her tone resembled the brittle rasping of winter leaves rustling in the cold wind. "I've been *home* for over three months now. Ever since you deserted my sister."

"Marie!" Catherine glared across the table set with her grandmother's hand painted china, hardly believing what she'd heard. Marie had spoken her mind to Catherine often enough, but Catherine had rarely heard her be rude to anyone else. "Please apologize." To Nick she said, "I can't imagine why she . . . I never implied—"

"It's all right, Catherine."

"Of course it is," Marie insisted with a flirtatious smile that never reached her eyes. "Nick and I understand each other, don't we, Nick?"

Laying down his spoon, Nick's gaze met Marie's. He couldn't deny that she was a beautiful woman, anymore than he could deny she spoke the truth. Unfortunately, he did understand Marie. At least enough not to trust her—or like her. "Yes, Marie, we do."

Catherine wished for some elaboration on that point, but got none. Nick seemed suddenly starved and attacked his rabbit stew and biscuits as if this vere the last meal he'd ever get. Which left Catherine vith nothing to do but eat—and think.

Her mind abounded with "ifs." She realized with a tart that she didn't know *if* she and Nick were still narried. She had no idea how long it took to get a livorce, but if he started legal procedures when he irst arrived in England . . . Maybe that's why he'd eturned, to have her sign the papers.

Or what *if* he'd decided that Marie really was the ister he wanted. Hadn't he just said they understood ach other? Well, that was more than Catherine ould say, because she didn't understand anything nymore. She didn't even understand why she vracked her brain trying to answer all these questions when all she had to do was ask Nick. And he would. As soon as she had a chance to speak with im alone.

"I think I'll retire to my room." Marie rose. "I'm ure you two have so much to tell each other."

Catherine didn't miss the smirk on her sister's face r the veiled reference to Catherine's news. She was ertain that Marie expected Nick's reaction to be egative. To be honest, Catherine couldn't under-tand why Marie hadn't already told Nick about the aby.

Nick moved around the table, taking Marie's lace, as soon as she left the room. He was close nough to touch Catherine which is about all he'd een able to think about doing for the last seven veeks. He couldn't believe he'd been home for five ours and hadn't taken her in his arms. If he only new what her reaction would be. He couldn't forget er dismissal in Richmond.

413

His nearness made her uncomfortable. For all that she carried his child, had shared with him the intimacies necessary to accomplish such a feat, she felt shy. Catherine cleared her throat. "I really am sorry about Marie. She didn't know you were back."

"I gathered as much. Has she . . ." Nick paused, thought better of his question, then asked it anyway. "Has she caused you much trouble?"

"No." Catherine jumped to her sister's defense, then surrendered to honesty. "Well, she has been after me to sell the mine and the house."

Nick grinned. "I can imagine the opposition she's run up against there."

Catherine's mouth relaxed into a smile, then straightened. "I do feel guilty about it sometimes. Marie doesn't like it here. She wants to travel, see the world. There just isn't enough money."

"That's one thing I wanted to discuss with you."

"What?"

"Money. For Marie."

"My my, don't this look nice." Before Catherine could ask him what he meant by that, Betsy entered the dining room, and began clearing away the supper dishes. "It sure is wonderful to have you home, Mr. Nick."

"Thank you, Betsy." Nick winked at Catherine. "It's nice to be home."

Catherine had to laugh at Betsy's knowing grin. A simple polite reply from Nick was all Betsy needed to assume a scene of loving domesticity. But Catherine needed more. And she needed to know now. But Betsy seemed intent upon pausing in her duties to chat with Nick. As much as Catherine loved Betsy, she had o desire to make this into an open discussion.

"Maybe we should go to the parlor, Nick. That way Betsy could finish her work without interruptions." And we could finish our talk. Why ever would he give Marie money?

But after she led the way to the parlor, Catherine turned to find Nick standing close to her. Not just close, near enough for her to feel the heat from his body through the frock coat he wore. His voice caused a ripple of anticipation to run down her spine. "We could take a walk."

"A walk?" Catherine forced herself to be logical. "Have you forgotten how cold it is outside?" And how could she have forgotten how tall and broad he was? She had to tilt her head just to look at him when he stood this near.

"The cabin isn't far."

The cabin? Memories of stolen moments spent entwined with Nick on the old rope bed sprang to her mind. She looked away to keep him from reading her thoughts, not realizing the message she sent him.

"What's the matter, Cate?" Nick gave into temptation and ran his knuckle along the curve of her cheek. "Don't you want to be alone with me?"

Always and forever—but only on those terms. She couldn't stand it if this were only a temporary visit. Her eyes sought his. "Nick, I don't even know if we're still married."

"We are." His fingers spread, tightening around her nape, tangling with the soft curls there. "I never started any kind of divorce proceedings."

"Why?" Her breath whispered against his lips as he lowered his mouth to hers.

"I wanted to stay married to you."

He was so close she could count the gold tipped lashes that framed his multifaceted eyes, smell the manly outdoors fragrance that surrounded him—her. His words wooed her, lulled her into believing in happily ever afters. Still the question remained. "Why?"

Nick's smile brushed his lips across hers. "Reasons . . . always reasons." The hand behind her neck tightened. His other arm wound around her moments before his mouth crushed down on hers.

He could still do it to her. His touch made her weak. She melted into him, clinging to the front of his shirt. Tongues, too long separated, slid with intoxicating familiarity across each other. Deep and wet, the kiss lasted until its suffocating heat forced them apart.

Catherine gulped in air, pleased to see that Nick did the same. She spread her hand, capturing the thundering beat of his heart. It pounded against her palm, matching her own frantic pulse. Feeling the magnetic draw of his eyes, Catherine looked up. Lips damp from their kiss smiled down at her.

"That's one reason," Nick said resting his forehead against hers. For weeks he'd remembered shared kisses, dreamed of them. It had taken only a touch to realize his memory had been a poor substitute for reality. Thoughts of more than kissing her flooded his mind, thickened his voice. "If you want to know any more you'll have to walk with me to the cabin."

She'd walk with him to the ends of the earth, Catherine thought, but felt too insecure to say it. His kiss spoke of forever. Yet how easy it would be for him to leave again. Catherine's fingers tightened, pulling the soft linen of his shirt.

"Cate?" Gray eyes, smoky with pent-up passion plumbed those of deep forest green. "I really do need to talk with you."

"I need to talk with you, too," Catherine said, thinking of the baby. But only if you tell me you're staying.

Covering the hand clutching his shirt, Nick led Catherine out of the room. "We're going for a walk," he called in to Betsy as they passed the dining room. "Don't worry if we don't come back." The older woman's snaggle-toothed grin contrasted with Catherine's mortified expression. He shrugged into his greatcoat after wrapping a blue wool cape around Catherine. "Well, what did you want me to tell her?"

"I don't know. But nothing would have been preferable to that. You have no idea the kind of erotic things that woman can conjure up in her mind."

"Oh, I think I do." Nick nuzzled his wife's neck, watched as her eyes drifted shut, reminding her that he sought privacy for more than just talk.

Catherine's breath formed a puffy cloud as she stepped into the overcast night. She should have been cold—dampness hung in the air like a chilling threat—but tucked beneath Nick's arm, surrounded by the promise of his warmth, she wasn't. He carried a lantern in his free hand, and as they walked along the path, light splashed out, spilling across walls of grizzled pine bark and a carpet of leaves that crunched beneath their feet.

Close overhead an owl hooted, and Nick lifted the lantern searching for the nocturnal bird. He found him perched on a branch surrounded by stubborn oak leaves that, though crinkled and dead, defied the night wind and clung tenaciously to the tree. It would take the new growth of spring to release their hold.

By the time they reached the cabin, a chilling mist had started to fall.

"Take this, Cate." Nick stepped inside the cabin and handed the lantern to Catherine. "I want to bring in some wood before it gets wet."

After he'd closed the door behind him, Catherine swept the lantern in an arch, reacquainting herself with the homey interior. At first, after Nick went to England, she'd used this room as her office, as he'd done. She'd found all his records neat and easy to follow. He'd made far more contacts with coal buyers than she or her father ever had. She had no trouble getting reorders from them.

But she'd given up coming to the cabin since she only spent her time there reminiscing about Nick. The fact that she did the same thing at the house didn't change the reality that she didn't want to be in the cabin without him—she didn't want to be anywhere without him.

"He's with you now," Catherine admonished herself. She could hear him moving about outside.

And you're doing nothing to keep him here. If you want him to stay, show him, a niggling voice whispered in Catherine's ear. He took the first step, if you could call sailing across the ocean merely a step. And all you've done is stand and stare at him. Let him know how you feel. What is the worst he could do?

"Leave me," Catherine answered herself. "He

ould leave me again."

But at least you'll know you tried. It isn't like you
ot to try.

"You're right. I—"

"What did you say?" Nick came through the door
s if propelled by a blustery wind. Logs that he'd split
ast summer were piled from the curve of his strong
rms. Tiny beads of water sparkled his hair, his
yelashes, the tip of his pugnacious nose.

"Nothing." Goodness, now he'd caught her
alking to herself. Catherine busily used the lantern
o light candles, ignoring the amused expression on
is face. With a shrug Nick knelt by the huge stone
replace. By the time the fire crackled to life, chasing
he chill from the air, the room glowed in the soft-
oun glow of candlelight.

Nick stood, brushing bark from his pants and his
yes met Catherine's. Their gazes locked. Gray
risms that reflected his soul melded with her
merald green that promised so much. It was the
erfect time to melt into each other's arms, bodies, yet
Nick hesitated.

Once he touched her there would be no stopping,
ot until the wee hours of the night, if then. No time
or talk. And talk, though not what his body craved,
vas what he knew their marriage needed.

Trying to convince his body that his mind was
rudent, Nick dragged a chair across the puncheon
oor, positioning it close to the fire. With a smile he
notioned for her to sit. He straddled his own chair,
eeping it a safe distance from her—a no touching
istance.

What had happened? Catherine was certain she'd

read desire in his eyes only a moment ago, ye now . . . Maybe he did bring her down here only to talk. Maybe the marriage was over. Maybe there was nothing she could do to keep him from leaving.

"The fire feels good," Catherine said, folding her hands in her lap to stop their trembling.

Not half as good as holding you in my arms, Nick thought, then stopped himself from letting his mind carry that to its natural conclusion. "How would you feel about dissolving our agreement?"

Catherine's heart plummeted. Dissolving the agreement meant dissolving them. "Well, I . . ." She didn't know what to say.

"Oh, you could still keep three quarters of the mine. Hell, you can keep all of it if you want," Nick hastened to add, misinterpreting her inability to answer.

What did she care about the mine when she was about to lose the only man she'd ever love? She told him as much then and there—at least the part about not caring about the mine.

"You don't care about the mine?" A grin worked its magic at the corners of his sensual lips, deepened the crinkles framing his eyes.

"No." How could she help not smiling when he looked so pleased?

"What do you care about?" There he'd said it, opened himself up for a repeat of the rejection he'd had in Richmond.

"You." The word traveled to him on a whispery breath of air. But he heard. Nick stood so abruptly that it startled her, kicked aside his chair and dragged

420

r into his arms.

"Do you think . . . ?" his voice faltered as she
estled more intimately against his body. "Can we be
arried . . . be together . . . just because that's what
e want?"

"Yes." Tears of joy sprang to Catherine's eyes.
Oh, yes. That's what I want." Her arms wrapped
ound Nick's lean waist, holding him tightly to her.
is large hands moved over her back, his heart beat
pidly against her ear, his smell permeated her
nses—she knew nothing but Nick.

Closing his eyes, Nick breathed in the clean
agrance of her hair, trailed his fingers over her
eek, corseted back to the petticoat layered softness
low. He cupped her, lifting, pressing her toward
e ache he'd carried with him so long. "Cate," his
oice rasped, passion thick, against her cheek. "I'm
red of waiting."

As was she. With deliberate haste, she raised her
ce to his. Lips to lips, heart to heart, they
onsummated the words they'd just spoken.

Firelight burnished the golden highlights in his
air, beckoning Catherine's fingers. She touched the
lken curls, then let her hands drift to the warmth of
is strong, corded neck. "Nick," she sighed into his
outh, feeling she couldn't touch enough of him.

"I know." Nick pulled away, thought better of it
ad recaptured her mouth while his hands searched
lindly for the dress fastenings. Their kiss ablaze, he
ulled the bodice of her gown off her smooth ivory
oulders.

His hands followed the silken descent, pushing
side the cotton chemise, shaping the mounds of soft

flesh beneath. Her nipples hardened in his palms, and she moaned deeply when his thumbs teased the torrid tips.

At the sound, so sweet and sexy, Nick's lower body thrust toward her. "I can't stand much more of this." He jerked away, tearing off his jacket and shirt, popping buttons in his haste, then pressing his naked chest against Catherine's breasts.

Scorching heat blazed through her, setting her blood to boil. Catherine's hands grasped his waistband, pulling at the buttons until they gave way. With hands made greedy by months of wanting, she pushed the fabric down his muscled flanks, smiling when it hooked on the hard proof of his desire.

"Witch," Nick breathed against her cheek, forcing his hands to abandon the sensual weight of her breasts to get out of his pants.

With a flurry of fingers, Catherine's dress and underthings lay in a heap on the floor and Nick and Catherine lay, entwined before the fireplace.

Catherine's cloak formed a flimsy barrier from the hard floor, but she barely noticed as her legs separated inviting Nick into her.

"Oh, Catie, I missed you so much." He thrust deep into her moist heat. "I missed this." His last word was more an anguished breath as Catherine closed her legs around his hips.

He wanted to take it slow, to savor the reunion, but nature and long pent-up desires dictated otherwise. His every movement was met by one of equal force by Catherine. Passion sizzled, screaming for release, and he grabbed her hips not wanting to spill his seed before she experienced all he could give her.

Catherine caught her breath on a gasp, then cried out Nick's name as tingles raced through her body. Lights, blinding in intensity, danced behind her closed eyelids, bursting into vivid colors.

Hot and sweet, her spasms surrounded him, demanding his surrender. He plunged deep, his body losing control as it convulsed and shuddered inside her.

Minutes passed, or was it hours, before Nick raised his head. Tracing the arched curve of her brow with his thumb, he smiled when her eyes opened. Still glazed with passion, they drifted shut again. Nick shifted. "Is the floor hard?" Nick teased after he thought he could control his voice.

"Not really," Catherine sighed. She hadn't noticed anything but his welcome masculine weight atop her.

"Liar." Nick grimaced as he rolled over on his back. "It's hard as hell." He smiled up at her surprised expression. He probably wouldn't have noticed a minute ago either. Actually, he knew he wouldn't have. "Let me cushion you for a while. No wait a second. Here." Nick wrapped her in the cloak, and standing lifted her into his arms.

Catherine supposed his destination was the bedroom, but instead he settled her on a chair. "What are you doing?" She didn't want to sit all alone.

"You'll see." He disappeared into the bedroom, and Catherine heard rustling noises. Moments later Nick came into the main room dragging the mattress from the bed. He looked so pleased with himself, pushing aside furniture and positioning the pallet in front of the fireplace that Catherine smiled.

"Why didn't we just go into the bedroom?"

"And give up this great fire?" Nick threw anothe
log on the blaze. "It's cold in there. And we might a
well be comfortable." His brow cocked suggestivel

"You weren't thinking of comfort a while ago,
Catherine teased.

"Catie, I couldn't think about anything a whil
ago."

"But now you can?" Catherine let the cape sli
down her shoulder, feeling warmth spread throug
her when she noticed passion flare in his eyes.

"For the moment," he growled, lying down an
lifting his hand in invitation.

Because there really was nothing else on eart
Catherine would rather do, she joined him, cuddlin
under the quilt he threw over them.

"Nick, I—"

"Cate—"

Both speaking at once, they interrupted each othe
Laughing at their silliness, they each suggested th
other go ahead. "No really, Nick. What I have to sa
can wait." At least a little while, Catherine adde
silently. She knew now that she must tell him abou
the baby. She only wished she knew what his reactio
would be.

"I know who my father was."

"What?" Immersed so fully in her thoughts c
Nick's impending fatherhood, Catherine's min
barely registered his soft-spoken revelation. One loo
at his face when she raised herself on her elbow mad
her realize she'd heard correctly. "Who?"

Catherine's sweet breath caressed Nick's cheel
drawing his gaze from the ceiling to her face. "Travi
Fielding."

"My goodness. Then that's why he—"

"Took me into his home, educated me . . . left me his fortune."

"Why didn't he tell you? How did you find out?"

Nick pulled his wife down, resting her cheek against his shoulder. "I don't know why he didn't tell me. Maybe he'd planned to, eventually. Or maybe he feared my reaction." His arm tightened about her waist. "Travis and I talked about my father a few times. At least, I talked about him . . . and not in the most complimentary terms."

Catherine heard the guilt lacing his words. "It wasn't your fault. You had no way of knowing. Besides you had a right to say what you did . . . to think the way you did. Perhaps Travis didn't tell you because he had a guilty conscience."

"But that's just it. He shouldn't have." While Nick's hand played over Catherine's neck, trailed down across her breasts, he told her what he'd learned from Lord Hawthorn.

"I'm so sorry," Catherine said when he'd finished. Her fingers, tangling in the golden curls covering his chest, rested over Nick's heart. "But you shouldn't blame yourself."

"You're right. It's just that I feel cheated. I never knew him as a father, he never knew me as a son." Rolling over, Nick positioned Catherine under him. "Sorry. I told myself I wasn't going to get all maudlin over this. I just wanted you to know." He bent down, brushing his lips across Catherine's, catching her chin in a playful bite. "Let's talk about something else."

"Such as?" Catherine rubbed her thigh against his swelling hardness.

"Such as how much I adore your breasts." Nick watched the pink crown pucker as his finger traced it in ever small circles. "Or how soft you are." His hand trailed lower, splaying over her stomach, and stopped.

Catherine sensed the exact moment he knew. Eyes, moments earlier engaged in recording sensual delights, sprang to meet hers—accuse hers.

"How long have you known?"

Not, are you carrying my child, or when is our baby to be born, but the demanding, how long have you known. Catherine tried to push herself up but his hand held her. Oh, why hadn't she told him right away? Why hadn't she followed Betsy's advice and written.

"How long?"

"Over three months."

Suspicion shadowed his face. "You knew before I left?"

"No! I swear I didn't." She hadn't even suspected, though thinking back perhaps she should have. Catherine had no trouble sitting up now, for he'd done the same, turning away to face the fire. Light danced along the honed muscles on his broad back as she reached to touch him. "Nick."

He jerked away. "You weren't going to tell me, were you?"

"Do you think I could hide it? Of course, I was going to tell you. Earlier when we both spoke at once, I—"

"What about if I hadn't come back. Were you going to tell me then, Cate? Were you going to let me know I had a son?"

She could lie, but the look in his eyes as he stared over his shoulder wouldn't allow it. "No," she whispered. "I wasn't going to tell you."

Jumping to his feet, Nick jerked his hands through his rumpled hair. He paced to one side, turned, paced to the other, finally leaning against the hearth. "Didn't it occur to you that I had a right to know?" When she didn't answer, just continued to study the quilt's design, Nick continued. "I was denied a father, Cate. And you would deny me my son, too." His forehead dropped to his arm. "I don't understand what I did to deserve this."

"You left me."

"I left you?" Nick's head snapped up, and his eyes fixed on hers. "Hell, you practically told me to go."

"You were going to anyway." Anger infused Catherine's thoughts. This hadn't been all her fault.

"I had to, and when you wouldn't come with me, I—"

"You didn't ask me to go to England."

Nick blew air through his clenched teeth. "Of course, I did." He watched Catherine shake her head. "Well, you should have known that I wanted you to come."

"How?"

"You're my wife, for God's sake."

"Ha!"

"What in the hell does that mean?"

Catherine jumped to her feet, oblivious to her nakedness until she noticed Nick's gaze flick over her. "Let's stop this charade. I know why you married me."

"You do?" Nick's brow raised in disbelief.

"Yes, I do." Catherine stood her ground.

"Well, would you please tell me, because right at this moment, I'm not sure myself."

"The mine," Catherine yelled, placing her balled up fists on her hips. "You wanted my money."

Nick's bark of laughter sent Catherine's chin up a notch. "You don't have any money, remember. And the mine . . . what profit I got from the mine didn't come close to matching the salary I received from Travis."

"I don't believe—"

"I don't know what you think you married. I'm wealthy now, hell, I'm stinking rich, but I wasn't poor before. Not since Travis took me in. The work I did for you in the mine; that was the first I'd done anything like that in a long time."

"Why?" Catherine's knees felt weak.

"Because I did other things like—"

"No. Why did you marry me?" If it wasn't for the mine, she wanted to know the real reason.

"Because I fell in love with you. I fell in love with you," Nick repeated more softly, realizing—at least saying—for the first time exactly why he had married Catherine.

Catherine stared wide-eyed. Nick stood before her, firelight outlining the tall, broad, planes of his body, unabashedly baring his soul. She took a step closer. "I . . . I love you, too."

"Then why didn't you tell me about the baby?" Nick still hated to think what would have happened if he hadn't come back.

"I know it was wrong." The hand Catherine had reached toward Nick fell to her side. "But I wanted

428

you to come back for me, not just because of the baby." Her eyes pleaded with him to understand.

Two steps and Nick reached her, folding her body with his arms. "I did come back for you, Cate." He held her away enough to rest his hand on the slight mound of her stomach. With gentle strokes he followed the curve from top to bottom, side to side. "When?" he asked, his voice full of emotion.

"Spring," Catherine answered responding to his smile. "But you know, the baby might be a girl."

Nick's laugh warmed her heart. "I know that."

"Then you wouldn't mind. I know you said about a son and all, and—"

Warm lips pressed sweetly against hers, silenced Catherine. "A daughter would be fine . . . more than fine."

Nick kissed the dimples that appeared beside Catherine's mouth. "But what about you? Are you feeling all right? Did I hurt you earlier. God, I should never have made love to you on the floor. If only I'd known."

"Shhh." Touching his lips Catherine smiled up into his concerned face. "I'm fine. Baby and I are both fine. We won't break."

"No?"

Tingles of desire shot through Catherine at the devilish gleam in her husband's gray eyes as he backed her toward the mattress. "No," she answered, and proceeded to prove it far into the night.

Chapter Twenty-one

Catherine had a twinge of disappointment. But the note helped ease it. Snuggling down beneath the quilt, Catherine read the message that, instead of the loving arms of her husband, had greeted her this morning. Actually, it had been the note that had awakened her, or she might still be asleep.

Rolling over, lost in a dream that hours earlier had been reality, Catherine's arm had encountered not hard muscle and warm inviting flesh, but crinkly paper.

Reading it again, Catherine smiled at herself.

Promised Simon I'd stop by the mine this morning. Wanted to wake you but figured you and the little one needed some rest after last night. Damn, I'm noble. I won't be late. Love, N.

She was tired, but the feeling was nothing like the fatigue that had plagued her for months . . . since Nick left. Lack of sleep or not, Catherine felt like she could conquer the world—at least her little corner of it.

But there seemed no need for that. She and Nick had resolved everything, for they had done more than make love into the wee hours of morning. They'd talked. Openly. Something they should have done long before. Now they knew how close they'd come to losing each other. Trust and openness would replace jumping to conclusions and easily bruised pride from now on.

Nick had told her his feelings about his father, his unborn child. Surrounded by love is the way Nick had described how their child—their children—would be reared. Catherine had decided that that's what she'd do with Nick, too—surround him with love.

Catherine stretched, and thought about ways she'd accomplish that. First of all she wasn't going to worry so much about Greenfield. It was, after all, only a place. He'd chuckled when she said that last night, his head resting lightly on her stomach.

"I mean it, Nick," she'd said. "It's not that important to me."

"What about your heritage?" he'd insisted.

She'd known he was teasing her, or at the very least using unfair tactics to divert her attention. His lips kept inching downward, and the hands that had lain quite peacefully below her knees started moving upward—slowly. But she'd refused to be sidetracked. "What about your heritage?" she'd countered, wondering just how long she could ignore what he did to her.

"What about it?" His breath had fanned auburn curls.

"You . . ." Her breath had caught. "You have a

birthright in England, a legacy to pass on to our children. We should take them there."

"All right." His whiskered chin had nudged her legs apart. "But Greenfield will be our home. We'll fix it up; purchase new equipment for the mine, buy what land we need." He'd paused, gazing at her over the slight bulge of her stomach. "Are you satisfied now?"

Catherine's body had arched toward him, all thoughts of where they would live drowned by the passion in his eyes. "No," she breathed.

Nick's grin had been wicked. Deliciously wicked.

"My heaven's," Catherine murmured, feeling the strong need to fan herself. She'd better get up and stop thinking about last night or she'd . . . She'd go down to the mine and drag her husband back to bed. Wouldn't everyone get a chuckle over that, she thought. Besides she had things to do today.

Marie. That's what she'd do—talk to Marie. How could she have forgotten Nick's plans for Marie? Catherine had been so excited about it when he'd told her that she'd rolled on top of him, peppering his hair-roughened chest with kisses.

Tossing off the quilt, Catherine rushed to the fire Nick had stoked up for her and pulled on her clothes. Now that she'd decided to talk to her sister, Catherine couldn't wait to get on with it. Not that Marie wouldn't like the idea. Catherine was certain she would. It had been what Marie had wanted all along.

But Nick wasn't doing it for Marie—he'd made that quite clear. "I don't like her, Cate. Nor do I trust her," he'd said. "I know she's your sister, but—"

"Don't. I know what Marie is. You needn't say it. But she is my younger sister, and I do feel a responsibility toward her."

"That's why I thought of this. You did say she didn't like being here."

Catherine had nodded.

"And she wanted money to travel?"

Again Catherine had agreed with him.

"The money I propose to settle on her will allow her to do both."

"But Nick," Catherine had protested. "It's so much. I can't ask you to do this."

"You didn't." He'd smiled, flashing white teeth in the pre-dawn darkness. "I'd pay any amount to make you happy, and I can't believe you like the way she talks to you."

"I don't, but—"

"And I never want her to cause another misunderstanding between us. Besides, I can afford it." The smile had become slightly crooked, tugging on Catherine's heart. If she hadn't loved him before then, she most certainly would have fallen at that moment.

Hugging the cape around her body, Catherine trudged toward the path. The sun had taken some of the chill from the air, but hadn't yet dried last night's rain from the trees. Droplets clung to pine needles, catching the sunlight and shimmering a silvery green.

Betsy looked up from her dusting when Catherine opened the parlor door. "You didn't sleep long." Catherine cocked her head questioningly and the black woman continued. "Mr. Nick stopped by this

434

morning for breakfast, and said you'd most likely sleep all morning. Sounded real happy about the baby, too."

Catherine couldn't help grinning, even if Betsy was leering at her. "He is. You were right, Betsy. I should have written to him."

"Well, by the look of things, everything worked out all right."

"It did." Catherine hung her cape on a hook. "Is Marie down yet? I want to talk to her."

"Down and gone," Betsy mumbled. "And I hope for good."

"What do you mean gone? Where did she go?" It had been agreed last night that Catherine would offer the money to Marie. But then maybe Nick had run into her this morning and decided to handle it himself.

"Went off with Mr. Parker. Said she knew when she wasn't wanted and she was going to stay with him. If you ask me, it ain't right her staying over there in that house with him all alone."

Catherine shrugged. She didn't think a chaperone necessary. John Parker didn't seem like the kind of man Marie would care for. All the more reason to wonder why Marie went to Windy Hill.

"Did Marie talk with Nick this morning?"

"No. She left before Mr. Nick come up to the house. She sent for Mr. Parker first thing this morning. Now where you off to? I was just fixing to get you some breakfast."

"I'm not hungry. Besides, maybe I'll have breakfast with Marie at Windy Hill."

"You going over there? I thought you and Mr.

Parker had a falling out."

"We did." Catherine had never elaborated on what the problem was, and now she was glad she hadn't. Catherine had a twinge of apprehension about going to Parker's house, but John knew Nick was back. He wouldn't dare try to hurt her again knowing what Nick would do to him.

Besides, Marie would be there. And once she found out what Nick planned to do, she'd be jubilant.

The ride to Parker's plantation in the buggy was pleasant. Catherine felt better than she had in months. When she arrived at Windy Hill, she followed the wide circular drive lined with magnolias to the columned portico. A wizened black man in immaculate livery answered the bell and told her that Mr. John and Miss Marie were in the stables. Assuring him that she could find them on her own, Catherine took the brick path that led past the summer kitchen.

She'd almost reached the double doors when she heard yelling. Recognizing the voices as those of John and Marie, Catherine sighed. She had no desire to walk into the middle of an argument. Backing up, Catherine decided she'd wait in the buggy. She turned to retrace her steps and that's when she heard her name mentioned in the argument.

She knew she shouldn't. Goodness knows she'd been taught better than to eavesdrop, but she seemed unable to resist peeking through the slit between the doors. To ease her conscience, Catherine told herself that she'd seen John really angry and Marie might need her.

Dust motes danced in the dim light inside the ~~st~~able. Catherine spotted Marie and John, but could ~~o~~nly see their heads since they were inside a stall. ~~T~~hey'd stopped yelling, and Catherine had just ~~ab~~out decided spying wasn't for her when John ~~sp~~oke again.

"Damn it, Marie. I'm not going to let you do it."

"Did I hear you right, John? Did you have the ~~n~~erve to say I couldn't do something as if you had *any* ~~c~~ontrol over me."

"Marie," John cajoled. "Someone could get hurt ~~w~~ith that."

"And that bothers you?" Marie's voice rose in ~~d~~isbelief. "Don't tell me you've suddenly acquired a ~~c~~onscience. Are you repenting your past deeds too?"

"I never did want anyone hurt," John insisted.

"Tell that to Sam Stevens."

Hearing the name of her former bottom boss ~~w~~ho'd died trying to steal from the mine, Catherine ~~m~~oved closer.

"Nick Colton is the one who killed him."

"Yes, but who sent him to do his dirty work, John. ~~W~~ho told him to set fire to the barracks. Who decided ~~C~~atherine would sell the Greenfield if there were a ~~c~~ave-in and told Sam to see how unsafe he could ~~m~~ake the mine. You, John, you."

"I wasn't alone, Marie. Don't ever forget that."

Marie's voice lowered, taking on a compromising ~~t~~one. "I know that, John. We've been together in this ~~fr~~om the beginning, and there's no reason to stop ~~n~~ow. I took this from Nick's room. We'll kill ~~C~~atherine with it, and everyone will blame Nick.

437

Both of them, John. We'll get rid of both of them." Marie sidled closer to John, her voice a mere whisper.

Catherine could no longer hear what was said. Her heart was pounding so loud against her ribs, and in her ears, she couldn't hear anything, not even the hinge that squeaked as she tried to back away from the door.

But Marie heard it. And John heard it. And before Catherine could turn to run to the carriage and back home to Nick, a strong arm grasped her upper arm. Air whooshed from her in a ragged breath as John rammed her against the splintery wall.

"What's she doing here?" he bellowed before jerking her further into the stable and slamming the door.

"I think that's rather obvious. She was listening. Weren't you Catherine?"

Catherine couldn't believe it was Marie standing before her. The features were the same—blue eyes, rosebud mouth—but it was as if some crazed magician had twisted them just enough to turn the beauty into a beast. But she didn't have time to contemplate how that could happen because John's fingers dug deeper into her flesh.

"Answer her. *Were* you listening?"

"Of course she was," Marie answered for Catherine. "She knows everything. Are you still so se against doing what must be done?"

Catherine didn't think she could be more shocked but as Marie spoke she looked down to her hand Catherine's gaze followed her sister's. Catherin gasped, and would have slid to the floor if not fo

438

John Parker's punishing grip on her arm, as she stared down the dark throat of a pistol.

"What treat are you fixing me for dinner?" Nick strolled into the kitchen and peered into the iron kettle slung over the fire. A long wooden spoon rapped playfully across his knuckles.

"You just stay out of that chicken stew, Mr. Nick. It ain't time for dinner yet."

"But I'm hungry," Nick insisted, favoring Betsy with his brightest smile.

"Should have eaten the breakfast I fixed for you," she fussed, while she uncovered a loaf of still warm bread and cut a chunk off the end. "Still I guess we can't have you going around starving to death." She handed him the bread she'd generously lathed with gooseberry jam.

Nick mumbled his thanks around a bite. Sitting down, he thrust his long legs before him, crossing them at the ankles. "What's Cate doing?" he asked when he'd finished the snack. He'd told himself that he hadn't left the mine early because of her, but he knew he was lying to himself.

"Imagine she's talking to Marie. Leastways that's what she said she was off to do."

"That's good." Even though he wanted to see Catherine, he was glad she'd decided to speak to Marie about their offer. There was something about Marie he didn't like or trust. The sooner she left the happier he'd be.

Betsy bent over the huge fireplace to stir the stew,

rubbing the small of her back when she stood. "This damp weather don't do my old joints one bit of good."

"Sit down." Nick indicated the chair across from him. "I'll stir the stew if it needs it," he added when he noticed Betsy's hesitation.

"Well, don't mind if I do." Settling herself on the chair, Betsy looked across at Nick. "Did I ever tell you about the time Miss Catherine . . ." From there she began a series of anecdotes that punctuated Catherine's life.

Nick balanced the chair on two legs and listened with interest. He chuckled over the time Catherine's pigtail got caught on the fence when she was trying to get away from the bull she'd teased. He laughed robustly at Betsy's description of Catherine's face when the pantaloons were found in the picnic basket. And he crossed his arms and smiled feeling love for her seep through him when Betsy told him about Catherine's sorrow over her grandfather's death.

"She used to go down in the mine with him, you know. Of course her momma didn't know, but then she never paid much attention to either of the girls. Catherine would just follow her grandpere anywhere. But after he was killed, she got awful afeared of the mine."

"She told me." Lost in thought, Nick felt the chair tilt further and righted it. He didn't know how long he'd sat here with Betsy but the combination of warm kitchen, savory smells and damn little sleep last night was having an effect on him.

He stood and stretched. I think I'll go upstairs. I'll knock on the library door and tell Catherine dinne

440

will be ready soon." He wondered if she was having any trouble with Marie. Their talk seemed to be taking a good bit of time.

"Oh, she ain't in the library."

Nick leaned over and gave the stew a stir. "Where is she?"

"Went looking for Miss Marie over at Windy Hill."

Nick dropped the spoon. "John Parker's place?" His eyes narrowed and he stared at Betsy with such intensity that she cringed. "Yes, but—"

"When did she leave?"

"I'm not rightly sure. Earlier. But what's wrong?"

Nick didn't answer. He didn't even hear the question. By the time Betsy had finished asking it, he'd run halfway to the stables.

What was in her mind? Oh, please let her be all right. Anger and fear raced through him as Nick galloped his horse toward Windy Hill. Catherine had never taken John Parker's attack on her as seriously as Nick thought it warranted. It hadn't been a lovestruck misunderstanding on Parker's part. There had been something in Parker's eyes when Nick had pulled him off Catherine. Nick couldn't put his finger on what it was, but it sure as hell hadn't been love.

Skidding his horse to a stop, Nick leaped off, and pounded on the front door. For a moment, in his mind's eye, he envisioned himself being escorted into the parlor, and looking like an idiot when he saw Catherine, John and Marie sharing tea. "Let that happen," he prayed, hammering on the door again.

The old man who opened it seemed barely able to

swing its weight. He looked at Nick from out of small eyes surrounded by wrinkles.

"My wife," Nick began. "Catherine Colton, is she here?"

The old man slowly shook his head.

Nick didn't know whether to feel relief or panic. "How about her sister, Marie Brousseau?"

"She was here. Both of them was. But they left. Along with Mr. Parker."

Now Nick had no doubt how to feel. "Was she all right?" He grabbed the old man's jacket without realizing it.

"Reckon so. Didn't really see them. Just the buggy."

"Which way did they go?" Nick noticed the fear on the wizened face and set the servant down.

"That way." He pointed toward a trail that led behind the house, toward the river. "But I'm sure they'll be back soon. Nothing down there but the abandoned mine."

"We can't just kill her."

"Would you stop whining and let me think." Marie climbed out of the buggy without John's assistance and bundled her cloak more tightly around her.

Catherine had done nothing but think since they'd forced her into the buggy. She let John haul her out of the seat without a struggle. His touch repulsed her, but this wasn't the time to act. She felt certain of that. But when?

After forcing thoughts of never again seeing Nick

and their unborn child from her mind, Catherine had bent her mind on escape. But how? Wedged between Marie and John in the buggy, the nose of the pistol, hidden under the lap rug, pointed at her midsection, she'd had no chance.

And now . . . Catherine glanced around her. They'd stopped in a small clearing. Buildings used when the played-out mine operated, stood silent and empty in ramshackle disarray. Though loosely boarded up, the mine opening yawned dark like a hungry mouth, eager to gobble up anyone foolish enough to wander too close. Above it the weather-worn basket that had carried miners down the shaft moaned eerily as a chill gust twisted the rope against the pulley.

"We'll put her down in the mine." Marie's words interrupted Catherine's survey.

"She'll die down there."

"Precisely." Apparently Marie took the stricken expression on John's face seriously, for she sighed. "Can you think of a better idea? Well, can you? She knows too much."

"I won't tell." Catherine figured lying wasn't wrong, given the circumstances. "No one will ever know. And you can have money. That's what I came to tell you, Marie. Nick is going to give you money . . . a lot of money . . . so you can go wherever you like." Now that Catherine had found her voice, she seemed unable to stop talking. Besides, maybe Marie would go for the idea. If not, at least she was buying herself more time.

"She's right, Marie," John said. "You could go away. I'll go with you. We'll tie her up and by the

443

time she gets loose—"

"Would you shut up? She'll scream everything she knows to that husband of hers the minute she sees him. Do you want Nick coming after you?" Marie snorted in disgust. "I can tell by the fear written across your face you don't. There's only one way, John. We have to kill her." Marie leveled the gun. "Now back up, sister dear."

Catherine heard the galloping hooves an instant before they diverted Marie's attention. Feeling her chances slipping away, Catherine lunged at her sister, catching her around her waist and sending them both onto the packed earth. Frantically, she grabbed for the pistol Marie held.

Nick leaped from the horse before it stopped, racing toward his wife. A flash of movement to the side caught his eye and he ducked just in time for the thick branch John Parker swung, to miss his head. It struck his shoulder with a thump and a quick bolt of pain.

In a flurry of petticoats and dust, Catherine and Marie grappled in the dirt. Nick had come. She didn't know how he'd found her, but he had. She'd seen him, and she knew everything would be all right if she could just get the gun from Marie.

Marie clawed at her hair, but Catherine ignored the pain as she clutched at Marie's hand. The gun. She had to get the gun. She had to stop Marie from hurting anyone with it.

Letting loose of a fistful of Catherine's hair, Marie punched at Catherine's breast, then lower. At that moment, the gun took second priority in her mind. Catherine had to stop Marie from hurting her baby. Catherine twisted drawing her knees up. The fist

Marie planted on her cheek knocked her back onto the hard ground.

Obviously shocked that he'd missed his target, John reached back to swing again. Twisting around, Nick grabbed the club, easily wrestling it away from Parker. Then with one quick, fluid motion Nick sent Parker reeling to the ground from a blow to the jaw.

Scrambling to her feet, swiping blond curls from her eyes, Marie aimed the pistol at Nick. He started toward her, leaving John slumped on the ground. "Give me the gun, Marie."

"You'd like that wouldn't you? Be a good girl, Marie and hand the gun over," she mimicked, aiming the pistol at Nick's chest. "Well, I'm not going to, Mr. Colton. I'm going to shoot you with it, and then I'm going to kill your wife."

A metallic click sounded, followed by Marie's gasp as Catherine yanked her arm sideways. The pistol fired, spitting its deadly charge. There was a groan of pain, and then nothing. The report seemed to freeze the moment in time. Catherine peered through the veil of smoke, no longer concerned with her sister, thinking only of Nick.

Someone grabbed her shoulders. Nick. Catherine looked up into the face she loved, then sank against his broad chest in relief.

"Are you all right?" The words seemed to leave him on a tortured groan as Nick's hands roamed over her back. "Did they hurt you . . . the baby."

"Fine. I'm . . . we're fine. Oh, Nick she tried to kill you." Catherine pulled away, searching Nick from head to toe. "Are you hurt. I thought she hit someone."

"She did. But thanks to you, it wasn't me." Nick

glanced over his shoulder at John Parker who lay on the ground, an ever blossoming patch of red, marring his jacket.

"Is he . . . ?" Catherine left the question unfinished.

"I think so. But you. Are you sure?" Emotion overwhelmed Nick and he hugged his wife to him, wrapping her tightly in the shelter of his arms. "When I saw you on the ground, I . . ."

"Shhh." Catherine clutched at his jacket. "It's over now. Nothing happened. Marie just . . ." Catherine stopped, looking up at Nick. "Where is she?" Her eyes scanned the clearing. "Nick, she and John were behind all the stealing at the mine. They sent Sam Stevens and . . . Nick we can't let her get away."

"She ran into the woods after she shot Parker. Knowing Marie's penchant for the soft life, she shouldn't be hard to find."

And she wasn't. Nick caught up with her barely a half mile from the abandoned mine.

"What do you think will happen to Marie?" That evening Catherine sat propped up in bed, watching as Nick splashed water on his face. He looked up, catching her eye in the mirror above the washstand.

"I don't know, Cate. That will be for the courts to decide." He dried himself and flung the towel in the general direction of the bar. "Does it bother you?"

"It makes me very sad, of course. But when I think what she tried to do."

Nick leaned over the bed and brushed his lips across Catherine's. Throwing her arms around his

446

neck, Catherine caught him before he could move away. She nipped at his ear, circling the whirl with her tongue.

"Now, Catie."

"Now, Catie, what?" Catherine kissed a trail along his sturdy jaw, then under his chin.

"Maybe we shouldn't. You've had a rough day. And I'm still not certain you're telling me the truth about being all right. Those two were pretty rough on you."

"Being noble again?" Catherine quarried, smiling into his serious face. How was she going to convince him that she was perfectly all right, and that he'd know if she weren't?

"Yeah, maybe I am." He touched the dimples beside her mouth.

"There's no need to be."

"Are you sure?"

"Positive."

Clear gray eyes searched hers then crinkled in mirth. "Good," he said, shifting onto the mattress, a devilish grin brightening his face. "Because I'm damn tired of being noble."